leave me behind

km moronova

FOR THOSE WHO CRAVE A VIOLENT LOVE STORY.

playlist

Jerk - Oliver Tree
Light Em up - Fall Out Boy
Can't Hold Us - Macklemore & Ryan Lewis
Waste - kxllswxtch
Enemy - Tommee Profitt
Ava - Famy
Brother - Kodaline
Hate Myself - NF
Fill the Void - The Weeknd, Lily Rose Depp & Ramsey
Tourniquet - Zach Bryan
Older - Isabel LaRosa
Pretty toxic revolver - MGK
I hate u, I love u - Gnash
Black Dahlia - Hollywood Undead
Bloody Valentine - MGK
I think I'm OKAY - MGK
To die for - sam smith
I am the Antichrist to you - Kishi Bashi
Animals - Maroon 5

content warning

. . .

The contents of this book may be triggering and disturbing to some readers. This is an dark military romance placed in a fictional "dark forces" setting. Some of the weapons and missions are highly unrealistic. Some places and landmarks are also fictional.

If you are sensitive/easily offended to any of the below subjects please do not read this book.

This book includes the following: Physical violence, explicit sex scenes, pain kink, blood play, morbid humor, explicit gore, death, explicit language, **extreme bullying,** harassment, sexual assault, **non-con,** dub-con, sexist behavior, war trauma/aspects of war, ptsd, mention of rape and home intrusion, murder.

patagonia - two years ago

. . .

BONES

ABRAHM'S EYES ARE BLURRY WITH DARK BLOOD. I TRY TO WIPE the red streams from his cheeks with my sleeve, but it flows relentlessly from the gash on the side of his head. His blond-brown hair that was always so bright is now burgundy and streaked with the call of death. Dirt and rocks cling to the stickiness of his skin. Panic flashes through me; it's through sheer will that I force the plains of my face to remain smooth and emotionless.

"B-Bones."

My chest grows heavy with the weakness that draws out his whiny breaths. The way his fingers tremble as he reaches for me. His black gloves are drowned in blood. I bury my teeth into my lower lip to quell the agony that seeps into my throat.

"I'm here, Abrahm." I shut my eyes to stave off the despair.

"I'm—" He coughs and blood splatters across my mask. I

don't blink. "S-scared." His green eyes are murky-yellow with red liquid, waning as death clings to him. I shakily remove my gloves and press my cold palm to his cheek.

Shit. We weren't supposed to be here, not like this. Riøt Squad was supposed to meet us at the checkpoint. Where the fuck were they? I duck as bullets pelt into the dry terrain and kick up dust around us.

Abrahm's chest gapes with a hole right next to his heart, the heat of his flesh quickly fleeing him. *Goddammit.* I lift my head and search through the smoke for the rest of our squad. Only three lifeless hostiles lie motionless in the clearing. I killed them mercilessly, cruelly, like I'd been taught to, but they aren't the ones who shot my second. They aren't responsible for his dwindling life. The bullet went straight through his vest and must be a higher grade.

My fists clench. Why didn't he stay back like I told him to? *Goddammit.*

The rest of my squad is firing back and securing the area, but it will be too late. I've witnessed many men die. I know when there's far too much damage. Abrahm isn't going to make it, and I find myself incapable of leaving his side. There are protocols I need to follow, and the mission isn't complete yet, but it doesn't seem to matter to me like it once had. Not now that he's going to die. I let my eyes fall closed and, with trembling hands, take my mask off slowly.

A face that no one is supposed to know. *I want him to know.*

I open my eyes and look down at him.

Abrahm's eyes widen, brows pinching weakly together with concern. "Bones, you shouldn't—" He tries to reach his hand up to cover my face, but he can't even lift his arm now. I catch his falling hand.

"Bradshaw."

His weary eyes are shutting slowly, but a small grin spreads over his chapped lips.

"My name is Bradshaw." My voice is a mere whisper, but I know he hears it.

Abrahm draws his final breath, and it sounds like a sigh of relief. It doesn't at all sound like the last noise he'll ever make.

His eyes are still on me, hazed over now but seeing straight through me.

The light has gone.

And vengeance is born into my heart.

one

. . .

I'M BEING REASSIGNED TO A SQUAD OF DEVILS. NO, NOT literally. Just men that come really fucking close.

The entire Riøt Squad was killed two years ago during a Level Red mission in Patagonia. Everyone except me. And what did my survival get me besides a heavy dose of trauma? I've been reassigned to the worst possible squad: Malum.

I let a long sigh roll from my lips and check my watch for the hundredth time. I tap my foot impatiently as I wait for the row of passengers ahead of me to grab their luggage from the overhead bins so that I can get off the plane and get to my next terminal.

Racing through the airport for my connecting flight, I desperately try to convince myself that my new squad's respect can be won with nothing more than blood and sweat. *Let's just hope they aren't as ruthless as Riøt was when I first joined.*

By the time I board, the window seat is already taken in my row. I pull out my ticket to double-check my number. *That asshole is in my seat.* I blow out an irritated breath. It's a three-seat row and two men flank each end, leaving the middle chair for me. The one in the aisle seat has his hood pulled up, hiding his face from view.

The other guy is also dressed in black with his hood pulled up, but he's staring out the window. He doesn't seem concerned about his surroundings. I stand there, annoyed, but people are already getting impatient behind me, so I settle for the middle seat. *God, I hate flying.* Everyone is angry and tired and so, *so* goddamn rude.

The aisle guy doesn't bother moving his legs or lifting his head, so I swallow the curse words building in the back of my throat and try maneuvering around him. I'm already regretting wearing the thin black leggings I threw on this morning as my thighs brush his knees. In hindsight, I should've worn sweatpants.

As I'm stepping around his feet, my back foot gets caught between his and I fall forward. My backpack falls into window-seat guy's lap and aisle-seat guy half catches me with a strong hand that splays over the center of my stomach; the other is wrapped around my inner thigh.

Instinctively, I snap out of his hold and shoot him a death glare. It's short-lived. Because now that he's looking up at me, I can see his lovely face. There is a frosty edge that radiates from his pale blue eyes. The set of his sharp jaw and blank expression don't add any warmth to his demeanor. A thin one-inch scar resides beneath his left eye, making him appear tired. Another crosses the bridge of his nose and two small scars rib his lower lip on the right side, almost appearing like piercings. The hollows of his cheeks are lined with muscle that defines the bone structure. He's easily the most beautiful man I've ever laid eyes on.

My senses return to me as I remember that civilians won't take kindly to my trained responses of profiling.

I take a deep breath and let it out slowly.

"Thanks," I say as casually as I can before sitting in the center seat. He doesn't respond and leans his head back against his chair. I glance at him and see sound-canceling headphones peeking out from beneath his hood. I don't think twice about the small encounter. I just want to get this final flight over with so I can sleep before the nightmare begins tomorrow. The window-seat guy gives me a brief smile and hands me my bag. "Sorry about that," I mutter, not bothering to look any higher than his lips.

I pull out my own sound-blocking headphones and shove my backpack under the seat before getting comfortable. Well, as comfortable as one can get on an airplane. I loathe flying, always have and always will. Anxiety used to pulse through my veins when I'd get on a plane, but I've been trained rotten out of the fear of it.

It's a six-hour flight to California. At some point, I fall asleep and am startled awake by turbulence.

Alertness instantly snaps me into focus before I recall that I'm not on a chopper. Any rivets in the air set me off. I've grown used to sleeping light. I snap my head up and look around urgently, pulling my headphones down around my neck as I blink away the drowsiness from my nap. I find that everyone is either silently reading, watching a movie, or sleeping.

Relieved, I look at the window seat passenger next to me. He's staring at me with a curious expression. My eyes widen as I take him in. It's dimly lit in here, but even if it was completely dark, I'd still be able to tell that he's handsome and, *wait*… I could swear he was sitting in the aisle seat before I fell asleep. Black hair peeks out from under the rim of his charcoal gray beanie, matching his dark brows. His eyes are a darker, softer blue than they were earlier.

But there's no scar under his left eye, across his nose, or on his bottom lip.

"I'm sorry, weren't you sitting in the aisle seat earlier?" I ask him hesitantly. He doesn't look like the nicest guy. So I'm surprised when he drops the analytical stare and gives me a small smirk.

"Nope. That's my twin," he says smoothly. His voice is husky and pleasant. Not too high, not too low, but perfectly in the middle.

I'm struck by his charm; it takes me a moment to collect my thoughts. "Oh." My brows knit and he seems amused by that. *Twins?* His eyes flick down to my lips and then back to my gaze. Is he a model? He certainly could be one. I'm eager to ask him questions that I normally wouldn't. There's something inviting about his wry smirk that taunts me. *It reminds me of Sergeant Jenkins.* I quickly push the thought down— thinking of Jenkins only brings a deep ache to my heart.

"Yeah, he doesn't talk much, unlike me." He winks. "But that turbulence spooked you, huh? You were passed out cold with your head on my shoulder." He chuckles, and my heavy soul lifts a bit.

Hold on—I did *what*?

Heat races to my cheeks and I lean as far away from him as I can in my seat, feeling entirely too close and embarrassed. But there's no escape, our thighs are literally touching.

I'm mortified. "I'm so sorry."

He chuckles lightly and shrugs. "It's fine; I just wasn't expecting it. You must be tired from traveling. What's your final destination?" My heart flutters with that boyish grin he shoots me. His lashes are long and thick, making those ocean eyes all the more irresistible. He looks to be in his late twenties.

"I don't think you can say *final destination* on a plane." I return the charm with the movie reference and let a small laugh slip. "Coronado, Cali. You?"

He shifts in his seat to face me more as he grins devilishly at my comment.

"Same, actually. I travel a lot for work, so I'm used to long flights."

I nod, thinking better of mentioning that I am too.

He takes my pause as me not wanting to respond, so he mutters, "Eren."

"Huh?" I glance back up at him and he smiles softly again.

"My name is Eren."

"Oh. It's nice to meet you, Eren. I'm Nellie." I use my nickname instead of my formal name. I offer him my hand awkwardly. Do people still shake hands? I'm used to saluting. Everything feels surreal out here on the civilian side.

It's not like I've had time to familiarize myself with society. I showed my true colors to the world when I was orphaned at fifteen. That's when the underground military faction first laid their hands on me. It's been ten years since then.

That's how you come to be in the company of elite killing machines. The dark forces take people like me who did something unspeakable and put us to use, rather than throwing us in prison. We don't exist, not on paper. We've been long forgotten by the people we used to know.

I am only a weapon. A rabid dog running from an inevitable death shot.

It's perhaps the government's darkest secret, the underside of the special forces that does all the dirty work they don't want to sully their hands with. Anti-terrorism, foreign combat, black market weapons raids. We get sent to stop it all and we don't get a lick of credit.

Basically, when it's all summed up, we're suicide squads.

The generals only want to make sure we get the missions done. They don't give a shit about us.

Eren takes my hand and gives it a light shake. "The feeling is mutual," he says.

He leans his head against the chair and stares at me. His eyes are so unrelenting, piercing me and daring me to look away. I'm the type of person who can't hold eye contact for more than a few seconds, but with him, I don't feel the urge to pull away. He's searching my eyes for something, studying me closely.

"Nice neck tattoos," he says with a smile.

My hand goes to my neck. "Thanks, they hurt like a bitch when I got them."

"I bet, but they look great. Got someone waiting for you in California?" he asks boldly.

I shake my head. I'm sure he can see the flush across my cheeks. "Nope—just work. No one special there."

Or anywhere.

Eren lifts a brow and tilts his head. "You're too pretty to be without a special someone." The kid sitting behind us kicks my seat and I blink like an idiot at his words.

He thinks I'm pretty? Being in the military, the only comments I get from men are: "nice ass," "you're fuckable," "love the long dark hair to grab onto," and "you have dick-sucking lips." But then there was Jenkins, and, although he never once told me I was beautiful, he certainly made sure I knew it with his stolen glances and heady kisses.

But when I think of Sergeant Jenkins, I only remember the blood he was drenched in that final night. After seeing him the way I did in Patagonia, it's difficult to recall his beautiful blond hair and the rare smile he spared for only me.

I blink away the flames that lick at my memories.

"How about you?" I ask. I'm sure Eren has a family or at least a wife. My eyes flick to his hand as I think it. *No ring.*

12

"Nah. I don't do relationships."

That piques my interest. Is he military? He must notice my curious stare and cracks a smile.

"I'm in the army," he admits. I can tell he doesn't want to speak on it too much, so I don't pry. I don't mention that I'm a trained killer as well. I'm supposed to be discreet with the squad I'm joining, so I keep it out of the conversation. But the thought of it reminds me of the hell I'm heading toward. *Malum Squad.* The dark forces team they send when they can't send any of the other suicide squads. Malum, who fucked Riøt when they didn't show up to the checkpoint before shit hit the fan in Patagonia.

"Thank you for your service, *sir*," I say slyly. His eyes widen with a flicker of interest that pulls at his lips. He wouldn't be anyone I'd run into at the base, right? I highly doubt it. Normally, I wouldn't flirt with fellow servicemen because it always ends badly, but the guys I normally work with aren't model worthy. They are depraved and murderous, like me.

I think he's in the clear. Besides, there's no way he could be in the dark forces. He doesn't have the hardness about him.

Eren laughs at that and shakes his head. "I'm just some low end officer. Oh hey, Bradshaw's awake," he mutters, looking past me. I follow suit and glance at the man on my other side, the other thigh that presses against mine. I'm met with those icy blue eyes again and that intimidating scar under his left one. The discoloration is just shy of his lower eyelid, but he doesn't appear to be impaired by it at all. *He's lucky to have evaded a blade that close.*

Jenkins wasn't so lucky. I shudder at the memory of the blood that spilled from his chest. My fists close over my thighs and I try to blink away the last images of him in my head. I should remember him as the soldier he was, not how he looked when I left him on the battlefield. He told me to leave him there and I did. I followed his final orders.

I'm haunted by that the most, the realization dawning over his eyes that I was leaving him there just as he commanded. He gritted his teeth in acceptance and smiled.

The ache will never cease, it only grows.

I force my fingers to unfurl.

Bradshaw looks at me calmly with his cold demeanor still intact. The uninterest that radiates from this guy is unreal. They are twins, no doubt, but now that I see them both up close, their eyes are different shades of blue and their personalities couldn't be more opposite. Like fire and ice.

"Nellie." I offer my hand to shake his like I did with Eren but Bradshaw just levels me with the same callous look. He doesn't even seem tempted to shake it. *Jesus, what's with this guy?*

Eren nudges his shoulder against mine. "He's an asshole to everyone, don't take it personally." Bradshaw doesn't reply or even seem offended. He simply pulls his headphones back over his ears and closes his eyes. His lashes are long and grace his pale skin. I stare a moment longer than I should. Admiring his ethereal features before returning my attention to Eren. He grins. "You want to join us for a few drinks tonight? Or do you have somewhere to be?"

He's inviting me out? A flutter skates across my chest. There's really only one person I'm worried about running into before tomorrow. They call him Bones. He's rumored to be the cruelest man in the dark forces. Apparently he likes breaking open ribcages and literally pulling people's hearts out. Sometimes their bones. Hence the disturbing code name he bears.

Unfortunately, he's my partner on Malum and I'm not sure how I'll survive.

But Eren isn't him. I'm sure of it. And if I'm going to be miserable for the next month, why not have a bit of fun?

I return his smile.

"Sure. I just can't stay out too late. Early commitments tomorrow," I say as casually as I can. My veins fill with adrenaline at the thought of going out on one last free night. Hopefully getting Eren on board for a one-night stand.

His grin is murder. "I wouldn't dream of keeping something as sweet as you out too late."

———

The bar turns out to be a full-blown nightclub. Not the gross ones in small towns, but the kind that has bouncers up front checking reservations and lists.

I pay the Uber driver and stare at the building. The music is bumping so loud it's even hard to hear the conversations outside. *Should I just go back to the hotel?* I consider it, but Eren is waiting for me and shouts my name.

The leggings and soft, body-tight T-shirt I wore on the plane seemed appropriate for a bar setting, but now I feel like I stand out amongst the younger women who wear belly shirts and short-shorts. Not that I have anything to wear like that anyway. I packed light; I don't own more than three outfits for street clothes. Traveling here is the first time I've been off base in months. The dark forces aren't exactly free individuals. We're halfway between criminals and military hounds.

Eren meets me on the edge of the sidewalk. "There she is. I thought you'd totally bounce if I wasn't up here to catch you." He winks and all I can do is smile awkwardly.

"It did cross my mind."

He chuckles and leads me straight to the doors. I glance over at the line of angry people waiting to get in, their impatience and rage palpable. I hate when people cut too. The bouncer gives me a gruff look but Eren nods at him and he lets me slide through without any trouble.

I didn't pin Eren as someone who frequents the club based on his appearance.

"Ever been here before?" he asks smoothly, laying his arm around my shoulders. A chill spreads up my spine and my heart beats faster. I shake my head and he smirks. "Get ready to have one hell of a night."

We enter the club's main floor. It's dark here and difficult to make out other people's faces. Blue and purple lights flash with the music bumping through the room and thrum excitement through my veins. Vapor curls in the air as the lights cut through shadows and the distinct scent of alcohol rolls over me.

I haven't been to a place like this since I was twenty-two, but this is way, *way* fancier.

Eren smiles down at me, clearly pleased with himself at my awe. He says loudly, "I'll get us drinks."

"Get me an unopened can," I shout over the music. A wicked look spreads over his face.

"Smart girl." He winks and disappears into the crowd swarming around the bar.

I laugh and shake my head, wondering how tonight will pan out. It wouldn't be the worst thing in the world to have a one-nighter to ease me into the dread that's coming tomorrow. Eren seems like the kind of guy that is good at flings. In our profession, that's not a bad trait to have. Our lives are fleeting at best and we're always on the move. But in my case, I'm underground; I couldn't have a relationship even if I wanted one.

It looks like Eren might be there awhile. I narrow my eyes as I watch him try to get the bartender's attention, but there are so many people shouting and waving their cards around that I have little faith he'll be back soon. My gaze sweeps over the sea of people bumping and grinding to the music on the dance floor. It's in the center of the club with seating lining the outer rim for people to take breaks and drink. Each beat booms so loud it reverberates in my bones. I smile to myself and push my way into the warmth of drunken, sweaty bodies. Where I'm sure no one will see me having the time of my life.

It's an entirely different feeling to be in a place where no one knows you. No one to judge you for letting loose.

I've been dancing for over ten minutes with casual movements when a club remix version of "Hey Mama" by David Guetta ques up and everyone lets out excited shrills. The sensation is exhilarating and my heart pounds lightly in my chest. I let my body follow their excitement and move with the bass, shaking my hips to the rhythm of the song.

My eyelids are heavy, chin tilted up and I happen to look at the far wall of the club. Up against it is Bradshaw. His arms are crossed tightly and he's wearing all black, hood still pulled up. A flash of purple light beams down on him for a moment, lighting up those cold eyes and revealing that they are focused solely on me, as if he's been watching me swing my hips this entire time. I didn't get a good look at his neck tattoos earlier but with the light hitting him, it's impossible not to notice the ink that follows and hardens his perfect jawline.

There's something in the way he stares at me, like a starved man who's contemplating a heinous act. You don't have to tell me there isn't one good thought in his head.

Red flags are flying all around this guy. But I can't look away. He captivates me, scares *me* even and I can kill a man in five seconds flat.

My veins chill under his scrutiny but I don't stop dancing. I hold his intense gaze for a few seconds to let him know I will not be intimidated by him before forcing myself to casually glance the other way as if I don't find him mesmerizing.

How did I forget about the psycho twin? I chide myself and roll my eyes. I refuse to let him know I'm affected by the way he watches me so carefully. My mom always said I was into bad guys. I doubt she knew I'd grow up to be into ones who clearly had psychological problems. The ones you don't tell God about when you pray at church to forgive your sins —the ones with dark backstories and baggage.

Curious and maybe a bit teasing, I lift my lashes slowly back to him and find him still staring at me steadily. Heat rolls through me at his brashness. He doesn't care that I'm looking straight back at him. He doesn't look the least bit unnerved as I continue to dance, unfazed by him, rolling my hips and putting my hands up over my head like everyone else, but I notice his fingers tightening around his arm and his lower lip flattening under his teeth.

Oh. His walls aren't so impenetrable after all.

As I continue dancing, someone comes up behind me, drawing their fingertips softly over my hips in a silent query. I smile, answering by leaning back into them and pushing my ass against a hard boner.

Yeah, it's been a while since I've been in a club like *this.* Where the air is thick with lust and alcohol. Where strangers will touch your body with the hope that you'll let them.

My new dance partner instantly responds by moving in rhythm to my hips. He buries his fingertips into my waist as we sway; his breath becomes heavier with each beat of music. I forget myself for a moment, letting my back fall against hard muscle and enjoying the sweep of cologne that fills my nose.

I glance back over to where Bradshaw is, but he's gone. The boner grinding into my ass has me not too concerned, but I don't have to wonder where he went for long.

"Hey, what are you doing?" the man behind me shouts furiously. His body parts from mine quickly and the cold air instantly makes me sour.

The music is loud, pulsating my heart for me at this point. I turn and find Bradshaw shoving the guy I was dancing with to the side. He looks like he wants to push Bradshaw back, but he takes one look at that intimidating build and settles with cursing and walking back through the crowd.

I scowl and shout, "What's your problem?"

Bradshaw snaps his attention back to me with the same coldness, but there's a tinge of interest there now. "You're here with *us*." He speaks for the first time and for a second everything else is silent. His voice is loud in my head even though he didn't shout. I want to hear it again.

I swallow and decide to just drop it, unsure of what exactly his intentions are.

The next song comes booming in, a remixed version of "Summertime Sadness" by Lana Del Rey. As I resume dancing, I keep my eyes locked with Bradshaw's. His icy gaze flickers with the flashing lights. His nostrils flare and his jaw flexes.

I turn to avoid his heavy stare, letting my body find the rhythm again. *God, I hope Eren hurries with those drinks.*

Calloused hands slide over my hips. I don't need to turn around to know they belong to Bradshaw. They're hard and demanding, as stiff as he appears, yet more sensual than any I've ever known. Maybe it's the malice behind them. The intensity of his grip. Heat floods through my entire body as he sinks his fingers into my flesh.

My traitorous body instinctively melts into the hardened planes of his chest. I'm pleasantly surprised with the muscles I feel beneath his hoodie. Is he in the military like his brother? I grind my ass into him and grin when I find him hard.

He keeps one hand on my moving hips while dipping a finger beneath my shirt, brushing the skin of my stomach as if asking permission. My smile is starting to hurt from this exchange. I slide my hand down to his and push it up a bit more so he knows I'm good with him exploring.

Bradshaw chuckles darkly, almost not loud enough for me to hear. It's a sound so voracious that I have to squeeze my thighs together to keep the urgent sensation in check.

Holy shit. Who is this guy?

two

. . .

I LOSE MYSELF IN THESE SHORT MOMENTS WITH HIM. DANCING like our bodies have known each other for years. His scent rolls over me and I breathe it in. He smells like a crisp forest —in the morning, before the mist settles.

His mouth comes to my shoulder and I bite my lip against the thoughts that thrum through my head. *Fuck him, it's your last night for God knows how long.*

At the start of the next song, Eren reappears with two drinks in hand. He grins mischievously at the both of us. I'm surprised he looks entertained with us dancing together rather than jealous. I stop dancing and embarrassment spreads across my cheeks.

Eren hands me the canned spritzer, unopened as promised, and takes a long sip from his can before shouting, "You've got *Bradshaw* out here dancing with you? Damn, what did you do grab his dick or something?" Bradshaw doesn't laugh. Neither do I. Eren laughs at his own joke on our behalf.

"You're okay with us dancing together? I was kind of—"

Eren cuts me off, "All cards on the table, I was hoping you two would hook up tonight." He shoots me a sly grin. *Why does that make me feel used?* I was supposed to be the one using him. His brows pull together as he sees worry clouding my eyes. "He has a hard time with women... you know, because he's an asshole. I thought you two might get along." He says it so innocently I can't possibly be irked. Not when they share the same lovely face. Why should I care what lies beneath that?

"No shit. He should try not being such a creep," I shoot back. Bradshaw's fingers dig into my hips with the comment. I look up over my shoulder at him. He flicks his eyes down to mine briefly, his intentions unreadable, before looking back at his brother.

I was after Eren initially, but I'd be lying if I said I wasn't more interested in Bradshaw. He has secrets and demons hiding behind that soulless expression he wears. Something damaged and broken being kept from view.

A sigh leaves my lips as I crack my spritzer open and gulp it down. Bradshaw moves to stand beside his brother as they exchange a few words. I can't make out what they're saying over the booming music, though. Then they look with bewilderment at the empty can I'm crushing between my hands.

"What? Expected me to sip on it?" I refuse to feel embarrassed about my drinking skills.

Eren laughs then slaps his hand on Bradshaw's back. "You two go ahead and get out of here. I'm sure I won't be far behind." He winks at us. My blood pounds loudly in my ears as make eye contact with Bradshaw.

"Get out of here?" I ask no one in particular. The one-night stand I wanted is looking promising, but with the

psycho brother instead of the guy I thought it would be with.

Bradshaw gives his brother a nod and Eren presses a kiss to my forehead before waving us off. *Wait.* Bradshaw guides me to the club entrance, where the music isn't as loud, before I start to slow.

He looks down at me in question. The cold edge has eased from his eyes and I wonder if it's because we both know where tonight is headed.

"Let's go to my hotel," I say boldly. I'm also going to make him check in with the front desk person with me before we head up. Can never be too careful. I've watched enough true crime to make any sane person paranoid, even if I'm trained to kill a man in more ways than anyone has the right to know. Bradshaw is one of the rare ones that has me on edge.

He smiles for the first time and it's a sight to behold. Somehow it makes him more mysterious too.

"Sure," Bradshaw says and flashes me that lazy grin again. *Holy shit.* He's the kind of guy I would take a three-day vacation for just to fuck for seventy-two hours straight.

My cheeks warm as he takes my hand and guides us out of the club. He leads me into the dark parking lot before mounting a crotch rocket. I force the smile that wants to bloom over my lips to remain small. *He's certainly full of surprises.* Bradshaw hands me his helmet and I raise a brow at him.

"You wear it," he says sharply, almost annoyed that I'd even be concerned about him not having one.

Asshole. I shove the helmet over my head and sit behind him, wrapping my arms around his wide torso and locking my hands together. It's not my first time on a motorcycle, but I get that same flutter in my chest with Bradshaw driving. He takes off at a wicked speed, maybe trying to scare me, but I just smile and let my head lie flat against his back.

The knowledge that this might very well be my last indulgence in pleasure sends a pulse of dread through me. But I'll make it fucking memorable. I haven't felt excited like this since Sergeant Jenkins cornered me against a shower stall when I was first transferred to Riøt.

We check in with the hotel clerk and head up to my room without any chit-chat. His lack of conversation makes the hair on the back of my neck rise. I'm keenly aware of the heat from his gaze as I slide the key card to my room.

I set my wallet down on the entry table, having fleeting thoughts of how stupid this might be. Admittedly, I've never fucked a stranger. But his hands smooth over my stomach, casting away any doubt I had as he pulls me back against his broad chest. My eyes widen. He's already taken his hoodie off and only his thin T-shirt hides those abs. He dips his head beside mine and presses his lips delicately to my collar bone. His breath is warm against my skin.

He spins me to face his chest and lowers his head to mine for a kiss. I open my mouth to say something rather than going straight into it, but he lets out a sigh and gives me a pointed look. This close, his scars are clear, more defined and red. Fresh. Maybe a year old. Two, max.

"I'm not here to get to know you." His voice is stern. Detached.

"*Oh*... sorry. I just don't do this often so..." I trail off and look down. Heat spikes through my veins with embarrassment. He's absolutely brutal.

Bradshaw tilts his head and guides my chin up with his hand, staring into my eyes coldly, like I'm a meal he wants to devour and be done with. My eyes trail to his ears where he has two black cuff earrings at the center of each. "I'll lead," he says placidly and brings his lips to mine.

In contrast to his personality, his lips are the softest I've ever kissed. His crisp forest scent falls over me and I'm instantly sucked into this moment with him.

It's not a romantic kiss people dream about. It's fervent and starved. Bradshaw guides me to the bed and dips me down to the sheets. He deepens his ruthless pursuit and our tongues meet aggressively. His teeth aren't far behind. I moan as he bites into the fat of my lower lip.

He breaks our connection and leans up, pulling his shirt off and tossing it to the floor. I watch him through hooded eyes and admire the sharpness of his body. There are many scars that caress each divot, making me certain that he's in the army too. The long grooves were from KA-BAR knives, I assume by the severity of the scars. Bullet holes have left starbursts on his skin. I want to ask him about them. I want to hear his stories. But he clearly doesn't want to talk and it's probably for the best. I'm going to be leaving tomorrow anyway. So, I admire him in silence and let his movements take my thoughts away.

Bradshaw's eyes find mine as he slowly removes his pants. I lower my hands to my waistband but he stops me.

"I like to do it," he confesses with a dark grin.

I swallow, trying to remain calm when my body is anything but. The throb of need in my core is enough to have me squirming, but I like the slow pace he's setting. He likes to be in control and clearly something depraved in me finds that erotic.

He frees his cock and tosses a condom on the sheets for when we're ready.

My eyes linger on his sheer girth. I expected nothing less, honestly. The assholes are always hung for some reason.

Bradshaw turns his attention to me now, lifting my shirt slowly and pressing kisses up my stomach to my chest. He unhooks my bra and pulls it over my head along with my shirt. He easily slides my leggings and underwear off after. My nipples pebble against the chill in the air. He lowers his lips to one while palming the other gently.

I writhe beneath him as he flicks my tit and mercilessly

swirls his tongue around. He rubs his shaft through my wet slit, coaxing and teasing my core until my nails are digging into the soft flesh of his back. A low grumble vibrates in his chest as he lowers his hand and uses two fingers to circle my clit. My back arches and he pulls me closer against his chest, breathing heavily and dotting my neck with kisses.

He gently pumps his hips, rubbing his dick against my stomach and wetting my skin with pre-come. *Oh my God.* He reaches behind me and grabs the condom, puts it between his pearly teeth and slowly tears it open, staring down into my eyes unfazed.

And just like that he made condoms sexy.

Bradshaw sheathes it over his twitching cock and grins at me as he reaches down and pushes two fingers inside me. I moan at the intrusion as he rubs my inner walls, fingering my G-spot and smiling as I beg him not to stop. He pulls his fingers out before my orgasm can build further and shows me the evidence of my arousal.

"You see how wet you are for a stranger? What a good girl. Are you going to scream for me too? I'd like it if you did," he whispers, but his voice isn't soothing. It's sexy and scary. Dominant.

Who the fuck is this man? I find myself wondering again.

He lines his tip to my entrance and starts teasing me, only pushing the head in before pulling it out. I can feel myself stretching for him, each thrust going deeper and penetrating small pieces of me at a time.

I whimper and the sound draws his attention back to my lips. He brings himself over me and whispers against my lips, "I like it hard." His brows are pinched with concentration and his thrusts are so painfully slow that my hips move of their own volition, trying to get him to burrow deeper inside of me.

My core throbs at his words and I nod, drunk with lust.

I feel his grin over my lips and let out a gasp as he rolls

me onto my side. He remains on his knees and settles between my thighs. He pulls my right leg up vertically with his chest. Good thing I'm flexible or this would've been painful. His cruel smile tells me he's having the same thought.

"Fuck, your body is perfect."

He wraps his hand around my upper thigh and presses the other around my waist. Then he thrusts into me ruthlessly. My cry is instant and I have to smother it by pressing my hand to my lips. The moans are just as loud, though. Bradshaw only lets out low grunts as he fucks me harder than I've ever been before. His muscles are flexed and working so effortlessly. He's a god in human skin.

Those merciless eyes stare down at me shamelessly, enjoying the twist of my expression between pleasure and pain. He stops for a second and flips me on my stomach, then resituates himself back inside me before he drags his hand down the length of my arm and cinches his fingers around my wrist. I moan as he wriggles his hips and his dick stirs up my pussy. He fills me to the brim, to the deepest parts of my abdomen and it feels so fucking good.

So good that I hardly notice when he pulls my wrist over my head and pins it to the sheets and wraps his other hand around my neck. I gasp, temporarily startled because he's completely dominating me, but he jerks his hips into me and my breath swiftly turns into a cry of pleasure.

He grinds further inside me until we're flush and his pumps slow, pulling all the way out before pushing to the hilt once more with enough force to make me scream each time, over and over until my eyes are lolling. He has me gasping and crying out like this is the first time I've been fucked.

"Oh my God!" I cry as my hips tremble, coming all over his cock. He doesn't let up. My next orgasm is already building back up. I'm not sure how much more I can handle.

Bradshaw drags his hand up my throat and to my mouth, forcing two fingers between my lips and breathing against my ear. "What God? Tonight, you only scream and cry for me. No God will bear witness to what I make of you." My eyes flutter shut at his words and I suck on his fingers.

He chuckles and ruts into me harder. I cry out again, fisting the sheets and biting down on his fingers. He groans and slides his hand out of my mouth and down my jaw to angle my head back so he can kiss me. He shoves his tongue down inside my mouth and consumes me. Our hot breaths mingle as we devour each other. His thrusts are getting faster and his breath more uneven. My entire body thrums with the release that shoots through my flesh like fire.

I cling to the sheets as he comes a few seconds after me, pressing his hips into mine harder and wrapping his arms around my chest as his engorged cock throbs inside me. He's all the way against my cervix and pulsing with each jerk he makes. I've never been so full and satiated. His teeth clench together and he grunts a couple more times before his body goes lax on top of mine.

Our breaths settle and he rolls us so we're on our sides. He holds me close against his chest, cock still planted deep inside me. I'd be surprised if the condom didn't break during that savage fucking. I don't usually do tender embraces—only Jenkins was allowed to hold me—but since I'm giving myself this one last night of pleasure, I shut my eyes and enjoy it for what it is.

Bradshaw lets his thumb graze my side a few times in long, languid strokes before pressing a kiss to my shoulder. He slides his cock out slowly and I'm left empty. I want to talk with him and get to know him even if it's just a little. But one look at his cold features has me holding my tongue. He has that detached air about him again like a flip of a switch.

We did what we came here to do. It's written on his face.

Right. I get my brain on the same level.

I offer him a genuine smile as I stand to pass him on my way to the bathroom. "You were a good fuck. You can see yourself out," I say with as much resolve as I can. I'd rather be the one to be cold about parting ways than him.

Miraculously, I stop myself from looking back at him one last time. I'll never forget those cold eyes and his heart-stopping face. The scars that hold a million questions and stories that I'll never know.

I shut the bathroom door behind me and turn on the shower, sliding in after I see steam rolling through the air.

It was a nice night. Tomorrow, I will be a killer again. I'll shed the sheep's clothing and be myself. *Today was fun, though,* I think as I lather my skin with soap. No matter how undeserving I deem myself of self-indulgence in things that bring me joy. I'd like to think my dead squadmates would encourage me to have a final courtesy before I'm thrown back into the blood and mud.

The door creaks as I'm lathering my hair with shampoo. I rinse my face and wipe my eyes before opening them. A flutter spreads through my stomach and a small gasp escapes my lips.

Bradshaw is in the shower with me, watching me with unreadable eyes.

"Why are you still here?" I ask, not sounding as cruel as I was going for.

The corner of his lip kicks up and he sets a hand on the wall behind me. "No one's kicked me out before and I didn't like it."

I huff out a breath and roll my eyes. His grin only grows.

"I have to get up early, so…"

He bursts out laughing and it shocks me. I legit did not think this man could laugh. I squeeze my hands at my sides at the warmth that spreads through my heart just at the sound of his raspy laugh. Perhaps because, although he's a stranger, I can tell it is rare. His laughter is unused.

"There it is again. It doesn't feel good."

I shift to turn away, but he catches my chin and brings his lips in for a crushing kiss. When he pulls away, his eyes are filled with curiosity and he studies my face intently.

"I thought you *weren't here to get to know me*," I say harshly.

He dips down and runs his tongue from the center of my throat up to my lips and kisses me a few times before murmuring, "Ask me something."

A new heat throbs between my thighs. I let him guide me to the wall as he strokes his tongue over my collar bone, tasting my wet flesh and feeling every inch of my body with his hands.

I suppress a moan and say, "I was actually kind of hungry and was going to wash up before going to that diner we passed down the block."

Bradshaw pulls back and assesses me, narrowing his eyes like he can't quite figure me out. But he smiles.

"Damn. Rejected *again*," he mumbles and raises a brow. "Want company?"

I break.

"Sure."

three

. . .

Bradshaw fits in with the whole late night at a twenty-four-hour diner vibe. His black attire is gloomy and his hood is securely back over his head where it belongs.

I thank the waitress as she brings me a cup of coffee and eggs benedict. Bradshaw ordered a cup of orange juice and a breakfast burrito.

It's now one in the morning. *So much for going to bed early.* But I don't mind being tired tomorrow. This is a much, *much* better night than I could've hoped for. I haven't felt anything like this in two years. And the longing to care for someone again is an ache I'm not ready to settle yet. I'll bask in his presence for as long as I can.

We haven't said a word to each other since arriving. He just keeps staring at me like he's trying to figure me out. At least he's not full-on glaring anymore.

I drop two sugar cubes into my mug and three packages of the small fake milk cups they leave on each table in a white bowl. Bradshaw takes a bite of his burrito and shuts his eyes.

"That good?" I tease, cutting into my eggs and eager to follow him into the food bliss.

He nods. "Best one a.m. burrito I've ever had."

I laugh. "How many *have* you had?"

He shrugs. "I guess this is the first."

"You've never gone out for late-night food?"

He shakes his head, the empty expression slowly returning to his eyes. "I was never allowed to leave the house at night growing up. And I joined the military young." He keeps it brief.

My throat bobs. I knew it. *Avoid the topic of work.*

"Why? Were your parents super strict with you and Eren?" I ask before shoving food in my mouth. I shut my eyes as the hollandaise takes over my tastebuds. *So good.*

He looks up at me and smirks.

"We were orphaned early on. The foster folks let Eren do whatever he wanted. They only kept me locked away because they thought I was going to hurt people if I had the chance."

My fork stills on my plate.

"Would you have?"

Bradshaw studies me inquisitively before ultimately saying, "Maybe. I was always sort of an *off* kid."

Me too. I want to admit but the words die on my tongue.

"Hmm, that's odd," he says, a darkness blooming over those icy eyes.

"What?"

"This is the part where you're supposed to be afraid of me."

I take a sip of my coffee before looking over the empty diner. My eyes move back to his. "You don't scare me." He does, though, just a little.

A sinister expression takes over his handsome face and sends chills up my spine.

"Is that so?" He lifts his drink and takes a few swigs. His Adam's apple bobs a few times and I hate how intently I watch it. He sets the cup back down and licks his lips. "What *is* a girl like you afraid of then?"

I try thinking of what scares me.

I was afraid of losing Jenkins and my squad, but that already happened.

"The ocean." My smile is mischievous.

He grins sarcastically. "Are you serious?"

I laugh. "Of course! Tons of people are scared of the ocean. It's fucking huge and it's so easy to lose control of things out there in the vast waters." I shudder just talking about it.

Bradshaw leans forward with his elbow on the table, his chin resting on his palm. Strands of his black hair are splayed over his forehead and make him all the more lovely. He blinks at me like my words are interesting and contentment tugs at his smile.

"What are you looking at?" I ask, annoyed.

"At the woman who fears the ocean but not me," he taunts.

My eyes narrow. "Well, what is a guy like you afraid of?" I playfully nudge his shoe with mine. I could be in a throwback movie right now, flirting with the man of my dreams. I muse about that as I watch him hesitate to answer. "Well?"

"Nothing scares me."

"That's bullshit." My nudging foot turns into a kicking one.

He shoots me a glare before breaking and shaking his head with another one of his soothing laughs.

"Okay, fine. I guess if I had to name one thing, it'd be outliving my twin."

I nod. "He's the only person that matters to you?"

His eyes flicker. "He's the only one left."

So there were others, but they aren't around anymore. I lean back and cross my arms. I'm no stranger to loss. "I'm sorry to hear that."

Bradshaw lifts a shoulder. "That's life." He pauses before changing the topic. "So what's a person like you doing here in Coronado?" He signals the waitress that we're done with our meals.

"Just trying new locations. Seeing what suits me," I lie. The waitress trots over with the check and my cheeks warm when he hands her cash before I can object.

"Thanks," I say as the waitress walks away.

He holds out his hand for mine expectantly. I slip my fingers over his.

"It's been a long time since I've met someone I enjoy talking to other than Eren." He brushes his thumb over the tips of my fingers before releasing my hand and nodding toward the exit.

"Same. But obviously without Eren," I mutter. Bradshaw makes a face and shakes his head with a smirk.

"See? You just say weird things."

"So do you."

"Maybe that's why I don't mind you."

I wait for him to walk ahead before smiling to myself. He sounded like Jenkins by saying that. *I don't mind you.* Those were the first hard-earned, kind words I'd won from my sergeant. Ones I never thought I'd hear from lips as cold as his were.

That's how I know Bradshaw, deep down, is a kind person too.

We walk around the corner, heading back to the hotel. I think to tell him he doesn't need to walk me back, but I doubt he'd listen.

"So, Bradshaw, what kind of guy are you really?" I bump

his shoulder with mine. The muscles in his neck feather but he steadily walks.

"I'm a devil."

"A devil?" I echo incredulously.

If he knew what I was capable of he'd think I was a devil too.

"Yeah. I've done things no one could fathom. Things I hate myself for." *Okay, ominous much?* "How about you? What kind of person are you?"

I think about that. I've killed many *targets*. Assigned and backed with paper. People I'd never met or knew why I was doing it. I have no clue how many children or brothers or sisters they had. I just followed orders, blindly and with little care. Jenkins always called me his little reaper.

"I'm a reaper," I say thoughtlessly.

He stops outside the hotel entrance and looks down at me, eyebrows raised. "A reaper, huh? That's a weird thing for a beautiful young woman to say." His eyes narrow.

If only he knew. But my life is a sinful secret, my actions nothing but a whisper in the wind.

It still wears on me, though, each kill slowly draining my soul more than the last.

"What do you do for work?" he asks as he brushes his thumb over my cheek.

I take a short breath and shake my head. "I'm in between jobs." I am *technically* between squads at the moment.

His brows knit in thought, but he pulls me into a hug, running his fingers down my back. I still as his fingers stop mid-way, close to my spine, over the bullet-sized scar that I know is piquing his interest.

"What did you do before?" He pushes. I can hear the gears in his head starting to turn.

My brain short circuits.

"Um, I worked at a library."

He pushes me an arm's length away and gives me a distrustful look. "Why are you lying?"

My lungs cease. "I'm not."

The coldness returns to his eyes, the hard set back to his jaw.

I reciprocate the callousness. "Why does it matter? What do *you* do?"

He doesn't respond.

"That's what I thought. Hypocrite." I attempt to walk around him and head inside to the lobby, but Bradshaw steps between me and the doors.

"Are you not saying what you do for work for the same reason I'm not?" His voice has a new edge to it, like a blade pointed right at me.

I look up at him and meet those scrutinizing eyes. His divine beauty should be illegal.

"What are you talking about?" I say as casually as I can. He studies me with disdain burning in his eyes before nudging me to the brick side of the building. There he leans over me, arms pressed to either side of the wall at my back.

I freeze. I can't breathe. I can't speak.

His words are careful. "You aren't *Penelope Gallows,* are you?"

Every hair on the back of my neck raises and he sees the shock roll through my expression.

How did he know my real name? Unless... no.

"You're not in the underground... the dark forces... are you?" My voice is shaky.

His eyes widen with the mention of our secret branch and his jaw sets with animosity. Bradshaw's muscles flex and his astonishment quickly turns into anger.

"You're the fucking *bunny* being assigned to our squad."

Oh. Fuck Me.

four

. . .

Bunny. They fucking call me *Bunny*! It better not be my code name for the squad or I swear to God I'll... I'll... I let out a scream into my pillow and punch the sheets.

After Bradshaw realized who I was, we stopped talking and he left abruptly.

I proceeded to my room where I am now freaking the fuck out.

"Goddammit. *Goddammit!*" My words fill the dark hotel room. I lie back on the bedsheets we just fucked on and spread my arms out, exhausted with the day and dreading meeting the new squad more than I already was.

I put my bulky headphones on and blare "Forget Me Too" by MGK with a scowl firmly planted on my face until I eventually pass out.

———

KM Moronova

My blood is thick with anxiety as I step off the bus and onto military grounds with only my small bag of personal items glued to my side. I hold it firmly beneath my arm as a sort of security blanket.

Jenkins always told me I had small bad habits. The bag under my arm being one of them. The hope I had in my eyes being another, though I don't have that problem anymore. That died many, *many* years ago.

This is fine. *I'm fine.* I take a grounding breath. I just hope that Bradshaw isn't on my immediate squad. There are three squads in our underground branch after all: Malum, Riøt, and Hades. My squad was the only one stationed on the East Coast. Hades and Malum are both located here, as they work closer together. But based on how he reacted last night to who I was... *ugh.* The odds aren't in my favor.

Worst case scenario, he's the sergeant or something. There's absolutely no way he's my partner, Bones.

The dread inside me only sinks further as I step foot into the cement fortress. The buildings on this base are all a mundane gray. The lawn is cut short and neat. Men run in groups around the fenced track for their morning exercises and I can instantly feel several sets of eyes on me. Judging, I'm sure.

Time to set in the cold bitch face Jenkins taught me. He made sure I knew how to survive in this male-dominated world. *"Otherwise you'd be eaten alive,"* he told me. I only wish he had taught me something in case I accidentally slept with one of my squadmates unknowingly. *Now that would've been useful.*

I take a deep breath and keep my eyes straight ahead. My legs move in a steady beat, almost a march. I ignore the looks and demeaning whispers that are huffed out under disapproving breaths.

It's difficult sometimes to remember that most of these men aren't aware the dark forces even exist. I mean, it was

44

only formed around twenty years ago with the rise of organized terrorism and black market dealings that the government didn't want their name attached to. Private sectors were formed to keep everything and everyone blissfully ignorant of the darkness that truly unfolds in this world. Sometimes we do truly morally corrupt things, like taking out scientists in other countries that are working on new methods of curing diseases. But we aren't here to question the missions, we just have to execute them. Follow orders.

I've come to the conclusion that we aren't the good guys. Hence why we're under the rug.

Getting angry will only fuel their taunts, I remind myself. *Show them you're worthy of their respect.* Jenkins told me this every time he found me crying in secret during my first few years. I'd never had such tender hands wipe away my tears before. He would sit beside me and wait until I calmed, then he'd tell me to show my comrades I deserved to be here as much as they did.

It's harder to hold onto those words as I enter the small war room with my new squad waiting for me like a den of snakes. They're all here already. They lift their heads and give me nothing less than harrowing scowls.

There are six of them in total. I instantly recognize Eren standing at the head of the room—his expression is the only one that has a bit of pity for me, but there's also a distinct sharpness there too. *Shit, that means Bradshaw told him everything.*

I sweep the room, not seeing Bradshaw's face. I almost relax, thinking that I've evaded the worst possible outcome, before my eyes land on one man who's wearing a black fabric mask over the bottom half of his face. Only his pale blue eyes, black hair, and scars are visible.

I could die right now from the anxiety coiling inside my stomach.

No one mutters a word. The room feels ten degrees

warmer than I'm sure it is as I awkwardly take the only open seat. Right next to Bradshaw. I pull my arms in tight against my chest, trying to avoid touching him. I swallow the shame that burns my throat. Why couldn't he have been someone else? *Anyone* else.

Eren moves toward the door and shuts it before addressing all of us. "Malum Squad, meet our new recruit, Private Gallows. Originally from Riøt Squad."

Malum. I had to look it up the first time I'd heard of them. When I was assigned to Riøt at the start of my military sentence, I didn't know there were two other dark forces squads that were just as lethal as we were. Hades: The hounds they send to wreak havoc. Riøt: The executors of traitors. And Malum: *The Evil*—the squad that goes where no one else can or is qualified to go, to snuff out the enemy quietly like ghosts in the darkness of night. Most of their missions are with secret organizations in remote locations. Busting black market weapons merchants or huge drug dealers that have integrated into society behind the facade of commercial retailers.

I straighten and keep my expression schooled into the hard and emotionless appearance that's required to be sitting here in this room. They all give me bone-chilling stares. Bradshaw doesn't even bother glancing my way. His arms are tightly crossed around his chest.

Anger swells inside my lungs but I keep it tamed. *Show them I deserve to be here.*

"I'm honored to be here, sir," I respond with a sharp tone.

Eren smirks at me. "We all go by code names here, so I'll only tell you your comrades' names once. You'll be good to remember them and protect them with your life, Private Gallows." I give him a curt nod, my lips pressed firmly. Starting with the guy on my right he points to them and goes down the line. "Jefferson, Pete, Ian, and Harrison." He skips Bradshaw and for a moment I think it's because he knows I already met him. "Their corresponding code names are: Jobs, Badger, Colt, Wasp, and Bones. My code name is just Sergeant."

Bones.

My eyes widen and that pit in my stomach sinks further with the confirmation of the worst-case scenario.

Please, God, tell me I didn't fuck *the* Bones, the dark ops guy who is rumored to be a death god. I once heard that he tore a soldier's arm off and used the broken humerus bone as a spear as he shoved it down another's throat. Not even his squad is supposed to know his identity. The same guy that I'm charged with being the direct second to. His partner in the trenches.

That guy.

"And your code name is *Bunny*," Eren says with a dark tone that sets my lungs ablaze. The corners of his lips twitch, suppressing a wry smile.

I look up at him sharply and glare. "I'm sorry, sir. That's unacceptable."

The men all burst into laughter except Bones, clearly not finding anything about this situation funny. He sits with his arms firmly crossed, refusing to look at me. His black compression long-sleeve shirt is tight against his skin, making those memorable muscles stand out.

Eren levels me a cruel grin. "Your squad chose your code name for you, Bunny. Are you implying that they aren't worthy to name their newest squadmate?"

My teeth bore a hole into the side of my cheek and blood blooms across my tongue. I can't decline it. Of course, they would do this to me. I'm not surprised but it still stings my pride. Even Riøt called me Gallows. They found my name to fit my personality and ruthless executions. With a deep breath, I force a hard smile. "No sir, Bunny… is adequate." God, those words are physically painful to say.

The men roar with laughter once more and I have to bury my nails into my palm to keep from losing my shit. It's ten thousand times worse than being laughed at by eighteen- and nineteen-year-old comrades; I wasn't as tough back then as I am now. These men are full-grown assholes. Early thirties, maybe mid to late twenties like me and they still act like pricks.

They can make fun of me all they'd like. It's me who's going to be saving their asses in the field. If they want to call me Bunny, then I'll be the most vicious little creature they've ever crossed.

"Aw, she's so cute guys," Pete says in a condescending voice. There isn't a hint of jovial lightheartedness in those dark brown eyes of his.

Jefferson tilts his head at me and scowls. "I don't even think she's cute. Riøt Squad must've been blind," he remarks as he nudges Pete with his elbow.

I stand abruptly and slam my hands on the table. That gets their attention. They shut up and stare at me with hatred.

"Don't talk about my squad," I threaten Jefferson. He sits tall in his seat, with short light-brown hair that's slicked back.

He narrows his eyes at me, clearly not caring about my fair warning, as he snaps back, "*Ex*-squad, *Bunny*. They're all dead."

I lunge at him to… I don't know, hit him or something irrational, but Bones grabs my wrist tightly and whistles. "Whoa, Bun. You'll only excite us if you get *physical*." I whirl on him and tear my arm from his hold, glaring daggers into his eyes. His brow raises with mild amusement.

"That's enough. Bunny, *sit*," Eren commands, opening up his black folder and organizing some pages for the briefing.

Reluctantly, I sit down and only look at the front of the room. This has already turned into the shithole I knew it would be. Bradshaw lets out a long breath. Harrison and Ian talk in a hushed tone, throwing me glares frequently. I hear my squad's name a few more times in their exchange. I dig my nails into the leather arms of my chair.

Assholes.

"You guys know the drill. When a new squad member joins the team, we take an extended training to bond and make sure they are a good fit. The last thing we want is a mission to go upside down due to lack of trust and skill set. Bunny was primarily the sniper on Riøt Squad, but we'll need to see how her long distance and close combat skills work with us."

"But Sarge, you said we don't have a choi—"

"Pete," Bradshaw snaps and levels him a glare.

Eren gives Pete a pointed look before continuing. "Yeah, we technically don't have a choice in whether or not she will fit with the team the way we want. But should she, say, throw in the towel"—his voice is thick with intent—"well, we just don't have control of that, now do we?"

All heads in the room turn to me, while I look hopelessly at Eren, who I thought was someone I could partially count on but apparently not.

"What does it take to get a bunny to quit?" Ian taunts.

"A *big* fucking carrot," Harrison says with a nasty grin pulling at the corner of his mouth. Bradshaw grunts beside me like he's trying to contain his laugh.

Anger thrums through my veins like fire. "Wait, so instead of accepting me as one of your own, you're going to try and bully me to quit? Because I'm a former Riøt soldier? What the fuck is wrong with you?" My voice is lead.

"What's wrong with *us*? You were the sole survivor while your entire team perished. What does that say about you?" Jefferson leans over the table and sneers at me.

My blood chills because he's right. And he's not the only person who's told me that either.

"The only good Riøt soldier is a dead one," Bradshaw says smoothly. Like it's his fucking slogan to live by. His eyes fill with pleasure the angrier I get. I shove him out of his seat and his ass hits the ground. He's back on his feet in a heartbeat and grabs my shoulders with a vice grip.

"That's enough, everyone! I don't want to hear any more trash talk. I've already told you I don't want to see any foul play out there in the training mission. I just want you to not hold back." Eren moves his eyes to me and his brother, pinning us with a glare. "You too, Bunny. I want to see everything you've got."

Bradshaw's hold on me loosens and he sits down with force, like a goddamn child.

I stare at Eren for a beat, trying to get a read on him, but his features are stone. I reluctantly nod and fist my hands tightly under the table.

"Any questions before dismissal?" Eren looks us over and when no one else seems to have any, I speak up.

"What's the mission that's *so* important the general sent me?" There are hundreds of other squadless soldiers in the dark forces that are just waiting for positions like these to pop up. They're already replacing Riøt with some new squad. So why not someone else? Why me?

Eren's brow twitches as he closes the folder on the desk. "You won't get the details until we confirm you're staying on the squad, Bunny."

I raise a brow and glance at the others. They don't question their sergeant's authority at all. "Yeah, because that makes sense," I grumble, but it's ignored.

Eren slaps his hands together. "Alright, squad, hit the showers and show Bunny the barracks. We'll meet at fourteen hundred at the chopper pick-up on the north end of base. Have your bags packed and get ready for a hell of a month."

They all salute him and stand in unison. "Yes, Sergeant."

An entire month in the training field is going to suck. But I try my best to stay positive. I give Bones a hesitant look, wondering if we'll be able to break past our awkward circumstances. In all honesty, it's not like I haven't had sex with other comrades. If he's worried that I know his identity, maybe I should try talking it out with him. I mull it over as the squad files out of the war room.

The twins share an uncertain look between them before Bradshaw walks out.

I stop beside Eren. He's easier to talk to, so maybe I should try to explain things to him first. "Sarge, I apologize about yesterday. I didn't know—"

He cuts me off sharply. "Bunny, I trust that you will keep yesterday's events to yourself entirely. Not a peep unless you want to be shipped out within the next hour." Eren's voice drips with disdain, though it's much softer than the other guys'.

I nod and look away pointedly before following my new squad through the cement jungle.

This is panning out to be way bleaker than I expected. I thought they might at least have a little sympathy for me for losing my comrades, but that's a hard no. They blame me and, by the sound of it, they're going to do everything in their power to get me to quit. If I'm anything, it's stubborn. General Nolan assigned me to Malum for a reason and the concern on his face while telling me I was being reassigned tells me it has a connection to what happened in Patagonia.

I have to stay no matter what. I won't let Malum scare me off. I have a fucking job to do, and I'll be damned if I don't see it through. I need to avenge my squad and bring down the enemy. By the end of our training trial in California, I'll have Malum's respect.

I take a deep breath and focus ahead where my squad-mates walk steadily. They know each other more than anyone, but that's about to change. I doubt they know my brain is one of my strongest attributes. *Cataloging brilliance,* Jenkins called it.

Jefferson is the tallest of Malum. Codename: Jobs. I try to go through my motions of memorizing them so I can start the internal profiles I keep of every squadmate I've had. It also might be a temporary reprieve from stressing about my situation.

We start training tonight and I need to have each of them down before then. Jefferson has short, light brown hair, dark brown eyes, and sun-kissed skin. He looks like he's in his late twenties and has a scar shaped like a bullet hole on the back of his neck. Scars can be weak points. If I find myself in close combat with him, I'll make sure to dig my knuckle into it.

As I'm walking behind them, analyzing, I can't help but notice one studying me in return. I look to my left and find Pete's brown eyes intently on me. His code name is Badger. Of all the men on my team, his eyes are the least judgy. There's a curiosity to them rather than distrust. He's taller than me but shorter than Bradshaw. His skin is darker than mine and his black hair is short like Jefferson's.

"Bunny," he says in greeting. His tone is void of sarcasm, which I am immensely grateful for at the moment.

"Badger," I reply just as curtly, and he flashes a tight grin at me.

"You're quick with names," he muses.

I don't return the smile.

Jenkins's first rule: No emotions. No weakness. Not when you're on duty.

"I'm going to know everything about you inside and out before your head hits the ground tonight." My voice is smooth but ill-willed. I'm not going to just forget how big of an asshole he was two minutes ago.

His smile vanishes and a flicker of uncertainty flashes across his gaze. "Uh, s-same," he stammers before redirecting. "You know you're dead, right? If you don't quit willingly, I think Bones just might kill you."

I set my eyes on the back of Bradshaw's head. "He can try."

"Trust me, he will. I hope it's gross too. You know he has a collection of teeth, right?"

I ignore his attempt to make me fear Bradshaw.

"Because I'm a Riøt?"

Pete's mouth molds into a sinister grin. "No shit. Your team is the reason we lost Achilles. You guys fucked us when you didn't show up at the checkpoint." His voice is laced with anger and he shoulders me before walking ahead. I noticed Bradshaw's shoulder flinch when he heard the name Achilles.

The soldier I'm replacing.

"Hey, don't bother talking to Bunny, she'll be on the first bus out before dawn," Ian mutters to Pete as they walk side by side. *Ignore it—catalog,* I order myself. Ian's code name is Colt. I narrow my eyes at him. He's the youngest of the group. His hair is an inch longer than Pete's, black and slicked back. His olive-toned skin is the same shade as mine and he has a cocky smile that I want to put my fist in.

I level him my most insidious stare. One that I hope tells him I'd kill him if ordered to. Because I would. I've done it countless times before whether I knew a soldier or not.

"She'll be crying like a fucking baby when we're done with her." Ian winks at me.

"Bunnies *will* consume their own under stress," I say nonchalantly, and the five of them stop walking and look back at me, shocked. Even Bradshaw this time, his eyes filled with fury.

"What the fuck did you just say?" Harrison barks, disgust muddled in his voice. Code name: Wasp. His hair is blond and he has pale skin that's been tanned by the sun.

His hair is short and he has a straight nose that has yet to be broken. *Yet.*

"Oh, *I'm sorry.* Are you hard of hearing? I said *bunnies* will eat their own under stress," I raise my voice, drawing eyes from other groups of men. My squad's earlier amusement in me seems to have been properly snuffed out. Their disturbed expressions are better than the sneering ones at least.

They know as well as I do that Riøt specialized in tracking and killing traitors in the armed forces. Sometimes even dark forces soldiers we worked with if their name ended up on Jenkins's receiver. A black bullet always indicated it was from a Riøt's weapon. If you were shot with a black bullet, you were dead.

"*Jesus Christ,*" Ian mumbles.

Jefferson looks at Bradshaw like he wants him to do something about it, then glares back at me. "Great. Our psychopath meets his match and now our lives are in their twisted hands."

"Make sure to remember that when I'm putting a three-inch bullet through an enemy's eye socket for your sorry ass, Jobs." My voice is filled with loathing. I strut past all five of them with my bag slung over my shoulder as I make straight for the showers ahead. Their brows are heavy with irritation, frowns pulling at each of their lips.

Especially Bradshaw. The fact that his mask can't hide his glower is chilling. He looks at me as if I'm gutter trash that swept in during a storm. It stings my ego, but I banish all the thoughts of him looking tenderly at me last night.

The second I'm alone in the women's showers I let out an exasperated breath and look at myself in the mirror with dull eyes.

How am I going to make it out of this alive?

five

. . .

My bruised leg and torn up feet burn as I lower them into the hot spring. The rest of Riøt went the remaining few miles to get back to base, but I can't handle another elbow to my ribs or one of them tripping me and laughing about it.

I blow out a long breath before letting the rest of my body sink into the warm water. My eyes close and, for the first time in months, I have a sliver of peace.

"Private Gallows, did I excuse you from formation?"

And the peace is gone.

I jolt and straighten at the sound of Sergeant Jenkins's voice. He's standing on the rocks lining the edge across from me and has a full view of my naked body. My arms go to my chest and my cheeks burn.

His face is stone like it always is. His blond hair is fade-cut on the sides and longer on the top, swept to the side perfectly. His sharp cheek bones and jawline make him intimidating, but tonight I find his dark eyes a little softer than usual.

"Sorry, Sergeant Jenkins." I stand and turn to grab my clothes. How could I be so fucking stupid. Of course he'd notice if I slipped away from the squad.

"Gallows." His voice is stern.

I flinch and stop reaching for my shirt. "Yes, Sarge?"

"I didn't say you had to leave."

My eyes widen at his soft tone and I look over my shoulder at him. His brows lift slightly and the first smile I've ever seen from him curls the edges of his lips.

My whole world ends with that smile. I know I'll never endure one quite like it again.

"Please, by all means, resume," he says as he slowly takes off his jacket and hangs it on a branch.

I slowly let my body sink back into the water and watch him curiously as he sheds every article of clothing. I avert my eyes when his boxers drop to the ground and don't look back at him until I hear the water break.

He lets out a low sigh as the steam curls around him. He's sitting directly across from me and when his lovely eyes crack open, I don't look away.

"You don't have to be formal, so feel free to be yourself, Gallows." The way he's talking makes my chest hurt. Like he's tired of people being so stiff around him. But what does he expect? He's ruthless. We've all seen him kill. The first time I witnessed him gouge a soldier's eyes out haunted my dreams for weeks.

Jenkins always prefers to use his ebony knife if he can. He loves the intimacy of it. I nod but don't offer anything for conversation.

His eyes are heavy but he stares at me. My heart rate spikes when he starts to wade over to me.

"Are they still giving you trouble?" I clench my jaw when his hand finds my knee and he pulls my leg up enough to examine it. The bruises and cuts are evident of either me being the clumsiest person alive or them pushing me to the ground. Jenkins knows better, so there's no sense in lying.

"Yeah, they are." I won't meet his gaze.

He hums in thought. "I know you're the one that killed Barlet." My blood chills and my eyes snap to his nearly black ones. He knows? "I know that Barlet was an asshole. He was next on my list of traitors."

But I killed him without orders.

Oh God. Fuck, he knows now how fucked up I am. Sweat rolls down my temple.

"Sarge, I—"

"Jenkins. Call me Jenkins when it's just us." His eyes hold me captive. A dark light flickers through them.

"Jenkins… please don't report me to the general. I'll never earn my cards if I'm found to be insubordinate." That's all any of us want. Our cards, so we can go back to society. It's the only ticket out of the dark forces.

"Report you? No, Gallows, I want to take you under my wing." My eyes widen as he grips my chin gently, tilting my face up so I look into his dark eyes. "I'm going to help you bloom into the monster you truly are."

A monster.

"Why?"

He moves his hand to my cheek and brushes his thumb gently across it. "Because you're just like me. I also happen to like you, Gallows." That's the second compliment he's ever given me. My heart thumps wildly inside its cage.

We stare at each other for a moment, the warm water soothing my entire body and making me want to melt in his arms. I shouldn't want to be held by a murderous thing like him. But I do. I crave it like a shot of morphine.

Jenkins's eyes lower to my lips, lifting back to my eyes slowly before he leans in and kisses me.

The world ceases to exist as the man I fear most adorns me with kisses and his dark dreams for us.

I knew it then. Jenkins would ruin what good was left of me.

six

. . .

I WAIT PATIENTLY OUTSIDE THE MEN'S SHOWERS UNTIL MY SQUAD reappears. Bradshaw isn't among them and they seem to catch my wandering eyes.

"Bones showers separately. None of us are allowed to know what he looks like, so if you're going to fuck any of us, it can't be him. Unless you're into mask shit," Harrison says snidely. I don't bother responding to his goading. *I am indeed into that.* Pete and Ian laugh cruelly as they throw their towels at me. I step aside and let the towels fall to the floor.

I remain quiet as they lead the way to our barracks. The dorms are in their own section of the building, down a long hall with other squad rooms. Though, the underground squads are supposed to room on the lower floor. Sure, normal units see us around, but they have no clue the dark forces exist. They think we're just special ops. We are required to room in different halls to keep the chances of discovery low, so my curiosity piques when they open one of the doors on this floor.

Our room is a small cement chamber with three twin bunk beds only a few feet from each other. A barred window sits at the far wall. It feels like a big jail cell. *Great.* At least we'll be heading into the field for a while and we won't be cooped up together like hens. I'd rather sleep in the dirt and bushes than in this tight room.

I get it, though. Tight groups make for a trusting team and efficient missions. But there is a fatal flaw to that. My eyes linger on the bed at the end, above Bradshaw's bunk. It's empty for a reason. They had to recruit me to replace the guy Pete mentioned and I'd bet he wasn't *just* another squadmate. Achilles. He was probably a brother to all of these men. But he was second to Bradshaw. The two of them must've been close. The loss was probably a devastation to the squad, but catastrophic to him.

And they blame the Riøt Squad.

My legs don't allow me to approach the bed. An ache resides deep inside my chest. I'm no stranger to losing a partner in this hell. Losing a fellow certified killing machine is not easy.

It hurts like a gaping wound that will not heal. No matter what you try to fill it with, it remains cancerous and starved for grief.

I think of Jenkins's icy blond hair, the dark brown of his eyes. How I'll never see him watching me from across a room ever again. Two years is not enough to forget him. No amount of time can erase his face from my mind.

I was his second. It should've been me who died, not him. I close my eyes and think of his last words.

"I love you, Gallows. Leave me behind."

I loved him too and I let him down in the end. I want to be dead alongside him.

I fist my hands at my sides.

Pete comes up behind me and nudges my shoulder, startling me from my thoughts. "You're at the end. Top bunk." I nod and hesitantly walk to the back of the room. Bones isn't back yet from wherever he showers, so I don't waste time tossing my bag to the top bunk.

We each have a small dresser at the foot of our beds with our names labeled. I frown at my drawer. The label reads Bunny. And there are kid stickers of bunnies placed around the name.

I take another deep breath and ignore it before opening my drawer, pulling out a black uniform. We're a dark ops team so we don't wear the typical gear the other branches do. Ours are entirely black and matte, non-light reflective and a shade darker than any black you've ever seen.

We'll be damn near invisible tonight and part of me rejoices in that thought. I haven't been in the field for a while. I miss the hum of unknown territory and the adrenaline rush of being in action.

My pants hit the floor and the four men watch me unabashedly and with a fraction less of disdain as I get dressed. It's nothing I'm not used to. As long as they don't touch me, we won't have a problem.

They talk amongst themselves like I don't exist.

"I can't believe General Nolan chose her for the replacement," Ian retorts as he pulls on his field gear. Harrison nods and gives me a dirty side-glance, though his eyes linger on my breasts.

Jefferson smooths his hand over his light-brown hair and laughs. "Part of me still thinks it's a fucking joke."

Pete has his back to me as he mutters, "At least she's nice to look at." My cheeks heat with rage as the four of them lift their heads and steal another look at me.

Ian laughs and gives me a nasty smile. "Yeah, she's got a pretty mouth, doesn't she?" I can see the thoughts sifting through their heads. *We'll bully her out by making sexual comments.*

Fuck you.

I force a smile that physically hurts. "You have the prettiest mouth of all, Ian. Don't worry, your dick sucking spot on the squad is safe." Harrison's hand flies to his mouth to muffle his laugh-gasp. The others only give me cold stares.

Jefferson opens his big fucking mouth to say something else, but Bradshaw opens the door and everyone falls quiet. It's good to know that he at least has respect amongst his comrades. They don't act the same when he's around. I force my eyes to the floor to avoid any more arguing with the men. *If I want their respect, I'll have to make Bradshaw accept me first.* God, that will be easier said than done.

Bradshaw walks past me as I secure my bulletproof vest and tighten the straps. I take him in as he sits at the edge of his bed. He's wearing the same outfits we are, except his uniform neck rises high enough to meet the end of his mask. His ebony hair is covered with his slick black helmet. A small skull is painted on the bottom side, a glossy black that shines against the matte.

He must feel my gaze because those pale blue eyes lift to mine, his brows furrowed with annoyance. My instincts tell me to steer clear of him, but I know that won't work. We'll have to get along eventually, even if he is the world's biggest asshole.

"I look forward to working with you, sir," I say with a manner of respect. Though, it tastes like poison coming out of my mouth. I just want to forget about last night and start this mission on the right terms.

He doesn't let his eyes trail away from me as he says cruelly, "I want you to quit, Bun."

My chest drops and the other men stop talking as their attention is drawn to us.

I can't hold back my offended scoff. "That's not happening."

Bradshaw stands and shoves me back by the shoulders. My ass presses against the cinderblock wall and heat spreads through my entire body like wildfire. *Stay calm. Stay calm. You can't punch your superior. Not on the first day, in the first hour.*

"I don't want you as my second. None of us want you on the squad, *Bunny*. You couldn't even keep your prior first alive. What was his name? *Jenkins?*" My heart stops and he sees the anguish race across my features. His eyes flicker with regret for a second, but the resolve doesn't leave. He's standing over me, hands braced on either side of the wall, trying to make me feel small.

Oh, fuck this. No one talks about Jenkins like that.

"You don't want me on your squad because I won't die as easily as your last second. What was his name? Oh, I guess it wasn't worth remembering because I sure as fuck don't know it. At least you've *heard* of Jenkins."

Bradshaw's pupils expand and his face is horror-stricken for a millisecond before he controls the emotions.

Yeah, that didn't feel very good. Did it, big guy?

I want to unsay the words the second they leave my mouth, but anger makes them stay. Bradshaw's eyes fill with hatred. He fists my vest and furiously slams my back against the wall. My head rocks back toward the cement, but instead of impacting on stone it's cupped by Bradshaw's hand, his knuckles taking the brunt of it. The force shakes down a few of the framed awards from the wall and they crash around us.

A few audible gasps sound from the opposite end of the room but all I can focus on is Bradshaw. Even he's blurry through the brimming tears that I furiously blink away.

Bradshaw's teeth are gritted together, keeping venomous words back I'm sure, but it doesn't stop the force with which he holds me against the wall, keeping me pinned with pure rage. My airways strain at the pressure and as my wits come back to me, my hand flies to his wrist. He doesn't let up; he only searches my eyes.

"You're as good as dead," he finally says darkly—a sinister promise.

The others watch us with twisted expressions. Harrison has his hand extended toward us like he's going to interject, but he doesn't speak out against Bradshaw.

"Not if I let the enemy kill you first," I spit back at him. Bradshaw's eyes widen with disbelief. "I'll bet that's how your last second died, saving your ungrateful ass. If I die, it's because I'll be taking a bullet for you too and that *fucking* sucks." I lift my knee swiftly, intending to nail him in the balls but he releases me quickly and steps back. His knuckles are bloody where he took the impact from the back of my head.

There's a new flame in his cold eyes and I know that this is going to be a long, *long* night.

———

The chopper pick-up is vacant with the exception of our small squad. The helicopter blades block out all other sound as it descends to the circular pad. The seven of us lower our heads and swiftly move into it with nothing but our backpacks strapped to our backs. Eren takes up the rear and boards last.

Bradshaw sits to my right side while Jefferson is to my left. Pete, Harrison, and Ian sit across from us. We each wear muffled headgear so we can hear the instructions for our mock mission and training. Eren stands in the center, holding a handle in the center of the helicopter ceiling and speaks loudly through his mic.

"Malum Squad, we've located a group of armed specialists for a Level Red operation. They've taken five hostages deep into the Rocky Mountains. Our mission is to find them, extract them safely, and return to the pick-up location by seventeen hundred exactly three weeks from today. I want you to take everything in this training seriously. That means if you get hit, you're out. Is that clear?"

"Yes, Sergeant," we all say in unison.

He hands out our guns, loaded with dummy bullets that pop with a red dust substance upon impact. I don't think it's been approved for general military use yet. They like to have the dark forces practice with all the new equipment "downstairs" before handing them out to the people who matter "upstairs."

I take the sniper rifle from Eren as he hands it to me. I'm used to handling them and the weight doesn't bother me one bit. The others eye me distrustfully. Ian even looks a bit arrogant, hoping for me to fail once we get out there. Not only do I need to prove myself as a marksman, but I have to excel at the hand-to-hand combat too. *Please, God, don't let my sparring partner be Bradshaw when the time comes.*

I bring my eyes back to my feet, reminding myself not to let the others get to me. It's hard to be the black sheep of the group, especially after coming from my last squad. It took years to get their respect. I only have one month with Malum.

My thoughts fade as I watch the others get their weapons. One of my specialties is, unfortunately, observation. I can break down a person's position and mannerisms in a matter of minutes. Though this squad is a bit harder to read than most, you can learn a great deal about a soldier based on the weapons handed to them.

Jefferson and Pete both get machine guns and assault rifles. They are our fireteam. The ones that have the heavy-duty weapons that can wipe out the enemy quickly and loudly.

Bradshaw shifts his leg and bumps my knee. I glare at him and he gives it right back. His hollow eyes pierce me and only fuel my hate-fire. *Focus on cataloging.*

Ian gets an assault rifle and a bag with radio equipment for airstrikes. He's the least armed and the one we need to rely on for communication. He's a signaler, but I already knew he was a dark air force member based on the raven wings tattooed on his neck.

Harrison gets a grenade launcher. Obvious, the grenadier.

Eren is our sergeant, so he hangs onto an M16 and pistol, while Bradshaw is our close-range assassin—he gets a fake blade, edged with red for marking his false kills and a silenced M16.

I shut my eyes and let my mind sort out situations we might have. Assuming they'll be difficult to work with, based on their reluctance to my presence, I think through a few additional scenarios. Of course, nothing is set in stone until we get to the site and see what we have to work with.

No one talks during the flight. We remain silent and on guard for any surprise emergency landings. After an hour I finally let my mind slack off and once I do I become acutely aware of how close we're all packed in here. Bradshaw's thigh is pressed against mine and his body heat leaks into me.

A mixture of different emotions thrum through me. I'm torn between wanting to tear his head off and apologizing for the shit I said. Even though he started it... we aren't children. I should just apologize; I decide I'll do so once we're alone tonight.

He takes a deep breath and lets his head fall back against the headrest. His hand is clenched over the fake blade, but it trembles like he's freezing. I frown and glance up at his face. His mask hides a lot of things—his lips and nose, the sharpness of his cheekbones. But it cannot hide the torment that racks through him. His brows are pulled in anguish, his dark lashes pressed firmly together, breath uneven.

I look over our squad in the small chopper and find all their eyes are closed, trying to get rest before we land.

Reluctantly and silently, I place my hand down on Bradshaw's trembling one. His eyes open instantly and he straightens his back. I see many things in his eyes, loathing and distrust, but more than that, I see a weary, hurting man. Very much unwilling to accept my comfort.

He looks down at his hand clutching the blade like his life depends on it and loosens his hold. The trembling stops so I withdraw my hand. I honestly don't know what I was thinking, but I wasn't expecting him to stand up and move to the center of the chopper, preferring to hold the handle attached to the ceiling rather than sit beside me because I *touched* him.

Bradshaw's eyes are shadowed as he stares at the floor, looking disgruntled by me.

I can't fucking stand him.

It's evident that he's the real MVP of the squad. The rest of us are expendable. And whether they want me here or not, I plan on executing my purpose flawlessly. Because it's all I have left—my usefulness.

I'll get revenge for you, Jenkins. This mission has something to do with Patagonia. I know it.

I'll paint the sky red for Malum, even if I fucking hate them. As long as I get to stay on the squad.

Eren stands and signals all of us. We stand with our sergeant and get ready to dismount from the chopper. I stand right behind Bradshaw. The sniper rifle is strapped to my back and I hold my pistol with both hands. I check it to ensure all the chambers are filled with the mock bullets. They're lined with streaks of red down the back to be easily identified. My thoughts hesitate on the fact that they aren't black, like they always were on the Riøt Squad, before I blink away the memories.

The moment the chopper hits the ground, we move rhythmically. Bradshaw leads the right-end exit while Eren leads the left.

I'm hot on Bradshaw's heels and do an initial area sweep before seeing the glint of a gun in the foliage. Raising my pistol, I pull the trigger as if it's as easy as breathing and fire into the brush. Bradshaw fires his M16 from my side; we're almost back-to-back. My instincts kick in and I spin, checking the far side where Eren's team is. They stare at us, surprised that we discharged our dummy weapons already. I fire again, twice in the opposite direction and then do a final sweep to be sure before straightening and using a silent hand gesture for *clear*.

The whole squad looks aghast and stares at us like Bradshaw and me are measuring dicks. In all honesty, we might as well be.

Not Eren, though. His lips pull up at the corners as three men step out from the bushes. They're wearing camouflage and all have red powder on their foreheads and chests.

Ian's and Harrison's jaws fall open. Jefferson's eyes narrow at me but there's a new fragment of respect there now. Pete stares at me for a second before letting his eyes shift behind me to Bradshaw. I follow the motion, turning and finding his pale eyes boring holes into me. If I thought the loathing there was bad before, it's ten times worse now.

I deflate.

What's it going to take to prove myself to him? I was the only one who was as keen on the enemy's presence as he was.

"Let's move out. Bones, Bunny, you two take up the rear," Eren orders and we follow without question.

Bradshaw jerks his head to let me know to go ahead of him and I don't argue. Ian walks in front of me. His helmet and gear make him almost indistinguishable from the others, but he has a tell in how he lets his foot drag for a fraction of a second before he lifts it. I occasionally get a glimpse of his neck tattoo when he scratches it.

I take in our surroundings. The Rocky Mountains are a tough terrain, very telling for what the environment of the real mission will be like. The woods are thick here, with many sharp rock formations along hillsides and cliffs as we ascend to higher elevations. The cold mountain air is brisk and the wind cuts straight through my gear, chilling me to the bone.

We walk single file through the thick forest brush. It's darker beneath the canopy of branches, even though the sun hasn't quite set yet.

It's cold and miserable—hours of hiking in mostly silence. I'm acutely aware of each step Bradshaw takes behind me. The crunch of the earth beneath his boots, the calculating thoughts inside his mind. I know he's going to do something to get rid of me, the question is what it will be.

Eren sets a brutal pace and we don't slow until we reach a thick underbrush that leads back to a rocky cliffside. By the time we get there, my feet ache and it's pitch black with no moon. We are far away from any civilization.

"Get comfortable, Malum. We're staying here tonight. I want team watch rotations. Myself and Harrison will take first watch. Stick to your partners… and Bunny—"

I lift my head and meet Eren's calm blue eyes.

"Good job today. If this were real, you'd have saved our asses. It's clear to me why you are so revered," He praises me, and it's the first time I've received acclaim from a sergeant so openly.

My eyes are wide and all I can muster is a curt nod.

Eren has the same gentle demeanor I sensed when we met on the plane. It makes me hopeful that I've grown a bit on his good side again. God, I wish it were him I'd brought back to the hotel instead of his psychotic twin.

The rest of the squad gives me dark expressions, but none of them are as grim as Bradshaw's. He looks like he'd rather eat dirt than share a post with me.

We get as comfortable as we can in the underbrush. Branches and insects make it difficult, but at least it isn't raining. It definitely could be worse. We're fortunate it's the middle of fall and not the dead of winter.

We eat our MREs in silence and then break apart into our sleeping posts. My shoulders can't be the only ones that hurt after carrying a pack all day. Bradshaw is tight against my side and I try as hard as I can to ignore his presence. Our altercation earlier comes back to me and guilt tugs in the back of my mind.

I know I shouldn't have said those things. No matter what he said to spur it on. It's eating away at me.

"Bones," I whisper.

He doesn't respond right away. I wonder if he's sleeping already, but I doubt someone as traumatized as him can find rest so easily. God knows I can't.

"What?" he says in a low, irritated voice.

"I'm sorry about what I said about Achilles. It was out of line." The words hang between us and stretch the silence until I'm certain he won't reply.

He shifts and I turn my head enough to look at him. He rolled to his other side to face away from me. My teeth gnash together but I force the muscles in my jaw to relax.

I knew I wasn't getting an apology back, but it still irks me.

My head is heavy and my thoughts falter before I eventually find sleep.

A boot against my arm snaps me awake.

I sit up quickly and blink up at Bradshaw. He doesn't look like he got a wink of sleep. Dark circles ring his lower lids. It's pitch black and I can only make out his features with the lighter he holds near his face as he lights a cigarette. He lifts the bottom of his mask to take a puff before nodding toward the night watch post and waits while I stand and grab my rifle.

Eren and Harrison give us a once-over before making their way to their brush bedding. Too tired for words, I imagine, just as I am. I watch Eren until his figure disappears into the dark. Dread swallows me whole as I sit down beside Bradshaw.

The first twenty minutes pass slowly. The forest is loud with crickets and the sound of bats swooping between pine boughs. My eyes remain trained on the distant bush lines, waiting for any signs of movement.

"I'm sorry."

He hadn't spoken for so long that his voice startles me. I stare at him blankly.

Bradshaw doesn't glance at me as he speaks. "About Jenkins. I shouldn't have dragged his name through the mud." His voice is low and husky. My eyes narrow with pain at the sound of Jenkins's name.

A beat of awkward silence follows because I'm unsure what to say. But I finally decide to try to make peace with the devil, if he's willing.

"You know, he was the only reason I survived in the dark forces," I say, voice raspy. I haven't talked about Jenkins out loud since he died. He lives solely in my mind. For some reason, it's easier to tell your secrets to people you don't know very well. Bradshaw turns his head in my direction and stares at me. For the first time it's void of loathing, instead I find a subtle curiosity there. "He was the only one who saw the real me and trained me to be like him."

Bradshaw blinks slowly and I spot a hint of a smirk from beneath his mask.

"Was he the only one who knew you were a little reaper deep down?" His tone isn't cruel, but somehow it still stings. Is it that obvious?

I force my eyes away and choose to ignore his comment. I shouldn't have told him I thought of myself as one. "I wasn't a reaper yet. I was only twenty. Stupid and emotional still. I think he saw bits of himself in me and the hazing I endured was hard for him to watch without stepping in... I also killed a squadmate and made it look like an accident." I glance back at Bradshaw. His eyes are hollow, patient. Unfazed by my admittance. "He helped me become a reaper because he liked that part of me. The part that killed against the rules."

"You don't think he was just trying to fuck you?"

A flash of heat spreads over my cheeks and my stomach twists with rage.

Bradshaw lets a couple low chuckles reverberate through the air between us. "Oh shit, you two did fuck, didn't you? Did you trick him like you tricked me?" The cold-hearted asshole is back. Or maybe he never left and he was only baiting me.

"What's your problem with me?" I ask and try to keep the bite out of it.

He gives me a stern look, those weary lines beneath his eyes pulling on my heart more than they should.

"You know, I was trying to hook up with Eren, *not* you." I blow out a breath and let my muscles slack. I lean into the tree behind us. "I just wanted one last night of fun, a small pleasure that I could indulge in before my last mission."

His shoulders tense. "What do you mean your *last* mission? Are you earning your cards out?"

The curve of my lips makes his eyes harden. He thinks I'm even close to earning my cards to a new life?

"No. I just have a feeling it will be my last. We all eventually expire, don't we?"

I look away, but I can feel his heavy gaze burning into my skin.

"Why?"

"Why what?"

"Why do you think it will be your last?" His voice is mundane but pushy, nonetheless.

Should I tell him it's because I *want* it to be my last? Or because Malum goes on missions that most soldiers don't come back from? Like Achilles. Or should I tell him the truth? That I know with the mission at hand we'll be going after the asshole who caused Patagonia to go upside down. Sure, Malum blames Riøt for their loss and we blamed them back, but the real enemy is the third party that invaded our operation.

I settle on shrugging.

He stares at me for a few more minutes before dragging his eyes away from me.

The hush around us digs into my skin. I'm glad he's not much for talking.

seven

. . .

NELL

I LIE ON MY STOMACH AND LOOK THROUGH MY SCOPE TO THE valley below. There's movement. I patiently wait, my camouflage cover heavy on my head. My neck started hurting thirty minutes ago, but I don't want to readjust in case I miss something critical.

Bodies shift into view below and I verify that it's the hostile squad.

"Four armed men," I say in a low voice.

Ian clicks on his radio and mutters the information and the coordinates to Eren. We remain still until we hear back from him.

The radio clicks and Eren's voice comes through with a small amount of static. "Stand down. We'll track them on foot tomorrow. Regroup at home base. Over."

The home base is made up of our shitty underbrush posts and a camouflage tent we were able to establish behind it. The first few days haven't been so bad, but the night watch sucks. I forgot how tired it makes you. Bradshaw hasn't uttered a word to me since our first night. It's awkward, but I think I like it better than the mean shit that comes out of his mouth. My legs ache and my eyelids are heavy, but I can't let it affect my performance.

"Fuck. All right, well, I guess we better head back then," Ian says. His black hair is still slicked back neatly, regardless of the paint and mud on his face. His cheeks are covered in dirt, as are mine.

I nod and start packing up my camouflage cover and unloading my sniper. He watches me in silence and I prefer it. There hasn't been much team bonding so far, even though Eren has strongly encouraged it. Everyone's been pretty quiet and when there is connecting, it's between them, not me. Even Bradshaw seems more at ease when he's speaking with them. Though, he doesn't speak much at all to anyone. I found him sitting alone with his head hung low this morning, reading a book and leaning against a tree. Meanwhile, his brother is the complete opposite. Eren smiles more than he doesn't and makes it a point to speak with everyone a few times during the days.

I haven't decided yet if it's a manipulation ploy or not. No one smiles that much.

I've been able to piece together some things. One of them is that none of our squadmates knows that Bones is Eren's twin. At first, I wasn't sure how they couldn't tell, but the two of them don't act like brothers while on duty and the difference in the shade of blue in their eyes makes them look unrelated. Add in Bradshaw's scars and his mask and no one suspects a thing.

"What did you do to get into the dark ops?" Ian breaks the silence. I glance up at him briefly before continuing to put equipment into my backpack. *Everyone does something unspeakable to get noticed by the underground.*

"How does anyone get in?" I retort. He knows as well as I do. Only bad people get recruited.

"Tell me what you did," he says firmly, as if this is an interrogation and I'm in the hot seat.

I stand with my gear and rifle strapped to my back. Ian studies my expression with grim eyes. It's no use; he won't get anything from it.

It doesn't hurt to tell him and I know he'll relay anything he learns about me to the others. They should know too.

"I killed a few bad people." *Horrifically. Borderline animalistically.* "I'm useless in the real world."

His eyes widen and he cackles. "Useless? I wouldn't exactly say that." I think that might be an accidental compliment.

I nod. "Useless in every other sense besides killing." His jaw flexes at that. Did he think they'd put a softie on their squad? "I was recruited because there's darkness in me and this is the only place I belong until I'm eventually killed too."

"Damn, Bunny. So depressing. How many people have you executed? I heard Riøt had a long list before you guys were wiped out. So, how many?" he asks as we casually start making our way back to the base.

I give him a confused look. "Are we supposed to keep track of that?"

He blows out a breath and shakes his head. "Damn, you're a cold bitch."

Yeah, and it's better that you know it now. I look up at the treetops ahead. I think of Bradshaw's pained eyes when he spoke of his prior second.

"What was his name?" I ask after a moment of silence. "Achilles, what was his real name?"

Ian swallows but blinks past the hesitance of telling me.

"Abrahm." Ian says his name softly, with respect. "His

code name was Achilles, but we often just called him Abrahm." I raise my brow but Ian isn't looking at me. He's focused on the pine-tree-thick hills ahead, in a trance of sorts.

"How long was he a part of the squad?" I pry.

"Five years... and you can't replace him. So, try if you want, but you'll never be able to fill his boots," he says venomously. I blink slowly, unbothered by his statement.

"Already filled, Colt." I keep my expression impassive. The rage that flashes across his gaze is quiet but promises punishment.

His animosity is hard to ignore, but I manage.

What I can't seem to ignore so easily is the team bonding activity Eren has planned out for our evening.

I get paired up with Bradshaw. His black hair is slicked back with sweat from the afternoon exercises and his jaw is set with anything but contentment at our matchup. I couldn't agree more. Aren't we forced together enough as it is?

Eren has it out for us.

Both of our arms remain firmly crossed while the rest of our squad mates have amused smirks. Bradshaw's face is unreadable beneath his mask, but the creases of the black fabric don't look like a grin to me.

Eren stands before the six of us with his arms behind his back. "Malum, today we're working on team bonding," he says bluntly, staring at me specifically. "You're tasked with reaching the destination marked on your map by nightfall. The path on your maps must be followed to the T, regardless of the obstacles. Both you and your partner need to arrive together, or you fail. Those who fail will be on night watch for the entire evening." A long groan escapes from the team. I'm assuming they've had to pull all-nighters as I have at some point in their training. It's as dreadful as it sounds.

"Come on, Sergeant, we all know it's going to be Bones and Bunny. Let's just skip the team bonding portion and make them do the watch tonight," Jefferson says breezily as he stretches his arms behind his head. Ian nods at his side, which earns him a glare from Eren.

"If I hear any more complaining, I'll have *everyone* on watch tonight," Eren threatens. His dark blue eyes shift back to me and soften. "I've marked your maps. I'll see you soldiers before nightfall."

————

God almighty. This could not have been a worse scenario for a worse pairing. Bradshaw's already rolled his eyes at me over ten times and I've withheld at least forty swear words.

I may have underestimated my patience.

"Can't you climb faster?" Bradshaw snipes at me as I'm hauling myself over a ten-foot-tall ledge. My gloved fingertips sting and the sweat running down my spine is making me more agitated by the second.

"Shut the fuck up," I retort between gnashed teeth. With one last pull I finally manage to drag myself over the lip of the edge. I collapse against the ground and stare up at the sky. Pine trees crowd the space above. Then *his* face appears and I scowl. His eyes are impassive, brows pulled tightly together and his frown is evident beneath the mask.

I hate this man more than insects.

"Get up, Bunny. We should be a klick further than we are." He fists my vest and yanks me up the remaining few feet, then sets me down hard. I smack his hand away and glare. He gives me a curious raise of his brow, nearing amusement.

"Don't touch me, asshole," I snap as I stand and stalk past him. "I'm not the one who couldn't fit between the two fallen trees and had to walk an extra five minutes around the riverbank."

He doesn't respond, but I can feel his loathing gaze

boring into the back of my head. I pull out the map Eren marked for us and go over the details once more. We already passed through the meadow and river. We still have at least five klicks before we reach the marked position and most of it is up this fucking mountain side.

I shove the map back into my vest pocket and take a deep breath to recenter myself. *What would Jenkins say to me right now?* I focus on the swaying pine boughs ahead as birds land on the thinner branches and chatter without concern for the rest of world. Jenkins would probably tell me that if I can't conquer my emotions, then I need to empty my mind. Let the stress and heavy things go. I can almost hear his laugh against the shell of my ear, his labored breathing when he carried fallen comrades through mud. *"When you let go of your thoughts, you can do anything, Gallows."*

I shut my eyes and even his scent still lingers around me. A cold breeze in a storm. Snapped branches and sap.

A chill shudders across my spine and I turn, finding Bradshaw's cold, icy eyes set on me. Then dread grows in my chest. There is nothing I wouldn't give to have Jenkins back. To have him behind me, tracing the lines of my face with his gaze. Cherishing every piece of my soul like no one ever has before. He saw darkness in me and held out a hand to lead me further into the shadows.

"What's wrong?" Bradshaw asks, surprisingly not as sharp as he usually speaks to me.

I come to a halt and stare at him for a moment. He observes me in equal silence, awaiting my response. "Sometimes I still hear them. Sometimes... I think if I turn around, they'll still be here." My lips are chapped and the words taste bitter.

Bradshaw's eyes dull with understanding. He takes a step closer to me before lifting his hand to my face. I flinch at the near contact of his palm against my skin, but he stops himself. A flash of horror flickers through his eyes as he seems to realize that he was about to comfort me. He withdraws his hand and clears his throat.

"Sometimes I dream of them," he confides, turning his face away from mine. He takes the lead and I follow behind. "Other times I see them in strangers, small things. The way a smile grows or a quirk I thought was only unique to them."

I consider his words before muttering, "Is that why you're so angry when you look at me?" He walks for a few moments in silence before curtly nodding.

"You have traits that should only belong to one person." His voice is callous and raw.

"Who have I stolen from you?" Please don't let it be his last second. When he doesn't respond, I swallow the knot in my throat and mutter, "Abrahm."

He stops like a rock thrown in mud and turns on his heels, fury racing through him. "Don't say his name. You never knew him." His shoulders stiffen. I can see it in his eyes. He loved Abrahm as much as I did Jenkins. The pain reflected in his eyes is a mirror of my own misery.

"I can't help how I am, Bradshaw. As you said, I didn't know him. The similarities you see are only in your head." He doesn't look at all satisfied with my words. "I just want to get along." I extend my hand out to him, hopeful that he'll take it.

Bradshaw's jaw muscles feather and he smacks my hand down. "Let's get moving, *Bunny*."

Asshole.

I let my mind drift as I watch Bradshaw's frame navigate the uneven terrain. The rocks and trees prove to be difficult and the thick underbrush is relentless. I'm relieved our boots can handle any kind of conditions.

That relief is short-lived when we come upon the last obstacle: another ten-foot, sheer-faced cliffside. My heart drops. There's no chance of climbing this one. At least the last cliff had rocks to use as leverage. This one is made of flat-faced stones that jut up from the earth. Bradshaw and I share a look. One of us will have to lift the other.

Goddammit.

"I'll have to go up first." Bradshaw smooths his hand over the back of his neck as he inspects the cliff. "You can't pull my body weight up," he says, then looks down at me like he's making a point.

I scowl. "I *can* pull you up."

He shakes his head. "I'm going first." His arms are crossed and his lips are flat with finality. There's no sense in arguing it, I guess. With an exasperated breath I lean down and cup both hands together.

Bradshaw gets a few steps of a head start before I lever him up. He grips the edge of the cliff and maneuvers himself over the side. I stare up at the ledge, waiting for him to peer down at me and help me up but his head doesn't appear.

"What are you doing up there?" I shout.

His masked face appears over the edge and when he doesn't lean down to help me up, an unsettling feeling fills my chest.

"You're wasting time. Come on, help me up." I back up and run at the cliffside, jumping and kicking off the wall while reaching. Bradshaw doesn't offer me his hand.

I fall to the ground, the force knocking the breath from my lungs. I stare up at him in disbelief.

You've got to be fucking kidding me.

His mask pulls up where his smile is growing. "Bye-bye, Bunny."

"You realize we'll both lose this *bonding exercise* and be forced to stay up all night, right?" I say as vehemently as I can. Emotions grip at my chest; it's really fucking hard to disregard the things I've gone through in the last two days.

He lifts his shoulders, letting them fall as he waves like an asshole. "I'll just tell them you couldn't make it over the hill. You'd be a hindrance in the field. Just give up." My jaw trembles and my fingers curl into the dirt.

I want to scream.

Maybe I can be assigned to the Hades squad. Anyone else's second other than this monster's. *But this is the only chance I have to avenge Jenkins.* I watch as the top of Bradshaw's head disappears and his steps grow distant. Eren's going to think I'm not good enough if I'm stuck behind this obstacle. He'll believe his brother no matter what I say.

I look to the sky, the sun beginning its descent toward the distant mountains. *There's still time.*

"Goddammit," I whisper as I push myself up to my feet.

After assessing the cliff, I come to the conclusion that there's no way I can clear it myself. The rock face is too sheer. Okay, what else can I use? I look around and see that the cliff extends far to each side. No good. I inspect the trees lingering nearby. One pine tree is larger than the rest; it has a thick trunk and the first branch is long and wide, stretching out over the edge of the cliff.

That's my only option.

It takes a few tries of losing my grip around the tree and falling on my ass, but I finally reach the branch and wrap my body around it. I'm going to wring Bradshaw's fucking neck when I get my hands on him. Thoughts of harming him fuel my hate-fire as I shimmy across the prickly branch. I ignore the splinters embedding in my thighs. It takes a great deal of effort to not look down.

I should cut off his dick. Break his lovely nose. What I would do to make him cry.

A smug, self-indulgent grin spreads over my lips at those diabolical thoughts. He deserves so much worse.

I finally reach the end of the branch and dare a glance down. The bough doesn't quite reach as far over the ledge as I was hoping it would. I'll have to swing. *Shit.* I'm easily twenty feet up and a fall from this height would probably break something. I draw in a deep, centering breath and slowly lower myself, clinging to the branch with trembling hands. Pumping my legs at the same time, I swing my body until there's enough momentum to get myself over the ledge.

I hold my breath as I let go. Then I'm falling like a downed bird. I extend my arms in case my feet don't catch the edge. The soles of my boots clip the gravel and for a brief, stupid moment I think I've done it. Then the earth gives out beneath me and my knees slam against the hardscape. A grunt escapes my throat as my chest hits the ground. I scramble to grip anything before sliding off the side and somehow manage to dig my fingertips into the dirt.

I wriggle myself up onto the plateau and splay out on my back. My heart hammers against my chest and all I can think of is beating the shit out of Bradshaw.

I fucking did it.

A laugh bubbles up from my chest and I lie here for several minutes until the shaking in my limbs ceases. I stand up and brush off my pants, wincing at the sting from my knees hitting the cliffside. Red smudges form beneath my uniform, but it's mostly hidden by the black color of the fabric, so I choose to ignore it until I can bandage it up later.

The sun is moving fast, casting its fading colors across the sky like orange strokes of paint. I run the remaining miles and finally catch up to Bradshaw by the time we're coming up to the marked point. His cocky stride is relaxed, making me angrier that he's without a care in the world.

I fist a rock the size of my palm and a wicked smile staves off the pain throbbing through my body as I get ready to deck him with it.

"Hey, *asshole!*" I shout as I baseball-pitch the rock at him. He turns, clearly startled. The rock strikes his helmet and tilts his head. I burst into laughter before adding: "Fuck you!"

Bradshaw stares at me hollowly, like something's been unplugged from his brain and an itch has formed. "You fucking brat."

My teeth burn with hatred but I'm still laughing. "Oh, *great* comeback, are you five?"

He charges at me, without warning or any sound. My instincts flare into a sharp scream. I dart to the side and sprint as fast as I can to evade him. His hands reach out and he snags one of my thigh pockets. I turn and land a back-handed punch to the side of his face. He grunts but doesn't let me go. He grips my braid and pulls my head back. We fall to the dirt together, wrestling like our lives depend on it.

"You make me sick." His voice drips with loathing. He pins my arm behind my back and I already know he's going to win this fight. My breath is too uneven and he has me pinned like an animal. I hold in the cry that swells in my throat. He twists my wrist and sets his knee on it. My face is planted against the earth and his weight spreads agonizingly over my spine.

"You're the only repulsive thing here," I say as scathingly as I can.

He mulls that over. "I'm not asking nicely again, Bunny. I want you off the squad. Fucking quit." There's nothing more I want than that too, buddy. I try to wriggle free but he only firms his grip on my wrist, forcing a cry from my lips. "You'll never have a place here with us. The only good Riøt soldier is a dead one. And I can make arrangements for that, Bun. Fucking try me."

My jaw trembles and my willpower to fight diminishes on a shuddering breath. Spit and blood bubble on the ground around my cheek. He settles his hips over my torso as my shoulders go lax and loosens his hold on my wrist.

Bradshaw leans forward until his hot mask coasts the shell of my ear. "If I really wanted to kill you, my blade would be buried in your back right now. You can't compete in close combat. You can't protect yourself. What if you were fighting an enemy soldier and they realized you're pretty and took you back to their base? You know what happens then?" My gut twists. Of course I know. Everyone knows. "Just leave. None of us want you here."

"Because I'm from Riøt," I bite out, glaring up at him with venom in my eyes.

"Because I don't trust you. I will *never* trust you."

He stares down at me with disdain and once he's sure I get the message he finally relents. He lets me go and pushes himself up, leaving me in the dirt as he walks ahead. I remain in the dust, breathing hard, unmoving, and thinking of anything more tragic than the predicament I've found myself in.

"*Soldiers don't cry.*" Jenkins's voice hums in my memory. His warm hands had spread over my shoulders. "*If you give up, you die.*"

Tears silently stream over the bridge of my nose. The sky grows dark as the sun sets. Footsteps approach but I can't find the will to sit up.

"Nell." Eren's voice is gentle and sympathetic as he kneels beside me. Dread sifts through me and my head aches. I force myself up. Dirt and blood cling to my skin and smears as I drag my sleeve across my face. His eyes soften and he raises his hand to my cheek, rubbing his thumb over the remaining grains turned red from my bloody lip. "Long day?"

I give him a dry, callous laugh. "You could say that."

Eren shifts to sit beside me, lowering to my level. He's so beautiful and lovely. His face is untouched by scars the way Bradshaw's is. Yet with his unmarked beauty, it lacks the characteristics and journey that his brother's hold.

"I hate to tell you this, but you two are on the night watch," Eren says with a bit of sarcasm to lighten the mood.

"Yeah, I figured."

"Do you want me to stay up with you guys? I know he's been... difficult."

"That's an understatement."

Eren chuckles. "I don't think he hates you as much as he lets on. He's been reluctant to have anyone replace Abrahm, but none of them want—" he cuts himself off.

"A Riøt soldier." I finish it for him, staring out into the dark woods.

He sighs and nods. "Yeah."

I raise a brow and ask, "Is that why the Malum Squad hasn't been sent out on a mission for so long?" He nods, his frown creasing his perfect face.

"Partly. But the main reason for the sudden push to get us back out there is because this mission is very, *very* important. Which is why—" he pauses again and meets my gaze. God, his kindness is getting annoying because he's making me finish his sentences.

"I was assigned."

He nods.

"I'm not giving up." My mouth is dry. There's no way I'm not going on this mission. It's the only chance I have to get justice for my squad. For Jenkins.

Eren's forlorn expression deepens. "I truly believe it's because he doesn't want what happened to Abrahm to happen to you. Not just because you're from a bad squad."

A bad squad. My chest deflates.

I shake my head and sigh. "Yeah, sure."

He lets the quiet air remain between us, then mutters, "Shall we get going?"

I follow him to the Humvee waiting at the checkpoint and endure the glares the rest of the squad throw at me on the drive back to the base and over dinner. I don't bother bandaging or looking at my injured knees. The pain is a dull throb, but at least it gives me something to focus on other than the disdain surrounding me.

eight

$\cdot \ \cdot \ \cdot$

NELL

BRADSHAW HOLDS HIS ASSAULT RIFLE LOOSELY AS WE STAND watch. My eyes are already heavy but we're only a few hours in. It's darker with the cloud cover tonight. Even the forest creatures are quiet under the grimness of it.

He hasn't said a word since our *scuffle* earlier. I shut my eyes for a moment. *It's better this way.* I'd rather be detached in case something happens on a real mission. I tried to be friendly with him, but he wants nothing to do with me.

"I think I heard something," Bradshaw whispers, the sound of his voice sends chills down my spine. My eyes snap open and I'm instantly alert, but I don't hear anything.

"Where?" I say back in a hushed tone. He nods straight ahead and I take the lead, walking slowly and looking in every direction for any sign of danger. I stop once I get twenty feet from our post. "I don't see anyone, it's clear—"

A foot plants squarely on the center of my back and I'm

forced to the ground. I break the fall with my forearms but pain shoots through my body regardless. My thoughts whirl.

I look up and find Bradshaw standing above me, Jefferson and Pete to either side of him. Horror sinks deep into my chest. "What the fuck are you doing?" I snarl as I try to get up, giving them a chance to say this is a joke and not what I think it is.

The second I'm on my knees, Bradshaw shoves my shoulders back and I'm flat on the ground again, only this time he straddles me, pinning my torso and arms to the ground with his body weight.

I wriggle desperately beneath him. Fear threads through my bones, increasing my breaths, making them strangled and raspy. "Two assaults in one day? You're a fucking productive psychopath," I shout viciously before spitting in his face. My heart beats rapidly against my ribs and the only thing I can see are Bradshaw's harrowing pale blue eyes. He ignores me but Jefferson and Pete share a mildly concerned look like they aren't completely onboard with whatever he's talked them into doing.

I try to focus on the anger. Fear makes you irrational, at least anger is a bit more grounding. I take a deep breath and calm myself. *He hasn't done anything yet. Maybe he won't do anything. They're just trying to scare me.*

Bradshaw leans forward and draws his KA-BAR. A real one. It's a black military-grade knife meant for plunging into other human beings' chests.

The blood drains from my face.

"Are you going to quit?" Bradshaw asks with no remorse in his voice. It's clear he isn't playing a prank, but I don't let my resolve falter.

Rage returns, fueling my words. At this point, it's fucking personal. "No. Now get the fuck off of me," I demand.

If he's fazed by my words he doesn't show it. Jefferson

kneels beside my head and Pete holds my ankles down firmly.

Terror spills into my chest and I shriek, "What are you—" Jefferson's hands come down over my mouth, muffling any sound from escaping my lips.

Adrenaline rushes through me and I thrash against them *hard*. I fight for my life, for my next breath. They're going to kill me? All because I won't quit? What the hell is wrong with them? My attempt to escape is useless; they have me pinned like a lamb for slaughter. Bradshaw brings his knife back up, sliding the flat side of it down over the softness of my stomach, searing the cold steel across my skin.

I try bucking him off and crying for help, kicking my feet desperately. Then cold air meets my sternum and it freezes every fighting limb I have—the very blood in my veins too.

My breath is rapid, feral. Tears spill down the sides of my face as Bradshaw unzips my vest. He drags the knife down my shirt, cutting through the fabric and my sports bra with ease, exposing my breasts to the chilly night air. My nipples harden and horror settles deep into my bones.

I attempt to bite into Jefferson's hand but his other one keeps my jaw shut tight. A muffled scream grows in my throat and I try once more to thrash as hard as I can. All their eyes are on my bare nipples. Shame floods me and I want to beat each of them senseless.

Why are they doing this? This is worse than anything Riøt ever did.

Tears make my vision blurry and my energy fades quickly. My mind is shutting off and going into survival mode.

I lie still and let my body go limp. My labored breathing is the only sound that rolls through the dark.

Bradshaw stares down at me with empty eyes. He doesn't care what he's doing to me or the impact this will have on my mental state. I keep my eyes locked with his, refusing to let go of the one thing I have left, my death glare.

He chuckles, brows pinching together as if he pities me.

"Still fighting? Damn, you *are* a tough one." Bradshaw brings the edge of his dagger to my right side, to the sensitive flesh just under my breast. He pushes the sharp tip in and I scream out against Jefferson's sweaty palm. The pain is a rush to my system but more than the pain, I feel Bradshaw's tender hand squeezing my ribs to steady himself. His crotch over mine is too hot and suddenly the fear that laced my blood has turned into arousal.

This is so fucked up.

My scream turns to a moan and Bradshaw's eyes catch mine, not missing a single detail of how my body responds to him and the pain. God, I hope the other two are too aloof to notice. I shouldn't be turned on by this, no, I'm *not* turned on by this. I bite my lower lip to quell the next rising moan.

Jefferson jolts and says, "*Bones*, you said we were just going to scare her. This is too far." He looks uncertainly from Bradshaw to Pete.

Pete's grip on my ankles falters. "You're hurting her!" his voice sounds genuinely shocked and worried. *Thank God for them not hearing the pleasure in my moans.*

Bradshaw ignores them both, keeping his devilish eyes on me and glides the blade in a crescent motion agonizingly slow, following the shape of my breast. I writhe and buck my hips. The pain gives me a high while his lustful eyes, gripping hands, and swelling crotch set my nerves ablaze. He dips his head down, pulls his mask up only enough to bare his lips, and takes my nipple between his teeth before bringing his lips down on my flesh and pressing one lonesome kiss there.

He stops the incision at the tip of my sternum.

Tears fall down the sides of my temples from the pain and shame, but mostly from the cruelty of all three of them.

Hot blood warms my skin as it races down my side and pools in the dirt. Jefferson releases my mouth and shoves Bradshaw off me. "Goddammit," Jefferson curses under his breath as he folds the vest back over my chest carefully to cover me up. His hands are trembling. He lifts me up quickly in his arms as if I weigh nothing and rushes me back to the base. As he carries my limp, tired body, I can only stare behind him at Bradshaw, who still watches me like an unfinished meal. I bet he's smiling underneath that mask of his.

I bet he thinks he broke me.

nine

. . .

Bradshaw

"What the fuck is wrong with you?" Pete shoves me back against a tree and I let him. I'm still thinking about all the blood that spilled from her supple flesh a moment ago. The fire that lit her eyes and the way her thighs were rubbing together beneath me, trying so desperately to give herself a bit of relief.

Of course she liked that. *Fuck.* She's messing with my head.

I drag my hand over my jaw and rub the soft fabric of my mask against my lips. I watch as Jefferson raises hell at the base. A flash of guilt rolls through me. I should have told him I was going to escalate things, but I didn't even know what I was going to do until it was already happening. When she stared at me with all of that hatred burning in her eyes, I wanted to carve it out of her myself and that's exactly what I did.

Eren is already stomping over here and looks livid.

Pete huffs and curses as he leaves, probably to go check on our little Bunny. It was just a small cut. I want to laugh at the dramatics my comrades are raising over it. Over a Riøt soldier, no less. Did they not see her enjoying it as I had? I think of how it may have looked from a different perspective.

Hm. Maybe I did go a bit too far, but the more she reacted to my touch, the more I wanted to see.

Eren reaches me and before he says anything, he strikes me across the face with his fist. It knocks the breath out of me.

He's never struck me before. *Ever.*

I look back at him and his eyes are filled with rage. Over something that isn't even his. My eyes dull and I regard him with little interest.

"*Bradshaw.* What were you fucking thinking?" His brows are pulled tightly in anguish. I know he's concerned about my mind. I've always known it. Sometimes I wonder if it's why we don't mind staying on the dark forces. Here, I can let out the darkness inside. I think he's known longer than I have. But I know about his inner monster too. "You'll be punished for this. You know General Nolan has a liking for her." He shakes his head and grits his teeth.

A pang of sorrow threads through my cold, dead heart. My brother is the only thing I have left in this life and I'm all he has too. But the sooner he realizes I'm going to die young the better. It's a miracle I've made it this long given the line of work we're in.

My thoughts trail off to Abrahm. *It should've been me.*

The coldness he left behind in my chest is like an infection that only continues to spread. I want to be in the ground and send him back in my place. It's where I should be.

Eren is talking and lecturing me, but I don't hear him. I look past him and stare at Bunny from afar. My comrades are swarmed around her, bandaging her side and apologizing relentlessly.

My eyes narrow and my teeth grind together. *She's bad.* But the thought doesn't carry to my chest with rage like it did a day ago, and that pisses me off.

If I have to break her hands to get her to quit, I will.

Bunny looks over at me, concern placed safely in those bright honey-toned eyes for me. I don't see the resolve to quit burning there like I hoped I would. Instead there's only fury and more willpower than there was before. More dark lust laying siege to those plump lips as she draws her tongue over them. No wonder her prior sergeant fell in love with her. He saw a little shadow and took it for himself.

I could never love a Riøt.

My fists clench at my sides. Why did it have to be her? Why did the only Riøt survivor have to be her? Her glare gives me an unwanted throb deep in my core. One that I refuse to look into and investigate properly.

I let my shoulders fall in a shameful slack and return my gaze to Eren.

He knows I didn't hear a word of what he said and throws his hands in the air with exasperation.

"She can't stay," I say with finality.

Eren's face is impassive at first, then his features soften with sympathy as he must see the pain in my eyes. He has always found things within me, even things I cannot see myself. I wonder if he sees how fucking tired I am. *That*, I feel.

"She's not Abrahm. We need her," he states.

I shake my head. "No, she's not. And she'll go worse than he did. She doesn't care if she dies or not. She's trained to be a suicidal death machine."

Eren's eyes widen. "You make it sound like you ca—" He cuts himself off and lowers his head, shaking it.

"Watch it," I growl, shoving his shoulders back.

"*Easy.* I'm already having a shit night thanks to you." He drags his hand down his face. His stubble has grown in since being out in the field. It makes him look five years older than me, but maybe it's the stress. "So what if she dies on the mission? We only have one objective and it's not getting her home. Stop fucking with the plan." He pats my shoulder and my eyes flick back to her. I picture her dying and it's a replay of Abrahm.

Memories of hot blood and sickening cries fall over me like a low tide, dragging me into the depths of my despair. This time though, instead of Abrahm's trembling cold hands reaching for the light, I see hers.

My voice is callous as I firm my decision. "I'll make her leave."

ten

. . .

NELL

PETE AND JEFFERSON SIT DEFEATED AS THEY TAKE THE NIGHT watch. Eren is making them sit out there as our replacements all night for their part in the ambush. A small reprieve that I'm immensely grateful for.

"Sergeant, there's no need to report the incident. I'm sure they were only trying to haze me as a sort of cruel introduction to the squad," I lie, and it tastes like acid. But the revenge I have playing on repeat in my head promises a reward. Eren gives me a look that says he doesn't buy it for one second.

We both know what Bradshaw was trying to do. What he *did* do.

"Are you sure?" Eren asks anyway.

I nod and wince as Ian finishes up wrapping the medical tape around my ribs. "I was just spooked by it. I'm mentally sound and can carry out the remainder of the training, Sergeant."

Ian lifts his head and stares uncertainly at Eren. But neither of them comment on it. Eren only nods and firms his lips.

"Okay. Well, get some sleep... Are you okay with sleeping beside Bones tonight?"

Of course I'm not. He hurt me, but he also awakened something really dark and disturbed inside of me.

I swallow the thoughts.

"You don't need to worry about me, Sarge."

Eren observes me for a moment and then nods before retreating to the tent. It would be a miracle if anyone gets a wink of sleep tonight. I finally have a moment to myself and take a long breath, staring down at my black tactical gloves covered in blood. *Great.* There's only one spare shirt each of us were able to bring so I change out of the ruined one and slip into a fresh shirt.

My eyes drift over to Bradshaw. He's already back at our post, lying on his side as he always is. The bushes around our sleeping bags make a perfect cave, keeping it relatively warm against the mountain's chilly air.

Rage filters through me, growing as it sinks further into my chest. He isn't going to be punished like the other two? Probably not, he's Eren's *precious* twin.

I don't think I've ever wanted to hurt anyone as much as I do him. *I could cut him back. He wants to scare me? I'll make him piss his pants. I'll make him face his own mortality.*

Dark thoughts seethe in my head as I settle beside him, wincing at the pain in my side. It's going to scar and I'll think of his stupid, gorgeous face every time I see it. For a second, I think about him pulling up his mask and the sensation of his lips on my nipple. It sends a shudder down my spine.

Stop thinking about it.

My knees throb and remind me they've been unattended to. But I'm so tired, they'll just have to wait until morning. A small whimper escapes my lips as I finally let my back hit the ground. Bradshaw tenses beside me at the sound. I don't bother speaking to him. I'm too tired and there's nothing I can do about it. He wants me to quit—I'll show him that I won't. I'll show them all.

Silence falls around our base once more and as the threads of sleep start to take me, his low whisper stirs me awake.

"You okay?"

What the fuck. No. No, I'm not okay.

I'm anything but okay.

I don't respond, feigning that I'm asleep. There's no reality where I can deal with him right now. I'm so close to unsheathing my blade and burying it in his chest.

He shifts to face me. His breath is hushed, but I feel it roll over my skin like a warm mist. I open my eyes enough to see his silhouette. It's dark and he's watching me. The black cloth mask covers most of his face, but it can't hide the anguish in his eyes as he studies my features.

Is this how he stares at me when I'm not looking? There's so much pain there. More than any person should have to carry. I know that weight.

His eyes lower to my side where he let the sharpness of his blade cut my flesh. Bradshaw lifts his hand and it takes everything I have to keep myself from flinching away from him. He lowers his fingers gently to my side, coasting his fingers softly against the wound beneath the fabric.

It stings, even with the delicate touch. My brows pull together and my lips part with a sharp breath. His fingertips are hot. Heat and pain coil between my thighs. His eyes lift to my face and I open mine so he knows I've woken. He doesn't pull his hand away from my side and he doesn't look away.

Those pale eyes bore into my soul. *What is he searching for?*

I take a shallow breath as uncertainty races through me. I can't get a read on him. My gaze lowers to his lips before I decide to close my eyes again.

He doesn't move for a while after that. But instead of rolling back to his side, he lies beside me, with the weight of his hand over my ribs, the warmth from his chest seeping into me. The ebb of pain slows and the heat from his hand reminds me that Bradshaw, as cold and uncaring as he is, does indeed have a sliver of a heart.

————

"Bunny, keep your hands low. You're smaller than your opponent so use their height against them," Eren shouts, bored. Ian shares a smug laugh with Harrison as I pick myself up from the ground.

"I know!" I hiss back, ready to call it a day, but only Eren gets to tell us when we're done. My ribs still hurt, but I'm not about to let it hold me back.

The sparring circle is a flat portion of meadow we discovered during the first week. Eren makes us come out here and beat each other up every morning before the sun rises.

My eyes connect with Bradshaw's. His hair is wet and pushed back. He crosses his arms as he watches me spar with Jefferson. The corner of Bradshaw's mask lifts in a nasty smirk and rage courses through me ten times more. He's been far more tame since the night he assaulted me, though I'm not sure how long that will last. Part of me believes it's only because Eren brought down the hammer on his brother. It's already been two weeks of trials and training, long night watches and uncomfortable meals around a campfire. And, somehow, I've managed to get only a few scalding glares from Bradshaw. Our conversations are one to four words max, but we aren't fighting like we were. So, *yay*.

My reluctance to speak with him probably helps. He

thinks this is over. That he's won. He thinks that I'll submit to him just because he caught me off guard.

Let him think that.

"Come on, Bunny. You're making me feel bad about this," Jefferson says in a sarcastic manner.

"Fuck you." I spit blood to my side, dirt instantly clinging to it.

Jefferson reaches his hand out and motions for me to come at him. His light brown hair is wet with sweat and clings to his forehead. I told myself I'd spar easy with them, let them think they have the upper hand before really letting them have it, but to hell with that.

I unsheathe my knife and charge at him head-on. His eyes flicker with my sudden boldness. He's too bulky to react to my swift movements. I easily duck and evade his attempt to land a blow on my chest. My leg sweeps beneath him and he lands flat on his back. He chokes out a strangled gasp from the impact. Without hesitation, I straddle his stomach, deck him across the jaw, and hold the sharp side of my blade against his stubble-covered neck.

Jefferson's brown eyes grow wide and he blanches. I sneer at him and lean down close, whispering sweetly, "Oh, Jobs, you're making me feel bad about this."

His nostrils flare and he opens his mouth to spout some dumb shit I don't care to hear. I increase the pressure of my knife against his flesh until blood bubbles up and he stills.

"That's enough, Bunny. Colt, you're next," Eren orders with a monotone voice, but I don't miss the glint in his eyes as he looks up at me. A fire that urges me on. *Good job.* I can practically hear him say.

Ian steps into the sparring ring and I hand his ass to him. Same with Harrison and Pete too. I can see it in their cold stares that they know I've been playing softball with them so far, hiding my true attributes.

"Leave it to a Riøt to be a fucking snake," Pete says loud

enough for me to hear. He's taking it harder than the rest for some reason. Poor loser.

"Leave it to a Malum to cry about it," I snap back. Pete's pupils dilate and his breath turns sharp as he stomps toward me like he can really do something about it. I ready myself, prepared to dislocate his shoulder this time if I have to.

But, of course, Bradshaw feels the need to step in. Pete halts immediately, pissing me off more that their loyalty to him is so strong.

"You think you're the toughest soldier out there, don't you?" Bradshaw says with a husky, angry voice that makes the hairs on the back of my neck rise.

Eren glares at him. "Bones, you aren't to participate in sparring. It wouldn't be fair," he warns.

Bradshaw ignores his brother and walks steadily toward me, unzipping his outer jacket so he's just in his protective vest. It's the first time I've seen his bare arms in daylight and, God Almighty, is he a fucking vision. His muscles are defined and his veins protrude as he grips his knife. His tight black tactical pants hang low on his hips and my eyes drift there momentarily. He is lethal and every instinct inside my body thrums on high alert.

I think he really wants to kill me.

"Bones," Eren warns once more to no avail.

"I'm going to make you wish you had quit the moment you got here." Bradshaw grins beneath his mask and it sends chills down my spine. Terrible things are playing behind his cold eyes.

I don't bother responding to him. Instead, I grip my knife harder and lower into a fighting stance. Bradshaw is the only one who I haven't observed sparring, which I'm assuming is to protect us, but to also keep his techniques secret. I'm not about to charge at him like I did Jefferson.

The four of our squadmates cheer for him, telling him to

break my arm and make me cry. My cheeks burn but I force myself to keep emotions out of it.

If he fights anything like Jenkins, I'm fucked.

Bradshaw doesn't let me wonder for long. He closes the distance between us with four long strides, faster than I could've predicted. My instincts kick in. My mind can't keep up with his strikes but my reflexes can.

He shoots a punch at my throat and I barely jerk back in time to dodge it. His smile is sinister beneath his mask and it only makes his eyes more ferocious. He blocks my counter-strike and I dodge his cheap shot to my kidney. I can tell he's having fun with this. Bradshaw comes at me directly and I fall for his trick, raising my arms to deflect a frontal assault. He tips to the right and hits me in the spleen. I choke, faltering in pain and he takes advantage of my slip up. His boot hooks mine and I crash to the ground.

My world spins for a second and I choke on the breaths I can't seem to take.

He has the audacity to laugh as he comes down on me, but I'm ready for it. I twist my ankle around his and roll us to the side. He stops us with his knee and pins my arm to the ground.

"That was a clever trick," he says in a low voice, pressing his cheek against mine as he kicks my legs apart and settles his knee between my thighs. "Unfortunately, I've seen it before." My cheeks flush and I desperately rack my brain for the technique to get out of this hold.

Nothing. My mind is blank. The only thing I can focus on is the heat of his bare skin against mine and the pressure of his leg at my center.

The others laugh and Bradshaw increases the weight on my spine and arm as he twists it back. I groan in pain and gnash my teeth together.

"Give up. I've bested you, Bun."

"No." I try to spin but it only puts more strain on my already throbbing arm.

"Such a stupid—" He only gets a gasp out before I buck my hips up into his crotch—*hard*. He arches forward and coughs as I roll beneath him and plant my foot on his chest, kicking him back with all my strength.

Bradshaw falls back and props up on his elbows, ready to come for me again, but I'm already tackling him back down to the dirt. I punch him in his perfect face and smile through the grit and blood that blooms in my mouth as he lands one against my cheek too.

All I see is red as we relentlessly punch the shit out of each other. Hands are wrapping around my arms and pulling me off Bradshaw before I can register what's happening.

"Jesus, will you two fucking knock it off!" Eren shoves me back and puts his palm on Bradshaw's chest when he tries to come back at me. His brow has a fresh cut and his mask is wet with blood. I sneer at him and he lunges once more. I'm glad Eren is between us—I'm not sure what we'd do to each other if he wasn't.

Bradshaw stares at me like I'm a wild animal that needs to be put down.

"I'm sick of you not obeying orders," Eren says quieter, getting in Bradshaw's face. The two of them share an uncomfortable silence before Bradshaw lets his shoulders roll back and he walks back toward base alone. He disappears behind the pine trees and I can breathe again.

I seethe all night as I scrub the blood from beneath my nails.

Devils *do* bleed.

eleven

. . .

EREN DIVIDES US INTO THREE GROUPS FOR THE TRIAL RAID. WE only have three days left in training to both infiltrate the enemy base and rescue the hostages. Once we do that, we need to bring them back to the extraction point. That alone is a one-day trip on foot, depending on whether the hostages are "injured." If they are, it might be longer.

It's hard to believe we're already in the final week. It's felt much, *much* longer than three weeks.

I'm stationed on a short cliffside that dips into a meadow, close enough that I can get a kill shot confidently. If I can't protect them today on the mock extraction, then I don't deserve to be on their squad.

It's easy to spot the six of them. Bradshaw is the only one on his own. He works alone with only his sniper counterpart as his backup. Those were his demands for a new partner. I'm guessing he wanted to work with someone specializing in long distance after Abrahm's death. Though I'm sure Eren

115

took his demands with a grain of salt, considering I specialize in close combat too.

We haven't received the real mission details yet, but from what I've picked up through eavesdropping on Eren, I know that it's going to be remote with little to no vantage points. I doubt I'll be using my sniper as much as my handgun and KA-BAR.

I watch as Bradshaw moves like a shadow born from the darkness itself, unsheathing his false blade marked with red. His broad shoulders flex as he readies his knife.

The others surround the small building we tracked the hostile squad to and lie in wait for Bradshaw to take out as many of the exterior guards as possible.

My finger curls slowly around the trigger and I take a deep breath as Bradshaw sneaks up behind the first soldier and draws his blade over their throat. The soldier falls silently and Bradshaw guides their limp body gently to the ground to avoid any sound. I raise a brow at the acting on the hostile team's part. I've only seen LARPers take a fake mission this seriously.

Bradshaw doesn't waste a second. He's already moving again, slowly creeping up to the next one. Watching him work so effortlessly sends a disturbing throb through my body. He's not actually killing them, but it's evident that he's done so many times before. A devil in human skin. Watching him move so fluidly gives me an itch I've been trying to ignore for weeks. Something inside of me yearns for him.

My blood burns through my veins.

A cruel grin pulls at my lips as the hostiles alert to Bradshaw's presence and start flooding from the building. Ian, Harrison, and Eren flank from the left while Jefferson and Pete come in on the right. They won't make it to Bradshaw before he's outnumbered.

I take a deep breath and hold it as I pull the trigger.

The sniper rifle bucks against my shoulder with recoil,

but I hold it steady; a red cloud of dust explodes on a soldier's temple. I wince, hoping their helmet took the brunt of the hit. *These new practice guns sure pack a punch.* I reload without blinking and hit the next target, who's about to shoot Pete in the chest.

Reload.

A flash of a scope makes itself known behind a wall of trees and underbrush. My body is rolling to the side before I can consciously process it. A false bullet hits the rock I just had my back against. Red powder coats the stoneface and the smoke plumes before being carried by the wind. *Jesus.* I roll back quickly and locate the marksman. He's about to shoot again, but I'm faster. My bullet hits his stomach and he goes down.

Reload.

Fuck. Where's Bradshaw? My eyes trace over the battlefield three times, but I don't see him. He must be inside getting the hostages. I shoot three more men before Bradshaw comes out of the building with two limping hostages on his shoulders. Pete and Ian help him while Eren rushes inside to get the rest of them out.

I take a relaxing breath.

So far, so good. If this is as hard as it gets, then I've definitely secured my spot on the team. If only it were this easy to earn their respect and trust.

All their backs are turned, having cleared the building and they're making their way back to the base. From my location I have clear sight of them the entire way. Looks like we can call it a day—

A man comes running out of the building with a dummy grenade. If the red powder gets on my squad, we fail the mock mission. It's easy to pull the trigger, second to breathing for me. The red plume that breaks on the man's helmet draws all their attention and every single one of them looks utterly shocked.

A wry smile pulls at my lips, but it quickly fades when I see that Bradshaw doesn't look impressed. He's the only one that seems displeased with the results. Of course, he isn't impressed. What will it fucking take?

I want to land a bullet in his chest as payback. But all that will earn me is an all-night watch.

I follow them with my scope the entire way back. There are a few soldiers hidden in the trees and I pick them off easily before my squad is even walking through the area. I finally lower my eye from the scope as they get back to base and let my forehead hit the ground with exhaustion.

I did it.

"If I were an enemy, you would've been dead ten minutes ago."

My eyes widen and I whirl, pushing up to my knees as adrenaline spikes in my chest. I wince at the pain across my ribs and knees.

"Bones? What the fuck, you're supposed to be back at base. When did you—"

"Shut up," he says harshly.

The air gets stuck in my lungs and my rage flares instantly. I stand and shove his chest hard. He isn't even fazed by it. His pale blue eyes only narrow at me with disdain.

"What do you want?" I say with venom, unsheathing my sharp, very real, knife. He looks down at it like it's a toy, as if he doesn't think I'll actually use it.

"I want you to quit, *Bunny,*" his voice is cold and there's something lethal about his demeanor today. He wouldn't try something again, would he? The blood drains from my face at that thought. Because unlike our prior fights, today we're completely alone and our squad is far out of earshot.

"I told you I'm not going to. Do you have any idea how many times I saved all your asses today?" I shove him again but he doesn't back up. Instead, he grips my forearm tight enough that it stings.

His eyes don't show any emotion as he pulls me closer. His cloth mask is the only barrier between our lips as he whispers, "*Nell.*" My name sounds more like a plea than a threat. More like Jenkins's voice than Bradshaw's. "I'm not letting you join our squad. You either quit... or I'll make you."

I tear my arm from his grip and turn my back to him so he won't see the tears brimming in my eyes. This mock mission has been draining and I don't have much mental endurance left. *Focus on something else.* I start unloading my sniper rifle and packing the gear up. There's no talking to this guy. No middle ground.

He's fucking insane.

His low sigh is the only sound he gives before wrapping his hands around my neck. It instantly triggers my fight or flight response and my elbow flies down into his ribs. He doesn't expect it and we fall to the ground together—his grip loosens instinctively and I take the chance to slip out of his hold.

I grab a fist full of dirt and throw it in his face. He groans and shuts his eyes but his hand reaches for me faster than I can crawl. His grip on my ankle burns as he digs his fingertips into my flesh.

A shriek rises from my throat as he pulls me toward him. He's scrambling to get me pinned under him. My mind flashes back to the sparring match and I refuse to be in that situation again. The cut on my ribs throbs and a hot, wet sensation spreads over my side. It's already broken open a few times over the weeks. It needs stitches to stay shut. I thought to mention it to Eren, but with everyone rooting for me to get off the squad, I thought better of it.

"Bradshaw, get the fuck off of me!" I scream and that seems to piss him off more.

He pins my arm to the ground as I kick him in the balls.

We both groan. *Fuck this.* Fuck this guy.

I dig my fingers into the earth to crawl further away from him.

"Say my fucking name out loud again and I'll *bury* you," he growls as he rises to his knees. He really won't let this go. He won't let me be on the squad.

I want to give in so fucking bad. I want to throw in the towel, because who in their right mind wants to protect someone like him? He deserves to die. But there's a small voice in the back of my head that won't let me give in.

I'll never find the truth about what happened in Patagonia if I quit.

Bradshaw grabs my wrists and spins me over to my back. He looks down at my face with hesitance before glancing at my wrist like he's going to snap it. "I'm sorry for what I'm about to do."

I don't wait to find out what he's sorry for. "Me too," I say as I hook my leg around his knee and force him to fall to the side, right off the edge of the short cliff. But he doesn't let go of my wrist and pulls me over the ledge with him.

It's not a far drop, maybe eight feet, but it feels stretched into many granular moments. All I see are Bradshaw's blue eyes—all the anger vanished and replaced with anguish. He pulls me close to his chest and wraps his arms around me. His hand cups the nape of my neck. Was it out of panic or does he not hate me as much as he tries to convince me?

His head tucks in close to mine and we hit the ground with enough force that it knocks the breath out of my lungs. Our bodies roll down the slight incline for a few feet before we tumble to a stop.

Dust rolls over my body and my face stings with gravel burns. Twigs and brambles are tangled up in my messy braid. I take a moment to take inventory of my pain before moving. It doesn't feel like anything is broken so I let out a small recouping breath.

"Shit." Bradshaw curses from a few feet away. He's already moving toward me and is at my side in a few seconds. His gear is covered in dirt. He looks fine, other than the red scrapes that line the skin visible around his eyes and the bridge of his nose. I'm surprised when he looks down at me with concern. "Are you okay?"

I groan as he rolls me to my back, wincing as he unzips my vest and lifts my shirt to the bottom of my breasts to check the cut across my ribs.

My mind goes fuzzy as a fresh wave of agony rolls through me.

"Fuck, it tore open." He unlatches his side pocket and grabs a new roll of medical tape. His hands are trembling as he lowers them to my bare flesh. The pads of his fingers are hot and that thin line between pain and lust lights up again. Something I shouldn't enjoy, but I do.

I grab his wrist and stop him from wrapping it. "Don't touch me, asshole," I rasp and take the tape from him, fumbling with my own shaking hands to get the damn thing open.

He watches me in silence as I pull the old bandage off. I have to bury my teeth into my bottom lip to keep from whimpering. Blood quickly leaks from the wound. My hands aren't moving as smoothly as I'd like. I'm not sure if it's because of the shock from the fall, the fact that my *partner* attacked me, or because I'm a second away from a mental breakdown.

Blood smears across my hands and stomach as I roll the medical tape around my chest. It keeps sliding and making it worse. I'm about to just pull my shirt down and deal with it once we get back to camp, but his hands reach out and rest over mine, steadying them.

I freeze and let my eyes flick up to his. He gives me an

apologetic crease of his brow but doesn't say anything. Slowly, he takes the tape from my hands and finishes binding the injury.

I observe him carefully as he does. There's a war waging in his mind right now. He's made it clear he wants me off the squad. He'll go to great lengths to make that happen. But then he gets upset after I'm hurt... My teeth set and I try not to think about it anymore. I try not to focus on the dark, wanton look in his eyes as he traces my skin with his fingertips.

Bradshaw's thumb digs into the flesh of my hip and I jerk involuntarily at the sensation of it. He smirks under his black mask. "You fucking masochist. I knew you liked when I carved you up. Your thighs were hot and rubbing beneath me. Is that why you won't go? Because I keep feeding your sickness?" His voice is hoarse. I know a crumbling man when I see one.

"You obviously enjoy dealing out pain. It's not my fault you discovered my kink."

His smile stretches under his mask but his eyes remain dull. He lets his hands, covered in my blood, come down to his sides and we share an uncomfortable silence before he seems to come back to himself. He stands slowly and, without a word, walks back in the direction toward base alone.

My head falls back to the ground and I lie there for a few minutes.

What the hell am I supposed to do to get him to trust me?

twelve

. . .

HER BLOOD IS SMEARED ALL OVER MY HANDS.

Fuck.

I take a deep, unsteady breath to center myself as I push my back against a tree and slide to the forest floor. My hands shake uncontrollably. This is usually when my panic sets in, when the anxiety spreads through my veins after training and all I can think of is death. But with her… My eyes linger on the bright red of her blood on my fingertips and it shoots heat to my dick.

"Goddammit," I say under my breath.

Don't get attached to her, I remind myself, leg bouncing with anxiety and the urge to calm the swelling in my pants. *Do not let her stay.*

I tilt my head back against the bark of the ponderosa and breathe slowly, letting my hand fall to my zipper and pull out my cock. I curl my fingers around the thickness of it and start pumping. Her blood slicks over my length and all I can think of as I beat myself off are her parted lips as I ran my fingers over her cut. The way her eyes rolled sensually back and her hips bucked at my touch.

My release is quick and unsatisfying. *I need more.* I let out a labored breath and stare out into the woods. Wondering why the more I show her who I am, the more she seems to be drawn to me. And more disturbingly, the more I'm starved for her.

thirteen

. . .

NELL

IAN TOSSES ME A WATER BOTTLE AND SLAPS MY BACK WITH A huge grin that spreads over his lips. "You fucking slayed out there today, Bunny!"

My smile is slow to reveal itself because I'm not sure if he's being serious or sarcastic, but his eyes flash with sincerity and my doubts drift a bit further as I rub the fresh bruises on my knees.

"Fall off that hillside, little bun-bun?" Jefferson jests, looking at my dust-covered uniform and messy hair. *If only he knew.*

I feign a laugh and force my hands away from my wrecked knees. I manage to pull a few twigs loose from my braid. "It's from laying on my stomach on those rocks all damn day," I lie.

The base is busy now with the mock hostages. Eren and Pete are tending to them and getting their sleeping arrangements put together before nightfall, which is already upon us as the sun sinks behind the distant mountains.

Bradshaw still hasn't returned.

My stomach turns and the worry must be evident on my face because Harrison raises a brow at me. *What could he possibly be doing out there for this long?*

"Don't worry about Bones. Ever since Patagonia he has to take breathers after every training," Harrison says indifferently. His blond hair is smeared with dirt from today's attack. His green eyes burn brightly against the dusk and campfire.

"Breathers?" I ask.

Ian and Jefferson share a grim look.

Harrison nods. "His PTSD after Abrahm is bad. If we weren't dark forces they would've pulled him from the squad. But even then, General Nolan considered it." My eyes linger over Eren to ensure he doesn't overhear our conversation about his twin.

He was almost removed from the squad? I can't imagine how bad it must be for it to get to that point. Dark forces soldiers like us are of little concern to the underground commanders. As long as we're ready to go on suicide missions and remain non-existent, they don't give a shit about our mental state.

"What was he like before? What kind of missions did you guys go on the most?" I ask as I take a bite from my MRE and warm my legs by the fire.

Ian sets his gloves on one of the big rocks lining the fire. They're soaked, I assume, from cleaning them in the river. He mutters, "I'm sure you've heard the horror stories about him and most of them are probably true, but he was a lot less of an asshole back then than he is now." Jefferson lets out a small grunt of agreement.

"Yeah, he was less likely to, uh… cut his comrade's shirts off, that's for sure," Harrison chides. I nudge his shoulder and shoot him a *shut up* look. He raises his hands innocently and laughs.

"Malum primarily did all the shit work the rest of the squads weren't likely to survive. Long operations in foreign countries where we'd stake out in apartments or way out in the middle of fucking nowhere like Patagonia." Jefferson pauses and looks at me, glances away, then holds my gaze. "Why didn't Riøt show up as planned?" His voice isn't harsh, but there's deep rooted pain and a yearning for the truth.

I keep my eyes on his, even if it makes me uncomfortable. "We were given different orders." I keep it brief. The distrust in Jefferson's eyes tells me he doesn't buy it.

"What happened to Abrahm?" I shift the conversation. If I keep it strictly informational instead of getting into the soft human side of it, they're more likely to share. A tidbit I'd picked up while listening to them speak to each other over MREs throughout the weeks.

Ian leans forward on his elbows and casts me a sidelong glance. "It was targeted."

My eyes flick to Jefferson and Harrison for more, but they only shake their heads. The loyalty they keep to their fallen comrade and Bradshaw is commendable. They needn't say it —their meaning is heavy in the air.

It's Bradshaw's story to tell.

"What about you guys? You seem fine compared to Bones," I say carefully. They become sullen and stare at the flickering flames of the campfire for a few seconds.

Jefferson rubs his hands together, a small tick he has when he gets uncomfortable. I meet his gaze as he mutters, "Just because a bowl looks fine doesn't mean it's absent of cracks. A horse that stands may not be able to run."

"So you're not fine." Blunt. To the point.

That earns me a firm frown from Jefferson, but he nods. "He was a brother to us all, but we weren't there in the last moments." Harrison and Ian shift uneasily, looking around the camp, worried, I'm sure, for Bradshaw to return during this conversation. Are they not allowed to talk about it at all? That seems cruel.

"And Bones was," I mutter.

The three of them nod simultaneously.

"He wasn't the same after that. A part of Bones died with Abrahm that night. And a darkness was born in his heart," Harrison explains. My stomach sinks hearing those words.

"You guys still think it's Riøt's fault. *Bones* thinks it's Riøt's fault." My voice is stern and cold.

Jefferson scratches his chin and looks at me like all his demons are waking up again. "No one can back up your 'we received different orders' story, bun-bun. All we know is that you never showed up."

I fist my hands over my knees. "You guys were supposed to get updated orders too." My eyes flick suspiciously to Ian. As the signaler, he should've been the one in contact with the air power.

Harrison takes a bite from his cracker and says through mouthfuls, "Well, at least we could hold our own. We only lost one soldier that night."

I lost everyone.

A part of me died when my squad was extinguished. *It was my fault.* My smile left and so did any morals I had left.

"How about you, Bunny? Are you *fine* after losing your whole squad?" Ian asks as he leans against his bandaged palm. The firelight illuminates his brown eyes. It's a cruel question.

The three of them watch me carefully. Unfortunately, it's a question I've answered more than I care to. The sting has been robbed from the words.

I stare at embers pulsing beneath the logs. "I'm not the same either. I don't think any functional person could be."

Harrison throws another block of wood into the fire and pries, "Sooo, what happened?"

Jefferson punches his arm.

"*Ow,* what? I want to hear it from the only survivor. She's like a legend now."

"It's okay. I don't mind talking about it."

I thread my fingers together and let my hands dangle between my legs. They sit straighter, perking to listen intently.

"As you know, we were supposed to converge in Patagonia a few klicks south of the drop-off. We knew it was dangerous. But we didn't anticipate the ambush that was waiting for us on the extraction route. We had instructions to stay put on the road until Malum showed up. The bombs came so suddenly and were so bright... We were blinded by them before the explosions blew our Humvees off the road." I swallow as the shouting and taste of iron that hollowed my throat that day roll back through me. Tremors planted in the deepest parts of my marrow awaken.

"Shit." Harrison breathes out, eyes hardening.

I nod and continue: "The first truck got the worst of it. The four of them died instantly in the first missile strike. Our vehicle flipped from the explosion and I—" My hands tremble as they always do when I think of the horrors we faced that day. I bring them to my sides, clutching my stomach in an attempt to comfort myself. "I pulled Sergeant Jenkins from the driver's seat and dragged him twenty feet away from the vehicle. Two of my comrades engaged in a shootout with the incoming hostiles. They protected us until we got to safety. There was so much blood... I knew I should've gone back to help them sooner, but I had to get Jenkins as far as I could. He was my commanding sergeant. I was his second. I couldn't leave him."

Their grim expressions hold misery. They already know

how this story ends, but it still sucks to hear how it all unfolded.

"I set him down once we were far enough, but when I stood up to help my squadmates, the second wave hit directly on them and the shockwaves blew me back."

My throat grows thick with emotion.

"It knocked me out and I didn't wake for several minutes. By the time I was aware of my surroundings, Jenkins had dragged me into the cover of the nearby trees. He had already lost so much blood and if it wasn't for me, he'd—" I flex my jaw and bite my lower lip to quell my bleeding heart.

My mind whirls as I picture his face perfectly—the last weak smile he gave, the way it made all his sharp features seem so soft and gentle, the soft caress of his calloused thumb over my bloody cheek. His words.

"You're going to be okay, Nell." He pushed me away from his *slumped body, the tree stained red with his blood. I stood shakily, shocked that a man I knew as invincible could look so broken.* *"Leave me behind. You can still live. Get as far away as you can, escape the dark forces, Gallows. Be free."*

The wood in the firepit shifts and the crackle snaps me back into the present. I blink twice and look up, startled for a moment. Pete and Eren joined the circle at some point and they stare at me like I'm a wounded puppy.

I press my palm to my forehead and sigh. *"Fuck.* Sorry."

They remain quiet, a knowing look of loss spreads over their faces. Eren looks particularly bothered but his eyes aren't on me, they're set on something behind me. I follow his line of sight and glance over my shoulder. I'm met with a black tactical vest covered in dirt, much the same way mine looks. My eyes move up slowly to his face.

Bradshaw looks like a ghost. The sliver of skin his mask reveals is smeared with dirt and his eyes are hazy like he's not present. He stares down at me, but there's a hollowness where his usual ire lives.

"Br—" I bite my tongue with the slip up before clearing my throat. "Bones?" I reach out my hand to his wrist. He doesn't move. His expression remains completely blank. He knows now. He knows I left Jenkins behind in battle.

I'm a coward.

Eren is at his side before I can say anything else. "Come on, you should lie down." He turns Bradshaw so the others can't see him and guides him to the tents. When I turn to look back at the rest of our squadmates, I find each of their gazes averted and sidelong. Unwilling to meet my eyes.

Bradshaw isn't fit for the field and they're allowing him to stay, knowing it could very well get him killed.

This might be the weakness in his armor I've been looking for.

———

The others head to their sleeping posts while Harrison and Jefferson take the first watch. Bradshaw and Eren still haven't returned from the tent. It's been at least an hour. I chew on my lower lip, not knowing why I give a shit about this asshole, but I decide to check on him anyway.

"Sergeant?" I stand straight, facing the tent flap and awaiting a response before I enter.

Eren's voice is smooth and calm as he replies, "Come in, Bunny."

I slip inside the dark green tent. My eyes take a few seconds to adjust to the dim, lantern-lit space. It's just Eren and Bradshaw in here, a few empty cots to either side of them. I still at the sight of Bradshaw with his mask off. His face is the mirror image of Eren's.

Something painful traces the edges of my heart looking at him in this state. I didn't think a man as hard and cruel as him could be this broken inside. He's never let on as much. I silently sit beside Eren on the ground and stare at Bradshaw's lovely face. Bradshaw's eyes lift slightly to mine and flicker with sadness.

"What's wrong with him, Eren?" I admire Bradshaw's empty stare as he takes me in. He's quiet and I can't tell if he's studying me or looking right through me. It's the loveliest I've seen him and I find myself wishing it would never end.

Eren takes a deep breath and exhales slowly, pushing his hair back and looking at me. "Honestly, I don't know. This is the third time in two years. He vanishes for hours and comes back like this."

"Why is he still active? He's a liability—"

He cuts me off. "You know what our line of work entails. No discharges. The only way you get out of the dark forces is in a body bag or earning your cards. Even if it wasn't that way, he wants to stay." I glower at Eren but he ignores it. "Anyway, I don't think he'll be fit to stay at his post tonight. I'll take over your watch. Can you stay here with him?"

I frown. I should tell him about what Bradshaw did on the hillside, but that would make me relive the unsettling things that went through my mind as Bradshaw covered his hands in my blood.

"Yes, Sergeant."

He gives me a cocky grin, warmth in his blue eyes. "Thanks, Bunny." He sets his hand on my thigh before standing up. Eren zips the tent behind him and his footsteps fade.

What a fucking day. I blow out a breath before moving to grab the lantern. Bradshaw's hand wraps around my wrist and the sudden contact startles me. I look down at him and find his brows pulled firmly together, as if he's fighting dark thoughts. His eyes are shut, lashes kissing his dirt-stained cheeks.

I lean down, hesitant to say anything, so I brush my hand over his forehead instead to check his temperature. He catches my hand and holds it against his cheek. As I'm about to pull away, he opens his eyes slightly, only enough for me to see the icy blue gems his lashes hide.

His expression is still absent.

"Bradshaw?" I whisper, staring at his features closer than I'd like to. His eyes flutter closed but he doesn't let go of my hand. *Well, fuck.*

For the first twenty minutes I admire his rugged, handsome face. The next twenty I study his scars and wonder how many more are hiding beneath his hair. I wonder if Abrahm once studied him as thoroughly as I am now and found the same lovely broken things I do.

My arms start trembling and I can't bear to stay in this awkward position any longer.

I pull away slowly, trying to wriggle my way out of his hold without him waking. Bradshaw's eyes open. He's dazed still, in the land between half asleep and awake. His eyes widen and he pulls me close. His voice is raspy and sharp. "What are you doing?"

My throat knots at his accusatory tone.

"You… wouldn't let go," I say slowly, my voice graveled.

His shoulders tense. "Bunny?" He flinches and we both look down at his hand firmly wrapped around my wrist. Surprise dawns over his features.

Bradshaw lets go and pushes me an arm's length away, hands planted heavily on my shoulders. We stare at each other for a moment. His eyes get their dark shine back, but he doesn't let my shoulders go.

"Bradshaw?" I whisper. Has he lost his fucking mind? He stares at me for a long time, his arms trembling, making my heart ache for him.

I think he's finally going to let go, but he pulls me down to lie beside him. I breathe in sharply, ready to escape, but he shushes me and guides my shoulders against his chest.

Maybe it's because of the pure shock to my system, or perhaps I've been drugged, but I stay still and lie with him.

If I'm being honest, maybe I'm just tired of being lonely. My jaw flexes at the comfort of his body and what it does to me. I allow my eyes to close.

"You do things to me, Bun," his voice is low, drowsy.

My breath is slow. *Does he know what he's saying?* Bradshaw's hold tightens around me and the swelling need in his pants presses against my inner thigh.

Every fiber of my being is telling me to pull away from him. All this man does is hurt me and awaken dark needs deep inside me. But it's been so long since someone's held me like this. I breathe in. He smells like blood and smoke. Slowly, my arms wrap around his chest and I hold him as possessively as he does me.

For some fucked up reason it feels like ecstasy. *I'd do anything for this forever.*

He trails the pads of his fingers over the nape of my neck, sending chills through me. Then his lips meet my forehead, hot and gentle in contrast to everything I know about him.

"My dick is covered in your blood," he confesses against my ear. His words send goosebumps over my skin. There's only one reason why my blood would be on his dick and that's if he beat himself off after our encounter on the cliffside.

"Sadist," I whisper and, for some reason, I'm smiling and turned on at the thought of him jerking off with my blood. *What's wrong with me?*

He doesn't move for a few stretched out seconds. Then he rests his head against mine and murmurs, "I couldn't control myself. You like the darkest parts of me and I wanted you all over my cock."

My throat dries. His filthy words send a throb between my thighs. "Have I seen the darkest parts of you?"

"Not even close."

I press my mouth further into the crook of his neck as he draws his fingertips down my back, slipping his hands under my shirt.

"Where did you go?" I try to breathe and keep this from going where I think it is.

"Nowhere." He lowers his face to mine, teeth skating over my shoulder as he tugs my shirt lower. I push away from him to look him in the eyes and when I do, I find a heady, lustful gaze.

"You went somewhere in your mind. You were like an empty shell," I pry, and his mouth firms with annoyance.

"Every time you talk, I want to shove my cock into your mouth. Stop fucking pushing me or I won't be so nice."

My stomach flips. *No. Don't get excited at that.* I glare at him. "Stop avoiding the question."

His lips part and a sinister smile stretches over his face. It does something to me. Twists the depraved part of my soul and pulls me in for more.

"How about you wash yourself off of me, Bunny? I only like your blood when it's fresh." Bradshaw unzips his pants and frees his dick. My eyes snap down immediately, taking in the sheer size of him and my dried blood that he's smothered over himself like some wild animal.

Any thoughts I had cease and are replaced with a craving I'm not mentally well enough to investigate at the moment.

"Spit on it," he commands, pushing me slowly off the cot and onto my knees. He sits up and hangs his dick over the edge. I swallow the saliva that rushes at his words.

Am I going to do this?

I stare at his pulsing, throbbing length and decide that I am.

I lower my mouth to hover over him and let the saliva

spill off my tongue and coat his dick. His hands curl over the edge of the cot and he throws his head back as he groans.

"Fuck, that's hot. Soak it, Bun. I want it sopping wet before I put your blood back into your body."

My jaw slacks at his words, but I continue to let the spit drip from my tongue. Bradshaw fists his dick and strokes it in long languid motions. Instantly, his veiny shaft glistens with a wet sheen and I want him to fill me up so fucking bad.

I'm going straight to hell when I die. For all the death on my hands. Further down, if there is something lower than hell, for what I'm about to do with the devil.

I reach down to put pressure at my core, but Bradshaw catches my arm and smirks coldly at me. "You don't get to feel good until I want you to."

He pushes me against the ground and comes down over me. He shoves my shirt up. His eyes flick briefly to the tent entrance before looking down at me, his legs straddled over my hips. He presses his length against my stomach and it reaches to my belly button. It's hot and wet and throbs eagerly as he leans forward and grinds his hips against my bare skin.

Pleasure rolls over his expression like he's taken a hit of ecstasy. His eyes loll and he licks his lower lip, biting it as if to keep himself from burying his incisors into me.

I squirm beneath his flexed muscles, trying to escape his gripping hands as he keeps me from easing the urge to find pleasure. I muffle a cry as he pins my wrists together above my head and brings his lips to my neck, nipping my sensitive skin.

"You want me to make you come?" he says in a deep tone that sends chills up my spine and a new urgent heat to my core.

I arch my back so my stomach presses to his and encases his wet cock between us. He continues to pump his hips and lets out another groan that is two seconds from unraveling everything I thought I knew about myself.

"I want you to break me," I mutter as callously as I can.

He lifts his head. Dark strands of hair fall over his forehead and those pale eyes scour into my very bones. A genuine smile spreads over his lips.

"Oh, baby, breaking you comes much, *much* later." He strokes his tongue up my throat and brings his mouth to mine. It's not a kiss I'd ever tell my mom about. Not even my best friend, if I had one. It's brutal. Devastating. Painful. Easily the most savage encounter two people should ever know.

He urges my tongue into his mouth and bites down on it. I let out a sharp moan and wriggle beneath him in pain before pleasure and heat coil inside me. My center is weeping, begging, pleading. I need him to touch me *now.*

Blood blossoms through our kiss and he laps at my mouth like a starved man. I force my lips away from his and give him the same treatment, letting my teeth meet his tender flesh. The starburst scar on his neck is soft against my tongue and he jerks sharply at the sting my closing jaw brings.

"*Fuck, Bun.*" Bradshaw groans, fists my hair tightly, and rips my head from his neck. I wasn't expecting him to force me off so suddenly—my jaw locks and his skin tears. His breath is heady as he rubs his neck and looks down at the blood that leaks from it.

"Oh my God. Bradshaw!" I lean forward and cup his neck with my palm.

The manic look that flashes across his eyes gives me pause. Foolish—I forgot his dick was out. I'm practically already sitting on it with our chests smashed together. He scoops my ass up and pulls out his pocketknife.

"Hold that cut tight, Bunny, and don't move unless you want a knife up your pussy." My body stills and I can't conjure any words before he's cutting a slit in the crotch of my pants. My body trembles and my brows pinch as I hold still. A low laugh rolls from deep in his chest. "Don't worry, I left your underwear, you'll need those to hold in my come."

My palm is slick with his blood and the focus in which I need to keep it firmly in place steals away my wit. So instead I mutter, "What if I'm not on birth control?"

He nudges my underwear to the side and presses his tip inside me. My pants are tight around my hips in this position. *I can't believe he fucking cut my pants open.* My opening instantly stretches around his bare dick. The intrusion makes my breath stutter and I have to clamp my free hand around his neck to support the other one.

His smile turns sinister and he does something that surprises me.

As I'm practically choking him, trying to stop his neck from bleeding, he leans forward, palms pressed down on my hips until I'm fully seated on his dick and he kisses me sweetly on the lips.

A real kiss. One that makes my heart beat faster and my stomach coil with butterflies.

Bradshaw's eyes are closed and he slowly guides us back until his shoulder blades are against a cot and he has enough leverage for his legs to support his deep hip thrusts.

"You're not stupid enough to come to a place like this without birth control, sweetheart." He pounds into me. The sound of him breathing heavily makes my insides twist with pleasure.

I don't bother telling him he's right. He knows he is.

His length fills all of me, stretching my inner walls until my eyes are rolling to the back of my head and my fingers lose their grip around his throat.

Bradshaw groans, trying to be as quiet as he can. I've almost forgotten where we are, who we are. He does that to me. I could be in a room with a thousand screaming, dying men and I'd only see him.

Hatred and desire aren't so different. Both are an obsessive, all-consuming emotion. It's a thin line to walk on.

And God, is it easy to fuck someone you hate.

Easier to feel that adrenaline and rush of confusion that follows.

"I'm fucking you because I want to show you who's in control between us," he says venomously, but his darkened eyes and bobbing throat betray his emotions.

He looks as confused as I feel.

Because this feels right. Two murderous, vile killing machines hurting and fucking each other like our flesh has nothing left to give us. Nothing left to surrender except this violent act of pleasure.

I never felt anything like this with Jenkins.

I've never felt this for anyone.

"Yet I'm the one on top, staring down at you as you pleasure me like I'm your master," I whisper, our lips brushing. The heat from our breaths makes my skin tingle.

Bradshaw's eyes turn cold and he grips my hips hard, then stills inside me, pressing agonizingly against my cervix. His cock throbs and I feel every sensation of it. I shudder and try to hold my composure.

"You'd rather I dominate you completely then, huh? Fuck, you're sick." He wraps an arm around my back and hooks the other one around my ass to hold me in place as he stands, his dick still entirely inside me. I moan at the pressure my weight puts on my cervix and bury my face into his chest to keep myself from screaming.

My hips buck against him as he walks us to the back of the tent. A laugh rumbles through his chest. "Who's pleasuring who now? Don't worry, I'll show you who's in charge here, Bunny. After all, you are my second, aren't you? You'll listen to every order I give you. And I expect you to follow them." He withdraws from me and the emptiness is a shock to my system.

He sets me down on the floor and before I can rise to my elbows, he's already on me. His fingers curl around the waist of my pants and he pulls them down to my knees. He wrestles me to my side until his chest is pressed against my back. Air becomes precious as his forearm secures around my throat and leaves me at his mercy.

"Shhh, there you go." Bradshaw draws his tongue up the side of my neck and slides his hand down my stomach until he reaches my core. He uses two fingers to swirl my clit as he pumps his dick between my thighs, rubbing my slit and making my breaths labored. "I'm going to fuck you hard and relentlessly. Until you cave to me. Until you beg me to come inside you and give your poor, sweet pussy some relief. You want that, don't you, Bunny?"

Shamelessly and high on adrenaline, I nod slightly in his death grip. Each breath is a sip of pleasure. Small whimpers roll from my lips.

His lips brush the outside of my ear. "I want you to submit to me, my little Riøt snake."

He wants me off the squad.

My only reply is a muffled cry against his tattooed skin as he inserts himself inside me again. Then the savage fucking ensues. He fucks me like I'm a nothing more than a doll for his pleasure. His fingers dig into my hip bones and he grips my throat with his other, squeezing until I'm certain I'll pass out.

A god of a man. A devil of demons.

Those are my only thoughts as he brings me to my climax faster than any man has ever done before. My legs shake with my release and I don't get a reprieve as he pulls my leg up so that he can fully rut into my pussy.

"*Fuuuck.*" He pants behind me, somehow increasing his

ruthless thrusts and making my sensitive walls quiver with each movement.

My mouth parts in a silent cry, my insides burning and building my next orgasm quickly. The pleasure is too intense, it hurts, I can't keep coming like this.

Bradshaw hears my whimper and shoves his cock in as far as he can, holding it there and grinding his hips to my ass. This time I can't keep my cry silent. The sound of it gets trapped in my throat as he forces two fingers inside my mouth.

"I think the question you need to ask yourself is, how many times can you come before you're a shell of who you are now? Hmm?" His grinding hips are unyielding. The sound of his cock stirring up my insides makes my brain foggy.

He pinches my clit just as he ruts into my cervix with brutal strength and I come completely undone. His entire body stills as my hips buck against his cock and ride out the wave of my climax. My lips are closed shut with his palm firmly placed over my mouth to keep the moans from being as loud as they were intended to be.

My body slacks in his arms and exhaustion floods through my limbs. My pussy is the most sensitive it's ever been. I want to beg him to stop, but my mind is unraveling at the pleasure and my body is reacting in a way it never has before.

Bradshaw hesitates, maybe because he thinks I've passed out from coming so hard. He removes his hand from my mouth and turns my head back to his. Our eyes connect and he can see that he's already broken what he promised to save for later. A flash of satisfaction flickers across that heart-stopping face of his. And he smiles. He fucking smiles and it puts a beating force back into my chest.

"You're done already?" He chuckles as he resumes

KM Moronova

pulling his dick out almost to the tip and thrusting it back in agonizingly slow.

What is this man doing to me? He's venom—poison injected directly into my veins. I wriggle to try and separate from him, but he grabs my side and holds me firmly against him.

"Just beg for my come and we can be done." Bradshaw's voice is cold, like I've deeply inconvenienced him by not begging sooner.

"Fuck you." I sound weak and it pisses me off, but my lax muscles refuse to give me any will to fight with him.

He lets out a deep sigh and pulls out. My eyes widen as he flips me on my knees. The breath is forced from my lungs as he pushes his hand down on my back until my breasts are against the floor. My ass is up and bare to him and I know this position will hurt if he fucks me as hard as he has been.

"I'll stop when you say you want it," he teases darkly. My pussy is swollen from the multiple orgasms and when he enters me again, he lets out a tender moan. "Goddamn, Bunny, every time I put my dick inside you, your pussy just grabs me more and more. You greedy little thing." He slaps my ass. I cry out into my arm.

He pistons into me and it doesn't take long before my knees are screaming for relief and my pussy yearns for that promise of come to bring an end to this pleasure hell I've found myself in.

Swallowing every ounce of pride, I say on a trembling breath, "P-please."

"Please what, Bun?"

He slaps my ass again and I can tell he's close by the way he's fucking me at an increased pace and the draws of his labored breath. My climax is already at the tipping point for the third time, legs shaking and arms trembling to keep me stable.

"Please come inside me."

"I'm sorry, what? You want my seed inside you?"

For the love of God. Why do my eyes loll and my core tighten when he says that?

"Yes, *please.* I want your seed inside me, Bones. Please."

He laughs and thrusts a few more times before he moans deeply and holds himself against me. I come moments after and ride the waves with him. His hips jerk lightly with each throbbing release of his semen inside me. The heat and pulsing of it steals all my focus, my swollen walls greedily taking every last drop he leaks inside of me.

"Fuck, it feels like you're milking my cock for come," he says on a shaky breath and I can feel his trembling hands as he sets them on my back to separate us. The swelling of my walls holds him tightly, and the friction that follows as he slowly pulls himself out has both of us gritting our teeth.

The second his body is apart from mine I collapse to the ground, too weak to do anything but breathe and watch him through hazy eyes.

Everything is wet. My knees, my hands, my face, my thighs.

He looks around and seems to come to the same conclusion. But he looks too tired to do anything about it. His body falls beside mine, his black hair slicked to his forehead with sweat. Bradshaw stares into my eyes.

"That was... holy shit," he finally says after a few seconds.

I just stare back at him, trying to figure out how I can hate him but feel such immense emotion for him at the same time. I see a broken shell of a man. I see someone who's been cast away from the world and thrown away like me.

He searches my expression for something but doesn't find what he's looking for, I assume by the pinch in his brows.

"We should get cleaned up. You've got come and blood all over you." He rises lazily and when he tries to help me up the world spins.

Spins. Until everything is black.

fourteen

. . .

BRADSHAW

BUNNY'S HEAD BOBS PEACEFULLY AGAINST MY SHOULDER AS I carry her down to the stream near the base. We bathe here during the day so I'm confident no one will be here this late.

It was a miracle no one heard what transpired inside that tent. It smells entirely of sex and blood in there and I'll be spending the rest of the night cleaning up.

It was worth it.

My eyes leave the dark dirt path ahead and focus down on Bunny's long lashes. She's out cold. *I didn't think I was* that *rough with her.* She certainly seemed to enjoy herself though.

A grin lifts the corner of my mouth.

The mountain is quiet tonight and for the first time in years, the silence is reciprocated in my mind. I'm exhausted. From fucking the daylights out of my comrade and from trying to figure out why I seem to be so infatuated with her.

I stop at the water's edge and gently set her down.

She stirs and blinks drowsily at me. Panic flashes across her face when she realizes we're no longer in the tent.

"Where are we?" She sits up slowly, wincing in pain. I feel a bit sorry for it, though I don't voice it.

"We need to get cleaned up. We look like carnage right now and I'm sure you're... sore." I try to put it delicately because my ire for her has been properly extinguished for the night. I'm mildly disturbed with the idea that I actually want to be gentle with her right now.

Her brows pull together but she doesn't argue with me. She tries to stand but her legs are still unsteady. I dip in and catch her before she can tilt and fall on her ass.

A sharp breath escapes her lips. Our noses are lined up and for a few moments we just stare into each other's eyes. Her irises are a sunset brown. I could stare into them forever and bathe in the peace she brings me. The scar over the ridge of her jaw makes me yearn to know the story behind it, to share sweet nothings while we lie together and fall asleep. I want to hold her and banish my loneliness.

But I know we can't do that. I don't even know why I want to.

I dismiss the thoughts.

Bunny's throat bobs and brings me out of my mind.

I straighten and hold her close to my chest.

She looks up at my face timidly before glancing at our surroundings. "Shouldn't you be wearing your mask?"

Ah. Is that why she was looking at me so intensely? I mute the idea, the hope that she was looking at my face because she finds me as alluring as I find her.

"It's fine. Everyone is asleep and the watch post is on the other side of camp."

She nods slowly as if she doesn't completely believe me. What should I say? That I'm not wearing it because I want to feel like a person when I'm with her? That sometimes even *I* need a break from being a muzzled beast?

Leave Me Behind

"I'll help you." I change the subject as I guide her toward the water bank. There's an off-channel pool there that is probably a bit warmer than the main stream.

I'm surprised she's being so compliant but, then again, she's filthy and weak from our little playtime together.

Her muscles tighten as I unzip the coat I loaned her. I let it fall to the riverbank. She's completely naked beneath it. My jaw sets at the cut along her ribs and the deep red of her knees.

I did this to her.

Why won't she just quit?

I force my eyes away and remove my clothes before guiding her into the water. It's cold and goosebumps trail up her arms swiftly. Her face is stoic, though, not letting a hint of the chill come across her features. Maybe it feels nice on her wounds. I'm sure they burn.

"Who was Abrahm to you exactly?" she asks softly as I set her down on my knee and rub the blood from her shoulders. His name isn't as painful to hear when she says it softly, like she is now. She seems so set on learning more about him, but what's the point in learning about ghosts and lost things? She'll never know him like I did. She'll never see how his smile was so like hers. How his stubbornness wore into me the way she does.

I don't like to think about him.

It's terrible to try and forget someone as precious as he was, but the agony always flares back to life when I try to remember what he looks like. I can't remember his eyes anymore. His jaw and smile come back with little thought, but his eyes... his *soul.* I can't remember it. And that makes me feel sick.

"He was..." I try to find the right words. "He was my peace."

She brings her hand to my neck and gently washes the blood from my neck. The bite is still fresh and stings, but I

153

let the dull throb of it numb me. My eyes close instinctively at her delicate touch.

"I know that probably doesn't make sense," I add, feeling stupid.

Bunny looks at me and a small, sad smile spreads over her lovely lips.

"No. It does… Jenkins was my peace too. He saw me for what I was and he accepted it. Whenever he sat beside me, I felt the world hush and the insects hum softly. I can still feel his smile, the way it made me lean closer and want to hold on to every word he said." She pauses and stares nostalgically out across the dark water.

Irrationally, I feel jealous that she still loves a dead man. I don't want her to feel that way for anyone… Though, I guess it'd be okay if she felt that way about me.

She looks up at me sadly and lets out a half-laugh on a sigh. "I always thought we'd die together. Or at least me before him. I was supposed to protect him."

My hand raises to her face before I realize it. I brush the pad of my thumb over her cheek and she startles, looking up at me with those shadowed doe eyes.

"I'm glad it wasn't you," I admit, perhaps because in the dark I feel like I can. "He wouldn't have been able to survive without his second."

The way I didn't survive without mine. But, somehow, I'm still here, as a shell of myself. I know if she follows me into battle, into the fire, I'd die if she took a bullet for me. Riøt or not. I can't deny that I care about her and that thought scares the shit out of me.

She washes the blood from my chest, delicately moving her fingers across my skin like a lover would. If I shut my eyes and imagine a different life, I wouldn't be a monster; she wouldn't be a killer. We'd be normal, maybe in love.

"You'll convince me you don't hate my guts if you keep

talking like this," she mutters and looks away. I scoot her off my knee and she stands steadily now in the water.

"Don't get your hopes up, Bunny." I dip my head back into the water and remerge cold and determined. "Let's get back before Eren notices we're gone." The edge is back to my voice and I leave her standing in the water alone and shivering.

She's too easy to talk to. If I'm not careful I'd tell her all my secrets, hopes, and dreams. I'd tell her everything.

But I don't exist on paper. Neither does she. No one in the dark forces does. So what would be the point of sharing dreams? When we die, it's for good. Nothing to mourn. My thoughts and words won't matter.

I glance back once to make sure she got out of the water. Her lithe figure steams with the heat of her body.

She might think I broke her tonight, but it's she who has broken me.

fifteen

. . .

NELL

When I get back to the tent, Bradshaw has already wiped the floor and arranged everything back to how it was. There is no sign of our wrongdoings anywhere.

He's lying on the cot where Eren left him, staring at the tarp roof. It reminds me that he may have heard what I said earlier around the campfire.

"Did you hear what I told the others earlier?" I ask in a hushed voice.

He hesitates, then slowly nods. It doesn't seem fair that he heard my story but I've yet to hear his. I think about it for a long while as I settle on the cot beside him and look at the same spot he does.

I must fall asleep at some point, because I'm nuzzled awake by a warm hand cupping my wounded side and a finger brushing the crook of my neck, where the collarbone greets the jugular muscle. It's soft and soothing. For a moment I forget where I am. Who I am. Then I see Brad-

157

shaw's weary eyes; the skin around them is red with rest-
lessness.

A weary man finding comfort in holding me while I
sleep. He's too callous to do it when I'm awake. I know he
has a heart that yearns for another.

He studies me in that cold way of his before he pulls
away, seeming troubled that I woke to his soft touch. The
warmth of his hand on my side fades. Bradshaw turns and
faces the other side of the tent. I wonder how long he
watched me sleep. Then again, I don't think I want to know
the answer to that.

My core is sore and throbs with pain. I wince as I sit up.

I check my watch and it's already twenty minutes past
my normal night watch shift. Eren said not to worry about it,
but I decide I'd rather sit out there with him than risk having
a heart-to-heart with Bradshaw. I snag a pair of extra pants
from a bag in the corner since Bradshaw cut through mine.
Hopefully no one misses them.

Bradshaw doesn't look back at me as I get up to leave.
His shoulders are slumped and he hangs his head. I wonder
briefly what could be keeping him up; he's looked tired
all day.

The tent zipper is quiet and I'm able to sneak through the
camp without waking anyone. Eren sits with his legs lazily
stretched out and his back against the tree we designated as
the watch post. He hears me coming but doesn't bother
turning to see who it is. He only lifts his hand in a half-assed
wave.

I sit silently beside him, not particularly expecting to
have a conversation, but his soft voice is always welcoming.

"Bunny."

"Sergeant."

His lip kicks up in a wry grin. I marvel at how strange it
is. How un-Bradshaw it is.

"You can call me Eren in private, Nell." He leans forward

and sets his elbows on his knees. "We are a bit past formalities."

I nod and return the smile. We sit in silence for a couple of minutes before he shifts his posture and looks at me more directly.

"Thanks for staying with him until he relaxed. He's always calmer when you're around," he says genuinely. Eren holds his gun casually, slumped in his lap as he rests his head against the tree behind him.

That almost makes me choke. If only he knew what transpired in that fucking tent. It wasn't calm. It wasn't relaxed.

"We don't really mesh. I think he'll hate me until one of us dies." I scowl at Eren's amused expression. The night air is brisk and sends a shudder down my spine. I wrap my arms around myself and he takes notice.

Eren scoots over smoothly and presses his side against mine. My cheeks warm. He says in a low voice, "You know, Abrahm used to complain about Bones hating him as well."

I lift my chin, a bit shocked. "Seriously?"

Eren nods. "He has thorns."

"No kidding."

A sharp laugh. "You do too, though. And I'm sure that's one of the reasons why you two clash so much. Yet, I've never seen two people work so fluidly together. Completely in sync." His dark blue eyes shift back to me and he pokes my forehead with his index finger. I blink like an idiot because the notion surprises me. "I've also never met such a deadly sniper. You've got quite the aim and trigger finger, don't you?"

I swallow before muttering, "They say I'm the least hesitant shot there is."

"Yes, so I've heard." His voice is dull. Thoughtful.

"That's why I was reassigned to Malum. To be useful."

Eren's smile fades. "Yeah." His eyes lose their playfulness and he stares at me solemnly for a beat. "Tell me something about you that isn't military related." He changes the subject sharply.

I open my mouth to respond but find my mind empty. *Something that isn't military.* That's all I am. Eren's brows furrow and he sighs.

"You think of yourself as only some war machine, Nell. But you're a person first. A weapon second. Would it help if I started?" He nudges me and I nod with a slight lift of my shoulder.

He's wrong; I'm a weapon first.

He chuckles before smiling and turning his attention to the few stars we can see from beneath the trees. At least the mountains make the world quiet and dark. "I always wanted to be an astronomer. The universe is fascinating and holds many unknowns. I wanted to know all of the constellations and the galaxies beyond galaxies. I wanted the world."

My breath catches in my chest. "You? An astronomer?" It seems laughable, because Eren is nothing but muscle and beauty. He looks to have been born for his current predicament. He certainly has the emotional off-switch for it.

He laughs. "I know. I'm nowhere smart enough to be one either, but I dreamt it once upon a time." His voice curls around me and breaks down a few walls I had firmly cemented up.

I let my gaze fall to my hands. *What did I want to be? Do I even remember?* That seems like a few lifetimes ago and after the life I've lived and all the things I've taken… anything I once wanted to be seems so senseless now. My perception of the world has changed. But, yes, I suppose there was *one* thing that I dreamt of once.

"I wanted to own a small coffee shop. I'd sell books there too." A smile stretches over my face as I remember my whimsical vision. I was fourteen and still somewhat normal. "The one I dreamt of was a sort of townhouse, stones on the exterior like you read about in fairy books. I would live on the second story of it. In the morning my husband would go downstairs and start early, brewing coffee until the bitter scent would wake me and I'd wrap myself in a robe and tiptoe downstairs to hug him tight. We'd read and open the shop at nine and then close at three. Spend the rest of the day gardening, exploring, or—" I once dreamt of a family, but I decide to avoid that. "Or just enjoying the afternoons together."

I realize I rambled and look up to see if Eren has lost interest, but it's the opposite. His eyes are intense and heartfelt. A shadow of a grin tugs at the corner of his lips.

"That sounds a hell of a lot better than being a fucking astronomer." His shoulders shake with his laughter. "Why didn't you pursue the coffee shop? How did you end up... well, *here?*"

That's a loaded question. I'm sure he's read my file four times over and knows exactly how. He just wants to hear me say it. But unlike with Ian, I'll tell Eren.

"Because real life isn't made of fairytales and sugar drops."

Eren stares at me patiently, waiting for the real story. I sigh.

"I discovered I was a good shot when my father took me hunting at a young age. We were really poor and had to hunt for most of our food. I watched the lights go out of that deer and it was then that I realized how disturbed I truly was. How thoroughly I enjoyed killing things. It was the only thing I was good at."

His face is blank. As I thought. He knew.

"My parents were murdered when I was fifteen. It was a home invasion in the dead of winter. The men woke me up and tied me to a chair. They were after my dad for something he stole from them. We didn't have much and anything he took was likely to keep us fed. I watched them beat him until he was unrecognizable. Until he was dead. Then I watched as they raped my mom. They put a bullet through her head when they were done and then I was next."

I let the words trail and the hush of the forest around us stirs with the breeze. Eren stares into the dark, listening with a set jaw.

"They thought I was pretty. They thought they could take me with them since I was young. They were fucking stupid." Eren's eyes shift to me, his face stone. "The second I was untied I tore a man's throat open with my bare hands. If you know the soft spots of the body, it's easy, almost designed that way. I shot the second one in the face three times. The third man I hunted through our woods. I made him beg before I cut his innards out and shoved snow inside him while he seized. I wanted him to feel the cold. The cold I always felt inside. I should've shoved his guts in his mouth instead."

Eren stares at me, a distinct sorrow in his gaze.

"You already knew that, though—what I did for the dark forces to collect me—so why did you ask?" I level him an appraising gaze.

He smiles, but it doesn't quite reach his eyes. "I wanted to see if you'd lie. You can tell a lot about someone that way."

I narrow my eyes at him. A bit calculating for the cheerful sergeant.

"I think the worst part was that I liked it," I mutter to see what his features will betray.

"Fuck… you really *are* like Bones. He's a monster too." Eren's voice is low and more withheld, but his eyes don't falter.

I try to picture how the two of them looked as children—one normal and one insane. How the two of them ended up here like me. Because no one gets into the dark forces faction without a fucked up past.

So what did Eren do to get here?

My response is callous. "What we do in the dark forces requires people like us. We're easy to throw away once the job is done."

sixteen

. . .

NELL

BREAKFAST AROUND THE CAMPFIRE IS QUIET. THE AWKWARDNESS from last night carried over and everyone is avoiding eye contact with Bradshaw. He has a new mask on today; it's sharper looking and has rivets on the exterior, still black, but somehow more aggressive with the added texture.

Eren sits beside me, eyes wearier than I've seen them. He took two watches last night and is still functioning perfectly. I eat my MRE as I stare out into the forest, thinking deeply about the anguish on Eren's face last night after I said that Bradshaw and me are the ones easy to throw away once the job is done.

He had become silent and I didn't mind the words that remained unsaid between us for the rest of the watch.

The march back to the extraction site is painful. My thighs ache and my bones cry out with each step. The mountain air is crisp today, fall is setting in quickly up here. Some of the highest peaks even have snow already.

Harrison's and Jefferson's expressions are significantly lighter toward me today. I wonder if it's because of how well I shot yesterday or if it's due to the sad story sharing we did last night. I don't let my mind linger too much on it. No sense in dwelling in Traumaville.

Ian and Pete walk steadily ahead of us, with Eren leading the hostages most of the day, while Bradshaw and me take the rear as usual. We make momentous progress and should reach the extraction point before sundown.

Relief floods through me with the idea of a hot shower and warm sheets.

Bradshaw won't even look at me. Back to his cold behavior, I guess. But it's better than his episode last night. At least he's composed right now. My eyes trace over the smooth lines of his face beneath the mask. I look longer than I should.

The last few hours of the trek are exhausting. Weariness tugs at my eyes and draws heaviness through my aching shoulders.

Bradshaw walks stoically beside me. It's as if he doesn't physically tire, *ever*.

There's a distinct tightness in the air that settles around us. It chokes me like a venomous adder coiling around my throat and waiting patiently for me to die. I want to talk about what we did last night. The brutal parts and the soft, sensual ones. I turn to face him, his eyes instantly lifting to mine and I open my mouth to speak—

A bullet flies between us.

My assault rifle rises instinctively and I shout, "Shots fired!" The scuffling and grunts that sound from ahead of us distract me momentarily as another bullet flies at us. This time it hits my shin and red powder coats my pant leg.

It stings like an airsoft bullet, but at least it hit me in the leg and not the chest. I'm still active in the training and not considered a fatality. *Yet.*

Bradshaw fires into the dark underbrush and it's followed by a grunt.

After waiting stiffly for a beat to listen for any more enemies, Bradshaw lets his eyes fall down to my leg. Disappointment flashes through his eyes. "You were hit."

"*Yeah*, I know, jackass."

His brows pull lower. "You're out."

"*What*? It's just a leg hit. I'm fine." I rise to meet his glare. The others come out of their positions and watch our interaction in silence. The air is cold and clammy against my skin as my blood starts to boil.

"I said you're out, Bun."

Eren comes up beside me and gives my leg a gruff look. "He's right. Our squad takes no faults, Bunny. You're out."

Heat races to my cheeks and I want to scream. Are they serious? After everything I proved to them this month, this is where I fail? I look to the others. Jefferson and Pete stare at me with finality. Ian and Harrison at least look a little bothered by the unfairness of it.

"That's not fair," I say, challenging the sergeant.

His eyes narrow at me and his voice darkens. "Bunny, you aren't disagreeing with my authority, are you?" He says it loud enough for everyone in the group to hear. The muscles in my neck flex with rage.

Of course he'd use his authority to try and get me to back down.

"No, Sergeant. I wouldn't *dream* of challenging your decision." My tone is harsh. Eren's brows ease, feeling like he's won. "But my hands are tied. I'm afraid I'll need to bring this to General Nolan's attention. How one of his dogs is feral and has a nasty bite. You think they'll put the dog down? I am Nolan's favorite, after all." I unzip my vest and lift my sweater, revealing the blood-soaked bandages. The wound throbs with the motion, making me wince at the pain.

Eren's eyes widen with horror. Bradshaw remains impassive; his cold gaze is enough to chill me to my bones. He's far scarier when you can't tell what's ticking in that mind of his.

"I'll let you think on it, Sergeant," I say callously. If they want to play dirty, then I'll play in the fucking mud.

I tuck my rifle under my arm before sauntering to the front of the squad. The men give me disdainful looks as I pass them. It's fine. I'm not here to be cherished like a doll.

I'm here to find out what really happened in Patagonia two years ago. And to put a bullet in the man responsible for it. The rest is bullshit.

———

The consensus, apparently, is that I'm being completely shunned from here forward. The remainder of our mission is quiet and without any more ambushes. When we finally reach the extraction point, my shoulders roll back with relief.

I'm not sure if my threat worked on Eren or not. But he seems more withdrawn and angry, so at least it's been weighing on his mind. We both know his brother will likely be thrown to the wolves for attacking a fellow squadmate. We might have different rules in the dark forces, but we hold our value. General Nolan has a soft spot for me and they all know it.

I take a deep breath as I board the helicopter and don't bother looking at any of the cold expressions that surround me. All I want right now is a hot shower and to sleep in a fucking bed for one goddamn night. The ride back to Coronado is long and quiet; everyone but myself, Bradshaw, and Eren seem to find sleep easily.

The second our boots hit the ground, Eren orders everyone to hit the showers except me and Bradshaw. I fight the urge to roll my eyes. This really couldn't wait until tomorrow morning? We're all barely holding onto our sanity at this point.

Bradshaw stares at his brother with the same energy as I do.

"You two have been a huge pain in my ass… Look, Nell, the team doesn't want you on the squad. I know that sucks, but we are looking for someone who meets the mission expectations *and* can bond with the squad. At the end of the day everyone needs to trust each other without a shadow of a doubt. I know it's not fair to ask, but I am asking anyway. *Please.* Let this go. Just quit." Eren's voice isn't far from pleading.

Show them. Jenkins's low voice trails through my memory like a river over stones. *Make them see you're necessary.* He taught me how to kill a man in every conceivable way. How to manipulate even the wittiest of minds.

"Fine. I'll give up the spot. But on the condition that you can find a soldier better than me. I want to be on the mock hostile squad. If you guys can overthrow our base and take the captives, then I'll throw in the towel," I say confidently and lift my chin.

Eren's brows raise with curiosity, but he looks at Bradshaw pointedly. "That's your best option." Eren looks tired —as if he's been thinking about his brother's fate and worrying every single night of his life instead of sleeping. Would I actually report Bradshaw's actions? No. Because I've done far worse to people who are now in the ground and will never be found. But to keep control over them is necessary. I need to be here.

Bradshaw looks at his brother for an uncomfortable minute, then gives him one curt nod before turning and walking back to the barracks.

Eren lets out a long sigh and gives me a sideways glance. "For the record, I voted for you to stay," he admits with an uneasy laugh.

I consider him for a moment before letting a smile spread over my lips. "Thank you, Eren." His lazy grin sends flutters through my stomach. "I really needed to hear those words."

He drops his hand atop my head. I look up at him and he chuckles softly. "Don't let them win. Show them like I know you will. I know *I* need you on this next mission." He winks at me and I let the sentiment sink into the depths where I need it.

Eren believes in me. It's better than nothing.

"Now, go get cleaned up. I'll meet with the general and have the backup marksman put on the squad. You'll be assigned to the hostile force we're invading in the next roll out." We walk together toward the barracks as he informs me.

"Where will I stay until then?" I ask, hoping that I'll be placed in other barracks for the two-day break until then. A weekend away, I guess, if you could consider it that.

Eren firms his lips in thought. "There's a spare bed in my room, but I'll have to chat with the general to see if we have other beds available. If it comes down to that, are you okay with staying with me?"

I'd rather sleep naked next to Eren than fifty feet anywhere near Bradshaw.

"Yeah, just get me away from your psycho brother," I say vehemently. It draws a frown to Eren's face and he stares off ahead, darkness clouding his eyes. If only he knew how thoroughly fucked I was last night by his precious brother. You wouldn't know it by the cold shoulder I've received all day.

"He's never been this—"

"Unhinged?" I interrupt. "Cruel?"

Eren glances down at me beneath those black lashes and his frown is replaced with amusement. "Yeah. He's never been this *interested* with his second." His frown returns.

I feel bad for Eren. He carries the responsibility of not

only the squad but also his brother, who's cutting new recruits across their ribs and being unreliable.

"It's because of Abrahm," I state matter-of-factly.

He nods, staring at the ground as we stop outside the doors. "Yes... but you being here has made it much, *much* worse."

"I'm not trying to replace him," I say hesitantly. "I just want to be on this mission. I'll be sent to the Hades Squad if I don't stay on this one. And they hate Riøt more than you guys do. The general would rather release me back into society than send me to them. And I can't go back into society." It sounds morbid but Eren only nods. Maybe he's seen the same demon in his brother.

His brow raises with interest. "You've earned your cards?"

I swallow. I'm not supposed to tell anyone that the general was going to sneak me out of the dark forces after Riøt's demise. But I refused it. I shake my head.

"No, I'm just saying I can't go back."

"Don't sell yourself short, Nell. You're more than a weapon." His words don't reach me in the way he intends.

"No, I'm not, Sarge."

He stares at me momentarily before pushing the door open.

"I'll come get you in an hour for your new room assignment. Have your things packed."

———

The squad is lounging in our barrack. Each one of them is spread out in their bed relaxing. It was a grueling month and seeing them in street clothes rather than their tactical uniforms makes them seem like completely different people.

Their eyes all move in my direction, making me feel misplaced in my T-shirt and leggings. I keep my eyes forward as I strut confidently across the cement room toward the last bunk. My bag is right where I left it on the top bed. I grab it, thankful that I didn't unpack anything before we left.

Bradshaw doesn't bother looking up at me. I let my eyes fall to him once more before we part ways. The next time I see him, it better be through a scope as I'm shooting a mock bullet at his fucking face.

He has a fresh mask on. The black is darker on this one, with gray stripes that run through it vertically. His lashes flutter against his skin, alluding that he's very much awake and choosing to ignore me. Such beauty is wasted on him, but still, I stare longer than I should. At the redness of the thin scar that curves beneath his left eye. At the grooves in the fabric over his lips as he draws breath. At my bite that drew his blood last night.

Without parting words, I walk back the way I came.

"Bye-bye, *Bunny*."

The muscles in my legs lock at the sound of his voice and I stop at the door, turning my head enough to look over my shoulder at Bradshaw. He's now standing at the other end of the room, his men between us, with his fists clenched and a sinister grin pulling at his mask.

"Eat shit," I say simply, as if I'm unbothered by this entire fiasco. I knew all his soft touches yesterday were empty, but his cruelness still hurts.

Rage flashes across his gaze and something about that small victory fuels me.

I turn my back to them and wait for Eren down the hallway. He arrives right on the dot, rounding the corner with a light smile.

I swipe my hair back behind my ear—wearing it down for the first time all week feels good. The dark strands are wavy down to my mid back.

"You clean up nicely," Eren mutters, winking at me.

I give him a weary smile. "Sergeant, you shouldn't compliment your subordinates and wink at them. We aren't in the club anymore."

He throws his head back and laughs.

"Sorry, Bunny. I'm so used to seeing grumpy men. I forget sometimes when I look at you because we met on a plane and it's all so unfair, isn't it?" Eren motions for me to follow him and I breathe out a sigh of gratitude that I'm not staying with Malum for the time being.

"Unfair how?"

His grin is contagious as he looks down at me. There's more warmth in his eyes than usual. No one looks at me with kindness anymore. Funny, I can't seem to place the last time anyone had. Perhaps it was Jenkins, with his dying light.

"Unfair that we're both in this line of work."

"How else would you have liked it?" I pry, and it earns me a hearty laugh. My cheeks warm and for a moment it doesn't feel like I'm in a cement grave anymore.

Eren glances behind us. Curiosity draws my eyes to follow. Pete and Jefferson are standing in the doorway watching us. It seems odd that they would do so, but I try to ignore them.

"I would have preferred if Abrahm had not died. We'd all be in different predicaments now," he says thoughtfully as we continue down the hall and turn the corner to another section of the barracks' wing.

Abrahm. How is it that the death of one man can change the lives of so many?

"What would your predicament have been?"

Eren's jaw flexes as he stops at a door and opens it for me. I step inside and take in the small room. There are two plain beds and two nightstands. It's the emptiest room I've ever seen, no sentiments or photos. No lingering care items from the mornings or nights.

"Patagonia was our last mission before we were to earn our cards." He lifts a shoulder and drops it. The cards of freedom. My eyes widen. Malum was on their last mission before their cards? The only underground squad that has earned their cards was Warsaw, and that was ten years ago. Most squads die out before they earn their freedom back.

They were going to be free. Riøt still had six missions to complete before we earned ours.

I set my bag on the bed he points at and let my aching body lower to the mattress. Basic sheets feel so precious after sleeping in bushes for a few weeks.

"Losing Abrahm cost you your cards?"

He sits on the other bed and stares out the sole window. "Everything went to shit after that. Bones was mentally shot and the squad was everywhere. We failed miserably and the general was furious with us." He stares at me with knowing eyes.

"We obviously failed too." My voice is low.

"This next mission is more than earning our cards, Nell. It's revenge. For Bones, especially. I can't get into the details, but we both know it ties in with Patagonia."

I wince at those words; our goals aren't so different.

"He has a debt to pay," I say sadly.

Eren's eyes flash at me. "You have one too."

I lower my eyes to my hands. They don't look covered in blood, but they are. I'm drowning in the deaths of my first squad. In the death of Jenkins. If I had stayed, he'd still be here. Or we'd both be dead, and that's fine too. *Why didn't I stay?* My eyes slowly shut.

The firm line of my lips is the only answer I can provide him. He doesn't press me further. He knows what I've done. The monster that lurks beneath my betraying features.

I lie back in the bed and let out a long breath. The ceiling is tiled here. Just as bland and soulless as the rest of the military base.

"So when do we start the next training?" I ask, as I absentmindedly brush the tip of my finger across the cut on my ribs. I'll think of Bradshaw's lustful gaze every time I see the mark, each time I feel it.

Eren notices me messing with my wound and stands, fumbling in his nightstand before approaching me with some clear liquid and supplies.

I sit at the edge. "I already rebandaged, Sergeant."

He gives me a stern look and I cave, lifting my shirt over my head and tossing it to the side of my bed. My sports bra meets the end of the bandage, so I scoot it up enough for him to easily change the wrapping.

"The next mock mission starts two days from now at zero eight hundred. You'll leave earlier with the hostile squad to get a head start toward your base. Same as before—few weeks of training and then we'll try taking the hostages back," Eren mutters as he gently unwraps the binding around my chest. He slows as he gets to the fleshy, blood-soaked layer. His eyes widen and his jaw clenches.

"Nell, we both know that this needs stitches." His brows furrow. He looks a lot more like Bradshaw when he's like this.

I lift a shoulder. "You made it clear that you didn't want anyone to find out. It's healing, so don't worry about it," I say indifferently, and torment fills his gaze. There are a million things on his mind; it's evident in the tired slump of his shoulders. "You don't need to feel bad. It wasn't you who carved me open and exposed my breasts to the other squadmates."

His hands freeze and for a moment I think I'll watch his mental state shatter with what his brother has done. But he pulls himself together the way he's been trained to as he dabs ointment on my flayed flesh. I know he's seen much worse in the field. His touch is soft and caring; if I shut my eyes I'll be consumed by the comfort of it.

"Don't let him hurt you like this again," he finally says after a long while of silence. *Too late,* I muse. He finishes the procedure using suture tape, which might actually work, and wraps my ribs better than I had. Delicate, but secure.

I let my eyes fall to his calloused hands, wondering how many men he's killed with them. I find solace in his presence. A kind soul that's dragging himself through hell. But Eren did something bad to earn his place in the dark forces too. I wonder if he'd tell me what it was.

"What if he does hurt me again?" I tease with a probing voice, knowing that our vicious dance is far from over. I've never seen death and hatred linger around a man's shoulders like it does with Bradshaw. Even with his imperfections and his violence, the reaper in me wants to break him as much as he's sought to destroy me.

Eren fists his hands at each side of me before looking up to meet my cold gaze. "He won't disobey my orders again." His voice cuts out as he lifts his left hand to coast his fingertips across my ribs. "It's my fault Abrahm died. My fault that Bradshaw is so fucked up." A single tear rolls down his expressionless face. I wonder if he even knows it slipped. The hard planes of his expression don't allude any emotions.

Eren is scary too, maybe more so than his brother. His ability to put on a facade is chilling.

Our conversation ends with an awkward lull in the room. The energy has gone cold and stale. Eren heads to his bed silently, his thoughts clearly weighing on his mind.

I like the way broken men grieve.

It gives me pause and makes me curious about the harrowing things he still has locked up so tight.

I think tediously about that as I stare at the now dark ceiling. Only Eren's soft snores from across the room keep the sound of nothingness from stirring my brain.

What could the sergeant of Malum possibly have weighing on his conscience?

seventeen

. . .

It's technically our weekend, but Eren nudges me awake just as the sun is rising anyway. I give him a very uninterested, groggy glare.

His dark brow lifts smugly. "Are you a breakfast kind of a girl?"

I keep my eyes narrowed, but my stomach betrays me and growls.

"*Yeah*, I'm a breakfast girl." My voice doesn't come out as sharp as I was going for. Eren's smile burns into my chest like a shot of whiskey.

"Get dressed in your civilian clothes. I'm taking us out to a diner I used to frequent when I was young," he says, sounding elated. I look down at his attire and realize he's not in uniform. His black T-shirt is form-fitting and clings to his muscles, sculpting out every inch of him.

"You *are* young," I tease as I pull my night shirt off and swap it for a basic gray tee.

"Youn*ger*." Eren grins and rolls his eyes at me.

I avert my gaze, securing my yoga pants over my ass. "Are we even allowed to leave base?"

He chuckles and pokes my forehead again. "What, Riøt didn't have street privileges?" I rub the spot and give him a scrutinizing look, though I secretly don't mind the sentiment of it. Jenkins would ruffle my hair anytime he thought I was being cute and I can't help but miss that small notion.

"No, we didn't."

Eren takes pause and looks at me for a second to make sure I'm not pulling his leg or something. I raise a brow and he smiles again.

"I'm the sergeant. I do whatever I want."

"And why are you bringing *me* with you? Wouldn't you rather take your dear brother?" I push, making eye contact. His smile is murder—those dimples will be the end of me.

"You'd prefer to stay here with all those assholes?" He juts his thumb in the direction of our squad's barracks. I stare at him for a moment before shaking my head. "That's what I thought. Now, hurry up before they run out of scones."

Sitting across from Eren, sharing coffee and scones while the sun rises behind him over the bay, is as awkward as you'd think it'd be.

Everything feels so normal and civilized. I watch the waitress go from table to table with a content and soft grin on her face. She remembers me from the night I came in with Bradshaw. She must think Eren is him because she mutters about what a darling couple we make. I change the subject instantly by telling her that her black dress is lovely. I almost ask her where she got it before remembering myself.

I could never wear such delicate things. My scars would

draw too much attention and I wouldn't feel secure in something as whimsical as a dress.

Eren must notice the longing look in my eyes because his hand falls softly atop mine. I meet his gaze and flinch at the cream mustache he has on his upper lip. He quirks a brow for the final humorous blow and I can't help but grip my stomach and laugh.

"What are you doing?" I manage to contain my outburst, scanning the diner quickly to ensure no one was disrupted by me.

Eren licks the cream from his lips and gives me that smoldering look of his. "Being a person. You should try it sometime." He winks.

I hesitate and glance down. "I don't know what you mean."

He laughs this time, leaning forward and setting his elbow against the table before resting his chin on his palm. There's a light that flickers through his eyes that's not unlike the one Jenkins had. It's secretive and daring. I could watch Eren exist for days on end without losing interest. He's unpredictable and amusing when he's not being a sergeant. Almost comforting to be around.

"Being funny, making jokes, enjoying the little things in life." He lists things like he could go on forever but stops before shifting gears. "Not looking so disconnected from the real world."

"I'm not disconnected," I say, sounding offended even though I know very well how disconnected I really am from everything. Even sitting here and watching the other customers go about their mornings disturbs me.

"No? Then let me take you out to get a dress. I bet you don't own a single one."

I frown at him. "Eren, I would never wear it."

"Why not? I saw you eyeing that woman's pretty dress."

I reluctantly look away. "Because I don't need anything for my squadmates to think less of me, *sir.*" I use the term for emphasis. Everything he's trying to do for me has me on edge. Why is he being so nice? Trying to get civilian clothes for me? My fingers curl against my pants anxiously. *He's trying to push me back into society. He's trying to nice-guy me into quitting. Does he feel guilty about it?* My stomach sinks.

His eyes soften on me and pool with anguish. Then, he taps his fingers on the table and banishes all his emotions.

"Bunny, we're going. It's an order." His voice is firm and his face stoic.

I stare for a few seconds before sighing.

"Fine." It's not like I'll have to wear it.

"We'll go after we catch some waves."

My spine stiffens. "What?"

"You can surf, can't you? Oh, come on, don't give me that look. You have to at least try," Eren says as he lifts his hand for the bill.

Did Bradshaw tell him I'm scared of the ocean? No. He wouldn't. But why is Eren staring at me with something lethal in his gaze? Can he see the horror in my expression already?

Goddammit.

Somehow, he gets me in a swimsuit. I stand in the sand with a board I have no intention of using clutched to my side. Just staring at the ocean makes me queasy.

Eren has already ridden a few waves with ease. His muscles slick with the ocean's spray. I watch and envy his fearlessness.

A hand lands on the nape of my neck. My elbow instantly flies back to hit their stomach and gets caught by the person's other hand.

"Easy killer, it's just your favorite fuck boy." Bradshaw's voice is heavy with a smirk.

I jerk out of his hold and, to my displeasure, there he stands looking like a god of land and sea. His swim shorts are black and hang low on his hips. They don't do anything to hide the bulge in his pants. His chest is all muscle, corded and tattooed. His jawline is rimmed with ink and the fresh scab on his neck makes my stomach twist. Those pale blue eyes flick down to me, interest dancing behind them.

He grabs the top of my board and leans against it with a smug grin. His maskless face startles me for a moment. I almost forgot he had one beneath it. I wish he didn't. It would make it easier to resent him.

"I thought you were scared of the ocean—now you're surfing?"

I glower at him. "Eren is surfing. *I'm* staying right here."

"I'll take you out there." He takes my board under his arm and my wrist in his free hand.

"Wait!" I try to pry off his fingers, but he has a vice grip. He wades straight into the waves and my heart drops when the water hits my knees. "I said stop!"

Bradshaw turns and pulls me into his chest, hooking his arm around my lower back and dipping down to speak quietly in my ear.

"You keep yelling and making people look at us and I'll really give you something to scream about, Bun." He pulls away and winks at me with a fake-ass smile. His white teeth flash and make my core heat. "Now, behave." I breathe in sharply as his cold hands curl around my sides and lift me up onto the board.

He makes me feel helpless and small when he controls me like this. It's a shot to my nervous system and I can't help but enjoy it. I'm always the most dangerous person in the room, but around Bradshaw I feel vulnerable.

The dark waves ahead look endless. Fear threads through my veins and I swallow the lump in my throat.

"Why are you doing this?" I ask in a low, defeated tone.

Bradshaw hops on behind me and pulls my ass to his crotch. His stomach warms my back, making me lean closer. "Because, have you ever had the chance to put a little rodent in the middle of the ocean and watch it squirm?" He laughs as he angles the board to the vast sea.

"Rabbits aren't rodents you idiot. They're lagomorphs." My retort loses its bite as I grip the board like it's a lifeline. My shoulders tremble as we get deeper and further away from the shore. I look for Eren, desperate to call out to him, but he's nowhere in sight.

"Why am I not surprised you know something as useless as that, Bun?" Bradshaw whispers against the shell of my ear. My skin pebbles.

What is he going to do to me out here? Throw me in and leave me for the sharks? I shudder at that thought and pull my knees to my chest.

Jenkins always laughed at my fear of the ocean, but he made sure I knew to keep it a secret. I could put our entire squad in jeopardy if I faltered in the water.

Maybe if I hadn't watched two children get eaten alive by sharks when I was a kid, I wouldn't be so afraid of them.

"Alright, hop off." Bradshaw's hands come down at my sides to throw me into the depths, but I lean back into his chest, hoping to appeal to his better nature.

My voice is a plea. "Please, don't."

His laugh vibrates against my spine and he turns me so I'm facing him. "What's in it for me? I'd really love to see you screaming in the water for my help."

My eyes widen and desperation makes me generous.

I swallow and look down at the bulge in his pants. He chuckles again and practically shouts, "You think a blow job will save you?!"

I glare at him and shove his shoulders back without

thinking of the repercussions. His eyes are wide as he falls into the water, but instead of anger or wrath, I only catch a glimpse of amusement before he disappears beneath the surface.

Oh fuck, what have I done? I cling to the board and start paddling away as fast as I can. I hear his body break the water's edge and dare to look back.

A dark smile reaches his eyes as he grabs the board and flips it. My scream is cut short by the water engulfing me.

I swim to the surface and choke out a few strangled coughs before blinking the water from my eyes. The first thing I notice is the empty surfboard bobbing in the waves. Panic rushes to my brain.

Where the fuck is he?

I don't have to wonder for long.

Arms wrap around my shoulders and my heart hammers against my ribs. He's going to drown me here, this is it for me. His words replay in my head. *"The only good Riøt soldier is a dead one."*

A terrified shriek breaks from my lips and my legs start to convulse.

"Hey, *hey.* Calm down, Bun," Bradshaw says gently, sounding genuinely concerned. He spins me in the water so our noses are pressed together.

I don't want him to see me like this. I swore I'd never let anyone see me this vulnerable. But this is what the ocean does to me. I fear it more than the battlefield, more than an M16 pressed against my skull.

He takes me in, shocked by my reaction. He treads water powerfully with his legs, keeping one arm wrapped securely around my back.

Fear makes me a different person. The ocean makes me weak.

I wrap my legs around his torso and cling to his shoulders. I didn't realize how much bigger than me he was, how strong his muscles were, but feeling them work between my thighs to keep us afloat makes it hard not to notice. His grip around me tightens as my teeth chatter together and my body trembles.

Bradshaw lets out a light-hearted sigh before letting his head rest against mine, breathing me in.

"You're really that scared?" His voice is thick with remorse.

"W-what, you don't l-like this as much as y-you thought you would?" My retort sounds lame with my shaking words.

He holds me tighter against his chest. "No. I don't," he admits. My breath evens out as he swims us back toward the board and pushes me on top of it. I instantly draw my legs back to my chest and shiver.

Bradshaw remains in the water, forearms folded over the surfboard and resting his head against them as he gives me a sidelong glance.

"What are y-you doing? Get back on." I try to pull his arm up, but he has it firmly in place. Even seeing him in the water gives me unease.

"Why? What's the worst thing that could happen to me, Bunny?"

"There could be sharks…" It sounds so stupid coming out of my mouth, but I can't help what terrifies me.

He stares dumbfoundedly at me for a moment before tilting his head back and letting out a ridiculous laugh. "Are you serious? That's what you're so afraid of?" His rare laughter starts to make me smile against my best efforts.

"Just get out of there, I can't sit here and watch you be eaten alive." My trembling voice is starting to steady out.

"And they say monsters don't have weaknesses," he chides me as he lifts himself from the sea. I scowl but watch the water drip from his abs and chin.

I sigh with relief now that he's not in the water. "What

are you doing out here anyway? Did Eren put you up to this?" I force my eyes away from his as he looks up at me. I scan the beach and water, but I still don't see Eren.

"I come out here every chance I get. Eren knows that."

Of course Eren knows. Is this his way of trying to get us to make peace with each other? Annoyed, I look back at Bradshaw. "Take me back to shore."

"Is that an order?" he muses as he leans closer to me, reaching his hand out.

"We aren't on duty, *Bradshaw*. I'll order you around as much as I want." I swat his hand away, but he grabs me anyway and wrestles me into his lap.

His amused expression quickly turns callous. "Does your cunt not ache enough from our lesson the other night? Have you forgotten who you submit to, Bunny?" He glides his hand down to my inner thigh.

My cheeks burn at his words. Why is he so hellbent on making me miserable? It has worn me down to the wire. I might as well just ask.

"Why do you hate me so much?" I wince at how sad it sounds coming out.

He brushes my wet hair back delicately and presses his lips to my shoulder. "Is that what you think? That I hate you?"

I bristle. "If you think your actions represent anything but hatred then I'm all ears."

"Are you upset because I didn't show you affection both mornings after I fucked you? You're delusional if you think you're anything other than a good looking, *average* soldier. I just used you for what I wanted in the moment. That's all." Bradshaw's breath is hot against my skin.

I try to push us apart, but he doesn't budge. "Stop dancing around the question, fuckface." *Don't let his words get to you.* I steel my mind the best I can.

He laughs again and tips us to the side until we're falling

back into the water. The icy water shoots straight to my bones and I rise to the surface with fury warming my tongue.

"What the fuck is wrong with you!?" I hit his chest and he only grins at my assault.

"I don't hate you."

I freeze, arm still partially raised for my next strike.

He snags my jaw with his hand and draws our foreheads together so there's nowhere else to look but into his soulless eyes.

"I want to dominate you. I want to break you into a million pieces and make you answer only to me. I want to keep you as far away from my squad as possible before I ruin what's left of you. Because if you don't leave, that's what's going to happen. I'll break you, just like I break everything. Is that enough? Will you shut the fuck up now?" He says slowly, cruelly, while squeezing my jaw.

A tear brims without my permission from pure rage.

Then I do something stupid.

I spit in his face.

My muscles tense as I wait for his reaction, but all I get is a lazy, curious smile.

"See? I told you your fear was stupid. You haven't thought about it once since I tipped us over."

My eyes widen before narrowing skeptically. He did that on purpose... He's fucking with my mind on a whole new level now. Taking my fears from me too?

"Just take me back to the beach... please."

He finally gives in and takes me back.

I wait on the shoreline for Eren while Bradshaw goes back out to surf. Reluctantly, I watch him for ten minutes before Eren taps my shoulder.

"Where did you go?" I snap at him. He flinches at the bite in my tone.

"You don't want to know." He pats his stomach and

gives me a sour face. *Oh God.* "Alright, let's find a dress, then get back to base."

I follow behind him silently for a few beats before asking, "Did you know Bradshaw would be here today?" He doesn't respond, nor does he stop walking.

I take that as a yes.

eighteen

. . .

NELL

EREN LEFT TO SHOWER TEN MINUTES AGO, BUT I CAN'T TEAR MY eyes away from the pastel yellow dress he bought me. It's simple. Mid-thigh length and sleeveless. I let my finger glide over the soft fabric and cautiously look at the door.

No one else is here. No one has to see.

I step out of my pants and pull my shirt off before slipping into the dress. There's no mirror in here so I can't see how it looks from afar, but I gaze down at the ripples the fabric makes, the way it makes my hips and waist look desirable. My hair is down and meets my mid-back; the dark brown strands complement the warm tone of the dress and my olive skin.

A timid smile coasts across my lips. I shut my eyes and, suddenly, I'm in the bookshop I use to daydream about. Lovely little dreams. Things that aren't meant for me.

The door clicks and my shoulders tense. I look up and

expect to see Eren, but I'm met with a masked man. It takes my brain a few seconds for it to click.

It's Bradshaw.

He looks completely different in his heather-gray T-shirt and form-fitting black sweatpants. His mask is thin and his black hair isn't swept back like it usually is. Messy strands fall over his forehead, still wet after his shower. His pale eyes widen on me and neither of us says a word. We just stand in this horrible fucking silence where both of us seem to be thinking, *Why are you here?*

Again.

Bradshaw's eyes slowly move down my body, taking in the dress and my figure. His pupils dilate and his fists tighten at his sides, making the veins in his arms protrude more prominently.

"Okay stop fucking with me. Why are you *here*?" He says calmly, but I don't miss the jealousy that flashes through his eyes.

I turn away from him sharply, an act of vulnerability that is purely instinctual and takes me by surprise. My cheeks burn and I feel so stupid for him to see me in a goddamn dress.

"I asked you a question."

Chills spread over my arms at the coldness in his voice. I reach for my pants to pull them back on, but Bradshaw is at my side in an instant and grabs my wrist tightly.

"Let go of me," I say vehemently. His eyes fill more with curiosity now than rage. He notices my duffle bag on the ground beside the bed and looks at me intently.

"You're staying with Eren instead of with the hostile squad?" Bradshaw sounds pissed. His features are hard to read, though, only being able to see his eyes. A small yearning to see his face again bubbles up in my chest.

I nod once. His broad shoulders loom over me and there's nothing more that I want than for him to just leave.

"There wasn't room for me in the other barracks," I explain, even though I should just tell him to go eat shit instead. I'm still unsteady after he took me out to the open ocean on a surfboard. He studies me thoughtfully for a second. I can feel his pulse against my skin, his palm still wrapped snugly around my wrist.

He releases me but doesn't take a step back.

"What do you want, Bones?" I grind my teeth at the way his mask shifts into the hint of a smile beneath it when I say his code name.

"Well, I was coming in here to see my brother, but I found myself a prettied up little creature instead. Were you hoping he'd fuck your brains out if you wore a dress? *Ah, wait.* Eren isn't into rodents… or lago-whatever-sluts." His voice has that pouty sarcastic sound to it. There's nothing more I want than to punch him square in the jaw.

"Lagomorphs, you dumb ass."

He doesn't blink. "I bet that word means a lot to you."

"Jealous much?" I shove his chest, but he doesn't budge an inch.

"Me? Jealous over a slut? Yeah, keep dreaming."

"Fuck you." I slap his face hard enough to tilt the angle he holds. He brings that deadly gaze back to me.

"You want to? God, you'll get me excited if you keep hitting me like that, Bunny." His eyes are filled with loathing and I reciprocate the hatred gladly. "Remember what I told you about leaving or I'll end up ruining you?" He runs his fingers over the back of my neck, sending chills up my spine. "I think it's time to break you bit by bit."

I look at the ground and swallow the knot that's building in the back of my throat. "I hate you."

"Am I supposed to care?" He pushes me and I fall back onto the bed. Before I can get up, he comes down over me like a tidal wave. His hands are pressed on either side of my head, sinking into the mattress slowly. Those icy eyes are like a cold winter day, hollow and empty of anything that once lived there. "I'm incapable of feeling things as petty as hatred, but if I could, I'd loathe you most. I thought we already hashed this out in the water, baby."

His masked nose is a breath away from mine.

I bite where his lips are.

He moves in time to evade most of my intended bite, but I tear the lining in his mask. It leaves a hole, revealing his gnashed teeth beneath. He stares at me like I'm a feral thing, evil lurking under his skin. My spine heats with dread and I know I've poked the bear too far.

"Oh, I knew you were into kinky shit like biting, but I guess you need to learn some manners," he murmurs in a low, dangerous tone. He lifts one hand and pulls off his ruined mask, using the back of his knuckles to wipe off a trickle of blood from his lip. "Let me show you the kinky shit *I'm* into."

His handsome face is shrouded with malice and promises unspeakable things.

Bradshaw stands and pulls his pants down without hesitation. His cock is swollen and already throbbing as he stares down at me. "Suck my dick," he commands.

I'm still sprawled out on the bed, elbows digging into the sheets. My teeth grit together with abhorrence. "Yeah, you'd like that wouldn't you?" He smiles at me and it's the cruelest one I've gotten out of him, mainly because of how genuine it is. He seems pleasantly happy with this scenario.

"No teeth or you'll *really* get me excited and you haven't seen me *really* excited yet, Bun."

I bury my teeth into my lower lip to keep myself from unsheathing the knife strapped around my thigh and burying it in his chest. "You think you're the first man to force me to suck his dick?"

"I think you're the first woman to spit in my face *and* bite my lips in the same day," he comes back harshly as he pumps his cock slowly, pre-come spilling at his tip.

The fact that I find it erotic disturbs me to my core. A beautiful, broken man who's working his dick while telling me to suck it. That's also why we're so drawn to each other, because we're both toxic and cruel.

Bradshaw must see the lust in my eyes, because his wicked grin grows. His curious eyes trace the curvature of my face and down my throat. He licks his lips and shifts on his feet.

"You like this, don't you?" His voice is smooth for once.

I continue to glare at him. There's no way I'm answering that question. And the sly raise of his brow tells me I don't need to. He already knows.

"*Oh, Bunny,* you sick little thing. Tell me you aren't into this too. The pain kink was already catching my heartstrings, but *this*? This makes me want to brand you as mine." Bradshaw smiles with his teeth revealed and it's both absurdly handsome and bone-chilling. He tightens his grip on his dick and the veins pulse more prominently, the head of his cock swelling with the pressure he's putting on it. His eyes narrow and his lips part as pain and pleasure dance over his features. He swipes the pad of his thumb over the tip of his cock and brings the drop of pre-come to my lips, sucking in his lower lip and biting it as he pushes his thumb inside my mouth.

Oh my god.

Oh my fucking god.

I taste him. The saltiness and the heat. My center aches for him and he can see it written all over my face and in the way I suck on his thumb as he pushes it further into my mouth.

I can't force my eyes away from him. The way his hips dip and form the V-shape down to his erection beckons saliva to pool in my mouth.

He watches me like a snake, patiently waiting for the perfect moment to strike. To constrict me and never let me go.

He hooks his thumb behind my lower set of teeth and guides my jaw to his cock. I try to pull back but end up whimpering at the way he digs his fingers into my jaw.

"Don't worry, I'll let you swallow." My eyes widen and shock rivets down my spine as his hand wraps around the base of my neck, fisting my hair and cupping the nape until my mouth lolls open. "Such a pretty mouth is wasted on you," he says, voice dripping with disdain.

Bradshaw drags the head of his dick across my bottom lip. His pre-come is still blooming from his tip. I savor the salty flavor as he smears it over my lip, lubing it like gloss. He watches every movement with hooded eyes. Darkness collects in his cruel grin.

"I don't hear you refusing this," he says as he continues to smooth the soft, pulsing flesh of his dick over my lip. I hate him so much. But the fire that burns inside my chest also trails down to my core, making a painful, urgent need throb through me.

I want it. I want him.

After a moment of hesitance and deciding that I'll just have to unpack my mental disarray at a later time, I let my hands move to his bare hips. I trace the grooves of his muscles and the abs that form a V tempt my depraved thoughts. My lips come down over his tip and I swirl my tongue around the soft flesh.

Bradshaw groans and lets his head fall back. His grip on my hair doesn't loosen.

I shut my eyes and let this moment just unfold. The deep sounds that roll from his chest send pulses of heat through my center. I let my free hand slide down to my clit and rub in a slow motion to get myself off. The dress is thin and makes access easy.

"Fuck," Bradshaw hisses between his teeth as I take him deeper, massaging the underside of his cock with my tongue and swallowing on his flesh to work him into madness. His fist curls tensely into my hair and his other grips my jaw like he's trying to keep me from consuming him so feverishly. "Who the fuck taught you to do this?" His voice is weakened by lust and pleasure.

If I could smile I would, but he's too deep inside my mouth.

I can tell he's close by the way he's bucking lightly into the back of my throat with need.

The door opens just as I'm performing my finishing move on Bradshaw—we're too connected and unable to part before the gasp rolls out of Eren's throat.

Bradshaw stills and tenses, his entire body like a statue, with the exception of his pulsing, throbbing dick inside my mouth. He's coming and I can't keep myself from swallowing multiple times. Bradshaw lets out a few shameful groans as his salty release flows down my throat.

"Jesus fucking Christ... Well, don't stop on *my* account," Eren says, laughing to himself and throwing his towel on the floor.

Bradshaw loosens his grip on my hair and jaw. I sit back on my haunches, wiping my lips with my wrist before growing increasingly horrified at the evidence of my pleasure that drips down my bare legs.

Both men are staring at my exposed thighs with front row seats to see my wet panties.

Eren curses and extends a hand to help me up off my knees while Bradshaw tucks his still very hard dick back into his pants.

Once I'm standing, the room becomes increasingly awkward as the silent seconds draw out.

Eren runs his hand down his face, his fingers lingering around his mouth and chin as he stares at me like I'm the biggest fucking problem in his life right now. I can practically hear his thoughts. *What am I supposed to do with her?* Then he looks at his brother and the same thought seems to flutter across his mind.

"You two are making my life really fucking hard right now, you know that?" Eren practically laughs, but the humor in his voice doesn't reflect in his dark blue eyes. "First you're fighting, then hurting each other." I open my mouth to argue that only Bradshaw has hurt *me*, but Eren's pointed look shuts me up. "And *now* you two are... what the fuck even is this? Are you fucking now?" He throws his hands in the air, exasperated.

Bradshaw rolls his eyes at his twin before glancing down at my wet thighs. The way his eyes become *hungry* with his unfinished business sends another throb of need through me. I refuse to waver, so I stand firmly, ignoring his seductive looks. But that becomes impossible as Bradshaw approaches me and slides two fingers up my inner thigh, an inch away from my core, before bringing the evidence of my arousal to his lips and stroking his fingers clean with his tongue.

My cheeks flare with heat and Eren's eyes widen.

"*This.* This is exactly what I'm talking about. What the fuck is wrong with you, Bradshaw? I've never seen you act this... this..." Eren's voice trails off and pain spreads across his face.

"Go ahead. Say it." Bradshaw stares at him emptily.

"Psychotic! You're acting like a fucking animal. The shit you're pulling... Do you have any idea how much I've covered for you? How much I've sacrificed to keep you here? You know the general won't put up with anymore of your shit." Eren is nothing short of pleading with his brother and it tears at my chest like savage claws. I've never had what Bradshaw does—his brother is fighting so hard for him and he just doesn't give a shit.

"I *am* a goddamn animal, Eren. Haven't you known? Don't pretend like I'm just some broken little thing that you can fix. You're just prolonging a shitty ending and you know it," Bradshaw says calmly. His words are like drops of rain. More sorrowful to be heard knowing that he doesn't care an ounce for himself. Is this why I'm drawn to him? Because he's... like me. A prolonged, shitty ending.

Eren's eyes narrow with anguish. "Get the fuck out." He says through gritted teeth and tense shoulders. The veins protrude in his neck and, for a moment, I think he's going to hit Bradshaw if he doesn't leave.

They hold a glare for a few dreadful seconds before Bradshaw turns to regard me once more, tapping two fingers on my sternum and knocking me back on the bed. I scowl at him and it earns me a cocky, careless grin before he heads to the door without another word. Eren hands him an extra mask he had in his nightstand, since I ruined the one Bradshaw wore coming in. Then he's gone, and I find an odd sense of loneliness filling the space where he just was.

Eren lets out a long, weary sigh before looking at me. He seems disappointed and maybe even ashamed. Though I can't discern who it's for—me or Bradshaw.

"I... um." I try to form words but fail miserably.

My thighs close together and rub with need. I have to take care of this ache. I'm still worked up from Bradshaw's cock in my mouth.

Eren's eyes catch the motion of my legs and his brows pinch with more humor than rage. "You two really will be the death of me." His gaze is heavy and he doesn't pull his attention away from me as his lips curve up. "Need help, or are you going to take care of it yourself?"

My heart clammers against my ribs. *Did Eren just offer to get me off?* He laughs at my widened eyes and tips his head down toward his swollen cock, not hidden at all beneath those gray sweatpants.

"I'm just a man," he says innocently, and my cheeks flush with his admittance. "I can't look at a woman in need and not get an erection."

Eren looks like Bradshaw in every way. Even the size of his bulge seems comparable. My conscience tells me that it's wrong to use him like this, especially if I'm picturing his brother in his stead, but he's just my superior. This can just be an indulgence, can't it? Just two humans who need to get off?

"No feelings attached, right?" I ask and Eren's grin is instant.

"Of course not." He takes a step closer to me, confidence and a gentle demeanor beaming through his eyes.

"You're not going to be weird after?" I pry because, my God, he's my sergeant.

His brow raises and he gives me a smug smile. "It's been weird since the club and we'll be parting ways soon enough," he mutters as he reaches down and grabs his bulge through his sweatpants. My tongue slips over my bottom lip.

Eren leans over me and, as he does, I realize his scent is starkly different than Bradshaw's. It's musky with smokey remnants. He must see something in my eyes that even I'm not aware of because he changes his direction. "Aw, Nell. Did you catch feelings for my brother?"

Eren tilts to his side and lies on his back at the bottom of my bed. He frees his dick and starts stroking it casually, like I'm not even here. My eyes dart to his length more than once while I try to form an answer.

"No." It doesn't sound at all convincing. I haven't caught feelings though. I really do hate him.

Eren watches me as he continues to pump his shaft. I decide to lie next to him and pleasure myself too. We stare into each other's eyes as I lift the edge of my dress up and slip my hand inside my wet panties. I circle my middle finger around my clit and try to remain as stoic as Eren is, but my brows pull together as my orgasm starts to build. My lips part and I stare at Eren's veiny dick, imagining it between my thighs.

"I think you do like him," he says simply with empty eyes. The more I observe Eren, the more I believe he's as psychotic as Bradshaw. He just hides and controls it better, which is immensely more frightening.

"What makes you think that?" I let my eyes fall back to his hand working over his length. The movement is languid and slow, teasing in a way.

"Well, for one, you're watching me whack myself off and not taking advantage of it, so there's a start." His eyes dip down to my hand rubbing my clit. "And you two look at each other in this way I haven't seen before. It's different."

My throat is drying at the sight at of his dick pushing out pre-come and growing as the veins protrude along his shaft. *Fuck.* I want it so bad. My hand isn't even close to enough friction. It's not the same when you're doing it to yourself.

"And how do I look at you?" I ask. I've found myself admiring Eren as much as I have Bradshaw, if not more. He has more gentle and caring features. He actually smiles like a person. Like a man I *should* be drawn to rather than the broken, murderous version of him.

Eren presses his lips together like he needs to deeply consider my question. "You look at me like I'm something untouchable. Like I'm a shiny glass figurine out of reach that cannot be disturbed." He gives me a shy smirk that worms its way into my chest.

"Well, you are my sergeant." *Not that that's stopped me before.*

He nods and shuts his eyes, saying with a frown, "A hard position to be in. Lonely."

I want to tell him he doesn't have to be, but it'd be a lie. Of course it's lonely. It was always lonely for Jenkins. I reach slowly over to his hand, the one that's currently fisting a throbbing, leaking eight-inch cock.

His eyes crack open and he stares at me through heavy lashes. There's so much pain and loneliness there. Guilt. I feel the same emptiness inside myself. I want it to go away. I want to think of anything but the gaping, agonizing hole that's left inside my soul. It's what we're taught, isn't it? To just let that shit go.

He flashes a sad smile as he accepts my invitation and scoots closer to me, pushing his cock between my thighs, slicking himself with my arousal. "I can see why you're so popular with the bad guys," he says, lips against my shoulder.

Bad guys? I can't tell if he's talking about Bradshaw, himself, or the general dark forces pond, but I reply simply, "I'm not exactly an angel, Sarge."

"No, you certainly aren't." He pumps his hips and fucks my thighs, rubbing against my clit and center. His arms wrap around my back and he holds me adoringly against his chest. It makes my heart skip a beat and my breath catch.

I'm not used to gentle. It makes me uneasy, the way my chest aches for him. "I'm curious to get to the bottom of you, though. I want to see the darkest things you're hiding. I want to know why the monsters like you so much." His voice is raspy as his thrusts quicken.

I'm half listening as I cling to his chest and cry out as my orgasm rolls through me. He pumps a few more times before he's shooting come on my ass and between my thighs. We lie here for a few moments, only our breaths creating sound, our hearts beating against each other.

Eren presses his head to mine and kisses my temple before untangling himself from me. He pulls his pants back up before sitting at the edge of the bed. He lets out a low sigh as he brushes his hand through his dark hair.

Who were they before becoming this? I ponder the

thought again as I watch him take a few breaths. His mind seems to be warring against him, but I can't figure out why.

"I'll leave your dark secrets alone if you leave mine buried," I threaten softly. I sit up and face him. Eren's eyes are on the floor and I can't help but take in his beauty. There's something almost divine about him. I'm sure he can sense my eyes on him but he lets me continue to stare without bringing attention to it.

"And what is it you want me to leave buried, Bunny?" He finally looks at me with a darkness settling into his features. I study him for a moment, not sure what to say in reply to that. His voice is hard as he mutters, "I'd have to bury you if you dug up one of my secrets."

nineteen

. . .

NELL

ONE OF THE SOLDIERS ON THE HOSTILE SQUAD NUDGES ME playfully and says something I'm not paying attention to. He's grown fond of me over these past few weeks, but I can't even remember his fucking name.

I only know his gear number, Eight-Seven-Four.

He's the air force comms personnel on the hostile squad and has been assigned to be my partner during the second mock mission. We were ordered to remain "inactive" in our pursuits up until the invasion day. At least *I* was, and it's driving me crazy.

I could've shot Bradshaw ten different times already. My finger has lingered more than once over the trigger this week with an open shot. But I remain patient, waiting for him and their new marksman to be fair game.

If Malum thinks I'm just going to forget all the shit they did to me, then they are dumbasses.

Eren's bonding exercises definitely worked, because I've felt nothing short of betrayal during this time without them.

Having to watch them laugh and get along with my replacement has been eating me up inside. There have been times during the night watch when I think Bradshaw can see me through the underbrush. He'll look out into the woods right at me and stare numbly while my replacement talks his ear off. He never responds. He only listens and looks into the dark. For me, I think.

This second mission isn't in the same location as the first, but we're still somewhere in the Rocky Mountains, north an extra hour.

Bradshaw looks like he hasn't been sleeping, I note while I nod to Eight-Seven-Four's endless chit-chat. I've already found his entry point and where he'll be slinking through the training field to extract hostages. I hate that I notice, but I do. He looks disheveled. *He never looked this fucked up when I was his second.*

I force the part of me that cares about him aside and brew on how I'm going to get my vengeance on him. I shut my eyes.

"Do you know how to break a man? I mean really break him." I remember Jenkins's words clearly. I was still newer to the dark forces then, eighteen.

I shook my head. "No."

Jenkins guided my hand across his chest and placed it over his heart. "You make him trust you, make him need you, and then you take it all away."

I was skeptical. "How?"

"Find his weakness, no matter what it may be and extinguish it." Jenkins's soft blond hair was smoothed back with his sweat after our training session. I stared at him longingly. He was perfect, always so stoic and wise.

My hollow heart shifted uncomfortably. "Even if it's a person? The thing that needs to be extinguished?"

Jenkins's green eyes darkened and a cruel smile spread over his lips. "Especially if it's a person. Take away what he loves and you'll break him irrevocably. You're heartless, Gallows. That's why I'm taking you under my wing. No one gets it quite like you and me."

I blink the memory away and force my attention back to the scope. Jenkins taught me many things, but I never got to ask him one question. *What if the man is already broken? What then?*

Bradshaw has already had his light extinguished. He moves like a ghost, uncaring and ready for the slaughter. He feels nothing when he takes a life. I'm certain he wouldn't blink twice if it came down to killing me.

Eight-Seven-Four looks through his binoculars and mutters distances to me. I ready my rifle for a *mock* massacre. There is one man I need to take care of before Bradshaw, though. The marksman who they think can replace me.

"He's there, up on the eastern ridge at two o'clock," Eight-Seven-Four says quietly, muttering the coordinates for me. I find the marksman quickly and grin. It's almost not fair to them. He isn't even looking in our direction. His cover is almost undetectable, I'll give him that.

"Eight-Seven-Four, I can take the field from here. Watch our backs so we don't get our throats slit." He nods and turns to watch our flank side. Bradshaw taught me that lesson and I won't soon forget it.

I take a deep breath and pull the trigger. Red powder erupts on the marksman's side. He rolls in pain and I bark out a laugh so loud it startles my partner. He doesn't say anything though as he holds his position. At least he can listen to orders without bitching about it.

I guide my scope to the field below and find Bradshaw quickly. He's moving like a panther, smoothly and with lethal intent. He hasn't had a chance to fell any of my squad-mates yet. I take a few more seconds than I need, savoring his ignorance of what's about to hit him. He doesn't even know he's vulnerable without his marksman watching his back.

"Fuck. *You*," I say slowly as I pull the trigger.

The bullet hits him straight in the center of his helmet and his head is thrown backward with the intensity of the strike.

The others freeze. Ian and Jefferson look at each other incredulously, while Harrison brings his hands to his mouth in horror. Bradshaw's comrades watch the plume of red powder that rises from his helmet like it's the single worst thing they've ever witnessed.

Their precious, lethal soldier is down.

"Holy fucking shit! Did you hit *Bones*?" Eight-Seven-Four says in disbelief, watching through his binoculars.

I chuckle and mutter, "Yeah, should I hit the rest of them while they're standing around like cute little ducks?" He doesn't respond before my next bullet flies and hits Ian in the ass. I have to suck in my lower lip to keep the laugh from bubbling up. I fire off again and nail him in the neck. We can hear the faint aftershocks of his scream from here.

Both squads seem to remember themselves and attempt to get back into the mission. I pull the trigger again. Pete hits the ground like a downed bird when I hit him in the balls and again in the chest.

Reload.

Harrison in the face. *Oops*. Then Jefferson right in the center of his spine as he runs for cover.

I leave Eren alone, seeing as he's laughing his ass off at his own stupid squad.

"Think they'll accept me now?" I ask Eight-Seven-Four, and he looks at me with raised brows and a newfound respect. Why can't it be this easy to impress the others? He looks at me like I'm death itself.

"I can't believe they didn't to begin with." He swallows

hesitantly. I can see the fear growing in his eyes as he studies me closely. "How many people have you killed, Bunny?"

Why does everyone ask me that? I shake my head. "I don't know. Too many." Jenkins taught me not to keep track.

He's quiet for a beat.

"Doesn't it bother you?"

I look at him with cold, weary eyes, saying numbly, "No."

His face fills with horror and I know then that he's still relatively new to the underground world. He's on the dark air force side. He doesn't slit throats and shoot people often. He has his missile team waiting on the other side of the radio for his coordinates.

"Look, at the end of the day, it's them or you. Them or your squadmates. I learned the hard way. So don't let it be you or your squad," I say somberly, thinking of my mistakes and the price I paid. Jenkins's warm smile that was stolen from me and the ache I've felt in my heart ever since.

"Oh." He shudders. After a beat of silence he mumbles, "Is it true that Riøt Squad used black bullets?" A rumor that literally everyone in the dark forces talks about. If a body is found with a black bullet, they are marked as traitors. If their bodies are ever found, that is. Jenkins did enjoy making sure some were never found.

I let my eyes fall on the young soldier again. "Yeah. It's true."

He goes white as a sheet and swallows.

I look back through my scope and find Bones still on the ground. A flutter of malice spreads through me seeing him that way.

Don't tell me he can't take a hit from a fucking powder ball.

A cruel smile spreads over my lips.

twenty

. . .

JENKINS GLANCES UP AT ME FROM HIS POSITION A FEW FEET away. His eyes move over my face slowly as if he's memorizing me. He does this before every mission starts, tracing my lips that he kissed so fervently last night.

I give him a slight nod so he knows I have his back. I always have his back. He gives me a solemn smile before looking back to the men moving crates over the dock of Black Bay. It's somewhere south of Anchorage between the national park preserves. It's not an official landmark, but it's highly frequented for the black market weapons trade.

They are dark forces soldiers we've been sent to eliminate as traitors. Riøt is spread out with every corner of this dock secured. No one is leaving unless we let them.

It's unusual to get other dark forces as a target. Usually we are hunting the upstairs traitors, which are immensely easier to take out because they don't realize a team like Riøt exists. Other underground teams? They know if they're involved in dirty operations that they'll need to watch their backs for us.

This is why our squad is stationed in a different facility from the other undergrounders, so we don't get close and have trouble pulling the trigger. General Nolan knows he doesn't need to worry about us though. Jenkins and me are the dream team. We don't care. If a name comes up on a screen, that's all it is. A name.

We obey. We eliminate.

Jenkins lifts his hand and gives us the signal to close in. I move quietly and keep on my sergeant's heels, looking every direction he doesn't. I find my thoughts harder to wrangle lately, especially when we're on a mission. The only thing I seem to be able to focus on is Jenkins. His sharp cheek bones and the whispers he tells me of dreams he has for us. *Together. I'll always be by his side.* My chest warms and I'm distracted for a second.

It was only a second.

A branch snaps under my foot and the target soldiers snap their heads up instantly.

My heart drops as they lift their M16s and start shooting at us.

"Get down!" Jenkins turns his back toward the gunfire and shoves me down. I fall on my ass and bring my scope to my eyes in my next breath.

I shoot both the men in the center of their foreheads and they drop like flies. A few remaining soldiers try to load the boat and drive away but our grenadier launches his missile and strikes the boat dead on. The explosion is bright against the night and burns into my retinas.

My eyes flash down to Jenkins. His shoulder is slacked and he breathes heavily. His blond hair is disheveled as he looks up at me with those lovely dark eyes.

I fall to my knees and tremble. "Sergeant..." My throat

tightens. "This is my fault." I try to take his gear off so I can assess his injury, but he shakes me off.

"I'm fine, Gallows," he says softly. "It's okay."

It's not okay. *I wasn't focused.*

"I'm sorry, Sarge." I dip my head with guilt but he places his hand on my shoulder and gives me a heartfelt smile, a rarity for him. It stops my entire world right on its axis.

"I'm glad it wasn't you." He brushes his thumb over my cheek before forcing himself to his feet. I follow his motion and pick up his M16.

The rest of Riøt is waiting for us on the burning docks. Our slick black figures are haunting against the flames.

Jenkins examines the bodies to ensure they're dead. He has me kneel beside him to teach me how to make them disappear.

"This one was just a grunt, so he's fine to be found by whoever comes looking for him." I nod and try not to think about the pain Jenkins must be in as he talks so smoothly. "This guy on the other hand has to go."

"What did he do?" I ask as I watch Jenkins bring out his KA-BAR knife.

"He stole secrets from a string of terrorists and was planning on using them against his own country. He hid them in the merchandise aboard his ship." Jenkins nods to the burning boat.

I cock my head to the side. "Who finds *that* out for us?"

Jenkins grins. It's one of his malicious ones that gives me chills. "We have snakes everywhere, Gallows. Trust no one."

My eyes widen. "No one?"

He looks at me for a while before he resumes cutting off the man's face and tossing it into the water. "No one but me, love." He shoves the body into the water and whatever the fuck is in those dark tides starts feasting on the flesh. My stomach flips and bile reaches the back of my throat.

Jenkins stands and blood drips from his gloved fingertips, dotting the old wooden dock with red. I glance back at the rest of our squad as they watch us like statues on the shore, waiting for the next order.

"Do you trust me?" I ask Jenkins.

His head turns toward me. The fire behind illuminates him in an orange halo, magnifying all his beautiful features. His eyes soften and he closes the distance between us. "I'm not sure I ever will," he says somberly. He lifts his hand to my chin and holds it still. "You are a dangerous little thing. Beautiful, but dangerous."

I think about that on our way back to our base and while I let Jenkins fuck me in his tent. His strong hands grip my hips and make me whimper, his come leaking from my center.

Before I fall asleep, I conclude that he is the beautiful, dangerous one. Wicked in his ways. Perhaps that's why he holds me so securely while he sleeps with his head on my chest. We were made for each other—molded by darkness itself.

I smile, letting my head fall to the top of his and breathing in his scent of pine sap.

As long as I'm by his side, I will follow him to the grave.

twenty-one

. . .

BRADSHAW

THE SKY IS CLOUDY AND GRAY. MY NECK FUCKING HURTS AND my ears are ringing.

Did I get hit?

What are you doing after we get our cards, Bones? Abrahm's voice fills my head. He often spoke about what he wanted to do after our last mission, but I never told him what I wanted. I always said I didn't know. Sometimes I even sat quietly, not responding and leaving the cruelness of my presence to speak for me. But he would smile anyway, so aloof and careless to my callous nature. He liked my silence as much as I enjoyed his refusal to shut up.

I wish I would've opened up more to him. I wish I wasn't such an asshole.

My eyes close and his smile resurfaces in my memory. I can't remember anything about his face except that fucking grin.

I wonder what his last thought was.

"Bones."

It's not his voice.

"*Bones*, hey—you okay man?" Is that Harrison?

My eyes crack open and I see six figures above me.

Eren's eyes are filled with amusement. Harrison, Ian, Jefferson, and Pete are covered in red powder. Were they hit too?

Goddammit.

My sight shifts last to the sixth figure lingering above me.

It's *her*. Eyes bright against her dirt-smeared face. Her dark brown hair is pulled back into a loose braid. I want to run my thumb over her bottom lip and tell her she makes my chest ache when she looks at me so tenderly. I want to tell her that the nights I laid beside her were the only ones I slept peacefully in fucking years.

I want to tell her that I fucking missed her.

Then that same wry smile that Abrahm had appears on her lips.

My eyes widen and I sit up abruptly at the pain that shoots through my chest. Everyone stops talking and they stare at me like I've lost my mind. I hesitantly glance back at her and the smile has vanished.

Why does she remind me of him so much? It makes me angry. She could never take his place and somehow there's enough of a difference that it soothes me. What does she see when she looks at me? A broken thing, a killing machine, someone who only knows how to hurt others?

Something that needs to be locked away... I need to know. What goes on behind those alluring eyes?

Weariness pulls at my thoughts and I let my eyes close once more, relaxing my muscles and falling back into the dirt.

"*Shit*. Get the medic, I think he's having an episode," Eren says sharply, and a few of my comrades run to get the med guy.

"I'm fine," I choke out, my voice raspy. Though, something does feel a little off. My hand trails up the side of my head and I unlatch the helmet, letting it fall to the ground beside me. It's completely red. God, she got me good.

"Stay with him. I'm calling in the chopper just in case," Eren orders, and his steps quickly fade.

"I don't need it," I call out, but no one responds. I let out a long breath.

Fingers thread through my hair gently. The comfort it brings me eases my shoulders. *Bunny.*

"Can't even take one hit, huh?" She laughs quietly. It's not in a bragging way; there's something sad in her voice. Pity, perhaps. I didn't think she was capable of it.

I open my eyes enough to see her. She's sitting beside me, so close that her floral scent is tangible. I wonder if she knows that she smells like flowers, even when she's bleeding and smothered in mud. *Flowers.* Like a field of wild, fluttering petals dancing in the wind. I want to sit with her for a long while. For as long as I can.

My jaw sets at her comment, but I'm too tired to fight with her. She continues to thread her fingers through my hair slowly as I watch her distrustfully.

Why is she being nice to me? I cut her... I scarred her beautiful body.

All I do is break things. But no matter how much I push her, she doesn't stay down. Maybe things that are already fucked up can't be ruined further. There has to be a point where there's nothing worse, right?

She gives me a small, gentle nudge with the back of her hand. "Looks like I'm the only one who can be your second, Bones."

I chuckle grimly. "I guess I probably don't have a say in the matter anymore," I say, softer than I intended. Instead of fighting with me she presses her palm against my cheek and the warmth of it is inviting. I let my temple lean into her and she guides my head to her lap.

My mind is so damn loud; I let her comfort me. For the first time, I don't care if others see me in a weak state. I just want her to hold me and continue to brush my hair back from my face. It brings back distant memories of when I was a child, when, for a brief moment under the sun, I was loved.

Right now, I'm not a dark forces war dog who cuts throats, and she's not the heartless soldier who blows brains out without blinking. Instead we're two wounded creatures, circling one another in our cage, curious about what will happen if we give in and collide.

At least my mask covers my grinding jaw and the anguish that pulls at my frown. She really is a beautiful, dangerous thing, just as Jenkins said she was. A warning he gave us when he'd only just got her himself. Eren worked with him often, but I only remember how much he spoke of his new recruit. I had no idea she lived up to his words.

A Riøt on *my* squad, I never thought I'd see the day.

And for the first time since I lost Abrahm, I feel distinct fear enter my soul. I cannot let her die like he did.

I will not survive it.

twenty-two

. . .

NELL

HE'S NOT AS EASY TO HATE WHEN HIS EYES ARE CLOSED. NOT when he's allowing himself to receive a bit of comfort. It's strange to me that I'm so drawn to wounded things—helpless creatures that I know can still turn and bite. Bradshaw holds himself well, the image of an impenetrable mind and body, but one hit in a training and he's a shell of a man.

Is it his pride? Or maybe he's just worn down from it all.

I look up at the others as they scramble to get medical personnel over here. He's not hurt physically. But something is wrong. He can hardly keep his eyes open and in his vulnerability, he's seeking my comfort. It makes my heart ache. I gently brush his hair from his face.

"What will you do on the other side? You know, after you get your cards," I ask, trying to keep him awake as long as possible. He cracks his eyes open enough to gaze up at me; there is a dark calm in them that sends a shudder down my spine.

"I'll be dead before I get my cards, Bun. I can't go back to normality, just like you can't." His voice is raspy and the determination in his gaze is stone.

My brows crease. "Not before I do. I've got your back. Have you forgotten? If you put yourself in danger, you'll have to watch me die first."

"You're so fucking annoying," he says, frowning. His defeated sigh makes me still. It's the first time I've seen him completely overcome.

What's that saying? Don't meet your heroes.

I wouldn't exactly say that he was my *hero*, but he was certainly a soldier I looked up to. So many of us have. He was unbreakable. But now that I'm close enough to see his flaws, it's clear to me that he's human and not some devil sent from the underworld. He is flesh and bone. He has trauma just as deep and red as the fallen comrades before us.

Ian lingers ten feet away, stealing glances at us. He seems too enthralled to stop himself. It's probably the first time he's witnessed this soft side from Bones. It makes me wonder if Abrahm ever had a chance to see this side of him.

Eren's voice booms, shouting orders at both the hostile squad and Malum before locking eyes with me. Shock rivets through his face as he takes us in. I quickly withdraw my hand from Bradshaw's cheek, worried that I'm showing too much affection on the field. But Bradshaw's hand shoots out quickly, grabbing my wrist and placing my palm back against his face.

"Don't let go," he murmurs. I wish I could take off his mask and let him breathe more comfortably.

"Everyone can see us," I whisper.

"I don't care."

His clear disdain for me has faltered and I find the same shift inside my own heart. We remain together while we wait for the chopper and even on the ride back to base. He's reluctant to stray too far from my side.

My skin pebbles under Eren's dark gaze. He hates how Bradshaw is clinging to me, but it doesn't explain the ill intent that lingers in his eyes. I try to focus on keeping Bradshaw's head comfortable on my lap, but I know Eren doesn't look away for one second.

———

Bradshaw was taken to the infirmary and hasn't come out for hours. I sit restlessly on the floor in the hallway, unsure why I feel so reluctant to leave. I decide I'll wait to hear how he is before going back to my room.

There's a row of chairs, but the tile is cool on the back of my legs, so I lean my head against the wall as I consider what might happen after today's mission. It's the second time I've proven my worth. I doubt anyone will try to step in my way again.

My arms are wrapped around my knees and I let my head rest on my shoulder. The entire front side of my tactical gear is covered in dirt and red powder from holding Bradshaw.

"Hey."

I glance up without lifting my chin from my jacket. Jefferson raises his hand in a feeble attempt at friendliness. I firm my lips and raise a brow in question. He's the tallest of us, but from where I sit on the floor he looks even more like a giant. He crouches beside me and lets his back hit the wall with a soft *thump*.

My head turns his way and I wait for him to say something, because it's sort of weird that he's here. They've been assholes this entire time. *Now* he wants to be friends? Jefferson's light brown hair is freshly wet and his clothes are casual. I guess the rest of the squad went straight to the showers when we got here.

"I have to admit, that was the shortest recon training I've

ever been on." His voice is genuine, which piques my interest more. He rubs the back of his neck. "You didn't even hesitate when it came to taking us down. Here I was worried I wouldn't be able to pull the trigger if I ran into you."

My head returns to my shoulder. "Does that scare you? That a *Riøt* could turn so easily?" His eyes dull and he frowns. "The replacement marksman was easy to pick off. He'd be dead in a heartbeat against someone like me. His camouflage was off from his selected location and he wasn't even trying to seek me out. You'd all be dead if this were a real mission." My shoulders tense as I consider that my words might come off as a threat. Fuck them. They deserved what they got for all the hazing. But I find a smug grin reflecting in Jefferson's soft brown eyes when I look at him.

"Yeah, that's an understatement, Bunny. You're fucking scary."

A foreign smile grows across my lips, born of belonging and finally feeling like they'll take me in.

"I'd hate to be on the side you're not on," he says with a low tone and a hint of a laugh.

"So you guys are done being assholes then?"

Jefferson narrows his eyes at me playfully. "Hmm. Probably not." We share a laugh and the door to the med bay opens a moment after.

Eren's eyes find us immediately. He's still covered in dirt like I am and he looks completely spent. He stares at us for a moment before deciding to engage with us. "Jefferson, what brings you here?" he asks. It seems obvious to me why he's here, same as me, to make sure Bradshaw is okay.

Jefferson lifts his shoulder and mutters, "Just thought I'd swing by to check in on you two. Well, three, I guess." He shoots me an apologetic grin for forgetting me.

The sergeant's eyes are empty, but he nods. "You can head back to your barracks, Jobs. Bunny and I will be heading back to our quarters as well." I share a curious look with Jefferson. Did they get in an argument or something? Eren seems so dismissive with him right now.

I watch Jefferson as he walks down the hall back to the barracks.

"Let's go," Eren says under his breath.

I spare a glance back at the med bay doors. "But what about Bones? Is he okay?" My voice lowers as I say the latter. I shouldn't care so much about his condition, but I do. Something was off.

Eren stops walking and looks over his shoulder at me. His features are grim and his eyelids are rimmed with shades of red. The happiness he usually shows the world is gone. I wonder if it was ever truly there to begin with.

"Is something wrong?" I ask more urgently. Something has changed since we arrived. I can feel it even in his posture.

He blows out a breath and smiles, but I can tell it's forced. "No. Of course not. Come on, Bunny, we can talk more in our room." Eren resumes his steady stride and I follow in his wake, silently thinking of a hundred different things that might be wrong. Then something sticks. Eren gave me a horrified look when he saw me holding Bradshaw earlier. Why? Is that why he's acting so off?

I hold my tongue until we step foot into the dark cement room with our two lonesome beds. My hands meet at the small of my back and I wait until Eren steps to the side of his bed and starts unzipping his bullet proof vest.

It's him who speaks first. "You know, I thought I saw weakness in my brother when he was partnered with Abrahm." He shifts his eyes up to mine and his hand stills at the end of his vest. "But I saw raw vulnerability in him today." He shakes his head and presses his palm to his eye, to quell a headache perhaps.

I sit at the edge of my bed, facing him. "Is there something wrong with him being human?" I ask impassively. This side of Eren is distasteful. The words themselves are not so awful, but the tone behind them and the way he's acting tells me otherwise.

Eren scoffs and glares at me. It's much more sinister than it should be. The hairs on the back of my neck rise.

"Yes. He is the only one who doesn't have the luxury of being *human*. He's a heartless killing machine that we need on this next mission. You need to focus on your position on the squad, Bunny. No more messing around. Got it?" Eren is using his sergeant voice and his hostile eyes portray just as much.

My brows knit together as I hesitantly nod. *Something is definitely wrong.*

"Say it," he commands.

"Yes, Sergeant."

twenty-three

. . .

AN ENTIRE WEEK OF BORING DRILLS AND BRIEFINGS PASSES before I get to see Bradshaw again. Eren told the squad that Bones is undergoing special training on his own in preparation for our departure, but the squad seemed to have a different idea on what he was really doing.

During one of the five a.m. drill runs around the base, I overheard Pete whispering to Ian that it was weird that Bones's second wasn't in "special training" with him. I thought about it for the rest of the day. A dark feeling ebbed in my chest. *Is Eren keeping us apart on purpose?*

Eren has been different since then too. Cold and distant, like a switch was flipped inside of him.

The briefing room is humid and quiet, with the exception of Eren's voice. We're leaving tomorrow at 0500 hours to set out on the mission we've been preparing for. My leg bounces with anxiety as Eren projects a map of the drop zone and where we're heading first onto the white board. The projector makes small clicking noises and it has Harrison tapping his pencil nervously against the table alongside it.

Before Eren can discuss the details, the door creaks open and all of our heads lift as Bradshaw enters the room.

Harrison stops tapping his pencil and Ian's jaw flexes.

I take Bradshaw in. He holds himself differently—his shoulders are lower and there's a distinct dullness to his eyes. He doesn't bother looking at anyone as he takes his seat beside me. His crisp pine scent alerts my senses and his low breaths ring in my ears. His presence alone is enough to start a fire in my heart and it takes every ounce of my willpower to keep from looking over at him.

Eren's eyes flick to me briefly and when he's sure I'll follow his orders as to not show attention to Bradshaw, he continues with the mission's details.

"We are going to Labrador, Malum. This is a Level Black mission, which is why I haven't shared any details until the night prior to departure. We can't risk any leaks and absolutely no bumps on this assignment."

Level Black? Oh shit. My leg starts to bounce now too. I've never been on anything higher than a Level Red, which is four levels lower than black. The only squad to come back alive from one was the Warsaw Squad over a decade ago.

Bradshaw sets his hand on my knee to stop the bouncing. I freeze at his touch. It's discreet but my heart flutters.

"There's no easy way to say this so I'll just come out with it: Hades has been compromised." *Compromised?* My throat goes dry. Another dark forces squad that's been targeted by this unknown operation. "They've been MIA for six months and we've managed to locate the group behind the attacks on the dark forces squads. Our intel tells us that they call themselves Ghosts." Eren's eyes are empty as he shares the shocking information.

Jefferson slams his hands on the table. "What do you mean Hades has been MIA? Why weren't we notified?" He stands and knocks over his cup of coffee. Pete curses under his breath.

"That can't be right," Harrison mutters, more to himself than to the sergeant.

"It's been confirmed. We didn't notify anyone because we aren't in a position to call the shots. We're being targeted as one of the last upper-ranked squads and it was strictly ordered by General Nolan himself that I keep my team in the dark about it until go time. Any more outbursts? Or can I get back to the mission details now?" Eren eyes Jefferson coldly.

Jefferson blows out a breath before falling back to his seat and crossing his arms.

Hades. They are reckless, sure, but they can wreak havoc unlike any other squad. The entire team is MIA? What could have possibly happened? My mind flashes back to Patagonia. *Were they ambushed too?* Who the fuck is hunting us? And why?

"Jobs, Badger—you two are going headfirst into the field. I'm anticipating an ambush and we need to go in fighting. Make it as loud as you can to draw attention." Jefferson and Pete nod, their expressions firming. "Wasp, you'll be hot on their heels, but you don't launch grenades unless you're signaled, understand?" Harrison grunts as he nods.

I've been on many missions, but none as severe as this one. The trust between us has to be tangible. We're all relying on each other, with our literal lives. One slip up and... fuck.

"Colt, you're going to stick with Bunny and Bones. You three will remain out of the line of fire and keep the backs of your squadmates safe." Ian glances over at me and I know a flash of uncertainty when I see it. He's not sure he can trust me as much as he does his other squadmates. It makes sense. I've been here for close to two months—they've been together for over five years.

Eren moves his pointer past the field on the map and

toward a heavily wooded area. "We will need to move through the cover of the forest and head to the first bunker, located here." He uses a red marker to circle a boulder somewhere in the forest. I do my best to memorize the coordinates of it before he moves on to the next ones. "The remaining bunkers will be on the charted paths dialed into your GPS. The locations will not ping until our boots hit the ground."

There's an uncomfortable shuffle of feet. We're going into this almost completely blind. Why?

Eren clicks to the next slide. This image is zoomed out farther than the rest and shows just how isolated the area is. "The operation running in Labrador is heavily unmonitored and dangerous. There won't be backup. We *are* the backup. I want you to keep your heads in any kind of situation you might find yourselves in. Our objective is to find the asshole running these attacks, take him out, and hopefully find the Hades Squad unharmed. We're looking at invading their base and the potential extract of wounded soldiers. If we follow the mapped location carefully and keep to the script it should be an in-and-out operation. Quiet, quick, and merciless. Are we clear?"

"Yes, Sergeant," we all say in unison. Though, my mind is whirling.

I zone out when Eren starts getting into the fine details with the fireteam regarding their part in the initial landing. My attention shifts to Bradshaw, who sits stoically beside me in deafening silence.

"Where've you been?" I ask casually, keeping my arms crossed like his are.

His head dips and the weariness rolls from his shoulders. When he doesn't answer right away, I look at him. A coil of emotions rolls through me as I stare at his empty expression.

"Not your concern, Bun," he whispers.

I've missed him calling me that so fucking much.

My jaw sets and my fingers curl against the sleeve of my jacket. What happened to him?

Eren moves down the line of our squad until he's dismissed everyone but myself and Bradshaw. The air is thick, a wordless conversation hashing out between the two of them.

"Bunny. You are to serve as Bones' double in this mission," Eren says in a low, gravelly voice. My eyes lift to his with surprise. His expression falters for a moment, revealing his discontent with the decision that I'm *really* hoping was out of his control.

Bradshaw leans forward and by the way his brows have furrowed I'm guessing this is news to him too. "What do you mean my *double*? She's supposed to watch my back from afar," he snaps at his brother.

Eren pulls a chair in front of us and sits on it backward so his arms are splayed over the back rest. "Bunny will dress exactly like you and will be provided a matching mask and helmet set. You will move together at all times and follow orders without fail. Is that understood?" Eren doesn't break eye contact with me once.

I flash a concerned look at Bradshaw and he returns the uncertainty, but the trust he has in his kin is strong. He nods, even though his eyes betray him.

I clear my throat. "But we are very *obviously* different in size…" My voice trails off because I'm still trying to process this and what the point could possibly be. "Sergeant, excuse my saying so, but I specialize in distance shots. What is the point of sending Bones in if I can't keep the area cleared and the squad safe?"

My nerves start to buzz in my limbs. *Something is gravely wrong.* But my hunch about the close combat being necessary was right.

Eren's eyes narrow as he replies, "Yes, and unfortunately it does not matter. As long as the enemy is hesitant on which one is the real Bones, that should buy both of you time to kill the enemy soldiers."

Bradshaw stands with a force that nudges his chair back and it shrieks across the tile. He stares down at Eren with fury blazing in those icy eyes. "Have Ian take her place. He has my same build," he says firmly.

Eren looks away but shakes his head as he mutters, "I'm afraid it's out of my hands."

I set my hand on Bradshaw's forearm as he's reaching to grab his brother by the collar. Our eyes lock and distinct emotions flash through his eyes, but I can't place them. I look back to Eren. "What's really going on? Something changed the night we got back from the last training. Tell me. You can't expect to keep us in the dark *and* have this plan go smoothly."

Eren blows out a breath, the stress evident on his features as he lets his chin fall to his arms. "*Goddammit*," he says. Bradshaw's jaw tenses but he lets his shoulders relax. Eren's eyes are dull. "Where to start... We first suspected foul play when Abrahm was shot. The bullet he was hit with was unlike the rest in the raid. It was a bullet meant for Bones." His fists curl with fury and he gives his brother a remorseful glance.

"What kind of bullet?" I ask, brows pinching.

A black one.

Eren stares at me for a beat before answering, "A black one."

My spine stiffens. I search his eyes as he does mine. *A black bullet.* Everyone knows only Riøt used black bullets. My stomach twists with the searing look he gives me.

Bradshaw's gaze is set on the door instead of either of us. Unmoving. I'm not certain he can handle this conversation. My grasp tightens around his wrist and it draws his eyes down to me. The pain in his gaze is a gut punch.

Eren stares at where my hand connects to Bradshaw as

he mutters, *"Then,* targeted for a second time, when Bones was poisoned on the training field. We think it happened sometime after you hit him and everyone crowded around. There was an injection mark found on his arm."

My eyes widen. *"What?"*

Eren nods grimly, avoiding my gaze.

I look up at Bradshaw and his eyes are back on the door, mouth twisting with fury.

Do they think I did it?

"Is that why you were gone for a week?" My voice wavers.

Bradshaw's arm flexes and I take that as answer enough, but Eren mutters, "Yes. And you will keep it a secret. I'm only telling you because I personally vetted your record and you've never betrayed your squad. So you're in the clear for *now* and you'll be his double until we can find out who the rat is. I have no doubt there will be soldiers specifically trying to kill Bones out there." His eyes hover on me distrustfully, but he must have a bit of faith in me.

My chest seizes. "There's a rat? On *our* squad?" I almost ask *why,* but it's obvious. Bones is the most dangerous soldier we have. Whoever we're on our way to kill must be powerful to be able to pull strings this deep. For them to even know that the dark forces exist is impressive. My stomach sinks with the idea that one of our squadmates could be a traitor.

Eren nods again. I glance between the two of them.

"How do you know someone else didn't get close enough? What about the med team?" I try to find the silver lining because Eren is wrong. Malum wouldn't do this.

"I was by his side the entire time in there and I found the syringe discarded in a bush near the chopper. You think I'd make this accusation without being sure?" Eren's voice turns sharp.

"This is exactly why precautions are in place." Bradshaw's voice startles me. It's hurt and strained. He points to his mask and I find loss in his eyes. Even if he doesn't know which of his comrades has done this to him, he's lost his faith in all of them... and with the black bullet knowledge, I think he's even lost faith in me.

"But won't the enemy know about me being the double if the rat is in communication with them?" I query, still wrestling with the fact that one of our teammates is trying to kill Bradshaw.

"That's why no one else is being informed of the plan. They won't know until their boots are already on the ground and all communications will be heavily monitored by me personally. I'm suspecting that whoever it is will be so stumped by it that they'll falter when they realize Bunny is masked as well and sticking close to Bones, rather than far away."

"What's stopping them from killing us both?" I ask.

Eren's eyes flick to Bradshaw's and they share another silent conversation.

"What?" I pry.

Bradshaw glances down at me, but it's Eren who says, "That outcome is possible, but highly improbable." He doesn't sound at all convincing, but I can't think of a reason why he'd lie to me.

"So you're betting both our lives?"

Eren narrows his eyes at me. "Don't talk back to your sergeant, Nell. You think I'd put my own brother in jeopardy?"

I shake my head. *He wouldn't, that much I know.*

"What will we do with them once their cover is blown?" Malice is laced into my tone.

Jenkins's voice rolls smoothly through my veins with an unpleasant memory. *"Traitors can be put down in two ways. In prison, fifty years after the crime, or when they choose to betray their comrades."*

I recall the way he shoved his blade into our comrade's chest. One of them we had known for years and Jenkins let his body roll off a cliff without hesitation. His body was never recovered. He was declared MIA, as most of Riøt's targets were.

I had asked, *"Even if it's not an order?"*

Jenkins smiled cruelly. *"Especially if it isn't an order. Don't let them die fifty years later after they've lived their life."*

His empty voice still haunts me from that cold day. Haunted me every time I watched the lights leave the eyes of traitors too. I didn't know what they did, or why I was killing them. Orders were orders.

Except when they weren't, then it was just Jenkins.

Bradshaw taps his arm uncomfortably.

Eren's face twists at my question. "Arrest them, of course. Nothing will be done without my orders to do so. Is that clear, Bunny?" There is a flash of distrust in his gaze but I only nod.

"Of course, but... should it come down to it?" The meaning in my question lingers in the air between us. I'm set in my ways, Jenkins made sure of it.

Eren levels me an icy look. "I can't imagine a situation where that would pan out." I hold his glare for a moment before looking down at my hands and allowing one curt nod.

I can imagine plenty.

"Alright, you're both dismissed. I'll see your asses on the plane at zero five hundred." Eren stands and leaves without another word.

Bradshaw doesn't move, so I don't either. I guess I'm his shadow now. A living bullet proof vest like Abrahm was. Somehow, that doesn't scare me. I welcome the noble death, but curiosity and revenge throb through my veins too.

I want to know what monster could do this to their closest comrades. I want to know who's after us.

"Was it you?"

My shoulders flinch. I look up at Bradshaw. His eyes are hardened but seeking the truth.

"Was it your bullet?" His eyes shift away as if he can't bear to look at me.

I remember that day like each grain of sand trapped in an hourglass. I've only rerun the scenes a million times, over and over, until my mind was raw.

I stare at Bradshaw for a few moments. He looks back at me, eyes studying me carefully, trying to read everything I'm not saying.

"Fuck. I'm sorry," Bradshaw says before I can respond. He nudges me softly before walking out, leaving me alone in the war room with dark thoughts.

Rats never seem to remember that snakes are hiding in the bird's nest too.

twenty-four

. . .

BRADSHAW

SHE WASN'T SUPPOSED TO FIND OUT ABOUT THE POISON. *Goddammit.* I slam my fist against the shower tile and enjoy the throb of pain that reverberates through my fist.

What is Eren thinking? He knows I can't let her be my double; I can't let anyone else die the way Abrahm did. It's my fault. They were trying to shoot *me*, not him. I swallow the bile that rises up my throat and I have to blink a few times to unsee the bloodstains on my hands.

Was she the Riøt soldier that took the shot? My blood chills and I shake my head. *No.* It could've been any of them.

I find Eren in his room and, thankfully, Bunny isn't back yet. He gives me an exasperated look before shutting his book. "What?"

My feet are heavy, but I walk to the edge of Bunny's bed and sit on the end. "I don't think this is a good idea... Why didn't you tell me your intentions sooner?" I try to give him the benefit of the doubt, maybe he was only instructed by the general this morning himself.

His dark blue eyes hold mine thoughtfully for a few seconds before dipping back down to his book carelessly. "This is the only way I can keep you safe. Just stick by her side and you'll be fine, okay?" I know him too well. He's keeping something from me.

I shake my head. "I don't want anyone else to die because of me. I don't want to do this anymore, Eren. She's not a bad person."

The plan was to have her be the sniper. Out of the way. Not tied to my side like a pig awaiting slaughter.

My brother stares at me.

He stands after a few seconds, walks to my side, and sets his palm on my shoulder. "I told you everything in the infirmary. She's the insurance, Bradshaw." I flinch at his tone. My eyes raise to Eren's. They're pleading. "Without her... I can't keep you safe. You understand?"

The muscle in my jaw feathers but I trust him. With my life. With hers.

"She stays safe?" I press him.

"We all do," Eren says with confidence.

I glance at Bunny's single bag on the ground. A worrying itch keeps making itself known in the back of my head.

"And you're certain she can be trusted?" I ask, hating that I am, but I don't trust her completely. Not like I did Abrahm. And this obsession I have with her doesn't make me any wiser.

Eren scans my features before replying. "To be honest, no. Her record is gruesome and disturbing. It's been flagged as odd that she was miraculously the only survivor of the mission failure two years ago. You seem to be awfully chummy with her, though."

My teeth feel hot. "Then why are you so sure the Ghosts

won't take her out? What makes you think she'll protect me?"

He flashes me a dark, calculating smile. "Keep your enemies closer."

I see the logic, but torment drowns me. She wouldn't hurt any of us. She already would've done something if it was her intention, wouldn't she?

"Is that why you had her stay so close and snug in your room?"

"Why else?" He threads his fingers together and presses them to his mouth as he stares at me coldly. "And if things go awry, I need your word that you'll kill her if she steps out of bounds. That girl is dangerous and we're already playing with fire."

A sharp prickle curls in my chest. My brows pull together.

"*Eren.*"

He doesn't blink. "Your word, Bradshaw."

My eyes lower to my hands. Could I kill her if it came down to it?

I look back up at him. "Why didn't you tell me that a black bullet killed Abrahm?"

Eren's face remains blank. "You already hated Riøt for not showing up at the checkpoint in Patagonia. If you knew about the black bullet, you would've killed her the first night."

My chest fills with unease because he's not wrong.

"You like her now, so at least you won't be stupid about it, but if it comes down to it, I need you to kill her."

Our eyes challenge each other and the pit in my stomach gets deeper.

"Do you think it was her?" My eyes linger on the floor.

Eren is quiet.

The door creaks open and Bunny strolls in with freshly

wet hair and flushed cheeks from her shower. Her eyes grow wide as she notices me sitting on her bed.

"Was just leaving," I say callously and shoulder past her. I can't bear to look at her. My resolve will crumble if I do.

If I have to kill her, could I do it?

I find myself asking that question over and over throughout the night and well into morning. Sleep on a night before a mission has never been a luxury for me.

But the thought pursues long into the flight. The transport aircraft is loud and we sit with our backs against the walls. The entire squad is on the other side of the plane facing us. Eren sits to my right and Bunny is on my left. Everyone is asleep except Eren and myself.

A family bloodline trait maybe—we can never seem to fucking sleep.

So instead of rest, I dwell on how I'd kill her if I had to. I watch her sleep soundly, her head hanging back against the seatbelts. Her lashes are long and dot kisses across the soft skin of her cheeks. I draw lines with my eyes over the rise and dips of the muscles in her neck. How could something so gentle and soft be as lethal as me?

My eyes shift down to her hands. They are small and scarred, but flesh colored—not a harrowing red like I'd expect to see when I look at the reaper's hands.

I would kill her swiftly, I decide. Maybe with a neck snap. The longer I ponder it the more certain I am that I cannot do it any other way. She's so lovely and the idea of ruining her in any capacity bothers me.

Sleep my bunny, your next breath is not promised.

twenty-five

· · ·

Nell

Dark clouds shroud the sky. Not a drop of moonlight leaks through the mundane wall of gray. The aircraft hums and rattles as another round of wind berates the metal siding.

Everyone's been silent for the majority of the nine-hour flight. Our gear has been checked twice and Eren has gone over the plan at least four more times while we sit, anxious and buzzing.

Bradshaw has a glum expression, as if he's already mourning the loss of comrades today. But he seems to be the only one who's deep in thought about it. Harrison has a manic smile and his knee bounces repeatedly. Jefferson and Pete look wired with adrenaline, studying their maps and cleaning their guns twice over. Ian strikes me as calm and not too concerned about anything. Air power gets to hang back with the sniper, but he doesn't know we'll be in the throes of things yet.

"Be ready to drop in three minutes. We're in Labrador, soldiers," the pilot calls out in our headgear. Eren motions his hands for us to unstrap and get ready to jump.

God, I hate this part.

We line up at the drop bay and grab hold of the handles that swing above us as the door opens. Cold, wet air rushes at us. I knew it was stormy, but I didn't think it was a complete downpour. The scent of rain and wet soil fills the space around us with a chill. The roar of the engine drowns out all other sounds.

Shit. This much rain isn't a good sign. Visibility will be low. But at least it might give us some cover. If what Eren said is true and we're anticipating an ambush, we'll need it. My shoulders tense as I pull the mask matching Bradshaw's over my face. It's a half skull, black-matte face shield. I take a deep breath and try not to let it bother me that one of the men standing before me is a traitor.

Bradshaw's hand plants firmly on my shoulder and I turn slightly to look up at his hardened gaze. His mask is a mirror of mine, with dark face paint around his eyes. He doesn't let anything show through them, but the weight of his hand conveys his wordless stare.

It'll be okay.

"Drop, drop, drop!" Eren shouts and, like mechanisms of war, we move like death, thoughtless and only as weapons. Jefferson, Harrison, Pete, then Ian. I pull down my goggles and walk straight off the edge and hold my breath like I always do as the butterflies swarm inside my stomach. They fade quickly and I'm able to regain my focus.

We don't fall for long before we deploy our parachutes. The rain instantly affects the descension. It's so fucking dark out here, it's hard to tell where the tree line starts and where the small clearing we're aiming for is. We're going in blind and trusting Jefferson to guide us down.

Rain crashes against the parachutes loudly and blurs my

goggles. *Fuck. Come on.* I can make out the shape of trees just as a gust of wind blows. The air catches in my parachute and thrusts me back. My teeth clench as I prepare to collide into a tree or fall to my death.

"Bunny!" Bradshaw's voice is loud and booming, competing with the storm that wails around us.

I don't have time to say anything before branches slap against my forearms and head. I'm waiting to be impaled by a broken branch but, luckily, I continue to fall through. My body jerks up as my parachute catches on the branches above. When I open my eyes, the ground is a few inches away from my dangling body.

A relieved breath escapes me and I don't waste time unclicking my deployment bag. My shoulders are sore and so are my ribs, but nothing else seems to be injured. I immediately click on my night vision and scan the area.

The top of Bradshaw's helmet glints, slick with rain. I head toward him. He's in complete stealth mode. The way his broad body moves so lethally sends chills up my spine. I say in a low voice through the headset, "Bones, coming up behind you."

He turns and squats beside me when I reach his side. I can barely make out his eyes beneath his goggles as he looks me up and down thoroughly. "You okay?" he asks quietly. I give him a sharp nod.

Ian comes in through the headset. "Bones, Bunny, ten o'clock." Our heads snap in that direction and, even with night vision, it's hard to make out his camouflaged figure.

We move like liquid through the underbrush. I try to orient myself, but I can't figure out where we are geographically. The wind has brought the pine trees to life, their rattling raucous and distracting. I studied that map until my eyes bled, but with the storm and crash landing it's useless to guess where we are exactly while under the canopy of trees.

Bones mutters with an empty tone, "Where are the others?"

Ian shakes his head as the pounding of the rain thrums against the leaves above. The plan has already unraveled so much. But, as with any mission, we're to get back on track immediately if we get separated.

"Wasp, Jobs, and Badger are probably fine. Let's find the clearing and get to the vantage point to watch their backs as planned," I say sternly. Ian notices my uniform and mask are the same as Bradshaw's and it gives him pause. He stares at me and only moves when Bradshaw nudges him and jerks his head.

It takes about five minutes until we get our bearings and find the clearing. The field is empty and a certain death sentence for anyone who walks out there right now. The rain has thickened and visibility is so low that I doubt I'd be able to make a clean shot.

"Wasp, come in," Ian mutters as we lower into a thick bush.

Silence.

"Badger, where are you?" Ian tries Pete.

No response. I shift on my feet uneasily and look at Bradshaw. His breaths are hard but that's all I can make out in the dark.

"Jobs... Jobs, come in." Ian's voice is laced with despair.

The worst-case scenario is playing out in my mind. Was the enemy waiting for them once they landed? Were they killed quickly? Taken as hostages? My throat dries with dread at the thought. I shut my eyes and try to refocus.

My headset crackles. "Colt? This is Jobs. What is your location? Over." The voice sounds too low to be Jefferson's. A warning signal goes off in my head, screaming that something is wrong.

Ian opens his mouth to reply.

I set my hand over his lips and he stills, eyes flicking to me with apprehension. Slowly, I shake my head.

"This is Jobs. Colt, I need the location, over," the man repeats.

Ian jerks away from me and opens his mouth again to reply. This time I unclip his helmet with his headset attached and toss it into the bushes.

"What the fuck are you doing?" He shoves me back on my ass.

I make sure my headset is muted before snapping, "That's not Jobs."

Bradshaw moves beside Ian, his goggles are set on top of his helmet, and glares down at me. "Jobs, what's the name of the book you gave me last week?"

There's a beat of silence.

"I've never given you a fucking book, Bones. What the fuck are you talking about? Where you guys at? Did Bunny eat shit?" The voice belongs to Jobs this time. I stare at Bradshaw. Can he really not hear the two different voices?

Bones nods his approval and tilts his head for Ian to go collect his helmet. I hear Ian list off the coordinates for our location. The blood in my ears roars loudly and my gut tells me something awful is about to happen.

"Those were two different peo—"

Bradshaw grips my arm and cuts me off. "You don't get to put your trust in yourself over us. If I didn't know any better, I'd think you're trying to fuck this mission up." He unsheathes his combat knife and angles it to my throat. "I don't trust you, Bunny. Pull something like that again and I'll cut your throat myself."

My heart pounds heavily. He's dead serious. "You think *I'm* trying to derail the mission?" My voice is laden with venom. The rain pummels against our gear.

Bradshaw's eyes narrow. "I think you're trying to keep the squad split up, which is a dead ringer for a conspirator."

I can't fucking believe this. He thinks after all the bullshit I've gone through, that I'd be the traitor? That I'd throw away my only chance to avenge Jenkins?

"Suit yourself. I'll watch through the scope." I say, a mere few inches from his face, as I tear my arm out of his grip. The moment I'm free he grabs my other arm roughly.

"Why? So you can blow all our brains out from afar? We stick together, you and me, remember?" His voice is low.

Footsteps are approaching and my mind starts to focus more on them than Bradshaw. He notices the shift in me and loosens his hold as he glances over to the approaching men. I take the chance and tear out of his hold. Once free, I don't waste a second. I sprint through the rain and remain low.

Get to a secure location and then snipe anyone who's threatening the squad, I tell myself. Giving orders as if you're talking to comrades was something Jenkins taught me that would help in times of panic. *"Let the monster in you take over."*

I slide in the mud and moss and turn so I lie flat on my stomach. The sniper rifle is already put together, but I have to load it and wipe the water from the scope.

By the time my eye is raised to the scope I can see Ian. His eyes are shifty as he looks for me, and... Jefferson. My heart misses a beat. Then Harrison comes up beside them and Pete.

I was wrong?

No. I studied them thoroughly; I know everything about their traits down to the wire. Ian was talking to someone else... Did he only pretend to radio them? Maybe he was signaling to someone else and Jobs responded to Bradshaw because he used his own headset. I continue to watch for a second before I realize Bradshaw isn't among them. I glance up and find him standing above me with his arms crossed.

"Get. Up." Each word is clipped with fury. He's been talking to me differently since he returned from the infirmary, like he's someone else entirely, or he thinks I am. He said he didn't trust me and I saw the resolve in his gaze. He really would cut my throat if he thinks I'm a danger to the squad.

"I'm telling you, something is wrong—" My reply is cut with the sound of a bullet ringing through the trees. It rings out from across the clearing.

"*Fuck*, let's go." Bradshaw grips the collar of my jacket and lifts me up. He shoves me toward our squad and I reluctantly move in their direction.

"Where's Sarge?" I say low enough so the sound of my voice won't carry far.

Bradshaw shakes his head. "No clue."

Something's wrong with this entire mission and I can already taste blood in the air. A low buzzing stirs in the back of my mind, saying over and over: *Get the fuck out of here.*

I know I'll regret this.

My leg juts out and I stop abruptly. Bradshaw's moving too quickly to evade my leg and plummets to the ground. I fall over him a second later. His voice is a loud grumbled sound but any words are drowned out by the explosions that shake the earth around us.

He goes still and I hold my breath as a wall of smoke rolls over us and through the underbrush.

The headset fires off with rushed shouts.

"Ambush! I repeat, amb—" Jefferson's voice gets cut short with gunfire.

"Fuck!" Pete curses through the radio, his breathing labored.

Bradshaw shoulders me off him and stands, charging blindly into the smoke toward his comrades. I grit my teeth at his inability to stay put.

I pull my knife out and grip it with the blade facing my ulnar bone. Killing in close quarters is not in my official file.

KM Moronova

It shouldn't even be in my skill set. I prefer not to do it either; it's messy and so much more personal.

But Jenkins made sure I knew how to slice a carotid from jaw to clavicle to ensure death beyond a doubt. He was keen on never having any ghosts come back from the grave.

My eyes close before I reopen them and slowly move through the thicket in a crouched position.

A figure forms out of the smoke and, although I can't see his uniform or mask, I can tell by the way he moves that he's not any of my squadmates. It almost isn't fair, the unnoticed movements I make as I creep up on him, straightening behind him like a reaper who's come to claim a soul.

My slash is swift and deep. He only makes a low grunt before collapsing to the ground like a sack of rocks. I move on without waiting for him to die. There's no coming back from the opening in his flesh. A quick glance down at my gloves, coated with hot, sticky blood, makes my throat tighten.

The next throat is easier, fewer thoughts invade my hollow mind.

I'll kill anyone who isn't Malum.

And then I'll kill the rat.

twenty-six

. . .

JEFFERSON IS SPRAWLED OUT ON THE GROUND AND COUGHING UP blood, his gloved hand clutched across his chest as red blooms from his vest.

My brain works on overdrive. I don't have time to be distracted by his wounds. I drag my gaze across the battlefield. The smoke is quickly fading with the pounding rain falling heavily on my shoulders.

A flash of movement draws my attention and I raise my M16, finger on the trigger. The soldier is dressed in different camo than ours, though it's a close resemblance—the difference of only a few pockets and designs on the front vest. I pull the trigger and don't blink as the soldier tilts back with the force, falling to the ground and twitching with their last breaths.

What the fuck is going on here? This is more than just an ambush. This is organized and they knew exactly where we were landing.

Any trust I had left in Bunny fades.

A gruesome snapping sound redirects my attention to a group of bushes. I approach with caution, aware of the fact that I don't see or hear any of my comrades or Ghost soldiers.

The leaves of the bushes are bathed in blood, lingering longer now that the rain is tapering off. The thick drops fall to the earth slowly, infusing the brisk air with a sting of iron. It hits the back of my throat and claws at the worry that this blood might belong to one of my squadmates.

A lone figure rises from the underbrush, wobbly from a fight. I still and unsheathe my KA-BAR, keeping low and waiting for the soldier to turn. With our uniforms looking so similar, it would be foolish to cut their throat before I'm certain.

They breathe heavily, the hot clouds of their breath plume around their mask. Then they turn their head and look right at me. My chest constricts as I instantly recognize her in my own image. For a moment it feels like I'm staring at myself, drowned in blood. The matte black of the skull mask and helmet are slick and glossy with red. She looks like a devil. The same one I see when I look at myself in the mirror.

I don't say a word and neither does she.

Bunny jerks her head up and her arm flashes before I manage to follow the motion of it. Twenty feet away a soldier cries out as her knife burrows deep into his spinal column. He falls to the ground and she's already darting toward him to finish the job.

I force myself to keep her pace and grip her wrist before she can pull her knife out of his back. Her head flicks up to me. God, I wish I could see her eyes past those goggles right now. Does she even look like herself when she kills like this?

"We need to keep one for questioning," I order in a low voice.

She hesitates but finally nods.

I take a breath and look back to the empty forest. Jefferson was in bad condition.

"Clear, half a klick west from the intended drop zone," I mutter through the radio.

Bunny remains settled on the soldier's back but keeps her head up and alert.

After a few terribly long minutes the radio clicks in my ear. "Clear on the eastern front, quarter klick from landing," Eren says calmly. *Where the fuck have you been?* My teeth grind together, but I wait for everyone else to respond before slowly standing. A few more gun shots ring out in the distance.

Jefferson was the only one who didn't respond.

"I'm going to go check on Jobs. Stay put," I tell Bunny. She doesn't acknowledge me, but I don't have time to wait for a response.

It doesn't take me long to find Jefferson. He's still groaning in pain and exactly where I saw him a few minutes ago. He clutches his stomach painfully and gasps for air.

I fall to my knees and start unzipping his vest. "You're okay," I bite out, but I'm not sure he hears me. Jefferson keeps taking in long unwavering breaths.

After I remove his vest, I quickly lift his shirt to inspect the wound. Jefferson groans again but I dismiss it. The bullet went straight into his gut, probably hitting mostly intestines, being so low. Hopefully it didn't hit his kidney.

"We need an evac, Jobs is down," I say as calmly as I can through the radio.

Eren responds instantly. "We're on the way. Don't leave his side; we're pulling out and regrouping at the alternate drop after we get Jobs out of here. This site is compromised."

I hold down on his stomach and watch Jefferson's expressions go from fear, pain, then to confusion. *Shit.* I'm not sure he'll make it through this.

A sharp cry rolls through the trees and my head snaps toward Bunny's direction. She wouldn't kill our only hostage, would she? I grit my teeth and force myself to stay put. If I leave Jefferson right now, he might not make it.

Pete and Harrison appear through the brush and spot me. I raise my hand and signal them to come quickly. They move silently and kneel beside me. They're covered in blood and their eyes are wide with adrenaline.

"Take care of Jobs. Sarge is on his way for an evac to the second drop location. I need to get Bunny and find Colt," I say with a ragged breath. They nod and replace the pressure I was keeping on Jefferson's stomach.

The blood in my veins pounds rapidly against my eardrums as I run back to Bunny. If she killed the hostage, then there's no doubt in my mind, she's a traitor.

I'll have to kill her. My fists curl tightly at my sides.

Her helmet comes into view and it's immediately apparent that she's no longer seated atop the soldier. I unhitch my handgun and point it at her. She turns as a branch snaps beneath my foot.

Her goggles are off and her blood-smeared eyes widen at me.

"Where is the soldier?" I bite out, finger caressing the trigger.

She stares at me callously for a few seconds before standing slowly. Her shoulders are slumped with weariness and my chest constricts at the realization dawning over her darkened eyes.

"You're going to shoot me?" She barks out a sharp laugh.

My jaw tightens and my eyes narrow with anguish. "If I have to."

Bunny nods down to her right, I follow the motion and find the soldier, dead and with her knife sticking out of the center of his chest.

Beside him is Ian.

Ian stares aimlessly at me with his mouth wide open. Blood leaks from his lifeless lips. My eyes widen and my voice booms with shock and fury. "What the fuck have you done?"

"He was going to kill me." Her tone is empty. "I found your rat."

She killed Ian?

No. She's fucking bluffing.

She stares at me like she's trying to read my very thoughts. *Ian couldn't have been the rat. Could he? I don't know what to fucking do.*

Abrahm's voice shifts across my thoughts, something he once told me. *"Don't pull the trigger until you're sure. Until you know you won't regret the last breath the other person will take."*

He wouldn't kill her. Not until he was certain of the facts. *Fuck.*

"Turn around!" I order her. She doesn't budge. Instead, she takes a step toward me. I secure my grip around the pistol, aiming it straight at her head. "*Bunny,* fucking stop. I swear to God I'll fucking shoot you."

Her grin is visible only in the way her eyes narrow at me. "If you're going to shoot me, then get it over with, Bones. If I'm going to die today, it will only be at your hands." She walks until her forehead is pressed against the gun, leaning against the weight of my hold and shutting her eyes. My hands are trembling uncontrollably. "I'm tired, so it's okay. If this is where it ends, it's okay."

My throat swells with emotions I won't dare to acknowledge.

"Give me your wrists," I say quieter, hoping she'll concede.

"Either you trust me, or you kill me. I won't let you keep me as a prisoner." Her eyes find mine. I'm entranced by her unwavering devotion, so much so that I don't realize her

263

gun is pressed against the bottom of my jaw until the cold steel burns my skin.

I almost smile.

She's fucking good at killing men like me.

My lips part with words that get lost in the sound of the forest being blown to bits. A wall of fire sucks out all the air and the two of us are thrown violently to the ground with the aftershocks.

twenty-seven

. . .

NELL

ASH FALLS LIKE SNOW FROM THE BURNING TREES AROUND US, embers flare and twist with each gust of wind. My head throbs and thoughts are scattered. My arms and wrists hurt too.

Explosions shake the earth from a quarter klick or so away. An airstrike? Who are the Ghosts that they have this much airpower in the remote mountains of Labrador? I cough a few times and black soot spills out. How long was I unconscious for?

As my head comes back to me, I realize there is a weight on my back. I try to force my arms beneath me and push myself up, but they won't move. My eyes widen and panic seeps into my veins.

I try again, this time noticing the bindings around my wrists.

"You're going to hurt yourself," Bradshaw says callously. He's draped over me, arms braced over my shoulders. He was protecting me from the explosions with his body, but tied me up while I was out? Cold.

He slowly shifts so he's lying beside me. His mask is still secure around his face, soot smeared over his eyelids. The back of his gear is burned and dried blood makes his black vest look maroon.

"Bones," I whisper, my throat stinging instantly.

He doesn't respond for a moment, just stares at me, wincing with each breath he takes.

He's a fucking idiot if he can't see what Ian was. My teeth grind as I think about how he pulled me off that hostile soldier and tried to cut my throat. I knew he was talking to someone else other than Jefferson.

Unfortunately, I doubt Malum will believe me.

My lungs burn and worry seeps into me at the weakness in Bradshaw's demeanor. He bound my wrists and if he isn't alert he'll get us both killed. "Bones," I hiss louder this time and flex my jaw at the pain that greets my throat.

He refocuses and a rush of relief floods through me. He lifts his head slowly. His body trembles to support the effort but he looks up into my eyes.

"Nell—" He groans out in pain as he says my name, then corrects himself. "*Bunny*. Where's—*ergh*, where's Eren?" He shifts to his back and splays out his arms, checking for damage.

I sit up and take a moment to check in with my own wounds. My back aches and my toes are numb. My wrists sting from being bound but they aren't broken. No burns. From the look of him, he looks unscathed as well. We were lucky.

"Bones, you need to untie me—"

"*Stop*." He cuts me off. His eyes are cold and more steady now. "Where is Eren?" I regard him for a few moments before shaking my head.

"I don't know."

His left eye is bloodshot and the corner of his mask is singed just over the edge of his lips. The breaths he takes are ragged and congested.

"Fuck. Fuck. *Fuck*—" Bradshaw curses repeatedly as he pulls off his headset radio. The receiver is smashed. My eyes widen as he checks mine too. It's useless, the mic snapped off at some point in the chaos.

Bradshaw stares at the broken headsets and a flicker of dread flashes across his eyes. He pushes himself to his knees, wobbly and unstable, before another wave of explosions rumbles over the ground. One lands relatively close and strikes fallen trees. Wood splinters in every direction. I manage to shield my head, ducking it into my shoulder before the worst of it hits us. Bradshaw is already lying back over me, his back toward the blast zone.

This close, his breath is loud and hot against my skin. I can taste the blood in the air as it mixes with the smoke and debris.

"Stay down," he says, mask pressed to my ear.

I groan at the pain his weight puts on my shoulders. "At least bind my wrists in front of me. It hurts." He gives me a skeptical look before conceding. He unties me briefly before retying the rope with my arms in front. The pain eases almost instantaneously.

He shifts up and quickly looks around. "Get up, we need to find the others." We limp back in their direction. He keeps hold on the rope leash connected to my bindings as we trudge through the forest, alight now with multiple fires burning. Thank God for the downpour earlier or the fire would be running rampant through this area. Everything's so wet and the air is frigid, so a wildfire is unlikely.

Ash falls and smoke rises. The visibility is harrowing and as Bradshaw slows, I fear the worst. My footsteps cease beside him and we stare down at three bodies. My stomach sinks. *Please tell me those aren't our squadmates.*

Bradshaw dips to his knee beside them and blows out a relieved breath. "It's not our comrades." My shoulders relax and I've never been so grateful for a sliver of mercy.

A headset crackles; I barely hear it but the electric sound whines in my ear and draws my attention. I look down and find one of Malum's radios. It must have been knocked off one of them during the assault.

Bradshaw looks at me and takes the headset from my hands. I glower at him.

It crackles again. "Sergeant, come in." Bradshaw's voice is raspy and dry. He listens intently. I can barely make out the other voice but it sounds like Eren. As the voice continues to speak, I watch Bradshaw's eyes grow darker and duller. He turns his eyes on me and a coldness I'd not yet known settles over him.

"Colt is gone," he says painfully.

My chest tightens. If he tells Eren I killed him, I'm done.

Bradshaw shuts his eyes. "It was Bunny." My jaw slacks. "She said he attacked her—"

He stops abruptly. I can hear Eren yelling but I'm not sure what he says.

Bradshaw lets his jaw tilt down. "Copy that, Sarge," he says in an eerily calm voice. Bradshaw looks at me like he's making the hardest decision of his life. Before I can process it he shoves me to the ground. He comes down on me before I can get another word out. His hands wrap tightly around my neck.

"Why did it have to be you?" He scowls in anguish.

I'm helpless with my wrists bound. I can't fight him off. Bradshaw's eyes flash with pain as I gasp for air. He releases my throat and pounds his fist against the ground mere inches from my face before dropping his head.

Eren doesn't care to hear what I have to say? He'll just throw me away and make his brother do his dirty work?

He shakes his head and sits back up, positioning his

hands around my neck once more with more resolve in his eyes.

"You don't believe me?" I choke out.

He swallows and bites into his lower lip, squeezing harder until my vision starts to blur. Hot tears drip on my cheeks and after another beat, he drops his hands.

"I can't fucking do it," he says slowly, sounding so disappointed in himself. Tears roll down over his mask and trickle to my skin. I take labored breaths and struggle to move until oxygen has returned to my brain. The only thing I can focus on is the pain in Bradshaw's eyes. He's crying.

The headset clicks beside us and Eren's voice booms, "Get back to the drop-off zone, Bones! You have two minutes before the pilot takes to the sky. Where are"— gun shots blur out his words—"did you exterminate Bunny?" Bradshaw hears it too and his eyes narrow in agony. It hurts to hear Eren say it so carelessly, like I didn't mean anything.

Bradshaw looks from the headset back to my bruised throat. A decision solidifies over his features and he sits back on his haunches. I scoot out from beneath him while he's still acting sane.

The sound of another incoming plane roars through the treetops. Bradshaw doesn't seem to notice. He looks completely lost in that lovely head of his. I grit my teeth, wrap my hands around his wrist, and drag him up. He grunts when he puts weight on his leg. My own are starting to feel weak already and tremble as I stand straight. I duck beneath his arm and take on some of his weight.

"Are you certain Ian was the infiltrator?" Bradshaw asks between breaths as we limp through the burning forest together. The smoke is thick from the damp pines.

"You think I'd kill him if he wasn't? I'm trying to keep you alive, Bones. Whoever he told our coordinates to, they were coming to kill you." We step over a log and he trips. I get dragged to the ground with him but swiftly find my footing again, hauling him up beside me the best I can with my hindered wrists.

"Why Ian?" he says quieter, hurt ebbing in his tone.

Groaning pine trees snap ahead of us and crash into one another, creating a domino effect and taking out surrounding trees. They fall like titans to the ashen ground, some on fire already and others just catching.

The force of the trees uprooting makes us lose our footing and fall to the ground. A widowmaker lands over Bradshaw's leg and he shouts out in pain. Dust and embers kick up around us like hellfire. I stare into his eyes as he does mine.

Eren's voice rolls through the radio once more. "Thirty seconds. Get to the drop zone, now!"

Bradshaw studies me, the blood smeared on my mask and my bloodshot eyes. "Go." His voice is stone.

My brows knit. "What—"

"Go back without me." I don't move or blink as I try to process this situation. He adds, "That's an order, Bun."

He can see the defiance in my gaze. He knows I won't.

"I won't let you die here, Bradshaw. And I can't return without you." I dip both arms under the tree and use all my strength to pull it up. He moves out from beneath it and staggers to his feet. He lasts two seconds before falling to his knees.

"Bun, please." The resolve has gone out of him. Desperation leaks from his pleading eyes.

"I'm sorry. I can't follow your orders this time, Bradshaw," I say quietly as I ignore the headset. Eren is shouting and urging Bradshaw to hurry. Another tree falls behind me and throws embers into the air at my back. They reflect in Bradshaw's eyes as he stares at me, not angry, but sad and remorseful.

We'll die here together, alone and stranded. We both know it.

twenty-eight

. . .

NELL

I DIP UNDER BRADSHAW'S ARM TO HELP HIM STAND. HE FORCES himself to his feet and instantly groans, keeping the weight off his wounded leg. Blood pools into his boot.

"Goddammit," he shouts, the smoothness of his throat exposed to the sky.

"We need to get out of the trees." I let him lean on me. My wrists are still bound but it's the least of my concerns right now. We trudge through the mushy terrain and underbrush of the forest, away from the drop site.

The chopper has already taken to the sky and grows further away until we can no longer hear it. Our only means of communication is the half-battered headset around Bradshaw's throat, and who knows how long the batteries will last on it. If Eren and Malum find us, will they hear me out for what became of Ian?

No. I doubt it.

275

Eren wants me dead. I think back to his empty eyes in the briefing room. He knows a Riøt soldier killed Abrahm. Bradshaw knows it.

I know it.

I think of Eren's easy smiles and how close my bed was to his. How stupid and foolish I feel for trusting him.

No one will believe me.

My heart drops at the thought and my step falters, nearly sending me and Bradshaw into the ground. The rope tugs on my wrist, making my jaw clench with pain.

This was meant to be a straightforward, smooth mission. Sure, it was high-risk, but we were prepared. I never thought we'd be trudging through the dark mountains in the opposite direction in search of shelter.

A black bullet. I consider the truth and what it might do, but my conscience tells me that Bradshaw deserves to know. I think on it to focus on anything other than my throbbing limbs.

The sun rose hours ago and beams down from midsky by the time we find a cave to rest in. My boots are soaked and the cold has seeped deep into my bones. I collapse to the dry ground and Bradshaw groans as his knees hit the dirt.

"You okay?" he asks. It's the first words he's spoken since the chopper left without us.

"Yeah. How's your leg?" I mutter between breaths. Now that the adrenaline has faded, I'm feeling every bruise and cut. I lift my tied hands to my neck and brush the spot where he choked me. The skin is tender and raw.

Bradshaw sits with his back pressed against a large rock, slumped slightly to the side with exhaustion and tugs his pant leg up. A pit forms in my stomach at the purple and dark blue bruises that spread over his shin near the split flesh over his calf.

"Don't make that face," Bradshaw grumbles, pulling his

pant leg back down sharply. His mouth is firm beneath his mask and tugs at the corners with weariness.

He looks so tormented by his decisions. I never thought I'd see Bradshaw this distraught, scattered. Any desire to argue with him died the moment shit hit the fan. He could've killed me if he really wanted to. God knows he has enough reasons. So why didn't he?

"Bradshaw... why did you let me live?" I pin him with a desperate look and shake my head.

He stares at me for a long time. His breathing is slow as he studies my face. Finally he looks away and takes his mask off, setting it down at his side. Bradshaw meets my gaze again and gives me a pained smile.

"Would you have been able to kill me if our situations were reversed, Bun?" He lifts his hand for me to come to him. I search his posture for any hidden agendas but don't find any. I slowly move toward him until we're sitting side by side, leaned up against cold stone.

Bradshaw slowly unties my bindings and tosses the rope a few feet away. I rub my raw skin softly before answering him. "No. I don't think I could."

Even now, after he choked me—I saw the anguish and hurt in his gaze. He didn't want to kill me.

I wish he had.

"Why did Eren order you to get rid of me instead of hearing me out?"

Now that we aren't moving and exerting energy, the cold air starts to permeate my bones. I shiver and pull my legs closer to my chest.

Bradshaw groans in pain as he shifts to sit up more. I'm more tired than I've been in years, but I know he needs medical attention now, not later. I unzip my bag and grab the med kit, bandages, and ointment.

"Here, bite on this. I'm going to have to stitch it," I

mutter as I hand him a roll of gauze. He shakes his head and grins even though his forehead is covered in sweat.

"Suit yourself." I clean his leg with a sterilizing wipe before starting.

His fingers curl into the earth, but he doesn't make a sound as I suture his flesh back together.

"Eren said you might be..." He stops himself from finishing that sentence.

My chest aches with his silence and reluctance to tell me.

I finish the last suture and apply the ointment. Bradshaw breathes out a sigh of relief when I secure the wrap and pat his knee to signal I've finished.

When I move to stand, he grabs my arm gently. "Wait."

My eyes find his and I try not to give away how much I'm affected by him. He pulls me closer until I'm seated in his lap. We stare into each other's eyes for a few moments. My heart beats faster than it did in the air raid. Then he pulls me into his chest and wraps his arms around me, squeezing a surprised breath from my lungs.

"I'm so fucking sorry." His voice breaks and his fingers curl into my hair. "I almost... I almost made a huge mistake." He shakes his head and tears wet my shoulder. I've seen more emotion from him in one day than the weeks we've spent training and fighting each other.

I don't know what to say. So I don't say anything. I just close my eyes and let my body relax against his. We mold together in this moment. His body is strong and muscular beneath me.

He caresses my skin delicately and I memorize every second of it. The way his calloused hands tenderly brush against the bruises on my neck and his torso trembling with each whisper of an apology he gives me.

Jenkins would've made me kill Bradshaw with my own two hands for what he's done. But I can't help but pity the broken soldier. He trusts his brother more than anything in this world. He always follows through on a command.

Just like I do.

"What do we do now?" I ask meekly, my eyelids fighting to stay open.

He rubs my arm anxiously and says, "Let's rest until nightfall. We'll make our way to one of the bunkers and go from there."

I shiver in his hold. My wet uniform is starting to feel like ice against my skin. "Eren will find us." I hate how scared I sound. But how can I not be? I trusted Eren with my life and he almost snuffed me out like I was nothing.

Bradshaw shakes his head. "He won't. The backup drop location is closer to the Ghosts' base. They'll skip over the first two bunkers before they even land. I'll protect you, Bunny. I promise."

Why wasn't I informed of the backup drop location? I wonder if the rest of Malum knew about it too.

"If it comes down to it and we run out of options, promise that you'll be the one to kill me," I say quietly. Bradshaw's muscles tense beneath me. "Don't let Eren do it. Don't let anyone else do it. I want you to be the one."

He pushes me an arm's length away before looking into my eyes. His pale blue irises have never felt this painful to look into.

"Okay," he says with a deep breath, the promise heavy between us.

He rummages through our packs and shakes out the two emergency blankets. They are thin foil ones, but it's better than nothing.

We reluctantly strip from our wet clothes and hang them on rocks to dry out before nightfall. Bradshaw spreads out one blanket on the ground. We lie side by side and warm up beneath the second one.

His body heat quickly warms against my back and my

shivering ceases. He holds me close, but my mind is a thousand miles away. I've never been in a position to not know what the next day will bring. Missions are straightforward and have backup plans. I didn't have a backup plan for this situation.

Bradshaw's hand smooths down my arm and he lets it rest over my stomach. The warmth from his palm is soothing and it urges my eyes to close.

"I'll take the first watch. You get some rest," he says.

I try to rest but can't. Instead I stare at the entrance of the cave for an hour. One thought on replay. *A black bullet.* Patagonia was a nightmare I will never escape from. The things I did there. The things I lost.

Jenkins's voice rolls over my body like smoke, as if he's standing right behind me whispering it.

"The target is the one in the mask."

"What's his name?" I had asked, steadying my rifle and staring at two oblivious soldiers talking. They wore dark forces tactical gear, but I couldn't pin what squad it was.

"He has many names. But the important thing is that he's a marked traitor. Hit him, Gallows." Jenkins watched from my side through binoculars. I thought it was strange that he was keen about this one. He usually didn't care to watch long distance shots. Jenkins only enjoyed the intimate kills.

"Yes, sir." I inhaled and just as I pulled the trigger the unmasked man walked into the shot path and took the bullet.

Arms dealers rose over the dunes simultaneously and all hell broke loose.

"Gallows, back to Riøt. We were never here." Jenkins pulled my wrist.

I tried to reload. "I missed him, sir!" I wanted to get the intended target. He was so easy to pick off, holding his fallen comrade.

Jenkins snapped, "You had one shot. Let's go. Now." My eyes flashed at him and I could see the rage boiling behind his stoney expression.

I swallowed the disappointment of failing him. "Yes, sir."

I close my eyes slowly and my breath grows weak with guilt. I've never felt remorse for a life I've taken. But why did it have to be him?

A black bullet killed Abrahm.

I killed Abrahm.

twenty-nine

. . .

BRADSHAW

BUNNY'S SOFT BREATHING COMFORTS ME. IS THIS WHAT IT'S LIKE to have a partner? I bury my face into her hair and let her scent soothe my nerves. I move my hand up from her stomach and trace her ribs, quickly finding raised skin from the scar I've left her with.

Eren's words on the headset replay in my head, buzzing in my mind like locusts. *"Kill her, Bones. I knew he'd set us up... He fucked me over. Kill her!"*

It was almost like he didn't give a shit about her killing Ian. Like the news of him being the infiltrator meant nothing to him. I've never heard him so furious.

Who was he talking about? I close my eyes and press a kiss to her head. Her naked body is pressed against mine and I've never been so warm in my entire life. Everything about her quells my demons.

I almost choked her to death today and something broke deep in my heart when the betrayal registered on her features. The pain in her gaze was enough to bury me a thousand times over.

Eren will hate me for this, but I can't keep his secret anymore.

I pull her closer against my chest and she makes a small, cute sound before rolling over and facing me. She tucks her head into my chest and wraps a leg around one of mine. A smile spreads over my lips.

"I have a secret to tell you." I stroke her hair back. Bunny's hands curl against my chest. I smile that she's trying so hard to pretend to be sleeping.

"My mother was sick most her life and she only got five years with me and Eren before she passed. I didn't know she was sick for a long time, not until our aunt started taking us to see her in the hospital. She always looked worse each time we saw her. She stopped caring to see us and stopped smiling. She became cruel. It took a year of hospitalization before she finally died, and by the time she did, I was calloused to the idea of her. She didn't even remember us and I hated it. I hated her."

I pause and stare at the dimming light to the entrance of the cave.

"I hated her because I didn't yet understand how her sickness took her mind. My aunt explained to us that our mother loved us very much, that she didn't mean the horrible things she said before she died. But I was a wicked child. I truly was born *off*. I didn't care. I was indifferent, ready to move on with life. But Eren? He thought about the evil that grows in the human soul and he broke. In more ways than I could ever describe."

Bunny looks up at me. She doesn't interrupt me, though, just watches my features. I refuse to meet her gaze.

"He killed our aunt when we were twelve. He grew tired of her senseless beatings and decided to take care of it. Made it look like an accident, but I always knew his secrets and he knew I'd always keep them. But then we grew up and we dreamed of a life better than what we had. Eren dreamed bigger. He wanted the world. He wanted *power*.

"I didn't so much care for it. I just wanted to stay by his side. So we signed up for the military. Eren read a lot of black market shit. He wanted to get involved with the underground dealers and sell weapons. It was a great gig for a few years. I became top of my platoon, and he rose to sergeant. But then we were caught red-handed by our general. At first we thought we were going to federal prison but, to our surprise, the general sent us to the dark forces. Something, at the time, we didn't even know existed. We were such a lethal duo that we were placed with Malum immediately. And *fuck*, did we love every second of it. The dead bodies didn't matter and neither did the terrible things that Eren's underground operation allowed really, *really* bad people to do."

I swallow and finally look down into her eyes. Her empty stare gives nothing away, so I press on reluctantly.

"Two years ago, he got into a fight with his dealing partner. He won't tell me what happened, but it was bad enough for him to pull his exports that were on their way to Patagonia. I think whoever he fucked over may have been the reason for the attack."

She sits up, spine stiff and eyes wide with rage.

"You're not talking about the attack on Riøt..." she says slowly, like she doesn't believe me. Her hand trembles and she pierces me with hollow, burning eyes.

I rise to sit beside her, but she scoots away. Our eyes don't part.

"I'm sorry."

Bunny stands swiftly. I raise my chin to look up at her and when I do, she decks me in the jaw. My head turns to the right and my skull clammers against the rocks of the cave floor.

"I deserved that." I rise slowly, wiping my bleeding lip with my bare wrist.

She lifts her arm to punch me again and this time I catch it. She doesn't miss a beat, her other hand is faster than the first and she slaps my face so hard my teeth dig into my lower lip.

"I hate you!" She screams, an inch from my nose. I shove her back so I can restrain both of her arms. Bunny is strong, but without her weapons she's not much of a match for me. I'm twice her size. I wrangle her wrists together and tie them up again. I tether her to a large boulder in the corner of the cave and cover her mouth with my hand, being mindful of her teeth and hoping she won't use them.

I glare at her and say coldly, "I'm telling you this because I care about you, Bun. I'm sick of lying. I don't give a shit about your squad, but I wanted to tell you because I can't lie for him anymore. Not when he wanted me to murder you."

The fight goes out of her eyes and she slumps against the stone, already worn out from the struggle. Her breath is ragged and heavy.

"I'm going to remove my hand now and if you start yelling again I'll have to tape your mouth shut until we reach the bunker. Understand?"

She nods, hateful tears filling her eyes.

I move my hand and she takes a few deep breaths before muttering in the most broken voice I've heard from her, "You knew the whole time?"

A dull ache ricochets in my chest.

"I had a suspicion after you joined our squad that the events were related." It sounds stupid. I don't blame her for glaring at me.

Her head lowers. "Is there more?"

My pause is answer enough, but I mumble anyway, "Yeah."

She doesn't say anything else, but tears roll down her

cheeks and crash against her legs. I force my eyes back to the entrance of the cave.

"There weren't supposed to be any survivors. But you lived. Eren didn't find out until a few months ago and he doesn't like leaving anything unfinished. So he made a few calls and had you recruited to Malum. General Nolan owed him a favor and he promised you'd be safe with us. Eren wanted to use you as insurance to protect me." My voice seems so loud even though I'm speaking just above a whisper.

Bunny writhes against her restraints, murder in her gaze. She wants to kill me and part of me wishes she would.

"You motherfucker!" She tries to kick me, but I stand before she can land a blow. "Did you know who I was the night we met…"

My fists clench at my sides. "*No.* I swear, I didn't know who you were. Eren did, but he didn't tell me until I stormed into his room that night after we…"

Her eyes are golden pits of fury. "You should've killed me… because I'll never look at you the same."

"I'm sorry." My gut twists at how choked up I sound. What use is an apology now?

"Insurance from who? Who's fucking after you two?!"

"I don't know." *The truth.* Her eyes narrow with doubt. "There are things Eren even keeps from me, Bun. My brother has made an enemy that actually keeps him up at night. I've never pressed him on it. He'd never tell me anyway."

She thinks for a long time in silence. Until the sun sets and our clothes have partially dried. I get dressed and help her with her clothes before binding her wrists again. We leave the cave and walk for hours in the direction of the second bunker.

She's quiet for so long that it startles me when she finally speaks.

"The only good Riøt soldier is a dead one," she says coldly, in the exact tone as I used before.

Guilt settles like a beast in my chest. There are no words I can say that will bring her comfort.

"You two are the reason my squad is dead."

I face her, my blood hot. "No. I'm not. My brother maybe, but not me."

Her eyes soften a moment before she swallows and gives me a regretful smile. "A black bullet killed Abrahm." Her voice breaks.

I stare at her. Why is she bringing that up?

Her eyes pool with tears. Guilt and sorrow twist her features. My eyes slowly widen and my chest constricts. I open my mouth and then shut it. She doesn't know what she's saying... because if she's saying that—

"It was me. I shot him."

The blood leaves my head and all I can do is look at her.

"I was aiming for you."

Bunny lets her shoulders fall in defeat.

Her admittance is like a shot to my nervous system. She killed him? Abrahm's last breaths resurface in my memory, his fading light, the blood. She... took him from me.

I wrap my hands around her neck and she doesn't fight against it. Tears fall silently down my cheeks. "What have you done?" I whisper shakily.

Her eyes are dull. "I felt nothing. I was upset that I didn't hit you."

My hands tighten around her flesh and my jaw trembles. Her eyes flinch at the pressure.

"Why?" I ask, and it's so quiet and broken it makes her eyes narrow in anguish. Did Eren know that it was her?

"I was following orders," she chokes out. Who gave her those orders?

Her body slumps and I guide her down to her knees. I can feel each strangled breath she sips as they flutter beneath my palms. My brows pinch together with despair. "Why would you tell *me*?"

Her eyes dim and she fucking smiles. It shatters my heart and my hands loosen, trembling. She mutters, "I didn't know the weight of taking life. Not until Jenkins died. Not until I met you. I wanted to tell you earlier..." Her lips are dry and chapped, smeared with black paint. "I'm sorry, Bradshaw."

My resolve breaks.

I release her and put space between us. My breathing is erratic and I feel like I'm two seconds from having a heart attack. I clench my hand over my chest. It hurts so fucking bad.

I can't hate her. No matter how much I want to. Even for taking Abrahm...

And that tears my soul apart.

thirty

. . .

NELL

BRADSHAW WALKS AWAY FROM ME. FOR SOME REASON, HIM NOT finishing me off triggers something deep inside me. *It shouldn't be hard for him to finish me. Everyone would understand.*

I push myself up and press my bound palms into the dirt. "Why won't you fucking kill me?! I've given you every reason. I've taken everything from you, Bradshaw. *Everything!*" I scream at him, tears streaming down my face and making his form blurry.

He stops and fists his hands at his sides. "You want me to kill you? You really want me to?" His voice grows louder with each word and he turns back to look at me. His eyes are rimmed with red and his features are contorted with misery.

"*Please.* Please. Bradshaw. Please just make it stop," I beg him and let my head hang. He walks back to me and falls to his knees before me. His hands fall on my shoulders and he shakes me until I look up at him.

His blue eyes pierce through me.

I expect him to yell at me, but his voice is a whisper. "Who taught you to beg for death just because you were a device?" My eyes widen and my lips part. "Nell… I know it wasn't personal… I know you were just going through the motions." He hiccups and reels back his emotions, tears still forming. "So why would I punish you? You're just the weapon fired, not the evil that wields it."

A sob bubbles up in my throat and I try to swallow it.

"I destroy everything I touch. I'm… the last Riøt soldier." I grab the hilt of his combat knife, slide it out of the sheath, and place it in his hand. "I'm tired of being the weapon. I'm tired of killing. I want to be free. Make me a good Riøt and kill me. Then, maybe, my sins will be absolved." I shut my weary eyes and focus on his breaths.

His knife grazes the side of my cheek and beckons me to look at him.

"Would you kill me? If I took Jenkins from you? Tell me you would and I'll give you what you want, Bun. But don't you dare fucking lie to me. Would you watch the light leave my flesh? Would you send the devil back to hell?" His gaze is smooth and doesn't falter. He searches my eyes for the truth.

My chin tilts up with my reluctance.

"*Never. I could never. Not you.*" *Because you make me feel things I've never experienced before. I could never hurt you. I could never let you go.*

He pulls the blade away slowly, letting it glide across my face before sheathing it. Our eyes don't bend away from each other once.

"I'm so mad at you, Bun, but if you think I'd ever risk losing you…" He shakes his head and pulls me in tightly, wrapping those corded arms around me and squeezing tight. He holds me like every fiber of his being relies on it.

His hands tenderly smooth over my skin and draw fire over the bruises around my throat.

"What have we let the world do to us, Bun?" he murmurs in a low, heady voice. It slips into my veins and I let the softness of it comfort me.

"We let them make monsters of us. Stolen vices."

He pulls me back and stares into my eyes. His hot breath plumes around us in the cold air. "I don't think I can keep doing this," he says slowly. My brows pinch together. "I don't think I can continue being Bones. Because Bones is heartless and ruthless. But ever since meeting you, I've been anything but those things. When I look at you, I feel like my thoughts are no longer blurry. This dark underworld I reign in doesn't have to be the one I die in."

He feels that way? My eyes lower and linger on his lips. *Even after the things I've done.*

"I want a world with you."

I flinch and pull back until we're staring into each other's eyes.

"When I saw you wearing that dress it broke my heart. I saw what you could've been. I want you to wear whatever the fuck you want and be a normal person. Not out here, with bullets flying between us. I want us to be out there in the real world." Bradshaw brushes the wild strands of hair behind my ear.

"Do you think we could make it out?" My voice is quiet, but his sad, boyish smile melts the ice around my soul.

"Together, our broken pieces can do anything."

———

By the time we get to the bunker coordinates, the sun is already starting to come back up over the far mountains. I hold onto the hope that there will be a shower inside and a few beds.

My eyes are heavy when they lift to Bradshaw as he tries a few different codes on the bunker hatch. It's a partially hidden metal door that's camouflaged to match the dark green underbrush. The mountains crowd this area and make it inconspicuous. A river can be seen down in the valley below, giving me a sense of where we are geographically. I memorized the map Eren showed us, the rivers were the key to most of the landmarks.

We haven't spoken in hours.

There really isn't anything to say. We've both done terrible things for awful people. And that darkness consumes the air between us.

The latch finally beeps and Bradshaw lets out a relieved sigh as the door unlocks. He lifts the hatch and hesitates before he looks up at me.

He opens his mouth to say something but closes it just as quickly before looking away. It's almost like we don't know how to talk to each other anymore.

I close the distance between us and take the steps down the long ladder. It's dark for the first five steps and then a sensor picks up my motion and fluorescent lights flicker on slowly.

The ladder leads into a large open area. The walls are made up of big white metal slats with bolts engineered into the edges, keeping them all lined up. Cots fill the sleeping side, enough for six people, and only one door lies at the end of the space—I'm assuming it's a bathroom. Opposite of the cots are small cabinets and a black table. It's simple and bare minimum for a bunker. *I hope there's food in the cupboards.*

Being in this confined space makes my chest constrict. There's only one way in or out of this bunker. My eyes lift to Bradshaw as he closes the hatch and locks it. There's a keypad on the inside as well, but he's the only one who knows the password.

Shit, maybe I should've been paying more attention when he was inputting codes. I watch him descend the ladder and he takes in the space like I did.

"How did Eren know these were here?" I ask.

His jaw ticks as he notices nothing about this bunker is military-grade. It was put here for hiding purposes by someone powerful and well-prepared. Someone paranoid. The Ghosts, I'm sure.

He turns and looks over his shoulder at me. "I don't know."

"At least tell me what the code was." It's not like I actually expect him to tell me, but the long frown he gives me still burns.

"You don't need to know it," he mutters.

"And why's that?" I eye him callously.

"It guarantees my safety."

I scoff. "From what?"

He levels me a broken stare. "From you betraying me."

The shock must roll through my features dramatically because he forces his eyes away. He really thinks I would? I guess our secrets catch up to us. I can't say I'd tell him what the code was if our predicaments were reversed.

The fight goes out of me with a pained breath. "Fair enough. You think there's a shower here?"

"There should be." He sits on one of the cots and lets his legs slide against the tile until they're relaxed and spread apart. "You go ahead and shower first."

I study him as he brings his hands to his head and ruffles his hair with distress. There are a million things I wish I could say. A million and one I wish I could take back.

But I don't say anything; I let the sorrow grow between us and head to the bathroom.

It's surprisingly spacious, but its only contents are a toilet, sink, and a round porcelain tub. One wall is entirely made up of a mirror. The fluorescent lights make a humming sound and brighten the room to the point where I can see every red stain on my skin.

The soldier I see in the mirror looks fractured. My eyes are bloodshot and my braid is ratted with forest debris. I let my focus linger on the bruises around my throat. It's funny that the same woman in the mirror was wearing a cute yellow dress a couple weeks ago. Did Eren feel bad about recruiting me? Why would he befriend me if this is how he was intending to throw me away?

I start to strip slowly. My body aches and each movement requires a tremendous amount of energy. It takes me a few minutes to get completely naked. Once I am, I hesitantly look back at my body. There are more bruises than there aren't. More skin that's scabbed, scarred, or bruised than not. I take myself in and wonder why I don't feel anything when I see the broken person staring back.

Nothing can be done about the past.

I scrub the blood and dirt from my skin and hair like I can absolve my sins this way. Like I can wash Abrahm from my hands. I have to drain the water for a second bath before I can soak, but as I do, I go over Bradshaw's story repeatedly. Eren knew who I was on the plane—is that why he took my window seat? Forcing conversation... but he was always so kind to me. *I let him touch me.*

A chill sets in my bones at the thought of him knowing what my fate held this entire time. How conniving he was.

I drain the water and dry my hair, deciding to leave my gear off and wash it after Bradshaw cleans up. There is a stack of white folded shirts in the corner shelf next to a single wardrobe that's much too tidy for my liking, as if someone frequents this place. We'll have to leave here once we rest up. I'd hate to be in the bunker with only one exit if someone returns.

The shirt falls down to my ass and I change out to a dry pair of socks. I expect to find Bradshaw still sitting on the cots when I finally emerge from the bathroom, but he's not there anymore. My heart rate spikes and I make for the ladder.

He wouldn't lock me in here. He wouldn't.

But as I look up at the metal door with a red light staring back at me, my hope fizzles out.

"What the fuck are you doing?"

I whirl, eyes finding him at the opposite end of the room, opening some canned food from the cabinets. My breath comes back to me and I try to slow it to steady my pulse.

"I thought you… left me down here." My voice is shaky. He narrows his eyes at me before waving me over.

He already has a few cans opened and hands me one with preserved apples inside. The scent reaches me first: cinnamon and tart. My stomach growls and my mouth waters. It's easy to forget your hunger when you're on a mission. I take it and the plastic fork he hands me, looking between him and the food before reluctantly biting into the soft apples and closing my eyes with the flavor.

"Can we call a truce now?" he asks haphazardly as he starts shoveling apples into his mouth too.

I swallow and laugh. "You think a can of apples can fix what we've done to each other?"

He continues eating as he considers me. "Why not?" His eyes are red and drift hesitantly down my body. "Jesus, Bun, you're all banged up." I grab the end of the white shirt and try pulling it over more of my bruised thighs.

"I'm fine."

"You call this fine?" He sets down his can and reaches for one of my legs.

I swat his hand away. "Yes."

Bradshaw raises a brow but drops it as he grabs my leg and slides me closer to him until I'm practically in his lap. "How was the shower?" he mutters mindlessly as he runs his fingertips over my skin, sending heat to my core.

"It's only a bathtub, no shower head." I set my can down and prop my arms up behind me. I don't know why I'm letting him touch me like this, but it's the only thing that doesn't make me feel absolutely nothing, so I accept the comfort for what it is.

He groans and mutters, "Great." His hands slide up an inch from my panties and he stops and looks up to my face. Bradshaw's eyes are pale oceans I could drift into for the rest of time. He gently touches my chin and presses his forehead to mine. He takes a breath, swallowing before whispering with a raspy voice, "I forgive you for Abrahm."

I jolt and try to push away, but Bradshaw only opens his eyes and stares into my soul with weary thoughts and forgotten sins. "All I want is to be by your side. In training, in war, in death. I can't picture myself anymore without you being there, Bun. You linger in my thoughts, in my fears. But mostly, you're the cause of all the emotions I feel again. I was dead until you tripped on my foot on the plane."

Tears form in my eyes—they burn as I hold them back. "You don't get to forgive me, Bradshaw." My voice trembles. I'm not sure if it's because I can't forgive myself for it or if it's because he's partly to blame for Jenkins's death. But if I sit on it long enough, I know deep down that I forgive him too.

He keeps me close against his chest and shushes me. "I'm sorry, Bun, I can't help how my heart feels. The only thing I know is that I cannot lose you." He presses a long kiss to the top of my head and I go limp in his arms. "And if you think I'm ever letting you go, you're wrong. You're mine. As much as I'm yours."

He leaves me with that, slowly slipping from beneath me and heading to the bathroom to bathe.

I don't move from my spot on the floor until he's been in the bathroom for ten minutes. When I get up and pass the door, I glance at the opening and see Bradshaw's naked form.

He's covered in fresh wounds, some still bleeding. His back is covered in long scars, old bullet wounds, bruises, and gashes. The area around his ribs is especially purple. The sight of it makes my chest twist. He must have at least a few broken ribs. His tattoos hide a lot of things. But they can't hide how hurt he is.

Bradshaw must sense me staring because he looks over his shoulder and our eyes connect. My cheeks flush and I swiftly avert my eyes and march to the cot closest to the wall. It feels like hours pass, but by the time Bradshaw comes out of the bathroom, it's only been thirty minutes.

He settles on the cot beside me, wearing a matching white shirt, which he fits in much better in than I do, and his briefs. Now that his skin is clean, I can make out all the damage beneath and it's heartbreaking. This must be how he felt seeing me, even though I felt nothing for my own pain when I saw it in the mirror.

I sit up and look at the sutures on his leg. He scrubbed it well and reapplied ointment. At least it doesn't look like it's getting infected.

"Eren told me you wanted to have a coffee shop. Was that always something you dreamt of?" I look up at him. His head is propped up with his arms folded behind his head for support. From this position his biceps are flexed and it makes that white shirt rise enough that I can see his V-shaped muscles at the waistband of his boxers. He gives me a relaxed smile. "Are you checking me out, Bun?" He chuckles and my brows draw together quickly.

"No. I wasn't."

He lifts one of his arms for me and beckons me to come to him. *You're mine. As much as I'm yours.* My throat bobs. What I feel for Bradshaw is dangerously close to love. I consider not going to lay across that rigid, corded torso and letting him hold me. But my heart shifts on an entirely different axis than my brain and wins the battle.

Tentatively, I slide my palm into his and a gentle smile forms on his lips. He looks so tired. I'm not sure he got any rest while we were in the cave. Bradshaw guides me down beside him. I rest my head on his bicep and close my eyes as he wraps his arm around me.

"The coffee shop, Bun. Tell me about it," he whispers drowsily.

I smile. "Well, it wouldn't just be a coffee shop."

"Oh?"

"Yeah, it would be a bookstore too. And my husband and I would live on the top floor." His abs flex with the mention of a husband. I ignore the fact that I just pictured Bradshaw in that role. I try not to dwell on it, but the more I think of the apartment above the shop, the more I only see him. All his imperfections. He wouldn't be hurt anymore. No more bullets to pierce his lovely flesh. No more blood.

My cheeks burn with the memory of him making me clean off my blood from his cock.

"You wanted to get married?" His voice sounds almost remorseful.

"At one point in my youth, I did. But life has a way of taking what you desire and shoving it down a garbage disposal." He laughs at that, and I cling to the feeling it gives me. Lightness. I'm able to breathe. "How about you? Were there any dreams in a younger Bradshaw?"

His thumb gently coasts over my arm as he thinks. "I always wanted a family, but I knew I'd never get one. Not with the way I am and the underground world that my brother and I fell into. I wouldn't be a good father."

My chin lifts so I can look into his eyes. He doesn't break his stare from the ceiling. His thumb just continues to stroke my skin slowly.

"Are you lonely?" I ask, knowing the desire for family but fearing it because of the way I am. It'd be impossible.

He chuckles sadly. "I wasn't." His voice has an implying lilt. Bradshaw shifts to his side so he's facing me. "But after you... I feel lonely whenever you're not around." His eyes are like ice shards straight into my heart.

Does he really feel that way? I can sense myself withdrawing and ready to end the conversation because it's getting too personal. But each time I think I can slip away, he pulls me right back with that smile.

"We should think about what our plan is. We can't stay here long." I change the subject. If he notices, he doesn't make it known.

He nods and lets his head fall to the side so his lips touch my head. "Let's get some sleep first. I'm fading fast."

Although sleep finds him quickly, I'm left staring at the ladder that leads up. The motion sensors cut out at some point and plunge us into darkness.

thirty-one

. . .

BRADSHAW KNEELS BESIDE ME AS WE SCRUB OUR UNIFORMS FREE of the excess blood and mud. Normally I wouldn't care too much about the dirty gear, but with the rain and stickiness of the blood, the material is too stiff to perform well in.

We've been sorting out ideas all afternoon, ranging from trying to regroup with the squad so Bradshaw can explain things to Eren so he doesn't want me dead, to proceeding as planned with the mission and hopefully running into Malum there.

"That's stupid," I retort, drawing my jacket from the water and shaking it out. I hang it on the clothesline we crafted from the rope Bradshaw used to bind my wrists.

"He'll listen to me, Bunny," he barks back. He sounds much more like himself today. He got his fight and banter back with rest. So have I.

Will he? Clearly Eren brought me here for a reason.

"I'm not so sure he will."

Bradshaw stops midway as he lifts his shirt over the clothesline and shoots me a glare. "We can't take the enemy fortress alone."

The exasperated breath I blow out has his jaw muscles feathering. "Can't we? I'm going to find out who's trying to kill you and finish the mission. Once they're dead, I don't care what happens to me. With or without the Malum Squad."

He shakes his head. "Stop talking like that."

"Why? Your brother won't let me live and I'm not even close to getting my cards—" I lower my head and stare at the bright tiles of the bathroom. The fluorescent lights flicker above.

Bradshaw moves to stand in front of me. "And?" His voice is back to being cruel and it makes me smile.

"So even if I come back from this mission, it's not like I can stay with you. They'll set you free while I remain a dark forces weapon."

Fury flashes across his eyes and he tips my chin up so I meet his gaze. "You think I'd let them keep you here without me?" I hold his stare. Steady and unmoving.

"I don't see what choice you have." I shove him back playfully and he doesn't waste a second before he's backing me into the mirror wall. My skin burns with its icy sting.

Bradshaw's eyes search mine desperately, a mix of emotions tangling inside him. "You almost sound like you want me to go without you." He presses his palms against the mirror on either side of my head.

I tilt my lips to his. "What if I do?"

His brow arches and he guides me away from the mirror by a few inches before he smashes his fist into it.

The mirror shatters and glass shards crash to the floor. When I stare into Bradshaw's eyes, only obsession burns there. He pushes his forehead against mine and pins my wrist to the wall. I don't fight him—I only stare back with the same lust and confusion eating my sanity away.

He presses his knee between my thighs.

"Are you trying to scare me? It's not working," I whisper against his temple.

"Trust me. If I wanted to scare you, you'd be scared. I'm only getting you excited," he murmurs back, his warm breath on my lips.

Then he kisses me. It's violent and passionate all at once. The pressure on my wrists increases and draws a mewl from my lips. Bradshaw quickly devours the sound with his own deep groan. He coaxes my mouth open and our tongues quickly tangle together fervently.

"Fuck," he moans into my mouth as he presses his groin to my core. His bulge sends an excited thrum through my entire body. He loosens his hold on my wrists and pulls me to the bench on the opposite wall.

"Wait." I gasp as he pushes me down on the bench and spreads my legs. I'm in nothing but the white oversized T-shirt and my undies. My hands come down over the shirt in a feeble attempt to cover my center. Partly because I'm embarrassed by how wet I already am and because we don't have time for this. We should be devising a plan to infiltrate the hostile base, not fighting and fucking and… whatever it is we're doing.

He looks up at me, dark strands of hair falling over his forehead, making my heart patter faster. "Wait for what? Don't tell me you're shy now. Does that mean you care about me, Bun?" His lip turns up and I shake my head.

"No. I mean—we don't have time," I babble, trying to find the words.

He laughs as he pries my hands away from my shirt and sets them on the edge of the bench. "Baby, who cares? We have all the time we need."

I shudder as he slips my underwear to the side and

strokes a finger through my wet slit. My thighs instantly try to close, but he catches my knee.

"Now, I want you to think long and hard about who's eating you from the inside out while I lap you up. I want you screaming *my* name. I want you to be as possessive as I am of you." His voice drips with lust.

I'm already possessive of you, I want to shout over and over, but my pride won't let me. What does that say about me? How depraved and starved I am for a man like him?

I guess I'm about to find out.

"Stare into the mirror and watch me consume you. I won't stop until you're trembling in my arms." He slips a mirror shard into my hand. "And I want you to punish me until you can forgive me for what I've done to you. For *everything.* I want you to make your mark on me, Bunny. Punish me so *I* can forgive me," he begs in a low voice.

The glass shard is as big as my combat knife. My eyes meet his as he dips closer to my core. "Eyes on the mirror. Watch me eat you. Watch yourself draw my blood."

What the fuck. Why am I so aroused by everything he says? Everything he does.

I let my eyes focus on the reflection. My cheeks are red, my dark braid messy, and my eyes roll seductively. Bradshaw is on his knees before me.

I find my voice. "Strip naked," I command.

He strokes his hot tongue up my center like an animal and removes his boxers at the same time. His obedience is new and it makes his tongue teasing swirls around my clit all the more sensual. My back arches and I let out a moan.

Bradshaw pulls away for only a second to take his shirt off before eagerly returning to my pussy like it's the best damn thing he's ever had.

I'm aware I've seen this man naked, fucked him, and have had the absolute displeasure of being his second for countless hours. But this is different and I can't seem to place why.

The hard planes of his body are bare. His back muscles flex as he spreads me out and sucks on my clit. A jolt of pleasure and pain shoots up my stomach and I writhe. But anger coils in my chest. I'm letting him pleasure me when only yesterday he was going to kill me.

I put that glass shard he gave me to use, sitting up, fisting his hair, and shoving his face roughly into my center. He groans and grips my thighs as he pushes his tongue as far as it will go inside me. I suppress the moan and focus on pressing the edge of the glass into the middle of his back, between two long knife-like scars.

"Carve me up," he murmurs against my clit before sucking in my sensitive flesh and making my vision blur with pleasure.

My orgasm builds and with sheer will alone I keep it from climaxing as I cut into his flesh. Bright blood rolls down his back and deviates over the grooves in his hips before dripping to the tiles below. He grunts and fists his cock with one hand.

This is for all the terrible things he did to me. This is for betraying me and humiliating me. For slicing my ribs and for choking me. For all the fucked up shit this evil man has done. But most of all, I do it because I forgive him. Because I want to leave my mark on his skin forever like he did mine. I want to own him as much as he craves to dominate me.

I cut the design until I'm satisfied and the anger inside my chest is satiated. Until I can't hold out any longer. The shard falls to the ground and clammers. Bradshaw shoves two fingers into me and rubs against my inner walls, flicking my clit with his hot tongue until I'm finally trembling with the orgasm. I brace both hands on his shoulders and cling for life as my hips buck involuntarily and I come all over his face.

He strokes his tongue through my center over and over, devouring me and groaning. I watch through hooded eyes in the mirror. Bradshaw slowly moves up on me, kissing my hip bone and licking up my stomach and chest. His eyes slowly rise up to mine and I bite my lower lip as need starts to build in my core again.

"You are where my sanity starts," he murmurs gravely, his jaw setting and brows knitting. He hates to admit these things to me—that much is obvious. But it warms my chest that he shares it with me anyway.

"You are where mine ends," I whisper back. His eyes soften as he leans up and kisses me. Our souls collide. He wraps his palm around the back of my head and coaxes my lips apart with his tongue, deepening the kiss. I let out a soft moan as he adorns me with his affection. His lips aren't demanding like before, not filled with animosity and rage. Each stroke of his tongue against mine is eager and curious. Soft and longing.

Bradshaw palms my breast and nudges my legs apart. I spread my thighs for him and he brings his hips to mine. His swollen cock is hot on my skin. Pre-come beads at the tip and smears across my stomach as he wraps his arms around my lower back and lifts me up. My legs instinctively loop around his torso and he chuckles darkly as his cock throbs between our flesh. I swallow hard.

"I like this shy side of you. It's cute." Bradshaw nips at my lips and gives me a provocative raise of his brow. He carries me to the edge of the bathtub and turns on the water. Steam rolls as the tub fills and my pulse steadily increases with each stroke of his thumb against my collarbone.

"I'm not being shy." It comes out higher than my usual tone and I die a little inside.

He smiles warmly and it hits me in the gut how sweet and unlike himself it is. "It's okay, Bun, you can be yourself around me. You don't have to always be tough. Let your walls down for once." He smooths his hand over my thigh as he positions himself at my entrance. My head falls back as he stretches my core with his dick. I brace my hands against the rim of the tub. He grabs my hips and buries his fingers into my flesh as he starts to pump into me.

I cry out as he pushes to the hilt.

"That's it, baby, you take me in so fucking good. Does it feel good when I stretch you out?" he says against my lips, thrusting into me at an agonizingly slow pace.

"Fuck yes," I mumble as I kiss him. He groans and sets a ruthless pace, gripping my ass and fucking me so hard my eyes start to water. My moans bounce on the walls of the metal-framed bunker.

My pussy grips his cock tightly as I climax. My entire body seizes and I dig my nails into his shoulders. Bradshaw groans and picks up his pace, staring down at where we are joined together and making a fucking mess.

"You're going to take all my come and you better not spill a drop of it." He grits his teeth together and the veins in his neck bulge. He ruts into me one final time and the force of it almost pushes me into the tub filling with water. His dick throbs inside me, filling me with his hot seed.

Bradshaw holds me tightly, our bodies still pressed together. The only motion is our breaths and the pulsing of him deep in my stomach. After his balls stop seizing and his breathing becomes even, he pulls away from me enough to share my gaze. We seem to come to the same conclusion. His pale blue eyes are alight with winter embers, flickering with the emotions a broken man has long since sealed away. I find secrets and words I'm unsure he's ready to say. And a part of me wonders if he reads the same sad lines in my gaze too.

I love you. I shouldn't, but I do.

thirty-two

. . .

NELL

BRADSHAW DRAWS OUT THE MAP FROM MEMORY ON THE TILE floor with a marker. He circles our location and taps where the Ghosts' headquarters is. "It's a day and a half walk from the bunker we're at now. If we keep close to the ridge line of the western mountain that follows near the remaining bunkers, we can keep an eye out for Eren and the rest of Malum."

I nod, but worry sits cumbersomely on my chest. "What if they attack me? I'm not so sure Eren will be willing to talk."

Bradshaw leans in close and smooths his hand over mine. I meet his gaze. "They won't. Eren won't tell them about his order to get rid of you. He'd never share the details of his shady side dealings."

"Don't you worry about what he's *not* telling you?" I query.

He shakes his head as his brows knit. "No. If it's impor-

311

tant, I already know about it. Anyway, you don't need to worry. I trust my brother."

Well, that doesn't make me feel better.

I doubt Eren tells him everything necessary. It's sad how ignorant to corruption we all are when we care about a person. I never noticed how cold-hearted Jenkins truly was, not when I was by his side.

"You're betting my life on that? I think he wants me dead no matter what."

Bradshaw lets out a breath. "Have faith in me."

I roll my eyes. "Like I have any other choice. You know the way in once we find their headquarters, right?" Bradshaw shakes his head and I groan, adding: "We can figure it out when we get there. I'm more worried about Eren than a security system to break."

He stares at the map for a few seconds before nodding and muttering, "Yeah, me too."

———

The uniforms dry by nightfall. We're dressed with masks pulled over our faces, ready to reenter the cold world above. My lungs are filled with fire. Who is targeting the dark forces? Eren knows, yet he won't even tell Bradshaw. It unsettles me that Eren knew how lethal I was. If he genuinely knew about my hand in Abrahm's death all along, why would he put me as Bradshaw's second?

I mull over those thoughts while Bradshaw tightens his vest and he finally gives the signal for *move out*. He starts to climb the ladder. I grab a step and start to haul myself up behind him.

BOOM.

The ground shakes and the fluorescent lights switch to red before we can even react to the aftershocks. Bradshaw looks over his shoulder at me and makes the hand signal for *fall back.* I hold my M16 tightly across my chest and duck behind the bathroom door. Bradshaw is a second behind me and takes the other side of the door. We both watch the bunker hatch, guns raised and ready.

I focus, listening for any footsteps, but there are too many to determine how many people are up there. It's an ambush. The Ghosts know we're down here. *Fuck!*

"Here they come," Bradshaw mutters as he pulls the pin to a flash grenade with his teeth. He times it perfectly, boots hitting the ground just as he tosses it. I shut my eyes against the flash of white. The second the light goes out I set my gun down and unsheathe my combat blade.

"Bunny, use your M16," Bradshaw hisses at me, but the weight of his words is lost as two soldiers rush into the bathroom. They were expecting us to be behind the door, but not from so low. I don't wait to see who it is and my blade is thrusting up before the man has any clue who he's fucking with.

The soldier notices at the last second and blocks my blade from being buried in his gut. I twist my hold on the handle to keep him from knocking it out of my hand with his counterblow. The butt of his gun hits my forearms. Pain crackles through my bones and I gnash my teeth at the ferocity this man fights with.

They have specialized training, but their goal is obviously to detain us. I can tell he's trying not to kill me. *Big mistake on their part.*

I sweep my leg across his feet and he hits the ground hard. His gun fires and shatters the mirrors. *Shit!* We're in a metal box. Loose bullets will be a problem if they ricochet.

My eyes flick to Bradshaw—he's wrestling a soldier to the ground and both their guns are two feet away from them. More voices sound from the other room. If we can't get control in the next few seconds, we're fucked.

His uniform looks familiar. It takes me by surprise. He takes advantage of my pause and grips my face mask. He rips it off, stinging the back of my ears. I clutch my knife and tear it behind the soldier's knees, severing the tendons. His legs go limp and he screams in pain. I take the chance his hysteria brings and go for his throat. My blade glides smoothly across his soft flesh and his pupils enlarge with the endorphins.

His body slacks instantly to the side. I grab my M16 and put three bullets into the soldier beneath Bradshaw just as he snaps his neck.

"I had him." Bradshaw glares at me, but I ignore him and kick him his gun. His mask was torn off in the scuffle, his bottom lip bleeding. He picks it up and stands in one fluid motion. "Night vision," he orders, knocking his goggles down over his eyes and shooting out the lights above us. I pull mine down too.

Going dark is the best option we have.

I shoot the ones in the main area and the bunker goes pitch black. The backup soldiers must've returned up the ladder because the room is empty. *Shit!* The hatch is open and I'd bet money they're waiting for us up there. We can't stay holed up in here forever; all they have to do is wait for reinforcements.

Bradshaw grips my wrist and I hesitantly look at him. He signals for me to follow him. He leads us to the cabinets and opens one door, motioning for me to get in. He pulls his goggles up and raises an implying brow. I shoot him a look that says, Are you crazy? but he just flattens his eyes more at me.

Goddammit. I crawl inside and he makes his way in beside me.

"Great. Now what?" I breathe uneasily. The space is cramped and although I can see with my night vision my stomach curls uneasily with our predicament.

Bradshaw gives me a shit-eating grin and pushes on the

inner wall of the cabinet. The thin board slides out of place, revealing a narrow tunnel that likely leads somewhere outside.

"Did you think Eren would plan on having our squad stay in a bunker with only one way in and out? I thought you were a bunny. That's like rule number one for animals, isn't it?" He laughs and I can't help but smile at his cocky comment.

I nudge him. "Let's get the fuck out of here."

He takes the lead, crawling on his hands and knees with his gun slung over his back. I slip inside the damp tunnel and close the board behind us in case the soldiers think to check the cabinets. The air here is earthy and thick with moisture.

The walls grow tight around us as we crawl and when Bradshaw turns to check on me for a second, I don't see him. I see Jenkins. He reaches his hand out for me. That's right... I've been in a tight place like this before.

"You can die anywhere, Gallows, but you don't want to die in a hole. So get the fuck out. Save the panic attack for after you're out."

I smile. He was an asshole, yet his words are what I need to keep going.

It can't be more than a few minutes, but it feels so much longer before we see moonlight dripping through an exit. Bradshaw stops and listens for several minutes to gauge where the hostiles are. I can't hear anything above my pulse hammering in my ears.

Bradshaw moves thoughtfully, quietly pushing through branches and exiting the tunnel. I wait for his signal. A second later, he dips his hand back inside and beckons me to follow.

Relief overcomes me as I hurry out of the tight space. Once I'm out, I move beside Bradshaw and we walk carefully through the underbrush. I'm facing a wall of trees.

There's no sign of hostiles, but I'm not letting my guard down now that they know we're out here.

We find cover half a klick east and crouch low to regroup and determine our backup plan. I keep my hand curled tightly around my knife. It's already slick with blood, parts of the handle sticking to my glove as it dries. Bradshaw checks his gear and points northeast. "That way. We're going to push until we hit the ridgeline and can find cover." His voice is low and firm.

I clutch my knife tighter.

"Did you see their uniforms?" My throat is raw from the fight and I sound scared. *I am scared.*

Bradshaw's concerned expression tells me everything. He nods.

My hand trembles. "And what did you see?"

He stares at me briefly before muttering, "It was the Hades Squad." He hangs his head and shakes it.

I thought so. I scan the forest warily for them. What the fuck are they doing? We are here to save *them,* aren't we?

"Bones... what does this mean?" I bring my focus back to him.

He lets his hands hang off his knees before lifting his head up. "It means we're fucked. If Hades is a part of this rogue operation, then who's to say who else is? This is bad. *Really* fucking bad." Bradshaw sounds uneasy. Nervous. And I've never known him to be nervous.

"Focus. Let's get out of here before they hunt us down." I tug on his arm and he stands, but his will to fight seems to have fled his spirit.

"God, this is so fucked up," he chokes out. He clasps his hands around his head and his shoulders tremble. *Fuck,* don't tell me he's having an episode.

I smack his cheek to see how together he has it and his head tilts, lagging to correct. *Goddammit!* "Bones, hey. Look at me. Bones!" I whisper-shout, but his body starts to slump against me.

No, no, no. What am I supposed to do?

Snap.

My head jerks to the left in the direction of the tunnel and spot three soldiers slowly sweeping the area for us. This couldn't be a worse situation. My chest clammers and my mind whirls.

Leave him. Run. My instincts have my legs twitching, but I refuse to leave him vulnerable like this. "It looks like this is where our mission together ends. Find Eren," I whisper against his parted lips. I kiss him gently before rolling him under the thickest part of the underbrush. I army crawl far enough before I'm ready to draw attention away from him.

This is suicide.

I stand and take off sprinting through the trees. Small branches and twigs smack loudly against my gear and a sharp shout rolls through the air behind me. *Good. They'll follow me.* I take off toward the river and ignore the shots they fire at me.

I'll get them as far away from Bradshaw as I can and then I'll take care of them. I slide on the beach sand and roll to my stomach, facing the pursuers, M16 aimed at the top of the riverbank. The first soldier that runs over the edge gets a bullet in his neck and the force of it sends him flying to his back. He squirms and covers his throat.

Two more rise over the bank and I fire at the one to the left.

Miss. Shit!

He shoots back and hits my shoulder. The impact alone takes my breath away, but I grit my teeth and shoot a second time. This time I hit him right in the dick. He screams and falls, rolling down the slope and crying like a fucking baby. I smile against the pain that blooms across my shoulder.

The third soldier is on me by the time I face him. He has

his knife unsheathed and goes for a thigh stab. I roll in time so he only nicks my calf, but the blood still pours from the wound instantly.

"Fuck you, bitch. You killed my partner!" He stabs at me again and this time he lodges it in my forearm. I scream at the pain and muster all my strength to strike him across the head with my gun. He's a tough motherfucker, he doesn't even flinch as blood gushes from the gash above his left eye. He grabs my arm with his knife sticking out of it and pounds it against the ground until I drop my M16.

A guttural scream rips from my throat and tears spring to my eyes, but I refuse to give up. I'll kill this asshole and anyone else who comes for us.

I buck my hips up as hard as I can and send him flying over my head. I roll to my side and unhitch my pistol from its holster—*bang, bang, bang.* I shoot him at point-blank range in his chest, but he's still coming. *Bulletproof vest—high grade too.*

"Fuck—" I choke out as his hands come around my throat and he pins me against the sand. His grip leaves no air, no hope of finding breath without knocking him off of me.

I gnash my teeth together and grab the knife that's still lodged between my radial and ulnar bone. *One, two, three.* I brace myself and pull the knife from my flesh, cutting his throat all the way to the bone with the same singular motion.

His body spasms violently and then slacks. He gurgles blood all over me. "Fuck you. Fuck you!" I scream at him as his eyes start to widen with death. I bury the knife between his collarbone and neck five times until it's mushy. His blood spills over my chest and neck.

I stagger to my feet and take a few labored breaths. The cold mountain air makes all the blood spilled on the sand steam in plumes.

My entire body trembles with adrenaline. The pain

spreads with each breath I take. I know if I can't stop the bleeding I'll be dead in twenty minutes.

Gasps and groans bring my mind out of its fog. I look slowly up and stare hollowly at the last two breathing soldiers. I limp to the closest one. He's still holding his throat and trying to keep himself from bleeding out. I bury my knife deep into his chest. He convulses and chokes on his own blood before going still.

For some reason, I think of Jenkins as I jerk the blade from the soldier's lungs. He loved killing this closely—loved making me do it too. I did anything he wanted me to, even if I hated it. And I do hate killing this sloppily.

That leaves only one man left. I look over at him, holding his dick and still crying about it. He sees me coming and tries to flee but I keep my limping stride steady. I reach him and tear off his helmet and mask. A scared man stares at me. He shakes uncontrollably.

I keep my tone as smooth as I can. "Are you going to tell me anything or am I wasting my time?" I lift my blade and he gasps, tears and snot mixing down his chin. His eyes trail over to his comrades, the ones I fucking butchered.

He shakes his head, eyes hardening. "Kill me."

"Done," I chirp, twisting the blade in my hand for the killing blow.

A sharp knife caresses my throat, giving me pause.

"Drop it." A deep voice seeps into my spine.

Jenkins taught me how to escape this very situation, although I'm fuzzy now with the blood loss. I breathe and slowly lower my arm as if to drop my weapon. Then I throw my head back against the man's face and grip the sharp part of his blade so it's not against my throat. My helmet strap is cut and flies off in the attack.

Blood spurts from my glove and my fingers go limp. *Shit.* Adrenaline keeps me moving. I reach for my pistol but the soldier already has his pressed against my forehead.

319

I breathe like a wild animal who's just run out of options. My chest rises and falls over and over with great burden. I expected him to pull the trigger already, so I slowly look up at him. His black mask covers the majority of his face, but those eyes... They're practically black as they bore into me vehemently.

I shudder but hold his stare.

"Always look them in the eye. Show them you aren't afraid to die," Jenkins told me many times. I do my best to follow his words.

The soldier stands silently for a long time. I'm starting to feel dizzy and my head bobs a few times before he pulls his gun a few inches away.

"Who are you?" he asks.

I don't move a muscle. I just continue to stare at him, waiting patiently for the bullet in my head.

He lets a sharp breath push between his teeth as he lowers to my level and studies my face, letting his eyes linger on my scars and neck tattoo. I lower my chin, but he grips my jaw tightly and forces me to look at him. He holds my face like this for a moment, his gun to the side of my head.

He clicks on his headset and mutters, "It's her."

He doesn't get to say anything else before a bullet flies straight between his eyes. His head is thrown back and I stare down at his lifeless body.

Who was he reporting to?

thirty-three

. . .

BRADSHAW STUMBLES TO MY SIDE AND BENDS AT HIS KNEE, looking over at the dead soldiers. He looks confused, but clearer now. His eyes aren't distant anymore.

"Bunny, are you okay?" When I don't respond, he manually searches my body for wounds and pauses each time he finds my flesh bleeding profusely. He swallows as he curls my sliced hand into itself with a cloth between my fingers to staunch the bleeding. He immediately moves to my forearm next.

"He said *'It's her'* to someone." I look Bradshaw in the eyes and search for secrets he might be harboring. "Who was he talking to?"

Bradshaw's eyes harden and his lack of response makes me twist in his hold as he tourniquets my arm at the elbow and wraps the stab wound tightly. My eyes narrow in agony and I try to stay focused.

"Who?" I demand.

"Bun, I don't think—"

Why is he keeping this from me? If he knows who the leader of the Ghosts is, why didn't he just fucking tell me? My heart hammers with the emotions.

"Tell me now or I'll blow your brains out," I say in a low, threatening tone and press the head of my handgun to the bottom of his throat.

He doesn't even blink.

"No," he says calmly and presses his forehead to mine, stealing a kiss and staring into my eyes, pleading silently for me to stop. "If you're going to kill me, then do it. It's not as easy as you'd think—"

Click.

His eyes widen and I whisper softly against his lips, "*Boom.*"

He smacks the empty gun out of my hand and glares at me. Horror spreads over his features. "Did you know it was empty? *Fuck*, Bunny, you make me so goddamn crazy." He grips my jaw hard, hand trembling. He shakes his head before resuming damage control on my body. He works on my shoulder next—I'm lucky it was just a clean flesh shot.

"Why won't you tell me?" My thoughts trail back to Eren. He's still protecting his brother... Is it Eren? My stomach sinks.

Bradshaw keeps his brows pinched as he works on me. I guess he really won't tell me.

"Of course I knew it was empty... I can keep my head even when I'm at my limit. Are *you* okay? You completely unplugged earlier. *You're welcome*, by the way, for saving your ass." I shove his chest. He ignores me as he finishes with my shoulder.

"I'm okay." His voice is gravelly and not at all convincing. He taps his head. "I'm fucked up, remember?" He tries to act like it's no big deal, but the weight of his words between us is heavy. He helps me up and I falter once I'm on my feet.

"Bones…" I start, but he puts his finger to my lips.

"No more talking. We need to get to the ridgeline before dawn. I'm guessing reinforcements will be on their way here." Bradshaw leads the way back up the riverbank, stopping briefly to make sure the coast is clear before we silently trek back into the forest.

My wounds slow us down and we have to stop to tend to them again before continuing. Bradshaw gives me one shot of morphine and the relief is so sweet I could cry. We only have a couple of them and I was hoping we could save them for when shit really hits the fan.

I sit and stare into the treetops, exhausted and fading as he picks me up. Next thing I know the trees are moving and it feels like I'm floating. Bradshaw's hands grip mine tightly and he keeps whispering something repeatedly. *"Hold on to me. It's okay. It's okay. I won't let you go."* I smile, aloof and drugged, but at least the pain from the wounds is gone. All I smell is his brisk scent and the pine trees.

By the time we reach the ridgeline, most of the drugs have worn off and the sun is coming up.

Bradshaw sets me down and covers us with foliage. He bends down next to me. He looks tired, but I know we won't be resting for long. We have to keep moving.

"How are you feeling?" Bradshaw whispers, checking each injury to make sure they haven't bled through the bandages again. The one that throbs the most is the gash in my forearm. Without medical attention, I'm not sure how long I can keep going before the meds stop working. Bradshaw's patch job probably won't hold longer than a few days.

I let my head fall back against the rock we're up against. "Like shit, but I'll manage."

He nods. "Two hours of rest and then we need to move," he says sternly, but his body must be weary because he lets his shoulder connect with mine. His head eventually meets my forehead before I start to doze off. He threads his fingers through mine and whispers, "I'm so sorry, Bun. I should have been by your side in that fight. I'm so fucking sorry." His thumb brushes mine soothingly.

If anyone can do this, it's us.

I hold onto those thoughts long after I fall asleep and long after I wake up. I think about it as we walk fifteen kilometers north through rain and freezing winds. We don't talk as we move; we only keep our hands on our guns and listen for any foreign sounds.

I watch Bradshaw move through the rocky terrain with ease, his muscles flexing with each step. Jenkins's voice rolls like smoke through my memories.

"Careful who you let hold your heart, Gallows. There are wolves out there. You know the saying, right? Fool me once, shame on you. Fool me twice, I'll bury you."

I stared at him like some love-sick pup.

He only laughed and pressed his hand to my cheek. "I know you'd never let me down. But you need to remember this for those you let close to you. Make sure they know it."

Bradshaw has fooled me twice. I'm still not sure what I want to do about it.

He stops and turns to look back at me. His goggles are up on his helmet and all I get are his icy eyes. "We're getting close to the last bunker. I don't know what's waiting there, but we need to stake out and watch until nightfall. We'll move out once we're sure no one is flanking us."

I nod and he lifts a brow at me.

"No arguing?" he taunts.

My eyes narrow. "You're in charge, Bones." A self-satisfied expression extends over his face.

"That must've felt like shit to admit."

I smack his arm and he laughs. "Don't make me eat those words."

He seems to be in a good mood for our circumstances and I can't help but let the energy seep into myself too. The drugs help, but his smile goes deeper.

"Think you can call me *sir* from now on too?"

"Whatever you'd like, sir." I don't miss a beat. He grins and is about to fire off something else to ruffle my feathers when an explosion brings us to our knees.

My eyes snap up to the bunker a quarter-klick away. Fire plumes from the underground quarters and shakes the earth with aftershocks. Bradshaw stands and rushes for the bunker.

"Bones!" I shout, voice raspy from the smoke already invading my throat.

He doesn't listen to me and continues to run toward the fire. *Fuck. He's probably worried Eren was in there.* My eyes lift to the sky to make sure it wasn't a grenadier. There's no trail from a launcher, so I rule that out. It seems too convenient to be an accident.

I stand and chase after Bradshaw, keeping my eyes on the forest wall surrounding the meadow and becoming keenly aware when I enter the burning debris how much easier it is for them to see me rather than the other way around.

Bradshaw kneels near the bunker. The flames are no longer licking out from the blown-off hatch, but the fire still burns below. I grab his shoulder with one hand and squeeze.

"We need to get out of the open. *Now*," I hiss at him.

He stares into the inferno below like it's hell's gates before he looks at me. "I don't smell burning flesh." His voice carries more relief than I thought I'd ever hear from him.

I nod. "Good. Let's go."

Bradshaw's eyes widen just as he's about to stand and he shoves me down. My back falls against the smoldering ashes as he takes a bullet to the chest. Another bullet flies and takes a piece of his left ear. He staggers back before lifting his M16 and firing off a few rounds above me. My chin tips up and I watch as a soldier jerks back from the bullets and falls to the side. Four more soldiers flank him and Bradshaw doesn't waste a second. He forces me to my feet and we run for the cover of the trees.

"Are you okay?" I assess his chest.

He nods. "It just got my plates." I look at his bleeding ear. A portion of it is gone and the sight of him bleeding and missing a part of himself makes my chest twist painfully.

"Damn it. So much for us trying to infiltrate their head-quarters without detection," Bradshaw mutters once we reach the trees and fall to the ground, splayed out on our bellies.

I pull out my sniper rifle and quickly wipe the scope, wincing at the pain as I try to steady my aim. "That explosion would've given us away anyway. Do you think Eren set it off?" I load a round and fire it. The closest soldier's head tilts back and he's down.

"Nice," Bradshaw mutters as he waits for the ones I don't pick off to get in range. "I hope not. That would be really fucking stupid and Eren is anything but stupid."

Sweat rolls down my temple as I pull the trigger again. Another headshot. There are only two left. If it wasn't Eren, then was it Hades?

"Maybe they thought we were in there," I say slowly, firing again but missing this one. "Shit."

Bradshaw lifts his M16 and pops the guy I missed. He hits his shoulder and throat and the soldier falls. That leaves just one.

"Maybe, but that doesn't feel right either." Bradshaw looks troubled and it distracts me from the last soldier charging us. I let my partner finish him off, watching thoughtfully as he falls ungracefully. What a stupid approach. They just ran at us, knowing we had the better cover and upper hand.

Sharp fear prickles through me.

No.

I turn too late. Men are on top of us before we can react.

thirty-four

. . .

NELL

"FUCK, THIS ONE BIT ME!" THE SOLDIER SEATED ON TOP OF ME shouts. He punches me square in the jaw and the world flickers for a second. My head drops back and he fucking laughs at my slackened, defeated state.

I try to stay alert, but remaining conscious is the best I can do for now. Two men restrain me and tie up my wrists. Bradshaw fights viciously. Our eyes catch multiple times as he thrashes and stabs a few of them with his knife. It's not a fair fight—ten to one.

He doesn't have a chance, but he takes out three of them before they get a hold of him. If they were intending to kill us we'd already be dead. The dread of what's to become of us builds inside my chest.

Bradshaw is thrown to the ground and three soldiers dressed in black Hades gear use the back of their guns to break his body. All I can do is watch as silent tears fall from

---

my eyes. Bradshaw grunts and protects his head as his ribs and back get the brunt of the assault.

Part of me breaks as I watch them ruin my cruel, lovely partner. In these moments that feel like eternity, I realize that this might be it for him. With each groan and pained glance he steals at me, my heart shatters irrevocably.

"That's enough. We need *both* of them alive," snaps one of the soldiers. The others stop and chuckle as they lift up Bradshaw. His head hangs as they force him to walk between them. Bradshaw can barely stay on his feet. He watches me through swollen eyes and blood that trickles down his face. The man carrying me tosses me over his shoulder like a sack of potatoes—his arms are hooked around my knees while my torso hangs down his back.

I wish I could hear Bradshaw's thoughts. I know I should be thinking of how to get out of this situation, but all I can ponder is what his kisses would be like in a life different than this. What books he hasn't read yet. How many nights we'd stay up late and watch TV until we fall asleep.

I hold onto those warm dreams for as long as I can, but they fade as we're taken to their fortress. The forest breaks and opens to a meadow. A lake sparkles in the moonlight in the distance. But the fortress is by far the most gripping sight.

The building looks new, the walls still untouched by the weather. The frame is cream-colored and modern, with black vertical windows, doors, and edges. It's in the shape of a rectangle and the smooth matted surface almost makes it look like a natural rock formation. Once we get closer, the camouflaged exterior paint is more noticeable and it's evident how they've been able to keep such a low profile out here. Armed men stand every twenty feet of the damn place and my hopes sink further into my chest as we pass four auto-locking doors.

What the fuck is this place? Who pays for all of this? The soldier finally sets me on my feet once we reach an elevator. Bradshaw is kept from entering and it's just me and two soldiers in the contained space.

A surge of panic rushes through me at the idea of being separated from him and I thrash, screaming and fighting to get to Bradshaw. His head is limp. Tousled, blood-smeared hair and flexed shoulders are all I get to see before the doors close.

My body stills and the men wrestle me back between them. "Damn, that was cold. He didn't even look at you." The one that carried me chuckles. His eyes move down my figure and it raises the hair on the back of my neck. He cups a hand between my thighs.

Bile rises in my throat. I know what happens to hostages in remote, untouchable places like this one. I keep my mouth shut and try not to give away the terror circling inside my chest. These monsters like it when you're afraid. They get off on it.

I shut my eyes and ignore him as he continues to fondle me and whispers disgusting promises for what's to come later tonight in my cell. *Stay calm. You've trained for this.* Techniques on ripping off a dick from a male's body filter through my mind and keep me relatively calm.

It's a mercy when the doors finally open on the B4 floor. *We're underground.* At least the soldiers aren't being unnecessarily violent with me. I'll remember that when I'm killing them. I'll make it quick for the ones who don't touch me. *Handsy,* however, I'll gut the motherfucker after I cut his dick off and shove it down his throat.

The fourth level down is the cell block. It's the nicest mini prison I've ever seen and I've witnessed my share of how degrading and filthy they can be. It's clear these have never been used. The white tiles are shiny and reflect the bright fluorescent lights above. The cells aren't barred except for a small square at the top middle of each door for communication. Our footsteps echo in the empty hall; only one armed guard stands by the elevator.

They lead me to the end of the hall and unlock the door with a key card and a fingerprint. I eye Handsy as he walks me into my cell. It's a good sign that there's no blood in here. But that does little to ease my nerves.

Handsy's partner closes us in, waiting on the outside. I assess the room while he unbinds my wrists. It has a single twin-sized bed, a toilet, and a sink—nothing else. All white. It isn't a tacky, hastily thrown-together design either; it seems purposeful and neat. Its design is to drive whoever is kept in these white walls mad.

Our weapons were taken and left in the forest. I feel naked without them. My hands twitch at my sides as I consider taking this guy on. But I think better of it. I'd rather not take my chance until I know I can escape with Bradshaw.

I wonder why he wouldn't look at me. My eyes close. *Maybe I'm no longer useful now that I've been captured. What use are weapons once dulled?*

"The captain will have you two brought to his war room in an hour, so if I were you I'd get cleaned up. Maybe he won't kill you if he fancies you." Handsy smirks and his dead eyes send chills up my spine. I give him a subtle nod and he laughs before touching me again. This time he grabs my ass. "They said you were wild, but I like the submissive ones."

I want to rip his brains out with my bare fingers. I act the part and smile sweetly at him and it charms him more. He kisses me on the cheek before leaving and once the door is shut and I'm alone, I let myself fall to the center of the floor.

The room is cold. The vent above constantly blows air down, intentionally I'm sure, to make this room miserable. I draw my knees up to my chest and rest my head on my forearms as I listen for them to bring Bradshaw down the hall to his cell. But as the minutes turn into the hour, I realize he wasn't brought down to this floor like I was.

I go over torture tactics they might use and what my best options are.

The videos I watched in my very first trainings replay in my mind and I have to swallow the bile rising in my throat. *Please, God, not my nails.* Considering Handsy's advice, I wash my hands and face. I'm better off playing the sweet, non-murderous girl if that's what they'll see. Blood and dirt cling to the bleached sink. I get my uniform as clean as I can before redoing my braid, hoping it looks decent. It'd be nice if there was just one mirror in here.

The door finally clicks as the locks shift and in come two soldiers—Handsy and his companion. I check their uniforms for names or numbers but am met with symbols instead—a snake on their top pocket flaps.

"I knew you'd clean up nice," Handsy says smoothly, offering his hand rather than grabbing me. I'm not going to subject myself to aggressive treatment, not when I know I can make them vulnerable and confused with my body and sweet smiles. Not to mention, I'm in agony and am hoping they'll offer me morphine soon.

"Thank you..." I leave it open, hoping he'll at least tell me his name. I slide my hand on top of his and he pulls me toward him softly.

"Lee. This is Paul." Lee smiles at me and guides me out of the room, keeping a firm but not painful hold on my uninjured hand. At least they don't have me in bindings this time. That's a good sign that my acting is working.

I study the hall again as I'm marched down the cell block —ten rows of rooms before the end where mine is. I can't be certain that there's no one else down here, but the quiet and cleanliness heavily allude to it.

"Am I going to be interrogated, Lee?" I ask innocently. His fingers squeeze a little tighter around mine.

"Maybe a little, but I don't think he will hurt you, cutie. I mean, you're just unlucky to be teamed with that monster. Did you see what he did to our men by the river?" Lee sounds pissed.

Oh, shit. Do they think it was Bradshaw who did that? I'm in deep water if they find out I'm the one who cut up their friends. I'm a little ticked that they assume it couldn't have been me, but I'm the prisoner here, I'll take whatever mercies I can get until the time is right.

I nod dramatically. "He's ruthless. You should see the scars he's given me." Not exactly a lie.

Paul is quiet and he gives me a cold glance from my right side. It's evident he doesn't trust me, not like Lee already does. But I force big, fake tears and his expression softens as he notices the hand bruises on my neck before he looks away.

Fingers crossed the soldiers are all like these two.

We step into the elevator again and go up to the second floor. Lee and Paul seem nervous this time, so I don't have to suffer any unwanted fondling. I'm beginning to get skeptical about the luck I've been getting. At some point I think the torture is going to ensue.

The doors open to a wide showroom. It's enormous. The ceilings and walls are all made of glass, and the night sky is on display above. The auroras dance near the top of a distant mountain. The view is enough to stop your heart. The room is lit from below and metal panes that hold the glass double as lights. If I weren't bleeding and being held hostage, I'd think this was the world's most extravagant resort tucked in the remote mountains of Labrador.

Lee leads the way with me in tow. I let my eyes explore as much as I can, searching for any potential weak points in their defenses. I'm assuming all the glass is bulletproof because it would be irrational if it wasn't. There are armed soldiers every ten feet, focusing on us as I'm led in like a sacrificial lamb.

At the end of the grand showroom are large black double doors—modern and slick. Paul takes one, Lee the other. They open them at the same time and Lee whispers under his breath, "Have fun."

I stare at him before looking ahead into the next room. At its center lies Bradshaw, blood pooling around his still body. My muscles seize and I can't force my legs to move.

"In," Paul snaps at me.

All I can do is stare at my broken, beautiful soldier. Is he dead? My stomach lurches and I can't find the rhythm of my breath.

Please don't be dead. I need you.

Paul grows tired of my paralyzed state and shoves my back, making me trip into the room. The doors close behind me and I press my back against them.

I've never felt this way before… so scattered and unable to compose myself. Even when Jenkins died I could at least partially respond. I didn't look back as I left him behind. I wasn't immobilized, but with Bradshaw, I feel everything and nothing at once. The things I want to say, the secrets I should've shared.

My hand curls over my chest and I finally start to stagger toward his unmoving body.

"Bring her to me." A bored voice echoes through the room. Two soldiers standing idly by move to grab me. I let them drag me by the arms to the man who did this. But I don't let my eyes break from Bradshaw's form. I watch him intently, waiting for a cough or a seized breath, but he lies motionless.

The two men toss me to the floor and only then is my trance severed. I force myself to my hands, wincing at the pain that shoots straight through my palms. I hesitate before looking up.

"It's okay, you can look at me."

I look up and find a masked man sitting lazily atop an oakwood table. His palms are pressed to the edge as he leans forward to see me better. His mask is matte black and covers his entire face. It's in the shape of a skull and the eye sockets have a mesh screen that hides his eyes.

The silence that fills the room makes me uncomfortable. I start to look over my shoulder back at Bradshaw, but my jaw is caught in the man's hand and he turns my face back to his.

"You care about that guy?" He has no tone, just odd curiosity that sends shivers up my spine. I nod slowly. "Why?"

Why? That's a great question. But regardless of what the answer is, I do. I care about him more than I'll ever admit.

"Did you… kill him?" My voice is weak.

He throws his head back and laughs before hopping off the table. "Let's go find out." He fists my hair and pulls me over to Bradshaw on my hands and knees. I bite into my lower lip to keep from whimpering at the pain of him pulling on my scalp.

He releases me a few feet away and I crawl to close the distance, pulling the bleeding soldier into my lap and brushing his dark hair from his face. Shock rolls through me as I stare down at Bradshaw's face.

It's not him.

"E-Eren?" I choke out. His eyes crack open weakly, but I'm not sure he can see me before they close again. "You fucking monster!" I scream and clutch Eren's body as if I can protect him.

Eren's face is drenched in his blood. I wipe away the excess from his cheeks and don't see cuts, so the wound must be on top of his head somewhere. His arm is broken and hangs to his side lamely while his torso has the monopoly on injuries. His jacket is soaked and leaves blood all over me. It breaks my heart to see him this way.

Even if he lost faith in me—I failed to protect him.

The masked man laughs. "I guess he's still kicking then? Good, I'd hate for him to miss all the fun."

I seethe and rise to my feet. I charge at the man and try to punch him in the face but he dodges it and grabs my throat with one hand. The force of it is so powerful it stops all airflow and makes me audibly gasp. Both my hands fly to his arm as I try to fight out of his hold. I'm so weak already that I can hardly put up a worthy fight.

He laughs again and drops me. I fall to my knees and choke as I take staggered breaths. Tears fall to the ground and I shake my head. "Where is Bones?"

"Who? I don't know a *Bones*," he taunts me.

I rise again and try hand-to-hand combat a second time. This round, I'm fighting with a more level head rather than pure rage. I kick him square in the chest, but he doesn't fall back, he grips my ankle so I can't pull away and twists it. I cry out at the ugly snapping sound that rings through the room, but I don't let the pain stop me. I lift my other leg and kick his kidney. He instantly drops my leg and I don't waste a moment as he clutches his side. I rush him, tackling him to the ground and struggling to get on top of him so I can wring the life out of him.

The soldiers standing by tear me off him and throw me back.

"Coward!" I scream.

The man rises and laughs again. I battle to keep my mind in control. He knew seeing Eren like this would make me distraught. But who the fuck is he? And how long has Eren been here? Where is the rest of the squad? I fight the tears that burn the back of my eyes.

"Bring in the brother," he says as he turns to return to the table. He sits like the unruly king of this underground operation, bored and seeking entertainment from others' pain and suffering.

My spine stiffens and I turn as the doors open. Bradshaw limps in. He's in the same state as when we arrived. Which is still beat to shit, but far better off than his brother.

Bradshaw's eyes flick to Eren's body and he only flexes his jaw before looking back at the ground. He still doesn't meet my eyes and my heart wars against my ribs with terror. Why won't he fucking look at me?

It dawns on me finally. It's guilt. *He knows who's in charge, he knows what's going to happen to us.*

thirty-five

. . .

BUNNY WATCHES ME FROM THE MOMENT I STEP INTO THE WAR room. Her gaze burns on my skin like liquid nitrogen. I can't look at her. If I do, I'll lose it.

It's my fault we're here.

My weary eyes lift to the masked asshole, to one of the monsters I've come all this way to kill. He isn't the leader of the group, but it's clear he's one of the higher-ranked generals. *I know who I'm looking for.* The real question is if he'll come out to play.

No one is questioning what this guy is doing. I bet he's from the Hades Squad just from the sheer cockiness with which he sits back on that table. I know he's smiling under that mask of his. Eren was always just the appetizer. They want to hurt me the most. I'm the primary target. I always have been.

It cost me Abrahm. It might cost me Bunny.

God, I hope it doesn't. I won't survive it.

"Aw, why are you looking so glum? Here, I know what will cheer you two up." He slides off the table and meets me where I stop beside Bunny. She looks at me with horrified eyes, continuously glancing back at Eren. He'll pull through. He's been through worse.

I have to believe that or I might lose my head right now.

I keep my eyes lowered as the man lifts my chin. Bunny watches with deadly silence.

"*Oh!*" He laughs and bends over from the sick pleasure he's getting out of this. "*That's* why she thought you were the one dying. You're twins. I wish you could've seen how upset she was. It would've melted your heart." He releases my jaw roughly and circles my back. "She called you *Bones*. I must say, your useless brother has fucked up many things, but he didn't fuck up when it came to keeping you safe."

I grit my teeth and try to believe that the rest of Malum hasn't been captured. We're all going to die here if they have. Bunny looks at me again and this time I meet her worried eyes. She deflates at our connection and must feel the same dread and hopelessness I exert.

"Let's see *how* much she cares about you. Come." He offers his hand to her and I still. *No. He won't do this. He won't.* I jerk against the two men who restrain me, but they firm their grip on my bindings.

She stares at me, confused mostly, but her eyes tell me she knows I've had a hand in this. The betrayal in the set of her brow pierces straight through me. She slowly rises and walks to him.

I shake my head. "Bunny. Get away from him."

Her eyes hold pain, but more than that they hold resolve. I know then that she's accepted anything she'll have to do to get us out of here. I want to tell her she's being stupid. The captain will never let us go. *Never let her go.*

"I want you to play nice. If you do I won't put a bullet in your boyfriend's head, okay? Be good and no one dies," he says against her bruised face and I thrash on instinct against the bindings again to no avail.

She visibly shakes but nods slowly. He turns her so she's facing me and I instantly look away. I won't watch. I can't. But the men force me to the ground and a heavy boot comes down over my head, making me watch in their direction.

The man pulls his dick out and grips Bunny's throat. He's going to make her suck him off.

No. No. No.

I shout and struggle to stand. I manage to knock the guy standing on my head off and the second guy raises his M16 to shoot me before another booming voice fills the room.

"What's going on in here?"

Everyone stops and turns to look at the double doors.

A man dressed in black tactical gear stands with his hands behind his back. His eyes are cold and distant, his pale blond hair slicked to the side, but he doesn't look at anyone except my precious Bunny.

He takes her in like he's seeing a ghost. His dark brows lift and his sharp jaw feathers as he swallows.

Bunny's breath of shock moves through me like cold water. She murmurs as though she has seen a ghost as well, "Jenkins?"

thirty-six

. . .

Jenkins.

There he stands. Not a ghost. Not dead.

My mind is empty of everything that isn't him. I only see our history. Our wounds.

He looks older now. The scars around his left cheekbone are from the night I last saw him. Two long, curved lines make his right jawline more severe. His eyes were never this dark and heartless. What horrors has he seen to have grown more indifferent than he already was?

His eyes widen as he recognizes me. Jenkins always had a slim figure, but the black tactical uniform he wears reveals that he's bulked up in the past two years. There are so many things I want to ask him. So many things I want to say.

I can't tell if what I'm feeling is happiness or heartbreak. He's alive. But how could he be a part of this organization? What brought him to *this*?

Jenkins takes a few breaths before looking at the masked

man beside me. Darkness falls over his eyes when he sees the man's dick is still out and in his hand. My veins chill as Jenkins walks casually over to us. The dullness in his eyes starts my heart again. I'm only the most savage soldier because I learned from him. He taught me everything. His thoughts are my thoughts.

Bradshaw watches with confusion and concern in his gaze. Our eyes meet for only a second before Jenkins speaks and steals my attention away.

His voice is gravelly, low. One I never thought I'd hear again but cling to desperately.

"And what is it you think you're doing, Greg?" Jenkins asks with a completely blank expression. I watch quietly as Greg pulls off his mask and sets it at his side.

It's then that I realize Greg isn't the boss. My eyes lift back to Jenkins and he meets my gaze. Our souls linger for a moment, as if we're testing the waters of time. Do we still know each other? Would we still kill for each other?

Jenkins is the leader of the Ghosts.

My thoughts get interrupted as Greg swallows and mutters, "Uh, well I was just going to have fun with—" Jenkins doesn't wait for him to finish that sentence. He twirls his combat knife in his hand before plunging it into the side of Greg's skull.

I've seen him kill like this hundreds of times. Maybe more. I don't feel anything as Greg's body violently convulses on the end of Jenkins's blade before falling off the table and going still. Jenkins keeps hold of his knife and brain matter spills out. The gash in the side of Greg's head twitches with probably his last flashbacks, if that's even a mercy we get.

Jenkins takes a deep breath before removing his black gloves and dropping them on Greg's lifeless body. He turns his attention to me and casts a curious look at Bradshaw, whose glare isn't at all curious like Jenkins's.

"Hey, Gallows." His voice is midnight rain, his gaze filled with lost time and stolen kisses of the past.

It never made sense to me how quickly he could go from a murderer to a sweet-talking man in the blink of an eye.

My mouth firms with emotion. "Sir," I say as calmly as I can, but my trembling hands give away my feelings.

He brushes back the hair around my ear softly. I fight not to shut my eyes at the endearment. God knows I want to lean into it, into him.

"What are you doing all the way out here?" His voice still has that caring tone that he only held for me. My entire being wants to become lost in it.

I falter. "A mission. To rescue the Hades Squad and to stop… you." My heart is in my throat and he knows it. A few blond strands of hair fall over his forehead. He looks into my eyes like he's memorizing each second of this.

"Rescue the Hades Squad? They joined of their own volition. Why the fuck would they rather be imprisoned to the dark forces than be a part of something so much bigger? They don't need to be rescued. But you already knew that, didn't you? You saw their gear." My jaw tenses and he sighs. "I got you out, you know. No cards. No promised lies. You were supposed to be out of the underground after our last mission." His eyes flick to Eren's unconscious form. "But it seems you were never going to get away from this dark part of the world."

"You got me *out*?" I repeat, not quite understanding. "Jenkins, how are you alive?" My voice wavers. There's a weight growing deep in my chest; it feels like I'll die if I take too deep of a breath.

He lets out a small sigh, then smiles with anguish brimming his eyes. "Yeah, I got hurt more than I expected, but my injuries weren't life-threatening. I was originally going to have you killed with the rest of the squad, but you didn't go out with the rest of them. I was already on the fence about it because, as silly as it was, I liked you. You were different. You had what it took to be like me. To stand here," he spreads his arms wide and alludes to the fortress, "with me. Gallows, I *let* you live. I even let you choose whether I'd take you with me or not. But you chose to leave me behind, as I suggested. I knew you'd be a weakness to me and, look, fate still brought you here. Taunting me."

He killed our squad. He planned for me to die there with them.

Something painful churns in my gut at those words.

Jenkins must see the pain in my eyes because he lifts his palm to my burning cheek. "Do you hate me, Nellie?" I think he'd be indifferent to it even if I did. But I can't force my heart to hate him. Not when I just got him back.

I stare into his dark eyes with anguish.

His loose grin fills with hints of malice.

"I knew you couldn't, even if you knew I was going to throw you away like trash. You were always foolishly loyal until the end." His words sting, but I take it. My chin drops and I grit my teeth. "But in the end, it was me who was the fool. I loved you more than I could stand. I still do." Jenkins brushes his lips across my cheek—his scent of a fresh storm hits my senses and makes me weak.

I missed him so much. But why does this hurt so badly? My body feels weak and sickness riles up my throat. It takes everything in me to keep from hugging him. No matter how badly I want his chest against mine and to feel his heart beating, I refuse to let myself reach for him.

Bradshaw shifts and draws Jenkins's attention.

"Ah—I almost forgot you were here. Well, enough reconnecting. We should probably get back to business, huh?" Jenkins shoves his hands into his pockets as if he's not threatened by us at all. He walks to check on Eren. He kneels beside him and observes silently.

Bradshaw's veins protrude through his neck as he

watches helplessly. Three guards are on him and they aren't weakened by injuries like he is.

"Greg was supposed to kill Eren. I guess he wanted to toy with you two first before finishing the job." He *tsks* and stands, pulling out his handgun and pointing it at Eren's head.

"No!" Bradshaw screams and thrashes. Two more soldiers rush to help keep him contained. Jenkins smiles widely.

There's the sadistic asshole I remember.

He loves watching other people's pain more than anything. Suffering is his favorite part of living. Looking at him now, I can't remember why I cherished him so much. Maybe it's because of Bradshaw… because I bonded with a new squad and felt what affection could be with someone else like me.

"Jenkins, stop!" I cry out and run to him. He raises a curious brow before narrowing his eyes at me.

"Since when did you get soft, Gallows? Don't you remember how many people you slaughtered when they begged for their lives? When their comrades begged? You killed them right in front of their brothers without so much as a glance at their pain. Don't pretend you're capable of caring for this piece of trash."

Jenkins's gentle demeanor vanishes and his voice turns cruel.

"Do you know what these dickheads have done? This is a really straightforward operation I run. We have a pecking order and things get done. We get paid an ungodly amount of money. Then do whatever the fuck we want. Well, we used to do all that back in the States. But guess who ruined that for me? For all of us? *Eren Bright.* He wanted a bigger slice of the pie, selfish motherfucker. He wanted the world for him and his brother and he wasn't willing to get it on his own. Why do so when I already had it? Eren tried to kill me after a private meeting. It was dirty. It was unforgivable, but I still needed him. So I ordered his brother to be picked off. An eye for an eye." Jenkins looks at Bradshaw, frozen and breathing heavily beneath five men.

Killing the squad was just a diversion so that the general wouldn't go looking for Jenkins. We really did mean nothing to him. My fists clench.

Jenkins brushes his thumb over my cheek. "I got you out, but he brought you back here, knowing that I wanted to protect you from this. He fucking brought you back to hell. He wanted to use you as a body shield for his stupid brother. Eren was counting on me not noticing that something I care about was on the field, and for what? For killing that nobody soldier two years ago?"

Bradshaw lets another shout roll from his throat, which comes out guttural and hate-filled. My chest aches for him.

"Why did you make *me* do it?" I ask in a hushed voice.

Jenkins studies me for a few moments before pulling his gun away from Eren's temple. He looks up at the glass ceiling and takes a moment before speaking.

"I liked that your hands were as dirty as mine. And you didn't care. You never did. As long as I kept you by my side, you didn't care about anything."

My chest constricts and I look at Jenkins with horror. He knows exactly what I'm thinking. "All those 'traitors' that I killed, were any of them actually guilty?" Anxiety moves into my stomach, prickling my blood.

"Some. I had you eliminate many loose ends, Gallows. Many were only guilty of being in my way. My own personal little reaper. To my surprise, you were the only one I couldn't pull the trigger on. You were so much like me. And you were such a pretty little thing. You still are." He lets his eyes fall down my body and sadness fills his eyes.

"You made me kill innocent people." I almost choke on the words. "How many?" The panic in my voice raises the hairs on the back of my neck. The rest of my body is taking longer to process what he just said, but my knees go first, bringing me to the floor and making me feel helpless.

"More than we could count, remember?" He smiles hopelessly at me. My shoulders drop and I start dry heaving.

I'm the Reaper. I don't deserve to live, not after what I've done. My throat swells and tears fall to the floor. If there's one thing I can do, perhaps I can save Bradshaw and Eren. I look at them both and try memorizing every last detail.

I don't think Bradshaw will leave unless I break his heart. Unless I make Jenkins see the misery he'll leave with.

"Let them leave, Jenkins. I want to stay with you... I'll kill them myself if they come back. *I'll* do it." My voice is hard and I force the feeling parts of me back into the depths. I tremble as I stand to meet my prior sergeant's eyes. I ignore the confusion and hurt that threads through Bradshaw's features.

His shoulders are shaking. "No, Bun."

Jenkins knits his brows at the nickname, then considers me. "We should just kill them—"

"I want them to live and to know that we are out here in the dark together. That if they dare cross a line again, we'll be the end of them." My gaze is hostile on Bradshaw and I limp to be in Jenkins's arms. Jenkins hesitates before opening his arms and holding me. I take a deep breath at the warmth that instantly falls over me.

He flashes me a wicked grin. "How could I refuse such a sweet request from my darling? Should we properly break his heart before we send him off? I know he thinks he loves you, but he doesn't know the real you. The monster that I know." Jenkins circles me, wrapping his hand around my stomach and kissing my neck. Bradshaw's eyes widen.

But all I can think of are the words: *He loves you.*

I want to tell Bradshaw that this is the only way. He doesn't know Jenkins like I do. He'll kill them both without a care unless I offer suffering. It's what gets him off. Jenkins likes when I make people hurt on his behalf.

"Hold him up so he can watch." Jenkins kisses my cheek and warmth plumes where he touches me. I hate him for what he's done. I hate him for what he is. Most of all, I hate him for making me a monster too. Hate and love dance a wicked line. Deep down, I know I will always love Jenkins.

But I'm relieved he'll spare them. I'll stay here in hell with him—my evil one.

His hands move as I remember, smooth and soft, lifting my shirt and pulling down my pants like a lover would. He touches my body and brushes his fingers over bullet holes and gashes in my skin, both fresh and old. I stare at Bradshaw. I look at him for as long as I can. Memorizing every detail of his face, every dip in his skin. He's going to be the last thought I have when I die.

I love him… I love him, and I'm never going to tell him that. He won't stay away if I do.

Bradshaw watches as Jenkins takes me. All the men in the room do. But my mind is steel. I hold onto Bradshaw's tears as they stream down his bloodstained face. I count them as they fall. Then I realize I'm crying too.

Jenkins licks the tears from my face and whispers sweet nothings into my ear. When he finishes, I sit slumped with his jacket over my shoulders, come leaking out from between my legs.

"Now *that* is a heartbroken man." Jenkins laughs. He guides me up tenderly and allows me to approach Bradshaw. I underestimated how much he truly loves misery. Or maybe I just turned a blind eye to it because I didn't want to see his darkest side.

I kneel beside Bradshaw and look into his icy blue eyes for the last time. "You will leave this place and never look back." That is the only thing I can manage to say. I make it as cruel as I can.

Bradshaw studies my face. His expression is so emotionally torn up that it makes my heart wrench. "You think I'm leaving you? This isn't goodbye." His raspy voice tears into my soul.

I shake my head. "It is. Live your life and forget about me." Bradshaw leans in and kisses me. I shut my eyes and let his lovely lips imprint on mine before remembering myself and shoving him off.

Don't let him stay.

"There is no life without you. There wasn't one before, there sure as fuck won't be one after," he whispers. His eyes narrow with misery. "I love you, Bunny."

He... *loves me.* I didn't know how much those words could hurt, especially when you can't have the only thing you love.

Jenkins shifts behind me and I tighten my hold on the coat covering my body. I let a small part of my soul grieve as I force out the words. "Leave me behind, Bradshaw."

He lets out a broken laugh, tears falling into his mouth. "Do you love me?"

I can't say it. *I can't.*

Jenkins's smile becomes grim as he waits for my reply.

If I tell him, it will only prolong both our pain. My hollow stare makes Bradshaw's jaw flex, and something changes in his eyes. I know a broken heart when I see one shattering in front of me and I don't know how I'll live with it.

Jenkins keeps his word. He sends Eren back with Bradshaw and we watch the two of them from the roof of the fortress. Malum Squad meets them half a klick from the fortress and they disappear into the Labrador mountains.

Bradshaw left without looking back, taking what was left of my heart with him.

thirty-seven

. . .

A MONSTER HAS MANY FACES, BUT JENKINS ONLY EVER SHOWS me the one I admire most. I cherish our morning walks around the frozen lakes, late mornings in bed, and the lavish plane rides to London and Florence. He dotes on my every wish. If not for meeting Bradshaw, I would love him entirely. I'm sure of it.

I'd let myself be the vile killing machine I once was. But I hold onto hope that one day I might see Bradshaw again, perhaps in passing. He must look older now, closer to his midthirties. Even I look older. Though, he would hardly recognize me now.

Three years is such a long time.

I haven't killed a person since that night we were captured. Jenkins lets me be by his side and watch his dirty work, but he never asks me to participate.

Eren would be happy if he could see me now, in the

dresses I wear and the civilian clothes I lounge in rather than tactical gear and vests.

Yeah, they wouldn't even recognize me. I muse.

"What are you smiling about, love?" Jenkins kisses the back of my neck as we roll in the sheets. I grin at the sun rising over the misty mountains.

It's been two years since we last returned to Labrador. The earth still holds many memories and heartache, but time is a savage thing. It makes the cruelest of things hurt less.

"Oh, nothing," I hum. Jenkins's pale blond hair is tousled with sleep still and his dark eyes lift with his drowsy smile.

"Let's go for a walk; some of the soldiers said a moose lingers around the lake this time of year." He breathes over my collarbone, pressing a kiss to my skin as his hand smooths down my arm.

"Really? It seems too cold for them to stand out there," I say as I slide out of bed and slip into leggings and boots. It's the dead of winter but I love seeing the ice crystals that form throughout the night. It's supposed to snow later, so we might as well go now.

Jenkins holds my hand in his, shoving them together into his coat pocket. We walk in silence as we usually do. I enjoy his silence. I often find myself wondering what his thoughts are. We only speak when we reach the frozen lake. The ice is beautiful and clear near the shore, revealing the visible rocks beneath. The trees are bare around the edge of the lake and the tall grasses have all been pushed down by the wind. The ice crystals that cling to the branches are beautiful. I smile at the complexity of nature.

"Can you hum me that song?" Jenkins asks, stealing a longing look at me. I smile and nod.

"Davy Jones" by Hans Zimmer. It's his favorite one. Jenkins took a liking to music more after our first year reunited. I often find him in his war room staring out into the terrain with weary eyes. He lost his ambition for the black market trade long ago. Now he primarily leaves his lieutenants to run most things while we spend time together.

I think I've changed him in these short years. The darkness in his eyes has faded and has been replaced with longing for things I can't give him.

Our sides are pressed together as I hum the song quietly. He closes his eyes and listens intently.

He's quiet for so long I flinch when he finally speaks. "Do you remember how that man looked at you before we sent them away?" Jenkins asks out of nowhere. His breath plumes in the frigid air.

I raise my brows. He hasn't spoken of Bradshaw since the night he let them go.

I nod.

"He looked at you and I saw the weight of the universe in his eyes." Jenkins looks down at me; our two black-clothed forms are the only contrast to the white snow. "You know… I saw you look at him the same way."

The pain of an old wound throbs in my chest. I will never forget the way Bradshaw looked at me that night. How I felt when I heard his words and how he looked at me with shattered eyes when I didn't say them back.

I close my eyes. I wonder if he was able to live a normal life—settle down and have a family like he wanted. It's been so long.

"Why are you bringing this up?" I ask softly.

Jenkins brushes my cheek with his thumb. "You've never looked at me the way you look at him. Not once."

The part of me that loves Jenkins aches. "Really?"

He's right.

He nods and breathes slowly, smiling mildly at the view. A crunch in the snow behind us makes me look over my shoulder.

I don't know what I was hoping for. Maybe I thought it might be Bradshaw, having seen right through my lies that night. My heart sinks when it's just the two soldiers charged with trailing us this morning.

"It's okay—I don't need your love in return. Your presence alone is enough for me."

Sometimes, I wonder if he desperately wants to hear me say it. My eyes lift to his. "Is it enough?" I rest my hand on his cheek.

He closes his eyes and strands of his soft hair tickle the back of my hand.

"My love is enough for the both of us. As long as you know you are my world, it is enough."

We hold hands during the walk back and don't speak of Bradshaw or that night again.

thirty-eight

· · ·

NELL

SIX MONTHS LATER

JENKINS LEFT FOR LONDON LAST NIGHT. HE'S BEEN ANXIOUS about something going down with his operations there. I know they've moved a big supply ship in the last week, but it's not unusual for him to not tell me what's going on. Nor do I care to know all the details.

I find solace in having time alone. Well, aside from the two soldiers who accompany me anywhere outside my room. They constantly remind me that my life with Jenkins is not a choice—even if I've long since made my peace with it.

Deep down I think Jenkins knows I might entertain the idea of leaving if I had the opportunity. But I don't mind my life with Jenkins. Our nights are warm and the days are peaceful.

I think that's what keeps him up at night. What has him gazing upon me while he thinks I'm asleep. His dangerous fingers that glide over my throat, his lips that kiss my scars. As much as I resent him for what he's done, I still love him. Our love is old, harrowing and rotten to the core, but it is ours.

It's late June now and the flowers on the hillside are finally blooming. I take a blanket and some bagels for a small picnic. Drake and Paul are my assigned guards and have warmed up to me considerably, especially after Jenkins made it known that I was special to him.

I think Paul is still a little sour over his old partner getting a knife to the head—like Greg did—for touching me though.

"Hey, the poppies are finally opening up!" Drake sounds more excited than I am. He kneels down in his military grade uniform and plucks a couple from the thousands we planted last summer. His light brown hair is short with a fade cut down the sides.

I smile at the bundle he hands me. Paul just spreads out the blanket and grabs a bagel. We sit in a small circle and share our boring lives as the three people who do literally nothing around here.

"Do you guys ever think about quitting? Leaving this world and living a normal life?" I ask absent-mindedly as I flip pages in a romance book.

They share a look before turning their heads to me. I take notice and wait for them to reply. Drake glances around uncomfortably before muttering, "No one leaves, Nell. The only way out is death."

My frown deepens. "*What?*" Jenkins doesn't give them terms like the dark forces? That seems unfair, considering how against that rule he was when we served for Riøt. He always thought the cards should be given out sooner. He knew as well as I did that the general leaned toward having soldiers "expire" in the field rather than earn their freedom. So I'm shocked he has adopted a crueler rule.

Paul nods. "It's a life commitment. No matter if you change your mind later. The secrets and knowledge we have of his arms deals are too sensitive to be leaked."

"That's awful," I say between bites of my bagel, thinking of my merciless Jenkins. "Would you leave? You know, if it was an option?" I study their expressions carefully.

Drake lowers his eyes. It's Paul who surprises me. "I would." Drake's head snaps up at him and his expression fills with alarm.

"You can't say that," Drake hisses.

Paul waves him off. "It's just Nell. She wouldn't say anything to Jenkins."

I smile at his faith in me.

"What about you, Nell? Is this where you want to be?" Drake finishes his bagel and leans forward on his knees.

My lie comes out filled with sorrow. "Yeah, of course."

I think of Bradshaw again. He lives in my mind as Jenkins once had. Funny how they've swapped places. I wonder if he got Eren back home safely. I smile as I imagine him on his surfboard, doing everyday things. What would his children look like?

My soul aches and I have to close my eyes at the reminiscent thoughts.

My home will always be with Bradshaw. I wish I could remember his smile instead of the pain I saw before he left.

The world is better without monsters like me in it. I don't fight my fate, even if it fucking hurts.

But sometimes, I imagine him coming back for me and wrapping his arms around me again.

We walk around the lake and pick more flowers before sunset. Then I find myself back in my room, sprawled over my expensive sheets and staring at the ceiling. I count the textured patterns in the paint like every night when I try to find sleep. But it evades me tonight.

The door to my room creaks open, but I ignore the guest.

Soldiers pop in every hour to make sure I'm in here and not making a break for it, sometimes sooner if Jenkins is feeling anxious while he's away.

The man walks to the edge of the bed and stands silently until I can no longer ignore him. I push up on my elbows and glare at him. "What do you think you're—" My breath catches in my lungs as I stare at a man dressed in a black uniform. His mask covers his lower face, but I know him just from the shape of his cheeks and the broken pale eyes that gaze down upon me with heartache.

"Bradshaw?" My voice is weak. I can't move. I'm frozen with the emotions that seep into my veins.

"Hey, Bunny." His voice falters, and he slowly goes down to his knees where my legs hang over the edge of the bed. His gloved hands gently touch my thighs and I crumble with him.

"You weren't supposed to come back for me, you idiot." I sob. He wipes my tears as he takes me in.

"I never left, Bun. My heart and every thought have been here with you all this time. If that makes me a fool, then I don't give a fuck. There's no me without you." He pulls his mask off and I get a full view of his handsome face. My hands tentatively move to his jaw, tracing the lines of his bones and taking in the way time has changed him in just three and a half years.

He looks like he's stayed up every single night the way I have. His eyes have lost their ire and rage, replaced with heartache and longing. He has a few more wrinkles around his eyes and his beard is a bit scruffier than his usual clean-cut look. Time hasn't changed his weary soul, but there's so much grief there now that hadn't existed before.

Bradshaw's eyes trace my face as if he's taking in who I am now too. For a moment I worry he'll hate what he sees, a defeated soldier who has given into the darkness. But his broken smile tells me he's just sad with all the time we've lost together.

"Are you going to kill me since I came back?" he teases and I shove him, tears still streaming down my cheeks.

"Don't even joke abou—"

His lips crash into mine, taking any words I had and swallowing them. Bradshaw pushes me back until we're falling into the sheets. He groans when my hands intertwine in his hair. His teeth skate over my bottom lip as he nips it gently before looking into my eyes.

"I'm never letting you go again, Bun. Never. You've always belonged to me. I don't give a fuck what you said to me that night. I know you lied to get me to leave." He dips below my chin and strokes his tongue up my throat as he unbuttons my night shirt. His calloused hands send a shudder up my spine.

"I've always been yours," I whisper.

He looks up and stares at me, completely taken aback. "Really?"

I laugh at how innocent he sounds.

"Really."

Bradshaw smiles and resumes kissing down my sternum before he gives attention to my breasts. He palms one while he sucks on the other nipple, his fingertips coasting down my side. His thumb brushes over my rib cage and stops on the scar he gave me so long ago.

His mark.

He pauses, his lips hot against my skin. "You liked it when I gave you this, didn't you?" His voice is nostalgic, but there's a drop of lust that slips off his tongue. "I saw how your legs squeezed together and how shadows collected in your eyes. I knew then that you were something dangerous I shouldn't crave."

A flash of heat pools in my core and my thighs press together to stave off the urgency at the memory of his cruelness. How many hours have I longed for him to be here? How many restless nights I've spent dreaming of his hands on me again.

"I loved every second of it," I say shakily.

He laughs and puts a small amount of pressure on my scar. A sliver of pain shoots across the sensitive skin and I instinctively grab his hand. My head tilts back into the crook of his shoulder and my hips roll against his groin.

Bradshaw doesn't let the motion fade. He drops his lips to my shoulder and bites into my flesh. It stings but doesn't break the skin.

My lips part to cry out, but he hooks two fingers inside my mouth and whispers in my ear, "No biting." He traces my canines before pushing his fingers deeper and pressing down on my tongue.

What god would make a man like Bradshaw? He's made the impossible mission to get back to me and instead of quickly whisking me away, he spends the time to greet me thoroughly. The wet arousal growing between my thighs shortens my breath with need.

My mouth closes around his fingers and I start to suck on them, giving him a playful swirl with my tongue. He settles on the bed behind me, a hard breath escaping his lips before he brings those venomous teeth back to the sensitive skin just under my ear.

"I missed ruining you," he says dangerously, pulling his fingers from my mouth slowly, dragging my lower lip with his fingertips like he's relishing in the way it feels.

His tactical gear is cold at my back.

I murmur, "I've ruined men much worse than you."

He laughs and rolls me over on my back, bringing himself to his knees so he's looming down over me. His pants are tented with that enormous cock I remember so fondly. It twitches with his muscles and he stares down at me like he's been starving for years.

"You don't hate this part of me?" He lowers his forehead to mine.

"Which part?" I ask, focusing more on his traveling hand that caresses my breast.

"The monster that only wants you."

He doesn't give me a second to answer; his lips are crashing down on mine and for the first time in three and a half long years, I feel whole again. The fire inside my chest that always burned hotter near Bradshaw comes back to life.

Bradshaw coaxes my lips open with his tongue and I eagerly allow him entry. Our tongues chase each other—hot, wet, devouring. Every sense is trained on him, the warmth of his body, the hardness of his cock, the deep feral groans that leave his lips as he lowers his hips to mine and starts dry humping me. My thin nightgown and his pants are the only barriers between us, making the sensation of his bulge drawing over my slit almost unbearable.

Our kiss breaks and he pulls away from me enough to take in my features. His eyes are hooded, tracing my face as he pumps his hips.

"It's the monster in me," I manage to say between hushed moans. His brow raises. "That craves the one in you."

That sick smirk of his that I love so much returns to his lips.

"I was hoping you'd say that." He drops his lips to my throat, kissing down my chest while he slips his hand beneath my underwear. "Oh, Bunny, *baby*. Did I make your pussy cry like this? How many nights did you pleasure yourself thinking of me?" He practically growls with his teeth cinched over my tit, teasing with gentle pressure and the stroke of his tongue over my sensitive flesh.

"So many." I moan as he pumps two fingers into me. My back arches and his chest vibrates with a soft groan. Bradshaw releases my nipple and continues his descent down my stomach with wet kisses and playful bites until he reaches my clit.

"Wait." I breathe out.

His tongue slips into me and I writhe in his hands.

My fingers curl into his hair as he strokes my center like a beast. My head falls back and I cry out softly. Bradshaw groans with pleasure, squeezing my thighs as he devours me.

He pulls away with saliva still connecting us for a second before it snaps. Bradshaw licks his lips and stares up at me with hooded eyes.

"I've been waiting for you for so long, Bun. I want to erase every trace of him from you." He unfastens his belt and button before pulling down his pants and freeing his swollen cock. "No heart is as cold as mine's been these past years."

Slowly, I sit up and crawl to him. He stands and brushes his hand over my head, threading his fingers through my hair and fisting it tightly.

I put his tip in my mouth and stare up at him the way I know he'll fawn over. His eyes go lax with pleasure and I see the demons he keeps locked up start to give him a bit of peace.

I'm his only way to escape the heavy thoughts that run rampant in his mind. He's my only escape too. And for years, we've suffered.

No more suffering.

No more hurting.

My tongue wraps around his veiny flesh as I take him in more. He fists my hair tighter and drops his jaw open. I take him in deeper, hollowing my cheeks and blinking past the tears that brim in my eyes. Bradshaw rocks his hips into my mouth and I follow the motion, allowing my fingers to find my clit.

"Your lips feel so fucking good wrapped around my

cock. Suck me dry, baby," he chokes out between jerks. Another throb of heat surges through me at his foul words.

He stops pumping and withdraws from my mouth, quickly fisting his dick and working the tip before commanding me to lie down. I do as he says.

"Do we have time for this?" I try to reason. Our breaths are the only sound against the dark of my room. Soldiers will be coming to check on me soon.

He raises a brow. "It's a bit late for that, don't you think?"

I nod, smiling as mischievously as he is.

"You're probably right. We don't have time." He leans up and checks his tactical watch. His eyes become somber and he sighs. "We don't."

"Told you," I tease, smoothing my hand over his jaw. He leans into it and shuts his eyes. I feel like I need to pinch myself to make sure I'm not dreaming. But he's really here.

A dull ache resides in my chest for how Jenkins will take the news of me leaving him, because I know he'll never let me go.

thirty-nine

. . .

BRADSHAW

I'VE WAITED FOR YEARS FOR THIS ONE NIGHT. I'D WAIT MANY more if I had to. I've moved mountains to rescue her. And it was worth every drop of sweat, blood, and tears.

Bunny cups my cheek with her soft hand. It feels so different than before. Her callouses are gone and so are all the stains of war on her skin. The last time I saw her this close we were covered in blood and slowly dying. She said cruel things to me and it fucking broke my heart.

It puts air in my lungs that she was relieved to see me.

"Come on, Bun. I brought your uniform." I pull my bag to the side and unzip it, handing her tactical gear. Her eyes harden as she looks at the set.

My brows knit. "What's wrong?"

She shakes her head. "I haven't worn a uniform since our last night together." Maybe not. But I still wouldn't want to tussle with her on a fighting mat.

373

"Can you still shoot?" I ask, concern blooming in my voice. My exit plan kind of included her being by my side.

Bunny laughs and it warms my heart. I've missed her so fucking much. My hands tremble thinking about how I forced myself to walk away. If Eren hadn't been on the verge of death... I shake my head. *Don't replay all the suffering,* I chide myself.

She grins. "Of course. What else am I supposed to do but practice? But promise me we won't kill anyone unless we have to. These men aren't bad. They're just loyal to an asshole, just like you are to Eren." She slips out of her night clothes and I search her skin for bruises or any sign of mistreatment. But she's unharmed. That alone lifts a weight off my chest that's been slowly suffocating me.

"Was he good to you?" I can't look her in the eyes as I ask. Guilt has been my friend for three terrible years.

She kisses my cheek and forces my chin to face her. "He treated me like a queen. I never wanted for anything." *Oh. Am I too late...* "Anything but for you. I could never love him like I do you, Bradshaw. He was good to me... but he isn't *you.*"

I deflate and press my forehead to hers. "Are you sure? I don't have these luxuries to offer you, Bun. I can't fly you to London and Italy on a whim and drown you with expensive wines. In fact, I'm not even sure I can offer much more than a warm place to lie down at night."

She lets a sweet laugh out before pressing a kiss to my lips. "Have you been watching me?" Hope lingers in her eyes for my answer, as if every time she laid out on the sundecks of London's finest hotels, she hoped I'd be watching.

She's not wrong.

"Always. I've been watching you all this time. Sometimes from binoculars or across the room. Other times from surveillance. I've been with you. Each starlit walk you took with him, every small look over your shoulder waiting for someone. *For me.* I was there. I never left you behind." Her eyes brim with tears and it's enough to make me crumble.

It killed me to never know if she loved him the way she did me. I watched him fuck her many times. I watched them sleep peacefully together and kiss like old lovers. But I never saw her tell him that she loved him. Not once.

Her smile is warm as she leans in to kiss me and murmurs, "What took you so long?"

I stare down at her and choke on my words. "Jenkins is as careful as they come. He has the tightest security in the world. Eren and Jefferson took out his main division in Europe a few days ago. The second Jenkins took the bait I was on the ground and en route. I promise you, Bunny, not one day has passed where I rested. Not one."

"You should've forgotten about me." Her eyes fill with pain as she glides her hand down my chest.

"Impossible." I take her hand and press it against my heart. "You feel that, Bun? It only beats for you. Bones has been dead for years. I just woke up again when I kissed you." Her eyes brim with tears but I know my words reach her.

"I love you, Bradshaw."

My eyes widen and a throb rolls through my chest. *I'd wait a lifetime to hear those words.* Her smile is everything I've dreamt about.

"I love you too. I want you to say it to me a thousand more times." I press a kiss to her forehead. "*After* we get home."

"Lead the way, sir," she coos, pulling up her mask and winking at me.

God, I fucking missed her.

"We're going to keep to the west wing and exit on the terrace viewing the lake." I know it's the one she frequents the most. I won't tell her that I've sat across that godforsaken lake for more hours than anyone should have to, watching her stare out into the wilderness like a lovesick pup. I watched Jenkins take her there and kiss her. She'd touch him adoringly and no matter how hard I tried, I couldn't look away.

It hurt. It always did.

And I know a part of her will always love him.

Eren knew their history. He warned me the moment he woke up back in Coronado.

"Are you sure she even wants to be rescued? It sounds like she wants to be with him. What happens if you show up and she doesn't want to come back?" Eren sat up in his hospital bed, hair messy and body bandaged. "She stayed for a reason."

I glared at him. "She saved our lives."

Eren looked away, he knew it too. He also knew he handed Jenkins the only leverage he could ever have on him. I saw how easily that man killed people.

I knew we were done with the underground shit. Eren wanted out of the game.

"I'm shocked he gave in to her demands. I didn't think he'd just... let us go like that," I said with an extinguished breath and hung my head.

Eren had let out a cruel laugh. "You idiot. He's infatuated with her and if he didn't let us go, he knew she'd go out fighting until either she was dead or he was. Letting us go was an easy choice for him... but you need to remember those two were together for years. She's loyal to him, Bradshaw."

No, she's not, I thought. I don't give a fuck what she said. She only said it to hurt my feelings. She gave herself up for us.

"I'm going to get her back with or without you." I stood and walked to the door.

Eren groaned and snapped at me, "Fine. But we can't just march back in there. He's going to be prepared and he has nothing to lose. His queen is tucked safely under his arm now."

I stood facing the door for a few moments before turning back to him. "How then?"

He lit a cigarette and breathed in smoke slowly. "Leave it to me. I'll get some of my buddies in Europe to stir things up. But it's going to take time, Bradshaw. We're going to need to be careful and wait. Patience is Jenkins's ace. We need to pull strings where we can and hope for the best."

My heart split at that moment.

"How long?"

Eren gave me a weary, pitiful look that tore through my soul.

"HOW LONG?" I closed the distance between us in a few strides and fisted the collar of his shirt. My brother plucked the cigarette from his lips and sighed.

"At least two years."

Two…

Then three.

Then I was done waiting.

I couldn't wait any longer, even if it was risky to push the timeline. I needed to come back for Bunny. To hold her and kiss her. To tell her I died more each time I watched her waiting for me to show up. Her sad eyes when Jenkins kissed her.

I'd left her small things that I hoped she'd see and know I was watching her. That I was with her always.

A bunny in the field. The drawings through the condensation of her hotel windows. The bunny stickers on restaurant menus where she frequented.

"Ready?" I ask, hand on the door, admiring the fierce expression I remember take its place back on her face.

She nods and I open the door.

forty

. . .

NELL

WE MOVE THROUGH THE WEST WING LIKE WE DIDN'T MISS A BEAT together, silent and lethal. I pray that we won't have to kill anyone. But I know if it comes down to it, we might not have a choice.

Our luck holds out as we slink through the last hall, but it ends abruptly when Paul and Drake turn the corner. I freeze, gun aimed up, finger caressing the trigger.

I'm not a monster anymore. Not when I know their dreams.

I set my hand on Bradshaw's shoulder and he looks back at me. "Not them. They're my guards." His jaw flexes but he nods with understanding. I'm sure he saw them trailing me constantly. We squat low on our haunches and wait to see what they'll do. For a while, they just linger in the hall and chat.

Please just keep moving. Don't make us confront you.

An alarm rolls through the hall.

"Fuck. Sorry, Bun. We'll have to—"

"*Wait*, let me talk to them." I rush to stand but Bradshaw grabs my wrist.

His voice is cold. "We don't have time. If they resist... We have to get out. This is our only chance." I nod and quickly step out into the hall.

Drake and Paul instantly raise their guns. I pull down my mask and run to them—their eyes cloud with uncertainty.

"Nell. What are you doing?!" Paul hisses and looks around quickly before leaning in closer. "Do you know what Jenkins will do if he finds out you're trying to leave?"

"Jenkins isn't here. We need to get out *now*. It's my only chance. *Please*," I beg them both. But I know they heard "*we*" more than anything else. Their heads snap up to Bradshaw, who cautiously approaches with his M16 drawn.

The two of them trace their guns on him. Sweat rolls down their foreheads.

"Jenkins is on his way back as we speak. He wanted to come back early to surprise you," Drake drawls, glaring at me. *Shit*.

"You two can come with us. You want out, don't you? This is your chance."

"*Bunny*," Bradshaw hisses, his finger trained on the trigger.

Their expressions are twisted. I know they won't shoot me. Jenkins would kill them mercilessly.

"Let's go," I say dully and walk between the guns pointed at each other. Bradshaw hesitates before lowering his weapon and following. We run to the terrace without glancing back. I'm not sure what will happen to those two, but at least they didn't do anything to stop us.

Bradshaw jumps down first and I trail him. The second my boots hit the ground, he mutters, "That was risky."

"If they wanted to kill us, they would've," I retort.

"They can tell the others what direction we went." We

sprint through the tall grass. The scent of the poppies in the field nearby tickles my nose.

I hope they don't. But I know Jenkins can make quick work of getting information out of people.

Anxiety builds in my chest as a chopper flies above us, heading toward the fortress. I know it's Jenkins and he's about to return to chaos. How long would it take him to hunt me down? My stomach twists.

Bradshaw doesn't look back at me as we slide down a muddy slope, but his voice is sure. "Don't worry. We won't let him take you."

My brows pinch in confusion as we stand and start moving forward again.

"We?" I ask.

He stops and turns back to look at me. He pulls down his mask and gives me a grin that sets my heart on fire.

"Did you think we'd send our favorite psycho out here by himself, little bun-bun?" Jefferson steps out from the underbrush, his face completely smothered in mud for camouflage.

"Jobs?!" I let out an embarrassing squeal as I jump into his arms. He laughs and pats my head.

"Malum doesn't leave their own behind," Pete says proudly as he emerges from the bushes and rests his hand on my shoulder.

Harrison stands next to Jefferson and winks at me. "Miss us?"

Eren comes to Bradshaw's side and offers me his hand. I stare at him for a moment. This is the man who planned on serving me to Jenkins on a silver platter—*dead*. He's the reason all of this happened. But time has a way of killing anger.

"Bunny. It's good to see you again," he mutters softly, remorse and guilt laced in his voice.

I take his hand and smile. "Happy to be back, Sarge."

He smiles at me before refocusing. "Well, let's stop wasting time and get to the extraction point, soldiers!" he shouts, and we all fall into form. He shoots me a wicked grin before nodding at his brother.

We slide our night vision goggles on and move quickly through the dense forest. It doesn't take long before we're further into the mountains than I've been since our last mission. Northern Labrador is a treacherous place; the wild animals alone are terrifying.

The first hour is bliss. We make it a great distance before hearing the four-wheelers roar somewhere beyond the trees. My heart rate spikes but Bradshaw sets his hand on my shoulder, assuring me he's right behind me.

One way or another, I'm leaving this place tonight.

I won't go back to Jenkins again, even if it breaks my heart.

"It's fine. They can't drive those things on this terrain. The woods are too thick." Jobs says just above a whisper.

I nod and try to focus on not tripping as we scale down a rocky hillside.

"How far to the extract point?" I ask as Harrison offers me his hand to help me down the slope. He lifts his night vision goggles as the moon emerges and looks into my eyes. I forgot how his perfect nose pissed me off when we first met, his blond hair still as soft and smooth as before.

"About four more klicks south. We got lucky that Eren has a buddy in Canada—" Harrison's head is thrown back with the force of a bullet. His blood coats my face and his hand is violently torn from mine.

"Harrison!" My shriek echoes through the small valley. Bradshaw is already forcing me forward away from our fallen comrade.

"Shots fired!" Jefferson shouts and we collectively sprint for the next grouping of trees.

I glance back at Harrison's still body. My stomach

lurches, but I swallow the bile that rises. *Don't let his death be for nothing.* I force my legs to move faster. The branches whip at us as we crash through the underbrush.

Eren leads with surety and sets a ruthless pace. A few more shots ring distantly through the treetops. I hope it wasn't for Harrison.

After two klicks, Eren slows down and has us group up in the cover of low-bearing trees. He speaks quickly and with ragged breaths. "We have to cross the plains to reach the extraction point. Jenkins wasn't supposed to be back this early, so we might have mines in the valley and air trouble. I want everyone tight and focused." He looks from Jefferson to Pete, me, and then Bradshaw. There's pain in his eyes for Harrison not being here. "There's no way out if we miss that chopper."

I nod gravely.

They came back for me. One is already dead for it.

When we reach the edge of the treeline, our feet slow. Eren raises his fist and we stop at his signal. He listens for the four-wheelers.

Bradshaw moves to stand beside his twin. Their shoulders move heavily with each breath and they share a hushed conversation.

"He refused to let you go," Pete says sadly as he repositions his M16 to give his hand a break. I nod, not breaking my trance on Bradshaw.

Jefferson chuckles, but his tone isn't happy. "He would've come alone if he had to."

My throat tightens. It must tear them up inside that we left Harrison's body back there. "I'm sorry about Harrison."

They lower their heads.

"Bunny, stay by my side while we move out there," Bradshaw mutters as he turns his attention to me and offers his hand.

"Stay vigilant," I say to Pete and Jefferson. They offer uncertain grins but nod.

"You too, Bunny."

I move to Bradshaw's side and firm my trembling hands over my gun. *We could easily all die out here.*

"Hey, we're going to be okay." Bradshaw pulls me close to him and he presses a sweet kiss on my cheek. I try to nod, but it's weak.

Eren stares down at me and hardens his gaze. "There's no reality in which I don't get you two out of here. I have sins to pay for and you're first on my list." He smiles at me and taps my forehead. "For what it's worth, I always did like you."

My brows knit and I give him a small smile back. "Right back at you, Sarge."

The clouds shroud the moon and darkness falls over us like a blanket of mist. "No matter what happens out there we'll always be connected. Should this be our last mission together, know I've never worked with finer soldiers." Eren's voice is reminiscent and for the first time since meeting him, I see fear flash through his eyes. Regret for the past, and perhaps hope for what remains of his underground squad to be free.

Jefferson and Pete step closer, setting their hands on his shoulder. Bradshaw sets his hand over theirs. I place mine on Eren's chest and a flicker of sorrow threads across his features.

"We'll get out, Sarge," Jefferson says quietly. Pete and Bradshaw nod confidently.

Eren shuts his eyes and smiles before nodding. "Let's go."

The valley is sloped and barren. The second our feet leave the safety of the forest my heart rate increases and thrums wildly in my chest. It's still quiet out here, but who's to say how long that will last. Jenkins is a smart man with many resources. I have no doubts that he knows exactly where our extraction point likely is and how to cut us off.

Bradshaw flanks my right while Eren moves stealthily to my left. It's the exact same way I met them, with me between.

"Wait!" Bradshaw snaps as he stops on his heels. We halt beside him. I search the ground for any IEDs but don't see any.

"What do you see, Bones?" Eren asks before I can. His eyes narrow on the horizon.

"Movement on the right, close to the riverbank, and the ground has been disturbed just ahead." Bradshaw keeps his eyes trained on the riverbank. My stomach sinks when Eren nods that he sees movement too.

Pete curses and lifts his gun. "I've got bad news, Sarge. Four hostiles to our left," he says under his breath.

"Fuck." Eren hesitates and looks around us, trying to think of the best way forward. "We'll need to move single file and far apart. If an IED goes off... at least we won't be bunched together."

"Sarge, they'll be able to pick us off easily if we fan out," Jefferson interjects, but Eren shakes his head with finality.

"I'll go first," I say firmly, swallowing my fear and stepping forward. They all share a look before Bradshaw gives me a stern look.

"Like I'd let you." He shoulders past me and all the unease in my chest doubles. Eren gives his brother a sharp glare before leading the way.

"Like *I* would let either of you guide us through hell. We need to keep moving. They haven't spotted us yet but that can change at any second. I have the best eyes of us all. I won't step on one." Eren doesn't sound as confident as I need him to.

But it doesn't matter what I say. We're already moving. Bradshaw takes slow, purposeful strides across the rugged terrain behind his brother. I wait a few beats before starting behind him. Pete flanks me and Jefferson takes up the back.

I stare at the back of Bradshaw's heels as they lift and move. We're three-quarters of the way across the valley when Eren steps down and a distinct sound tears through my soul.

Click.

My eyes flash up, wide with horror.

The sky is angry behind Eren's form. His gentle smile trembles with the promise of death. Bradshaw tries to run forward, but I grab his shoulders.

"Walk around me, slowly. Come on, it's okay." Eren orders, his voice sharp. Pete and Jefferson pass us and walk ahead at a steady pace. Each nods their respect to our sergeant silently. Somehow, the weight of the lack of words makes my chest twist more.

Bradshaw takes one staggered step and then stops, his entire body trembling. "I can't go on without you," he chokes as tears stream down his cheeks. "Not without you, Eren."

"Look at me," Eren says softly. Bradshaw looks up at him and Eren makes an effort to seem calm. "I'm fine. But I need you two to get the fuck going. I love you. Both of you. Now go." His tone is desperate. I've never seen those deep blue eyes so weary, tears brimming and his jaw trembling to hold back the emotions.

Bradshaw slowly moves past his brother, taking one last look over his shoulder before walking straight.

I stop at Eren's side and tears fall like drops of rain from my soul.

"I'll take care of him, Eren," I promise. His eyes shift with peace and he taps my forehead gently. His fingers feel so cold it makes my heart twist.

"I know you will." I hold onto his gentle voice and the way it wraps around my heart.

My teeth chatter as I force my legs to move away from him. Bradshaw is already out of the field, with Pete and Jefferson at his side. I reach them and together we continue down the sloped valley, stealing last glances at our sergeant alone in the minefield.

By the time the sound of an explosion rings through the quiet, dark mountains, our eyes have dried and my body jerks painfully in response to the sharp, echoing blast.

No one speaks.

Bradshaw's shoulders shake with his silent cry. We keep marching forward without Eren.

forty-one

. . .

The sound of the IED setting off and knowing Eren stood on it hollows out my chest. All I can feel is the blood that seems to pool in the cavity. I feel like I'm fucking drowning inside myself.

I can't live without him. I... can't.

My legs come to a halt and Bunny stops, looking back at me with red-rimmed eyes and a quivering frown.

"I can't go on, Bun. I need to go back for him."

Her eyes narrow with sorrow and she shakes her head. "You know we can't do that, Bones. He's... he's..." She can't even say the words. My throat knots and I feel sick.

Jefferson and Pete glance back and realize we've stopped. "Bones... I know this hurts so fucking much but we can't stop. We have to keep going," Jefferson's voice breaks.

I shake my head, fists trembling at my sides. "No. I can't live without him. I can't." I hang my head and tears fall down the bridge of my nose.

Bunny wraps her hands around my head and strokes my hair as soothingly as she can. Her tears tap against the back of my skull. "I'm so sorry... but we can't let his sacrifice be in vain. We have to keep going," she pleads, and I know she's right.

I give a hesitant nod and force my body to move with them. Each step makes me feel sick to my stomach.

Bunny walks close to my side and slips her hand in mine. I can't bear to look at her. I'll lose all my composure again if I do.

"One klick away. Chopper is inbound and touching ground in twenty," Jefferson says in a low voice. I nod and secure my hold over my M16.

"They're not going to just let us walk out of here." My comment sounds grave, but my brother is dead. If they didn't spot us before the explosion, they know we're here now. It's only a matter of time.

Bunny stills and snaps her head to the left, raising her rifle with no hesitation before letting her first bullets fly. The four of us kneel and raise our scopes to our eyes.

"Two incoming on our left," she says as she pulls the trigger again. "One."

Pete and Jefferson fire to the right and front. Goddammit. We can't get surrounded, not this close. The blood in my ears beats erratically. I face our flank and spot three soldiers approaching.

"Give them hell, Malum." I grit my teeth as I shoot the closest flank-side soldier in the throat. He falls to the ground and the others don't even blink as they move past him.

Chaos unfolds as gunshots pepper the night sky. My lower side gets hit as I shoot a soldier in the thigh. We both grunt and before I can lift my rifle to shoot the next guy, he shoots again. My upper arm flares with pain and the shock in my system makes my hand stop functioning. The M16 slips from my hold. I quickly unlatch my handgun and shoot the soldier three times in the chest at point-blank range. His body falters and crashes into me. I use him as a shield as his comrades open fire at me.

Fuck. I spare a glance at Bunny as she unsheathes her knife and cuts a throat without a second thought. My eyes narrow in misery. She didn't want to kill anyone, but look what it's come down to.

Once the bullets stop, I drop the carcass and shoot the two men in the face. One of them looks right into my soul as I pull the trigger. I recognize him as one of Bunny's guards. So much for them trying to help her escape; they'd drag her right back to hell if that's what their master wanted.

His eyes dull as soon as the bullet shatters his face. His counterpart falls beside him. I stagger to my feet and press a bloody hand to my injured side. Pete and Jefferson engage hand-to-hand with three soldiers while Bunny fights off two.

I start to move toward her when I hear *his* awful voice.

"Bradshaw. What an unfortunate end to the Bright brothers, don't you think? You just couldn't let her be." Jenkins stands ten feet away with a black knife and a handgun. His uniform is matte gray, making his slicked-back blond hair stand out even more. His sinister, dark eyes trace my features carefully, enjoying the despair he's caused.

"It's not my fault she can't love a monster like you," I say venomously.

Jenkins throws his head back and laughs. His smile is genuine—the malice that rolls off his shoulders is unbelievable. Strands of his hair fall over his forehead as he points his knife at me.

"If only I had a heart," he says with a curl to the edges of his lips. Then he charges me. I'm slower in drawing my KA-BAR but block his heavy-handed blow. It sends sharp pulses of pain through my injured arm and my blood makes the hold I have on my knife waver.

Jenkins takes advantage of my agony and knocks my feet out from beneath me. The force of the ground knocks the breath from my lungs, but I prepare myself for his attack.

He tries to plunge the knife into my throat, but I block it with my forearm. I stab him in the thigh and he doesn't even flinch. He just uses my momentary victory against me, letting his knife sink deep into my shoulder. My body convulses and I clench my jaw to keep from shouting in pain.

Jenkins smiles and laughs as he pulls my blade from his thigh and twirls it in his hand. "Who do you think raised our lovely soldier? She was nothing but a murderous little thing when I found her. Who do you think took her under their wing? Taught her everything she needs to stay alive? And you think you can just take her from me?" He claims to not have a heart but, clearly, he's bothered by her disloyalty to him.

"She'd choose me over an evil fucker like you any day. You were better off as a memory to her. She loved you then." I grin as the words sink into him. His eyes lose their malice for a moment before he shakes it and buries my blade into my other shoulder, pinning me to the ground and letting my blood seep into the earth.

I groan and try to shake him off, but he's planted firmly on my torso.

Bunny shouts as a soldier shoots her in the stomach. She buckles and falls to her knees. Blood is smeared over her face and hands. Bodies pepper the battleground.

My chest seizes and every moment after feels drawn out and slow.

"Bunny!" I shout. Pete snaps his head up and runs to help her. Jenkins lifts his pistol and shoots Pete without a thought. The bullet strikes the side of his head and he falls like he was never anything more than a body thrown into war.

No.

Jefferson is nowhere to be seen. My eyes lower to the bodies where Pete had stood. My gaze meets Jeffersons's lifeless eyes, his throat cut and oozing blood into the earth.

My throat dries and all the fight flees from my body.

Jenkins laughs and tears the knives at the same time from my shoulders. I cough at the violent force he uses to rip them from my body. He turns me on my side and presses his hand down over my head, letting his weight make my face sink into the ground.

"I want you to watch him kill her." He chuckles darkly as he waits for his soldier to finish Bunny off. She fights valiantly for someone just shot in the stomach, but the man sparring with her is uninjured and lands a brutal strike against her face.

"Bunny!" I struggle with every ounce of strength I have and throw him from my back. Jenkins staggers to his feet. I deck him across the face and he falls on his neck. I fist his ebony knife and plunge it into his chest furiously. He cries out as I withdraw the blade one final time and slash his face. The sharp end of the blade catches his lip and tears half way up his jaw. My breaths are uncontrolled and my body rocks back and forth with the adrenaline coursing through me.

Bunny gets the upper hand while the soldier is side-tracked by his boss getting overthrown, and she buries her blade into his temple. His entire body convulses and he falls back lamely.

I return my attention to Jenkins. A darkness falls over me for all the lives he's stolen from me, and I set to punching his face over and over. I want him to feel everything in his last moments. I want him to feel all the pain he's caused. His teeth break and blood spurts over my face as he chokes on his incisors. I keep hitting him until his face is almost unrecognizable and raw.

A soft hand falls on my shoulder and I stop. My breath is heavy and uneven as I look up at Bunny. Her eyes are rimmed with red and she looks so fucking tired. Her hands tremble at her stomach, where blood streams from her small frame.

"Let me finish him," she says sadly, with a grim set to her jaw.

I hesitate. The urge to strangle the life from him still vibrates at the ends of my fingertips.

"*Please.*"

I struggle to my feet and watch as she lowers to his side.

Jenkins's eyes soften almost immediately.

He loves her. I look around at the carnage left in the wake of his so-called love. The number of soldiers he brought with him is evident in his intent. He wanted the fight to be fair. Jenkins was anything but unfair in the end. Perhaps even he wanted her to escape him.

Yeah, he loved her. In his own wicked way.

forty-two

. . .

NELL

JENKINS LIES STILL; HIS NECK IS AT AN AWKWARD ANGLE AND HIS breath is strangled. His blond hair is dyed red with blood and he's beaten so terribly it threads sorrow into my heart. His teeth are bare on the left side where the knife tore through his flesh and his chest trembles weakly with the ounce of life he holds onto.

I brush his cheek gently with my fingertips, his eyes never leaving my face. They're narrowed and fight to stay open.

"Look at the mess you've made," I say softly, like tucking a child into bed.

He coughs blood and gives me what looks like a small smile. "One last dance, you and me. It was fun while it lasted, Gallows. Can you"—he winces in pain and coughs again—"c-can you hum that stupid s-song for me?" He lifts his hand slowly and caresses his thumb delicately over my cheek.

I nod.

"Davy Jones" was always his favorite, perhaps because of the sad tune. Jenkins, my wicked, lonely soldier.

Our blood mixes as we bleed out next to each other. I hum and stroke his hair back softly until his eyes flutter closed.

My throat constricts as Bradshaw hands me a pistol and my tune sounds off as I press the cold steel to my lovely Jenkins's temple.

"Do not cry for me, love. I wasn't meant for this world. I am darkness... Thank you for showing me a splinter of the light." His voice is a mere whisper.

"I love you, Jenkins," I say with tears streaming down my cheeks. His eyes widen at my admittance and a smile unlike I've ever known curls his dry lips. He sets his hand on his left breast pocket and clutches it as if his heart aches.

Pop.

The sound reverberates through me.

Jenkins's head is tilted to the side now, but his broken smile remains, and I let out a cry that will haunt me for the rest of time.

I crumble on Jenkins's chest and wail. *Why did everything have to come down to this?* I slide my hand over his and feel something beneath it. Tears drip down as I gently move his hand and open his breast pocket. It's a silver round music box with bunnies carved into it. My fingers are shaking so violently that it's hard to get them to twist the key, but once I do, the same lullaby I hummed for him drums out softly. I lift the lid to the music box and a small note is carved into it.

To think of me when I'm away.
Gallows & Jenkins

I shut the music box and place it against my heart. Bradshaw lowers to my side and rests his hand on my shoulder. The touch brings me back into myself and the pain that spreads through my injuries makes my head bob wearily.

"I know," Bradshaw whispers when I give him a broken look. "*I know.*"

He helps me up and we sway on our feet as we stare over all the death.

"Do we even want to go back?" I say absently. Part of me wants to stay here with the dead. And all go together into the night.

Bradshaw squeezes me a little tighter. "I'll die here with you if it's what you want, Bun."

I look at him, our cheeks stained with blood and dried tears. Then I shake my head. "We should head to the extraction point… Otherwise, all this death was for nothing."

He nods and we support each other as we limp toward the pick-up location.

After five minutes, we hear a chopper cutting through the night.

"We're almost there," Bradshaw whispers, kissing my temple.

A shout sounds behind us.

Eren? My eyes widen as I hear the faint shout once more.

Bradshaw heard it too and his face reanimates. We move as fast as we can and backtrack until we see two soldiers, one carrying the other.

"Eren?!" I shout, and my pain subsides as adrenaline rolls through me again. I recognize the man carrying him instantly. "*Paul?*" I knew he was good.

When we reach them, Bradshaw falls to his knees and desperately hugs his brother. My eyes fall to his legs. One is hardly still hanging on while the other is gone below the knee.

An ache pulses through my chest at the idea that we left him when he was still alive. My eyes meet Paul's. "Thank you isn't enough," I choke out. Bradshaw clings to his brother helplessly and cries.

Paul smiles. "Let's hurry up before any of you bleed out." I nod and give him a painful hug. Paul made a tourniquet for Eren's leg the best he could but he won't last long like this. None of us will. "We need to get to the extraction before the chopper takes off." Paul carries Eren as his consciousness dips in and out.

The three of us cry silently as we make it to the evacuation point. Paul keeps his grim expression as he pushes us on. More tears fall as the chopper descends and medical personnel come out to help us get on board. They aren't from the dark forces. I assume they are Eren's friends from his other endeavors. Harrison was saying he had Canadian allies just before he was hit.

Does this mean we're free?

The chambers of my heart fill with grief as we leave Labrador. I shut my eyes and think of Jenkins's last smile. I think of his bones that will forever rest here.

I press his music box tightly against my heart.

———

Bradshaw lost a lot of muscle mass while being wrapped up in the hospital. So did I, but it's much more noticeable on him. He smiles as I step into his room. It's only a few doors down from mine, so I sneak in here more often than I should.

"Is he still asleep?" I whisper, looking over at Eren's bed. He's sitting up and shoots me a glare. I let a laugh slip and he can't keep his serious ruse up anymore.

"How could I possibly sleep with a bunny running rampant in this hospital?" Eren teases me. I shrug, knowing damn well that I'm much too noisy every time I come in here. But I can't help it. I look from Eren's bed to Bradshaw's across the room and grin. He narrows his eyes and motions with his finger for me to come to him.

A few weeks in the hospital is too much for anyone. I get bored too easily to sit still this whole time. Paul parted ways with us when we got to Calgary. I wish I could thank him somehow, but his freedom seemed more than enough to him.

I set Eren's mocha latte on his side table before bringing Bradshaw his.

"Ah, the simplicities of civilization," Eren says as he sips his drink.

Bradshaw grins and takes a swig of his. "I have to admit, it's pretty fucking nice. I could get used to it." He pulls me onto his bed and I laugh.

"Careful, I'm still on bed rest too." I wince at the stitches on my stomach and Bradshaw presses a kiss to my lips.

"Sorry, Bun. How can I make it up to you?" He raises a brow suggestively.

Eren chokes on his drink. "*No.* No. I will not be subjected to watch, not again!" He starts pressing the button for the nurse to check on him. "Help!"

Bradshaw breaks out laughing and I can't help but join him. By the time the nurse comes to check, Eren is throwing his pillows across the room to keep us from kissing each other.

In the madness and laughter, Bradshaw whispers against my ear, "Promise me forever, Bun. You're where my sanity starts." I can hear the smile in his voice.

"You are where mine ends."

forty-three

. . .

SMOKE ROLLS FROM THE TOP OF OUR CHIMNEY IN THE DISTANCE. Winter in Thornhill, Scotland, isn't too bad. We moved out here four years ago and found that we like the seclusion from the rest of the world.

The dark forces will likely always be searching for us. But there's a good chance they think we died in Labrador.

Our cottage is an old stone-framed one with moss and ivy growing along the walls. In the summers, the green rolling hills are welcoming, and the four of us enjoy walking along the stone fences that line the dirt roads.

This life isn't grand or dangerous, but it's what we want.

The three most important people in my life are alive and with me. I couldn't ask for more.

Eren shivers and wraps his arms around Bunny. "It's so cold. Can we go back now?" I shoot him a glare and he lets her go. She's carrying a handful of firewood like I am.

"You're the only one not doing anything. Stop complaining," I snap at him, and he grins at me. My eyes lower to his artificial legs. He walks so well on them that you'd never know he had them amputated.

"Hey, I'm on nanny duty remember?" Eren narrows his eyes at me before laughing at Nathan's scowl.

My three-year-old son says as carefully as he can, "I dun need a nanny."

"Don't," Eren pronounces it correctly for him and Nathan's scowl deepens.

Bunny laughs and her eyes soften on our son. My chest warms at the second chance life's given me. The family that I'll protect no matter what.

"We should go to the pub tonight and see if Rei is working," Bunny chimes in, smiling at the way Eren's face drops and turns red.

"Yeah, Rei seems to enjoy chatting with you, Eren," I add nonchalantly. He tries to hide his grin, but I know he's really into her.

Nathan's red cheeks grow with a smile. "I like Rei!"

Eren laughs and squeezes Nathan's hand. "You too?"

The woodpile is stocked, and we sit down at our table to eat lunch. The hearth is warm and the fire lights our cottage well. Orange flickers over photos we've hung on the walls. Some are of Malum, Abrahm smiling at my side. Others are of Jenkins and Bunny in London, sharing a kiss on a balcony. My heart aches for all the faces that are no longer here with us, yet soars with the ones that still are. The new ones too.

Bun stares at the silver music box that she keeps on top of our old piano sometimes, and I know she misses him in the way I'll always miss my Abrahm.

She gets up and brushes the part on my back where she carved a symbol into me. It took me a while to figure out what it meant.

In the end, I fell in love with a Riøt soldier after all.

Leave Me Behind

acknowledgments

This book was incredibly fun to write. I let the characters have their way with the story and I really enjoyed bringing them to life!

Thank you to my readers for following me through my author journey and for reading my books!

I would like to thank my husband, Mr. Moronova, for all this help in story boarding and being the alpha reader. He really gives me the encouragement to keep writing when I feel like my story isn't piecing together.

Thank you to my editor, Kelsey, and my evaluator, Leanne. These two keep me on track and really made this book shine!

Thank you to my beta reader, Jay. You always read in a timely manner and help me meet my deadlines.

Thank you to Cierra, my proof reader and PA for always reminding me of things I've forgotten to do!! I don't know how I'd keep my head on straight without you.